DISTANT VOICES

BARBARA ERSKINE is the author of the internationally bestselling novel *Lady of Hay*, which was translated into seventeen languages and has sold over a million copies worldwide. This was followed by another bestseller, *Kingdom of Shadows*, and by a collection of short stories, *Encounters*, which met with wide popular acclaim. Her third novel, *Child of the Phoenix*, was based on the story of one of her own ancestors, and provides a link between some of the characters from *Lady of Hay* and *Kingdom of Shadows*, again encapsulating the author's dual themes of the supernatural and of history. *Midnight is a Lonely Place* enjoyed the same international bestselling success and was shortlisted for the WH Smith Thumping Good Read Award of 1995. It was followed by her most recent bestselling novel, *House of Echoes*, which has been shortlisted for the 1996 WH Smith Thumping Good Read Award.

Barbara Erskine has a degree in mediaeval Scottish history from Edinburgh University. She and her family divide their time between the Welsh borders and their ancient, crumbling manor house near the coast of North Essex.

'Written with imagination, and spiced with a sharp observation of human foibles. You'll be hard-pressed to find a better book for your bedside table.'
                                        Yorkshire Evening Post

DISTANT
VOICES

Barbara Erskine

HarperCollins*Publishers*

HarperCollins*Publishers*
77–85 Fulham Palace Road
Hammersmith, London W6 8JB

This paperback edition 1997

1 3 5 7 9 8 6 4 2

First published in Great Britain by
HarperCollins*Publishers* 1996

Drawing of ostrich plume by Jane Conway

Set in Postscript Linotype Galliard by
Rowland Phototypesetting Limited
Bury St Edmunds, Suffolk

Printed and bound in Great Britain by
Caledonian International Book Manufacturing Ltd, Glasgow

In Memory of
'Uncle Stuart'

STUART ERSKINE BIRRELL

1887–1916

a kindred spirit

CONTENTS

PREFACE   ix

Distant Voices   1
The Drop Out   15
Moment of Truth   23
The Duck Shoot Man   35
Frost   51
The Fairy Child   61
Who Done It?   74
Watch the Wall, My Darling   77
OBE   149
The Gift of Music   160
Island Shadows   176
A Test of Love   192
Witchcraft for Today   200
The Poet   209
The Toy Soldier   216
To Adam a Son   233
Writer   242
The Fate of the Phoenix   252
When the Chestnut Blossoms Fall   267
The Inheritance   296

CONTENTS

Dance Little Lady   304

Rosemary and Thyme   330

Flowers for the Teacher   339

A Family Affair   346

Networking   428

Catherine's Cat   435

Stranger's Choice   456

Aboard the Moonbeam   462

Choices   475

Two's Company   482

PREFACE

When my first collection of short stories, *Encounters*, was published in 1990 I did not expect to be asked to compile a second, so I was enormously pleased to find myself writing some new stories, and making a further selection amongst my old ones, for *Distant Voices*.

I still very much enjoy writing short stories. For me they are the sorbet between the courses of longer novels. They freshen and stimulate the palate. They indulge the writer's and the reader's whim with a quick glimpse into shadow or sunlight. They intrigue, they titillate, they frighten or they amuse.

As in *Encounters* those stories that are not new have been chosen from more than two decades of writing and are very varied in theme. To select a few for comment or explanation might help to put the collection in context. Three of the stories, for example, *A Test of Love*, *To Adam a Son* and *Flowers for the Teacher* are unsophisticated and sentimental, written in the early seventies for the so-called true-life market, while others like *Witchcraft for Today* and *When the Chestnut Blossoms Fall* depict incidents in an older world where romance has grown a little cynical.

There are of course ghost stories – two inspired by my own garden. The core story in *Frost* came from a sad tale told me about a greenhouse here, thankfully perhaps, now demolished; *Rosemary and Thyme* is based on an experience which I had myself whilst weeding in my herb garden one morning in early spring.

Catherine's Cat has laid to rest (or perhaps not?) a terror which haunted me for a while as a child and made bedtime a torment for many months – the suitcase on the wardrobe.

The Duck Shoot Man was based on an incident which happened to my mother and my grandmother and myself when we paused on a journey to Edinburgh and spent the night on Lindisfarne.

Dance Little Lady (purely imagination, this one!) was written in the brash eighties; *The Toy Soldier* (inspired by a toy we found in our cottage) in the more thoughtful nineties, a time of redundancy and re-evaluation.

There are many more, about different times and different places, depicting different moods and both the strange and the mundane.

Three of the stories are much longer than the others. *Dance Little Lady*, *A Family Affair* and *Watch the Wall* are almost novellas – two mini thrillers and one a historical romance – something to get your teeth into.

Whatever the length and whatever the subject, I hope you enjoy reading them as much as I enjoyed writing them.

DISTANT VOICES

Distant Voices

THE LOCK WAS STIFF and the door swollen. It was several seconds before Jan could force it open and peer at last from the bright sunlight of the porch into the darkness of the house.

As she had climbed out of the car, which was parked on the overgrown gravel of the drive, and looked up at the grey stone façade, she had felt a strange nervousness.

'Go and have a look round, my dear. Take as long as you like.' David Seymour had pressed the large iron key into her hand the day before, when she had met him for the first time. 'I want you to get a feel of how it was.' He smiled at her, his gentle face dissolving into a network of deep wrinkles, contradicting his initial wariness. 'Then we'll talk. Later.'

His grandson, Simon, had been with him. 'Simon's an architect. Clever chap.' The old man had introduced him fondly. The young man was tall and fair with his grandfather's piercing eyes. Where the older man had the look of a buzzard, hunched, predatory, the younger version was an eagle, right down to the aquiline nose. He had held out his hand to Jan, but his appraisal of her was anything but friendly. Clever he may be, she decided instantly, but also hostile, defensive, and summoned, she suspected, to guard his grandfather's privacy.

Of all the people there on that fatal night fifty years ago, David Seymour had been the hardest to approach. And without him she would get nowhere. He had been, after all, the husband.

She had looked forward so much to this part of her research. Interviewing the people concerned; comparing their memories; putting the pieces of the jigsaw together. But it was harder than she had imagined. Some of the people there had suppressed what had happened for over fifty years. The memories were painful, even after so long. To have an inquisitive journalist raking over the past was the last thing many of them wanted.

She took a step into the darkness of the house and paused. It smelled damp and musty. The floors were dusty and cobwebs hung festooned across the landing window. She peered along the corridor towards the staircase which swept uncarpeted up towards the light and then round and out of sight.

That must have been where she fell.

Behind her the door creaked. A wind was getting up. She could hear the rustling of the leaves on the oaks which grew on either side of the long driveway and she shivered, half wishing now that she had brought someone with her. 'This is silly.' The sound of her voice in the intense silence was an intrusion, but a necessary one. She reached into her soft leather shoulder bag and brought out her micro cassette recorder.

'Monday the fourth,' she said firmly, holding the machine close to her mouth. 'I have just arrived at The Laurels. I am standing in the front hall. The house is empty and has obviously been closed for a long time. No one lives here now and there is, as far as I can see, no furniture or anything here.'

She moved to a door on her left and put her hand out to push it open. The room inside was empty; pale light filtered through round the edges of the shutters, diffused green by the ivy which clung to the outside wall. The parquet floor was scuffed and criss-crossed with old, long-dried muddy footprints.

'This must have been the drawing room. It's large. Beautiful. Ceiling mouldings; candelabra, lovely carved mantel-piece,' she murmured into the machine in her hand. She sounded, she thought with sudden wry amusement, like a house agent preparing particulars for the sale of an especially desirable property.

The silence was intense. She turned off her little machine and walked slowly around the room, trying to feel the atmosphere. Had they all been in here, talking, drinking, smoking, when it had happened? Dinner was over, they were all agreed on that. And the ladies had withdrawn. But what had happened after that? John Milton said they had all gathered in the drawing room and that someone had agreed to sing. Sarah Courtney said the men were sitting over their port whilst the ladies were still upstairs, powdering their noses. Stella had finished and had gone on down alone. . .

Walking back to the foot of the stairs, Jan peered up. 'The staircase is shallow, graceful, curved elegantly around the wall,' she murmured into her machine. The banister, polished and smooth, was almost warm beneath the light touch of her fingers. 'Stella Seymour's body was found crumpled at the bottom by the other guests who ran from the dining room, and presumably from the bedroom, when they heard her scream. At the time her death was widely thought to be suicide. It was only four years later, after the war had ended, at the instigation of the man who claimed to have been her lover, that the first accusation of murder was heard.'

Slowly Jan began to climb. Half-way up she stopped suddenly. She could hear something. The intense silence of the house had gone and instead, she realised, she could hear a gentle murmur of conversation coming from somewhere quite near her. She was almost at the bend in the staircase. Frozen with embarrassment she looked up and then back. David Seymour had promised her the house was empty. She could feel her heart beating fast. This was ridiculous. She had permission to be here.

Squatters? Was that it? Could there be squatters in the

3

house? Uncertain what to do, she clutched her tape recorder more tightly as she tiptoed on up the stairs and peered along the upper landing. Several doors stood open up there; all the rooms were empty of furniture.

The sound of voices was louder now. She could hear the occasional chink of glass, of cutlery on china. It sounded as if a dinner party were in progress. Flattening herself against the wall she squinted back down the stairs where she could just see the door opposite the drawing room. It was closed. Why hadn't she looked in there? Had she not noticed it in her anxiety to see the staircase? Whatever the reason, she thanked God she had not gone barging in, for that seemed to be where the noise was coming from. Get out. That was what she must do. Get out now, without anyone seeing her.

Taking a deep breath she crept back down the stairs, intensely aware that this was where Stella Seymour had died.

The sounds were quieter again now that she was nearly down. Gradually the hall fell silent. The front door was still ajar as she had left it. She could see the wedge of sunlight thrown across the dusty floor. How strange that the noises had been louder from upstairs.

She stopped. She could smell cigars. Then, quite near her, she heard a man laugh. Spinning round, she faced the sound. There was no one to be seen. Her mouth dry, she switched off her tape recorder. Pushing it into her shoulder bag, she tiptoed towards the dining room door, holding her breath as she edged closer. She could see now that it was not quite shut. Cautiously she moved forward. She could hear the voices again. And subdued laughter. Smell the tobacco. There was a sudden crescendo in the noise and a shout of laughter as she brought her eye to the crack in the door.

They were sitting around an oblong table – some dozen people – no, she saw suddenly, just men, all at one end of the table. The air was wreathed in smoke. They were all wearing dinner jackets.

A sudden sound behind her brought her upright swiftly,

her heart pounding. She could hear footsteps on the landing.

'David, darling –' The voice was clear and high. Excited. There was a rustle of skirts, the quick patter of feet and then suddenly – horribly – a high-pitched scream.

Jan froze, her hand still clenched on the door-frame behind her back. She could hear it. The sound of a body falling, but there was nothing there. Nothing at all. The dust was untouched on the steps save for the scuff marks where her own shoes had been.

Whirling, she stared behind her at the door. Beyond it there was total silence. Her heart was hammering so loudly in her ears she felt sure it must echo all round the house as she pulled the door-handle and swung the door open. The dining room was empty. There was no table. No scent of tobacco. The room smelled merely of damp.

Only when she was sitting at last in her car peering back at the house did she start to breathe again. She flung her bag onto the passenger seat beside her and slammed down the door lock, then she sat for a moment, her forehead resting against the rim of the steering wheel. She was shaking all over.

David Seymour had poured her a cup of coffee himself, from hands which were considerably less shaky than hers, despite his ninety-four years. 'You've just come from The Laurels now?' He stood looking down at her, his expression curiously neutral. 'My dear Miss Haydon, I am so sorry you should have been so frightened. There is no one there, I can assure you. My grandson keeps an eye on the place for me. He went over there only a couple of days ago.'

'I shouldn't have come straight to you like this.' The black coffee was taking effect. This was an old man and his memories of the house must be bad enough without her adding to them with wild stories about ghosts!

He shook his head, sitting down opposite her. 'I'm glad you did. Who else would you go to?' He reached for the phone from the table beside him. 'I'm calling my grandson now. He can go over there straightaway to check that there are no intruders.' His voice was strong and alert, like the rest of him, Jan thought, as she leaned back against the cushions and sipped her coffee gratefully.

She realised he was watching her intently as he replaced the receiver. 'Simon is coming over here first.' He reached for his own cup. He paused. 'You are irrevocably set upon writing my wife's biography?'

Jan frowned. 'There are a great many people who would love to read it. She was a very great painter. She's been a heroine of mine for as long as I can remember.'

'And that is a reason for raking over her bones?'

The sharpness of the words brought Jan up with a shock. 'I'm sorry. I understood you had no objection to the book.'

'Would it matter if I had?' His gaze was suddenly piercing.

'Well . . .' She hesitated.

'No. Of course it wouldn't. In fact my opposition would whet your appetite. It would make you curious. You would want to know what the old buzzard was hiding!' He glared at her.

She smiled shame-facedly. 'I expect it would, if I'm honest.'

He nodded, seemingly satisfied with her answer. 'Good. You'll do. Now, do you believe that I murdered her?' The directness of the question was shocking.

'I – no – of course not.' She was embarrassed.

'There is no *of course not* about it, my dear. You must search the evidence. You must be a thorough and honest investigator.'

'But they never charged you.'

'No.'

'You loved her.'

The old face softened. 'Indeed I did. I worshipped her.'

'And she didn't have an affair –'

'Didn't she?' He seemed suddenly to be looking inside himself, searching for pictures which had long ago grown

6

fuzzy and out of focus. 'She was a vibrant, sociable, lovely person and she was lonely. I had been away so long. It was the war.'

Jan bit her lip. 'Then the article in the American paper was true?' It had appeared only a few months ago, reviving old memories, claiming that the baby Stella had been expecting was the result of an affair.

'I did not say that.' She could see his pain. 'I didn't know if I could father more children; I had been wounded. But the American had long gone and Stella was above all honest. She said he had meant nothing and I believed her. I did not know he had taken so many of her pictures away . . .'

'Surely the pictures didn't mean anything.' Obscurely she felt she had to comfort him. 'He could have been going to sell them or exhibit them for her –'

'Perhaps.' He sighed. 'The fall was an accident. A catastrophic, disastrous, tragic accident. She would not have killed herself. I'm sure she wouldn't. And yet how can I be sure? And how will I ever know about the child?' He took a deep breath and looked up at her again, suddenly almost pleading. 'You will make your own mind up as to the truth of all this, and I think you will make the right decision.'

Was he asking her to decide? To find out the truth for him? Jan bit her lip as the old man sighed again, a bone-weary sound which tore at her heartstrings.

'In a way I'm glad all this has happened,' he went on after a moment. 'Simon has been trying to make me face the rumours and think about that house for years. It's an albatross; a Pandora's box. If there are people squatting there, which I doubt, then it's time to let it go. I hope Simon will get married, then he could live there, but it's too big for one person alone.' There was another short silence. 'Stella wouldn't have liked squatters. She loved that house, you know. All her best painting was done there.' He levered himself to his feet. 'Did you see her studio?'

Jan shook her head. 'I'm afraid I left rather quickly.'

The old man grinned. 'Ran away, did you? Can't blame you. I've always thought the house was rather spooky, myself, but Stella always filled it with people. There was never any silence. Only when she was painting, or when she said she was painting . . .' He turned away sharply. For a moment Jan wondered if he were sobbing silently. She could see the movement of his shoulders and she ached to comfort him. But as she watched he straightened himself and with a visible effort he turned and went over to the window.

Jan too had heard the car draw up outside. She waited, watching, as David Seymour turned to face the door.

Simon's first words were to the point. 'If you have been upsetting Grandfather –'

'No, Simon!' The old man's interruption was peremptory. 'She has been doing nothing of the kind. I gave the girl permission to go to The Laurels. And I want her to write Stella's story. It's all so long ago now. No one is going to be hurt . . .'

Simon swung round. 'But Grandfather –'

'Enough.' David threw himself back on the chair with a groan. 'I want you to tell her everything she wants to know. And go with her to check out the house.' He gave a short laugh which after a moment changed into a cough. 'She thinks someone is squatting there. She heard people in the dining room.'

They went in Simon's car. Jan had followed him out of the house reluctantly, sensing his hostility. 'I'm sorry to inflict this on you,' she said as she slotted her seatbelt into place. 'I'm sure you have better things to do than chase out to the country at a moment's notice.'

'If there are squatters something must be done about it,' he replied. Engaging gear smoothly he swung the car out into the traffic. 'How long were you in the house?'

'Only a few minutes.'

'But you saw no one?'

She hesitated. How could she tell him what she saw? 'No.'

'And the door was locked?'

She nodded. 'It didn't seem to have been opened for ages.'

'I have the back door key. I imagine that if there are intruders, they too have gone in that way. Only Grandfather still has the front door key, as far as I know.'

'Do you remember your grandmother?' Jan glanced at him curiously.

He gave a short laugh. 'Hardly. She died long before I was born.'

'I'm sorry. Of course.'

'You've seen her self portrait? The one in the town gallery?' Jan nodded. 'She was very beautiful.'

'Yes.' He turned onto the bypass and accelerated away from the traffic. 'I suppose the idea is to bring your book out in time for the exhibition they're planning for next year to mark the fiftieth anniversary of her death.'

'It will be wonderful to have so many of her paintings together.'

'Even the ones in the States. Quite.' His voice was dry. 'We're almost there.'

He pulled the car around the back of the house and they climbed out, looking round. The house seemed as deserted as before. There was no sign of life at all as Simon pulled out his key and opened the back door.

'No one in here, anyway.' He walked ahead of her into the kitchen.

Jan looked round. Oak dresser, table, chairs, deep sink, rusty range. It was obvious that no one had cooked here since that day in the war when David Seymour had walked out of the house after his wife's funeral, locked the door and gone back to his squadron.

She could feel her stomach clenching with nerves. 'Perhaps they are camping in some other part of the house.'

'Perhaps.' Simon reached into his pocket and produced a torch. He did not switch it on however. Enough sunlight filtered through blind and shutter for them to see clearly as they walked slowly through the ground floor. Outside the dining room door he stopped. 'You heard them in here?' He had his hand on the knob.

She nodded. She knew what they would find. Only dust and cobwebs decorated the room which had glittered with such life. 'I suppose you think I'm going mad?'

He grinned. It made him look suddenly and unexpectedly approachable. 'No more than dozens of other people who have seen and heard it too.'

She stared at him. 'You mean you know about it – what I saw? You knew! Your grandfather knew?'

He nodded. 'Ghosts. Memories trapped in the walls. Who knows. None of the people in the village will come near this house. Which suits us fine.' He pulled the door closed. 'Come and see Stella's studio.'

He gave her no chance to say anything as he strode back to the kitchen and out of the house. She followed him, almost running, over the long grass of what had once been the lawn and through an overgrown shrubbery to a low, thatch-roofed building which overlooked a reedy pond. He reached for the key which was hidden beneath a moss-covered stone. 'I can't think why this place hasn't been vandalised. But it seems Stella's secrets are still her secrets,' he said shortly. He stood back and let Jan go in ahead of him. 'Did my grandfather not tell you about this place?'

Jan shook her head. She stared round.

The studio stood on the edge of the water, its large windows allowing the sky and the willows and the glittering ripples to explode into the room, filling it with light. All Stella's painting equipment was still here: easels, canvases, paints, sketchbooks curled with damp, the pages stuck together, an ancient sofa, draped in a green silk shawl, the fringe trailing on the ground, black with mildew, vases of

10

flowers, long dried and faded beyond recognition, on the table a straw sun hat amongst the scattered brushes and pencils and dried-up tubes of paint.

Jan bit her lip, fighting the lump in her throat. 'It's as though she only left a few minutes ago.'

'He would never let it be touched.'

She picked up a palette knife from the table. The lump of paint dried on its tip matched exactly the colour in the foreground of the painting on the easel.

'What do you think really happened that night?' She was staring out at the water. A pair of mallard swam into view, the pond rippling into diamond rings around their gently paddling feet.

'No one knows for sure.'

'The article in the American magazine said that she was pushed. That it was murder.' She turned and looked at him. He was very handsome, Stella's grandson, with her colouring, if the portrait in the gallery was anything to go by, even if he had inherited his grandfather's nose. 'It said that she was pregnant by another man. An American.'

Simon's eyes narrowed. 'Grandfather should have sued them. But he didn't want to. He didn't want anything to do with the article. He thought everyone would forget, and her memory would be left in peace.'

'Instead of which I come along.'

'Instead of which you come along.'

'He told you –'

'To tell you everything. I know.' He had strolled over to the windows and was looking out, his shadow falling across the floor to the green shawl. He sighed. 'I expect you know about the letters. To the GI. And that he had sent so many of her drawings and paintings back to the States. That rather supports the gossip in a way.' He turned and faced her. 'What do you think you heard in there? In the house?'

'People? A tape? A radio? Echoes? Ghosts?' She could feel her skin beginning to shiver even though it was warm in the

11

studio. The air was heavy suddenly with the scent of oil paint and linseed and turpentine.

'Did you hear a woman laughing?'

'Yes, I did.'

'And she sounded happy?'

'I heard her calling him. Your grandfather. She sounded ecstatic. And then I heard her fall.' She paused. She had heard the voice, but where had David Seymour been? Downstairs in the dining room with the others, or had he appeared suddenly on the landing next to her? She bit her lip. No. Surely it had been a happy voice. 'I think it was an accident. I think she wanted me to know that. You've heard her too?'

He nodded. 'I think at that last dinner party they were enjoying themselves. They were all deliriously happy. Stella and Grandfather and John and Sarah and the Daniels and Peter Cockcroft. It was wartime. There was rationing. So many of the fit young people were gone, so many of their friends had died, but Grandfather had been invalided out after being terribly wounded. He was safe. He had recovered. They were all there and they were happy. After my father was born Stella had hoped and hoped for another child but none came. Then suddenly Grandfather was back and she was pregnant again. They were celebrating. It was the happiest moment of her life.' Simon turned away from the window and looked at Jan. 'I'm guessing. No, it's more than that. I'm almost certain that's what happened. Grandfather trusts you. He likes you and I think that when he heard that you had seen something – heard something – in the house, he knew that she trusted you too. Only nice people hear her laugh –' He stopped abruptly as Jan's eyes flooded with tears. 'Oh Miss Haydon – Jan – I'm sorry, I didn't mean to upset you.' He delved into the pocket of his jacket and produced a handkerchief. It was slightly painty.

Jan wiped her eyes. 'You are an artist too?' She was feeling rather silly.

'A bit. If I've inherited half her talent I count myself a very lucky man.' Gently he steered her to the sofa. 'Sit down a minute. Get your breath back.'

'How could he bear to think of selling the house?'

'He can't. Not really. He'd have done it years ago if he were going to. After the inquest he went back to the war even though he wasn't really fit – I don't suppose they asked too many questions – they needed all the men they could get. As far as I know he never came back here, but I think he must still love the house in a way. And the house must have happy memories as well as sad ones. They shared so much here. Besides, don't you feel it? She's still here –' He gestured at the easel. It was another self portrait, this time in Edwardian dress, unfinished, a few details completed: the face, which was vibrant, happy, glowing with life; the sparkling jewels around her throat and wrists; her hands, the ostrich feather fan. . .

As they sat down Simon had left his arm around Jan's shoulders. She was shivering. The sun had moved a little, and the studio was no longer lit across the water. It filled with weaving, drifting, green light.

'If only she could speak to us,' he went on. 'Give us a sign. Something to tell Grandfather that the baby was his. It's such a sad story, but at least then that last awful doubt would be gone and he would know once and for all that it was an accident; that she didn't, couldn't, have had any reason at all to kill herself.'

Jan smiled. 'What sort of sign?' This was scarcely objective research, but she was beginning to enjoy the feeling of his arm, so lightly draped over the back of the sofa.

'I don't know. Move something. Say something. I'll leave it to her. Anything.' He grinned. 'Listen, Grandfather asked me to take you back to tea. He wants to lend you her letters and diaries.'

'Then he really does trust me.'

Simon nodded slowly. 'I told you. He wants the whole

story of her life to be known at last. He said he was too old for them to hang him.'

'But that's admitting –'

'No. It's not admitting anything, except that he loved Stella more than life itself.' Simon stood up. He held out his hand. 'Let's go back to the house.'

For a moment she didn't move, then, reluctantly, she stood up. For a second she stood looking down at the face on the easel, then she followed him outside.

At the back door of the house she stopped. 'Can I go in once more? To see the dining room?'

'Of course.' He stood back so that she could go ahead of him through the kitchen and out into the corridor. The dining room door stood open, a wedge of light pouring from it across the floor.

They could both hear the music. Glen Miller. And the talk and laughter. The chink of knives and forks on crockery; they could both smell the cigar smoke, and through it all the faintest trace of oil paint.

Jan found she was holding Simon's hand. She was trembling, but she could not resist going nearer. Slowly, step by step, they crept towards the dining room as gradually the noise of the dinner party got louder. She could smell other things now. Cooking. Carefully hoarded coffee. Wine. A woman's scent. One hand firmly clutching Simon's, she reached forward with the other and gently she pushed the door open a fraction.

The room was empty.

In the echoing silence she gave a little sob of disappointment.

It was Simon who spotted the soft curl of an ostrich feather drifting on the bare boards.

The Drop Out

OF COURSE he wouldn't really come. The idea was too bizarre. But then, a husband is a husband, even if this one had hardly fulfilled his matrimonial duties to the letter.

Zara leaned forward and gazed into the mirror. If he did come he was going to see quite a change in her after all this time. She vaguely recollected that her hair had been not only a different style but a different colour then. Her figure had improved out of recognition and maturity had brought sophistication and confidence.

'I wonder if he's got a paunch?' she asked her reflection out loud. And giggled. Gerald with a paunch was unthinkable.

She looked at the letter again. It began, 'Darling,' – That too was unlike him. Gerald had never been one for endearments. He must be in trouble, she decided as she slipped on her elegant silk suit.

Money? She had always understood that he had plenty. He had been 'something in the city' when they married. She had never bothered to find out what. Certainly he had from time to time continued to pay handsome amounts into her account. For old times' sake and when he remembered, she always thought, rather than for any mundane idea that he should support his wife. Not that she had needed supporting for years, of course, thank God. But, come to think of it, there had been no money now for nearly a year.

She stood sideways to the mirror and ran a critical hand

down her flat stomach. No. She was the kind of woman who did well in business and thrived on it. Gerald's conscience money or whatever it was had brought her some nice little extras, like the small Mercedes in the driveway. It had in no way gone towards her upkeep.

Well. If not money, what? Women. She knew some wives were called on to extricate their husbands from the clutches of too-persistent girlfriends, but Gerald had never had that problem. She had heard in fact that he merely turned the latest woman onto the last with a cold-blooded delight which often shocked both parties into flight. She paused for a moment. Perhaps he wanted a divorce? No. It was unthinkable. He, like her, found the state of absentee matrimony far too useful and pleasant an arrangement to end it.

The police? She looked at the mirror for a moment, her eyes wide, and then shrugged the idea away. It was too ridiculous to contemplate.

Zara gave up the idle speculation with a glance at her watch, ran downstairs, collected the car keys from the mantelpiece and went to the door. She was not usually given to conjecture and certainly not to day dreaming, and she had made herself uncharacteristically late for the board meeting.

He was sitting on the doorstep.

In rags.

For fully two minutes Zara looked down at her husband without speaking. Then, bleakly, she stood back and motioned him into the house, wrinkling her nose ostentatiously as he passed in front of her.

He walked straight to the drinks table and poured himself a Scotch. Then he turned and looked her up and down. He was slim still, no sign of a paunch, lean and hard, brown and fit, and his eyes twinkled mischievously.

'Go and run me a bath, Za-Za, dear. Then you can stop holding your nose, and we can talk.'

'But, Gerald!' Her usually well-modulated voice had risen to a squeak. 'What's happened to you?'

'Fate hasn't been kind, lady.' He put on what sounded like a very professional whine. But still his face was laughing. 'Go on woman, before my fleas start hopping onto your Persian rugs.'

With a cry of horror she fled upstairs and, turning both taps on full, groped for the small bottle of Dettol in the medicine cabinet. It smelled very strong in the steam, but anything was better than Gerald's . . . aroma.

While he bathed she washed his glass assiduously, sponged the outside of the whisky bottle and then got out the vacuum cleaner and ran it over the carpet where he had been standing. Fleas indeed! She shuddered.

With a sudden pang of guilt that she could so completely have forgotten her meeting she went to the phone and called the office to instruct her PA. 'I don't feel too well,' she explained quietly into the receiver and was amazed to find it was the truth. She felt sick and slightly feverish.

He reappeared in half an hour wearing her bathrobe. Voluminous on her, it sat on him like an outgrown coat on a gangly schoolboy, exposing long muscular legs and arms, and an expanse of hard brown chest.

'No sign of a man up there,' he commented as he threw himself down on the leather sofa. 'I could have borrowed his razor.' He sounded faintly aggrieved.

'I suppose you're hungry?' Zara ignored his remark loftily. She was indignant to find that her heart had started to bang rather hard beneath her ribs as it had, she distinctly remembered, when she first knew him.

'I'm starving, lady. Not eaten since the day before yesterday.' He reverted to his whine. She ignored it.

'I hope you don't still expect oysters for breakfast,' she commented sarcastically from the kitchen as she filled the kettle, remembering some of his more extravagant tastes. Her hands were shaking.

'A crust will do, lady, just a crust.' He appeared immediately behind her suddenly, and put his hands gently on her shoulders. 'I suppose you want an explanation?'

'I think I do rather.' She gave a small laugh.

'You could say I'd been down on my luck.' He looked at her hopefully, then on second thoughts shook his head. 'No, I know. It's not me is it. Would you believe that I did it on purpose?' He paused. 'You'd never credit the things people put in their dustbins, Za-Za. Someone ought to write a monograph on it: *The world's great untapped source of wealth.*'

'I'm sure the dustmen tap it successfully,' she commented acidly, slipping two slices of bread into the toaster. 'Judging by the things they nail to the fronts of their vans.'

'Teddies,' Gerald said reflectively. 'Your dustman here nails teddies to his van. I saw him as I came up the road. How anyone could bear to throw their teddy out I shall never know. It's worse than homicide.'

'Gerald! You never kept yours!'

'I did!' Her perched on the edge of the breakfast table to take the toast as it popped up, snatched his fingers away and blew on them hastily. 'Didn't you even search my trunks and the things I left?'

'Of course not. They were private.'

Gerald stared at her. 'You are truly a wonderful woman Za-Za. I wonder why I left you?' He buttered the piece of toast thoughtfully. She was also, he noted, slimmer, taller, if that were possible, and overall a thousand times more stunning than he remembered her.

'You couldn't stand me, dear.' She smiled. 'It's a shame because I really rather liked you.'

'Liked?' He raised an eyebrow.

'Loved, then.'

'Still in the past tense?'

She smiled. 'Stop fishing Gerald and tell me what you've been up to.'

The black coffee had steadied her, and she sat down opposite him, elegantly crossing her legs, waiting for him to begin.

For a few minutes he ate in silence, giving every impression that he really hadn't eaten for days, then he sat back with a sigh and reached for his own cup.

'One morning on the way to office, I thought, Gerald, old chap, what does it all mean? You know, the way one does? I couldn't find a convincing answer. So I thought, Right. If there's no reason for doing it, don't.' He grinned and reached for the sugar.

'There's always the need for money, Gerald.' She tried not to sound prim.

'Money for what?' You earn a damn good salary, so *you* don't need it. *I* don't need it. You had a house, I had a flat, did we need both, for God's sake? Why should I risk a coronary for the sake of a subscription to a golf club full of bores and for the Inland Revenue?'

'Gerald, that's a very trite and short-sighted remark, if you don't mind my saying so. And how,' she flashed at him suddenly, 'do you know how much I earn?'

'I own your company, dear. No,' he raised his hand as she put down her cup indignantly, about to speak. 'No. You got your job on merit alone, and I am totally uninterested in policy. Now, as I was saying, I thought, Why don't I drop out like all those delightful chaps one sees singing in the underground. The trouble is, I can't sing. I expect you remember that. I can't paint, or pot or woodcarve, to earn enough money to subsist, so I had to resort to begging. More coffee, please.'

She poured it for him without a word.

'I told James to stop the car. I told him to take a month's salary in lieu, drive the car home, lock it up, turn off the gas and the electricity in the flat, stick the keys back through the letter box – oh and empty the fridge. I thought of that. Then I called the office and said, "I'll be away for a year or so," and gave my solicitor a ring, about power of attorney and that sort of thing. I bought a large cream doughnut, simply oozing cholesterol, and a can of beer, put all my loose change in the hat of one of those pathetic young men you see sitting leaning against walls with their dogs beside them and started walking. Right then and there, in my city suit.' He threw back his head and laughed. 'I bet you didn't recognise it when I came in.'

'Did you enjoy yourself?' Zara tried not to sound shocked or angry.

'Marvellously.' He reached for the breadknife, cut an enormous wedge of bread and began heaping butter onto it. 'I've been all over the south of England and right down to Cornwall, to all the little off the road places one misses in a beastly car. I've stuck it for eight months.'

'Why did you come back here then?'

'For one thing I was hungry this morning. For another, I wanted to see you again.'

'Gerald. How could you afford the stamp and the paper for that letter?' She was suddenly suspicious.

He looked embarrassed for the first time. 'Well, the trouble is Zara that I've begun earning money again. First it was only casual jobs: car cleaning, fruit picking, even potato lifting once – God! What a job that was. Then one night in a pub, I happened to recite one of the poems I'd been making up on the road as I walked along. They passed the hat round and I made about seven pounds fifty. A fortune! Well, I've gone on from there. Each town and village I visited after that I'd chat up the landlord and stick a notice in his pub saying I was going to give a recital. Then afterwards I'd pass round the old hat.'

'Gerald, you're not serious!' Zara looked at him with real admiration.

'Well, the truth is dear,' he looked down at the cup, half embarrassed. 'I think I need an agent or something. You see I want to have them published. I know it's silly, but I've got ambitions for them. I've found out what life is all about, you see. For me, it's poetry.'

'And you'd like me to act for you?'

'Would you?' He looked up eagerly.
'Of course.'

Zara enjoyed dressing her husband as a poet. She spent the morning buying him jeans and shirts and a rather expensive-looking leather jacket. She even debated whether he would wear beads or a necklace, or a thong around his neck with a bead on it, but decided finally against it. He had after all been in the habit of wearing a pinstripe suit.

She had left him before setting out on her spree, reciting his poems to her dictating machine. When she got back, her cleaning lady was standing open-mouthed at the drawing room door, listening.

'It's filth, Mrs Lennox, real filth,' the woman complained, jumping guiltily when she saw her employer. 'But it's beautiful. I could listen for hours, so I could.' She giggled skittishly.

Zara stood beside her and together they heard Gerald reciting. It was indeed beautiful.

After a moment he swung round, microphone in hand, and saw them. To Zara's amazement he broke off abruptly, blushing. 'I didn't know there was anyone there,' he murmured and then he laughed. 'They're not really for ladies' ears.'

'Nonsense. They're damn good.' Zara went in and reaching up planted a quick kiss on his cheek. 'I'll start putting them on the word processor for you this afternoon.'

They decided they would call him Noxel, which was Lennox inside out. No other name. It looked right in print, and would sound good, Zara thought, on the radio. She ignored his comment that it made him sound a little like a lavatory cleaner.

Gerald Lennox had been, they both agreed, a bore.

She took him round London, showing him off to her new, trendy friends, and she bathed in reflected glory as Gerald's exquisitely metred adjectives and highly coloured phraseology assailed their ears. She had always suspected they cultivated her acquaintance for her money and contacts. Now she had produced someone who belonged to their world. More than belonged. He actually did things. Most of them, she now discovered, claimed themselves passive rather than active participants in the arts. Zara felt herself to be one-up at last and was very pleased with her eccentric, wandering poet.

Together they giggled over the raised eyebrows of the neighbours. It seemed no one recognised him.

Then Zara's lover came back from two months in Cape Town. He let himself in half an hour before she was due home from the office and found Gerald sitting at her computer.

'My dear chap,' Gerald glanced up and then rose, his hand outstretched. 'I knew you must exist, but she never admitted it, bless her.' He grinned amicably.

The other's mouth fell open, and he felt uncertainly for the nearest chair and sat down heavily. 'I'm sorry,' he said at last. 'I don't believe we've met?'

Gerald leaned back in his seat. 'I'm Zara's husband, actually. But not to worry –' as the other man rose abruptly to his feet, Gerald lifted his hand to reassure him. 'I'm off. I've been wanting to move on for some time now, but I didn't like to leave her on her own. She's been a brick these last few weeks.'

He shuffled his papers together and collected the pages he had been printing. 'Give me ten minutes old chap. We'll manage the turn-round before she gets home.' He took the stairs two at a time.

The new arrival sat, looking rather stunned, for a moment. Then, a trifle wearily, he rose to his feet and went to pour himself a drink. When Zara came home he was in the bath with a large gin.

She saw the note from Gerald on the hall table and knew without reading it that he had gone. She considered for a moment and then breathed a deep sigh of relief. It had been an interesting interlude, but not one she had wanted prolonged. It spoiled her concentration at the office.

Moment of Truth

STEVE AND I had known each other since we were children, brought up in the same village, growing together, and at last, realising that we were in love, we became engaged on my eighteenth birthday. Then began our struggle to save enough money for a deposit on our own home. Steven didn't want us to marry until, as he put it, he could support me properly, or at least put a roof over my head, and in spite of my pleas that it didn't matter, our engagement stretched out for one and then two years. Steve was a mechanic at the local garage in the village and was hoping desperately to be offered a partnership by the owner, so the future looked good, if only we could save enough for that deposit. And then something happened which was to have a profound effect on our lives together. Steve's great aunt Irene who had looked after him when he was a little boy suddenly had a stroke and they said that she would never be able to manage on her own again; even when she was strong enough to leave the hospital she would have to go into a home for elderly people where she could be properly looked after.

As soon as she was well enough to have visitors she called Steve and me to her bedside. She could hardly speak, and her poor withered hand lay paralysed on the sheet but she made it clear, with tears in her eyes, that her cottage was ours. It was to be a wedding present.

Six weeks later we were married. The cottage was tiny, but

it was our own home at last and I adored it. The low oak-beamed parlour had two rocking chairs and a table and there was room for little else. The bedroom window opened out under the thatch and wisteria and honeysuckle climbed round it. I remember I leaned out of that window on the first morning after we moved in and took a deep breath of the fresh air and I could have cried for happiness.

I worked as a waitress at the local Tudor Tea Rooms before we married and I kept on my job. For one thing I enjoyed it; for another we were still saving all we could. The cottage needed modernising badly and we wanted to start a family of course, so it seemed sensible to work all the hours we could fit in, putting every penny we earned into the bank. Although we were both tired and strained more often than not, we stayed happy. Or I thought we did. But perhaps without our realising it, earning money had by now become for us both an end in itself, more important even than our love for each other.

The trouble started in the summer two years after we were married. We were always very busy at that time of year in the café, for hundreds of tourists crowded into our tiny Cotswold village to see its beauties and its famous manor house, and often I would come home too exhausted even to give Steve his supper before I tumbled into bed, falling asleep as soon as my head touched the pillow. I was much too tired to make love.

It was about then that Steve started working overtime in the evenings. 'I might as well, for all I see of you,' he said rather bitterly. 'And besides, I can't bear to see you so tired.' And he had weighed my heavy blonde hair – the same colour as his almost – in his hands, and kissed me rather wistfully on the cheek. 'If I work extra perhaps soon you can give up the waitressing altogether.'

I glanced up at him gratefully and tried not to feel guilty as I noticed, for the first time, that he too was tired, and his face pallid from lying all day under cars when everyone else in the village was deeply tanned from the summer sun.

And so it happened that we had hardly seen each other for the last three months or so at all. We were saving, yes; but without my realising it, our marriage was fading away.

I was feeling especially tired and depressed when one day, as I was serving at the front tables, the ones which looked out of the mullioned windows across the green, a young man came in. He was of middle height, not terribly good-looking, rather swarthy, but he had the most incredible eyes. Light grey, so light they were like silver streaks in his tanned face. He beckoned me over.

'What's your name, sweetheart?' he asked in an American accent.

I smiled at him easily, whisking crumbs off the table with my cloth. I was used to this.

'I'm Linda,' I smiled. 'What can I get you, sir?'

'Tea. An English tea with cream cakes and scones please, Linda my love, and later perhaps you can show me the town?'

'Sorry sir, my husband will be expecting me home,' I answered with a practised smile. I turned to get his order.

Usually I dismissed passes like this man's without another thought, but something about his eyes, and the way his face fell when his gaze rested on the wedding ring which I waved under his nose, tugged at my heart.

When I took the tray to his table I asked casually, 'You all on your own then?'

He nodded. 'I'm over from the States for a few months. I'm a photographer and I'm doing a series on beautiful old England.'

There was something so wistful about his smile that I felt my heart do a quick bump.

As I moved quickly round the tables with my tray I could feel his gaze following me and every time I re-emerged from the kitchen with a new plate of scones and clotted cream, there he was watching.

When I took his bill to him he grabbed my wrist. 'Honey,

wouldn't your husband spare you for half an hour – just to have a drink with me at the pub? I hate going alone.'

I felt my stomach lurch. I had told him Steve expected me. It wasn't strictly true, of course. He had told me that there was a rush job on at the garage again that night, and he might not be back until even later than usual. As I said, I was depressed, and bored.

I took a deep breath. 'Okay,' I said. 'Perhaps I could manage a very quick drink, but not here.' I thought of the prying eyes and quick tongues of the village folk. 'Have you a car?'

He nodded.

'Then pick me up outside the post office.' I glanced at my watch. 'I'm on till we close this evening, at six. I'll see you then.'

His name turned out to be Graham, and he told me at once he had a wife and two kids in Wisconsin. We spent a couple of hours driving round the leafy lanes and then went to the fifteenth-century pub in the next village. He brought me home and dropped me at the end of our lane before going back to his hotel.

It was a perfectly innocent and very enjoyable outing, and so was the next, three nights later when Steve was again especially late. After that Graham took to dropping in at the tea rooms every evening as we were closing and I would tell him whether or not I would be able to spare an hour or two.

Steve was more and more regularly late at the garage as they seemed unusually busy so I saw more and more of Graham. I never mentioned Graham at home. The first time, Steve had come home in a temper from work, very unusually for him, and I knew it had not been the right moment. Then after that it became increasingly difficult.

Then came the time, inevitably, when Graham kissed me.

It happened so gently, so naturally, I hardly noticed it coming and before I could help myself I had returned it, passionately allowing him to draw me against his chest till I could hardly breathe.

'Oh no Graham. No!' I pushed him away suddenly. 'No, don't. I love my husband.'

'Sure, honey.' Gently but firmly he drew me back again. 'He won't miss a kiss or two, for a lonely man.'

But I was scared. I turned my head away and pushed with my fists against his chest. 'Don't Graham. No. I want to go home, please.'

Reluctantly he released me. 'Okay Linda, if you're sure that's what you really want.' He looked at me closely and as those silvery eyes met mine I felt my heart give a disloyal little lurch. It wasn't what I wanted at all.

He dropped me off at the end of the lane as usual and I made my way through the fragrant twilight to the cottage. Steve wasn't home, so I let myself out of the back door and into the garden. I could smell a whiff of pipe smoke from next door. Ian Johnson and his wife were sitting on their porch chatting quietly.

I had kicked off my sandals to walk on the dewy lawn, so I suppose they didn't hear me. The cottage was in darkness so they must have assumed I was still out.

'It's that pretty little wife of his I'm sorry for,' came Ian's voice, low but clearly audible. 'She doesn't suspect a thing.'

' 'E deserves to be shot 'e does,' came his wife's voice. 'Such a lovely couple they were. And I was so pleased when old Irene said they could live in her cottage. Hoping for some little ones next door, I was, and now this 'as to 'appen.'

'She's bound to find out.' Ian again, and a fresh cloud of smoke wafted over the roses as he drew on his pipe.

As I stood, listening, I was shaking with cold. My hands gripped the skirt of my dress and crushed the fabric convulsively. I felt terribly sick.

What were they talking about? I wanted to run next door, to scream, to cry, to ask questions, but in my heart I already knew the answer.

Steve's boss had never been all that keen on overtime in the past, so why should he have started working till all hours

27

this summer especially? Certainly not just to help us with our finances, and I had never bothered to go to the garage to check. I could feel a great sob, like a lump in my chest, and I turned and fled into the cottage before it could come out like a scream of misery.

I sat for an hour or more in the dark listening to the steady calm ticking of Aunt Irene's grandmother clock. Then I heard the front door open and close again softly.

'Linda, are you home?' Steve called quietly.

I couldn't say a word. I sat in the dark, my hands still clutching my skirt.

'Lyn?'

He pushed open the parlour door and clicked on the light.

'Lyn! What are you doing here?' He gazed at me in astonishment.

I hadn't actually been crying, but my face must have told him everything for he sat down suddenly on the edge of the rocking chair and ran his fingers through his hair. 'You know, don't you.' It was a statement, not a question.

I nodded dumbly.

'Oh Lord, Lyn. I'd have given the world for it not to have happened.' He stared at me miserably. 'What am I going to do?'

'You'd better tell me the truth,' I whispered at last. And I waited, my face in my hands, while he told me.

'Her name's Lauren. I met her a few months before you and I were married. She went to work in London, and then three months ago she came back. I serviced her car and we got chatting.' He shrugged. There was a long silence, then he raised his head and looked at me. 'She's going to have my baby, Lyn. I don't know what to do.'

'Do you love her?' I couldn't recognise my own voice, it was so cracked with fear.

He nodded. Then he shrugged desperately. 'Not as much as I love you. You mean everything to me, Lyn, you know you do, but . . .'

28

'But! While I've been working my fingers to the bone, struggling, saving . . . you've been spending money on someone else. The whole village knows except me. You louse! You hypocrite. You foul, beastly rotten dirty beast!' I was screaming at him now, and I saw him stand up, his face pale.

'Quietly Linda, please,' he tried to interrupt me, but I couldn't stop.

'You mean, unkind, disloyal bastard!' The tears were streaming down my face now. 'How could you! How could you? Well, if you don't want me, thank goodness there is someone who does!'

Blindly I pushed past him and groped my way out to the front door. I opened it and ran down the path between the hollyhocks in my bare feet.

I don't think he tried to stop me. I didn't wait to see.

I turned out of the gate and ran down the road. I had only one thought in my head. To go to Graham. I was so hurt and angry and miserable I didn't think at all beyond that one thing.

I ran most of the way to his hotel, not caring about the cars that flashed past me in the dark or the one or two passing pedestrians. My feet hurt terribly on the tarmac and my hair whipped in tangles against my burning face. The receptionist looked at me in horror as I pushed open the revolving door, but she rang through to Graham's room without comment and ten seconds later I was in his arms.

He helped me to his room and rang down for drinks and some coffee. Then he sat me down firmly on the bed.

'Calm down, Lyn honey. Tell me slowly,' he ordered. He reached over into his bedside cabinet and produced an enormous box of tissues.

Somehow I blew my nose and stopped crying. Then, gulping, I poured out my story to him.

After a few moments there was a knock on the door and a maid brought in the tray with the coffee and drinks. She stared at me curiously, then I saw her eyes widen as she noticed my feet. They were bleeding. At the sight of them suddenly I burst into tears again, and she was bustled off on Graham's instructions to get a bowl of warm water and antiseptic.

By the time they had finished fussing over me I had managed to stop crying and when we were alone again at last I gave him a watery smile.

'I'm sorry, Graham. Forgive me. It was all such a shock.'

'Of course it was, honey.' He took my hands and held them gently. 'The guy sounds no good to me at all. You're well out. Do you want to go back to London with me, Thursday?'

I nodded dumbly. I never wanted to see Steve again or our beautiful cottage which I couldn't even think of as home any more. All I wanted – was out.

Later, much later, I crawled into bed. Graham's bed. He turned off the lamps one by one, then he climbed in beside me. I was exhausted and still very tense and when he rolled over towards me and reached out I shrank away suddenly.

'Okay honey. No hurry.' He turned onto his back and lay staring up at the ceiling and after a few moments I heard his breathing grow deep and regular and I knew he was asleep.

I barely slept that night. Every time I dozed off I awoke with a start, clinging to the edge of the bed. As dawn broke I crept from the blankets, my eyes heavy with lack of sleep, and drew back the curtain to gaze out into the garden.

We breakfasted in the room, then as soon as I was sure that Steve would have gone to work I let Graham drive me back to the end of the lane. He had a day of appointments he couldn't break so he persuaded me that I may as well go home and collect some things.

Quietly I let myself in and not letting myself stop to think I ran up the stairs.

Steve was lying face down on the bed. I stopped dead when I saw him and turned to run downstairs again but he had heard me and he raised his head. His face was strangely red and swollen and it struck me suddenly that he too had been crying.

'Where have you been?' he whispered. 'I've been out of my mind with worry.'

'With a man of course.' I wanted to hurt him as much as he had hurt me.

'Oh Lyn.' He bit his lip, painfully sitting up and swinging his legs to the floor. 'What has happened to us?'

'Nothing happened to me,' I retorted. 'I trusted you; I was working hard, for us, and look what happened.' It didn't cross my mind that perhaps if I had been less preoccupied with Graham over the last few weeks, things might never have gone so far.

I stamped across to the window and looked out. Ian Johnson was cutting roses next door. I could see the curl of blue smoke rising from his pipe.

I heard Steve coming across the room behind me. Then his hand was on my shoulder. 'Linda, my love. Can you ever forgive me?'

I shrugged off his hand, and shook my head.

'I'm leaving you, Steve. Even if I wanted to stay, it seems to me you've got commitments elsewhere now.' I was so weary by now that my voice was quite unemotional and flat. I hardly cared what was going to happen.

We stood in silence for a moment, then Steve said, 'Who is this man?'

I felt suddenly dreadfully guilty. 'He was just a friend. Someone I met at the teashop.' I turned and nearly spat at him, 'He was just a friend to me, but I knew he loved me. He cares. I'm going to London with him. There's nothing for me to stay for, is there?'

As I felt the tears welling up in my eyes again I turned back to the window. 'Go away Steven, please.'

I held my breath. Would he go? I desperately wanted him to stay suddenly, but I heard his soft footsteps on the rug and then the sound of the door shutting behind him. Then I let the tears run down my face unchecked.

I don't know how long I stood there. Perhaps it was hours. Slowly my tears stopped and dried in streaks on my cheeks. I felt completely drained and empty.

I nearly didn't answer the knock on the front door. But then I slowly dragged myself down the stairs. There was a young woman on the doorstep. Instinctively I knew it must be Lauren. She was tall and slim with auburn hair. There were great dark circles beneath her eyes too.

'Are you Linda?' she asked bluntly.

I nodded, still clutching the door-handle.

She swallowed. 'Will you tell Steve I'm going back to London. I don't want to see him again.'

'But the baby!' I blurted out.

She blushed crimson. 'There isn't any baby, Linda. I made it up. I knew that was the only way I would get Steve, make him divorce you. But I couldn't go through with it. I'm sorry.'

She paused as though she was going to say something else, and then she turned and ran down the path.

I didn't know what to do. I just stood there for a while, looking after her, then I went slowly into the kitchen and made myself a cup of black coffee. It made me feel rather sick, but I hoped it might help me to think straight.

What was I to do? My brain raced in circles. Steve, Graham, the cottage, my beautiful little home. Steve, Graham, Steve . . . oh Steve.

I hardly know to this day what made me do it, drag a comb through my hair, collect my purse, and take the bus into Minster. The old people's home was near the bus station, set in a lovely garden.

Aunt Irene was sitting on the porch, gazing out at the rose beds when I arrived. She smiled at me when she saw me and

gestured at the chair near her. Her poor hand was still paralysed but she looked much better than when Steve and I had
last seen her.

I felt her looking at me closely as I sat there not knowing
what to say. I didn't want to tell her anything; I just wanted
the comfort of being near her, I think because she was Steve's
aunt.

'It's good of you to come, my dear,' she commented at
last. 'I've been thinking a lot about you and Steve.'

I felt myself blushing and I looked at my hands. Me and
Steve. It seemed strange that she could still refer to us
together like that, as if nothing had happened.

I looked up and smiled wanly, and I was quite embarrassed
to find her looking at me so shrewdly. I felt it was almost as
if she knew exactly why I was there. I suppose it can't have
been difficult to guess that we had had a row.

'You know, Linda, I often think of my life in that cottage
when I was young. I'm so happy to think that you two live
there now, to fill it with happiness and laughter. I never told
Steve this, but when I was a girl,' she paused and there was
such a long silence I thought she had forgotten what she was
talking about, the way old people do, but then she went on,
'I was engaged once, you know. To such a nice boy.' Her
faded blue eyes twinkled at the memory. 'We nearly got married, then I found out that he'd done something very bad –
he'd stolen some money. I told him I couldn't marry him.
He went away to the war of course, in 1914, and he was
killed in the first month.' There was a long silence. I could
see that even now, after so many years, it still hurt her to
think about it. At last she went on, 'If I'd stood by him, in
spite of what he'd done, I often think perhaps he might not
have been killed. I might have had children of my own . . .'
Her voice tailed away again, and I felt my eyes fill with tears.

She smiled suddenly. 'You won't wait too long, will you
Linda, you and Steve? I would so like to see your babies
before I die, my dear.' Then she became suddenly brisk. 'Why

not go and find the housekeeper and ask her if you can stay and have lunch with me. I'd like that. Don't look so sad, dear. Take no notice of an old woman's ramblings. After all, you do have Steve; and I know you love each other so much, that nothing could come between you the way it did between Robert and me. Nothing, however bad, should come between lovers. They must forgive.'

I got up and dropped a kiss on her head. 'I'll go and see about lunch,' I said, my voice catching in my throat.

Of course it was very hard to forgive and I could never forget, but somehow we managed to get through that summer, Steve and I. When Graham came for me that afternoon I told him I couldn't go to London after all and he shrugged philosophically. 'I'm sorry, honey; if you change your mind you know where to find me . . .' I think he was secretly rather relieved. After all, he was happily married in Wisconsin.

And I didn't change my mind. I loved Steve and I realised that whatever he had done I was prepared to give him another chance. I knew I had been lucky too. Graham understood and he had not taken advantage of me when I had, I now realised, been playing with fire. I might so easily have found myself in the same situation as Lauren.

And now, the leaves are blowing from the trees and I've lit a fire in the grate and the room is filled with the scent of burning apple logs. I've given up my job; somehow we'll get by on the money we've saved already, and by the time spring comes I shall have a baby and if it's a girl I shall call her Irene. Steve doesn't know the real reason I chose the name, but of course he's pleased, and he's thrilled about the baby. And I love him so very much.

The Duck Shoot Man

ALTHOUGH THE SUN WAS SETTING in a blaze of livid gold behind the distant hills Harriet Cummins had her back resolutely towards the sight. Instead she was peering doubtfully through the windscreen of her stationary car at the retreating ripples of water on the road in front of her.

'Extraordinary,' she murmured to her friend, Cathie Hamden, who was seated apprehensively beside her. 'You wouldn't expect that the last bit to be uncovered would be the nearest bit to us. The land must be lower than the sea or something.'

'I still think we ought to wait, dear.' Cathie was looking at the shining mudflats and the road which snaked across them. A flock of ducks was wading happily across the causeway, not pausing to discriminate between mud base and thin mud scum.

'Rubbish. I'm going now.' Harriet reached purposefully for the handbrake before she switched on the ignition. That way the car already had a little impetus before the engine spluttered into life. 'I wonder,' she went on, gently malicious, 'if there's enough petrol to see us across. Wouldn't it be awful to be caught by the tide and have to climb into one of those baskets!'

Cathie let out a squeak of fear as Harriet knew she would. She smiled to herself, but even she cast a slightly apprehensive glance upwards as they passed the first post with its plaited straw refuge.

She noticed that Cathie was sitting upright, clutching the top of the dashboard – the way she usually sat, in fact, when Harriet urged their old car over forty, which she was constantly trying to do, even in the short High Street at home – and spitefully she jabbed the accelerator. 'Silly old woman,' she murmured scornfully to herself. She always thought of Cathie, with her fresh pink face and still-blonde hair as old, although at sixty-five Harriet's companion was three years her junior.

The car coughed momentarily, a frequent occurrence from its bronchial engine, and Harriet clutched the wheel more firmly, ignoring the subdued groan on her left. The wheels were sending up a fine spray and in the strange slanted evening light it was sometimes hard to see where the road ran. The water flowed impartially before them disguising their route in a silver tissue of reflections.

They gained the upslanting firmness of the island with undisguised relief, stopping momentarily to gaze back over their shoulders at the winding road through the mudflats. Already the tide had ebbed away and in places the causeway was drying in the cool sea wind.

Harriet groped in the glove compartment, leaning without apology across her friend. 'Where's the address? I want to get to the guesthouse and have a bath.' Maps and books were rummaged unceremoniously to the floor.

Cathie tightened her lips a fraction. 'I think, dear, you'll find that you put it in your bag,' she murmured at last, half apologetic.

'Rubbish. Why should I do that?'

Cathie smiled bitterly. 'Because you said I'd be sure to lose it if you didn't.' She watched as Harriet turned to the back seat for the battered leather hold-all she was pleased to call a handbag. Sure enough the instructions were there.

'Humph!' That grudging snort was the nearest Harriet ever

came to apology, the glitter in Cathie's eyes the nearest to triumph.

The car shuddered forward again, and they began to thread their way through the network of lanes which led to the island's only village.

The guesthouse was not hard to find. It stood out at the end of a row of whitewashed fisherman's cottages, a modern bungalow with cream and red paint and ornamental scroll-work on the nameplate, *Castleview*, which hung on a gibbet by the front gate.

Harriet parked the car with its near-side wheels in the thick lushness of the hedge and sat back, squinting at the house.

'*Castleview* indeed.' She craned her neck to see if the claim were true. 'I do hope it's going to be all right. One can never tell, booking from so far away. Well, what are you waiting for?'

'I can't get out this side, dear.' Cathie moved round slightly and slid half an inch to the right to show she intended climbing across the handbrake, as soon as Harriet had herself moved. Beyond her the heavy greenery pushed against the car window.

Harriet gave a little smile. For a moment she considered making Cathie slide across. Then she relented. She made a great show of restarting the car, backing off the verge, waiting for her passenger to disembark, and then reburying the car in the hedge. Then at last she herself climbed stiffly from the driver's seat.

The air was strong: a combination of salt and honeyed ripeness from the heavy hedgerows and the evening breeze off the cool of the sea. She sniffed loudly and allowed herself to grin happily at the scarlet and golden remnants of the shrouded sun as it sank into heavy bruised cloud on the inland hills.

Then she turned her attention to the bungalow before them.

'I can't think why they were allowed to build such an ugly

house,' she commented tartly. She pulled her tweed jacket down neatly over well-padded hips. Her right eyebrow had risen an indignant half-way to her hairline.

Cathie, knowing the signs, licked her lips quickly.

'It does seem out of place,' she ventured.

Already Harriet had opened the gate and was making her way up the concrete path. Half-way to the door she stopped.

'Look at this garden,' she appealed, not so much to Cathie as to the limpid blue of the evening air. 'Geometric! Could have been designed by a town clerk with a ruler.'

Town clerks were for some reason one of Harriet's pet hates. She blamed them for most of the twentieth century's more uncomfortable problems.

She waved her hands at the neat beds of salvia and the short-haired grass. 'You know,' she confided over her shoulder in an echoing stage whisper, 'I shouldn't be at all surprised if they have flying ducks over the fireplace.'

'Ssssh!' Cathie glanced in agonised embarrassment at the heavy lace curtains, and then permitted herself the luxury of wondering quickly why they bothered with net curtains with such a large front garden and such a deserted lane which was in any case firmly hidden behind the high hedge.

Harriet rang the bell and smothered a giggle as the pretentious chime rang out in the silence. 'I wonder if we could transfer to one of the cottages,' she hissed, as somewhere in the distance a dog began to bark. Cathie smiled nervously. Someone was coming. She patted her fair hair into place.

The lady of the house, Mrs Cosby, was large and red-cheeked and determinedly jolly. She beamed benevolently at her guests as she led them across the house to show them their rooms. 'I've no one here now, but a gentleman come for the birds and yourselves,' she explained cheerfully. 'The season's more or less over, you know, once the kiddies are back at school.'

She threw open a door. Inside was a small room with a single bed, a blue straw-plaited chair and a dressing table.

Harriet glanced at the window. The lace net curtain reached only half-way up the window here, a gesture showing that this was the side of the house with, some fifteen feet away, a thick holly hedge blanketing the view. She did a lightning toss-up in her mind. 'You'd better have this one,' she murmured to Cathie over her shoulder.

Cathie nodded gratefully.

Harriet's own room was on the opposite side of the corridor. She breathed a sigh of relief as the door was flung open. Her gamble had paid off. The half span of intricate net showed a view over miles of mudflats, and at the end of the promontory, the castle reflected stilly in the low of the tide.

She carefully regulated the broadness of her smile.

'The gentleman is next door to you here,' Mrs Cosby was saying. 'And the you-know-what is opposite, there.' She coyly indicated a door on which was a small enamelled label bearing the inscription, *This is IT!*

Cathie saw her friend's mouth twitching and prayed she would be able to suppress whatever remark was about to burst forth.

'I'm afraid –' Harriet began, and then continued to Cathie's extreme relief, 'that we've left our cases in the car. I hoped perhaps your husband . . . when you get to our age, it's hard to carry things.' She eyed Mrs Cosby closely. The woman was probably Cathie's age – perhaps a year or two younger.

'Oh, I'm a widow. I thought I told you in my letter.' Mrs Cosby fell into the trap at once. 'But never mind, I dare say I can carry them for you. If there's anything too heavy I'm sure that Mr Danway will fetch them up later when he comes in.'

'Mr Danway?' Harriet had thrown her jacket on the bed – a gesture of possessiveness.

'My other guest. A strange one, he is, but very quiet. No trouble at all. Now, my dears, tea is at six as a rule, but as you were late arriving I've put it back today. Just this once.'

Her expression was suddenly threatening. 'It'll be ready in about ten minutes, if that suits?'

She did not wait to hear them agree.

Harriet watched the door close. At once came the expected outburst. '*This is IT* indeed! Do you think she *knows* there's such a word as lavatory?' She sat on the bed and gave a gentle experimental bounce.

'Hush dear. As a matter of fact it's a bathroom. I looked.' Cathie walked to the window and raised the net to look a little wistfully at the view.

'Have you got a screwdriver?'

Cathie jumped and looked round apprehensively. 'What for?'

'To unscrew the notice of course. No? I'm sure there'll be one in the car. Come on. At least help me get that net curtain down.'

'You can't.'

'Who is going to stop me?' Harriet stood and gave orders as Cathie struggled to pull the hook of the curtain wire over the screw which held it. At last she managed it, panting. The wire dropped to hang down the side of the window, the net a heavy bridal train, trailing to the floor. 'I hope Mrs Cosby's not offended.'

'Why should she be?' Harriet sat down heavily at the dressing table and began to rub her face with the licked corner of her handkerchief. 'Ought to be glad I've let some light in!'

Five minutes later they were summoned by gong to the guests' sitting room. Four tables stood regimented on the carpet, two by two. Only two were laid; one for one and one for two.

Cautiously they sat down. Harriet peered into the teapot and sniffed. 'I knew it. We should have brought our own tea. I wonder what she's going to give us?' She peered at the other table. 'She's made him wait to have it with us, old devil. I bet he's usually in the pub by now.'

Cathie had already helped herself from the loaded toast-

40

rack. She was buttering enthusiastically as their hostess came in with a heavy tray. She was hungry and not even Harriet's scornful remarks about her weight – Cathie was the lighter by a good ten pounds – were going to put her off her food this evening.

'Is your other guest going to eat with us?' Harriet asked pointedly as Mrs Cosby began to unload her tray onto their table.

'Oh yes, I daresay,' she answered comfortably. 'I just heard him come in.' They waited in silence till she'd gone back to her kitchen, then Cathie leaned over the table. 'Do you think he's a boyfriend?' she simpered a little.

Harriet's eyebrows shot up. 'That woman must be your age if she's a day!'

Cathie looked taken aback. 'Well, even at my age, Hattie . . .' She broke off as the door opened.

A man came in. He was tall and sturdy, with rugged features and ruffled wiry hair – a man perhaps in his late forties. He stopped abruptly when he saw them, then he strode across to his own table in silence.

'Good evening Mr Danway.' Harriet's voice rang across the room.

He stiffened, then half turning he nodded in their direction. He chose a chair with its back to them, and sitting down leisurely moved his place setting round the table until it was in front of him.

'Well!' Harriet made no attempt to lower her voice.

Cathie frowned at her, embarrassed equally by the behaviour of both. She was relieved when Mrs Cosby appeared with a new tray. Obviously familiar with Mr Danway's taciturn nature their hostess made no attempt to talk to him as she put the plates on his table. It was to the ladies she turned at last.

'Got everything, have we? Is there anything else I can fetch you, my dears?'

A dog had bounded into the room after her and it ran to

41

Cathie, its tail wriggling obsequiously. She patted it, flattered that it should have singled her out.

'That's Rudie,' Mrs Cosby volunteered. 'I hope you don't mind. Soppy case he is.' She stood for a moment surveying him fondly.

'I think,' Harriet's voice was frosty, 'we'd rather he were kept out of the dining room. Wouldn't we, dear?' She shot a look at Cathie who guiltily snatched her hand away from the soft slobbering head which was lovingly pushing against her knee.

Dog and landlady vanished and the meal continued in silence. From time to time Harriet threw dark, meaningful glances at the man's back. She seemed preoccupied and Cathie, snatching at the opportunity, helped herself to more sausages from the serving dish. The room was quite silent save for the sound of knives and forks on china; the large clock on the mantelpiece had stopped at ten past eleven.

When Mr Danway pushed back his chair and threw down the newspaper he had been reading, both ladies jumped nervously. Cathie focused all her attention on the bowl of sugar from which she had been about to help herself.

He stopped beside their table for a moment, looking down at them in silence, then abruptly he strode from the room, slamming the door behind him.

Cathie found that her knees were shaking a little. 'What a *peculiar* man,' she commented and reached for her teacup.

'Did you see his eyes?' Harriet's voice was almost awed. 'The were yellow, like topaz. Weird.'

'Do you think he's . . .' Cathie hesitated a moment, hardly daring to voice her question, '. . . well, *normal?*'

'He certainly didn't look it to me. Remember to lock your door tonight, dear. I certainly shall.' The shudder which shook Harriet's sturdy frame was not entirely faked.

Cathie laid down her knife and fork. Her appetite had vanished of its own accord. Regretfully she eyed the sausage left on her plate and comforted herself with the thought that probably the dog would get it.

The two ladies made their way back to Harriet's room. By unspoken consent it had become their headquarters and neither woman had felt like sitting in the two formal armchairs before the defunct clock – no flying ducks, Harriet had noted with something akin to disappointment.

The door of the room next door was ajar.

'I must go to the loo!' Harriet announced loudly, intending to be heard well beyond the confines of her room. She advanced sideways across the hall, towards the bathroom door, her eyes glued to that of the opposite bedroom.

Abruptly she stopped. Cathie saw her expression change to one of horror before, after the briefest hesitation, she groped for the handle of the door marked *This is IT* and dived out of sight.

It was a nerve-racking five minutes. Cathie waited, not liking to close the bedroom door in case a rescue was needed, not liking to walk away from it, in case – well, in case. But supposing he came and saw her standing there? She trembled at the thought.

Then came the welcome noise of a cistern flushing and Harriet emerged. She closed the bedroom door behind her and leaned against it, breathing heavily.

'He's got a gun.'

'What?' Cathie's voice rose up in a squeak.

'He's got a gun. It's lying on the bed. I saw it.'

They looked at each other in silence for a moment. There was a strange suppressed excitement in Harriet's eyes.

'What shall we do?' Cathie breathed the words tremulously and Harriet, probably for the first time in her life, shrugged, at a loss.

'Do you think *she* knows? Do you think he's got some kind of a hold over her?' Harriet carefully left the door and went to sit on her bed. Her legs were trembling a little and she raised her chin defiantly to hide the fact from Cathie.

Cathie's eyes widened as she considered the possibility. 'He had an unpleasant face; thoroughly unpleasant.' It was as near as she ever got to being critical of someone's appearance.

'Capable of anything, I'd say.' Harriet forgot herself so far as to lick her lips. 'I wonder if he's escaped from somewhere?'

'We'd have seen it in the paper.'

'Not necessarily. They might not have wanted to spread panic.'

Somewhere close by there was the sound of a door slamming and both ladies jumped violently. Cathie ran to the window. The garden was dark and deserted. Beyond the low wind-flattened hedge at the end of it, the salt marsh and fields spread out towards the luminous sea. Dusk had closed in now and the wind was gathering strength. One or two leaves whipped from a stunted apple tree at the corner of the garden and flicked against the glass near her face and she flinched. She drew the curtains, making sure there was no crack between them, and returned to her seat on the bed.

It was then that they heard the heavy footsteps outside in the corridor. There was a loud knock on the door.

They clutched each other in fright. Harriet rose to her feet. With considerable dignity she went to the door.

'Who is it?' There was only the slightest quaver in her voice.

'Danway.'

She closed her eyes and swallowed. 'What do you want, Mr Danway?'

'I've brought your cases. You and the other lady. Leave them out here, shall I?'

There was an instant surge of relief on Harriet's face. 'If you please, Mr Danway. That is kind of you.'

They listened to the double crash of the heavy cases being dropped on the floor, the tramp of his footsteps and the bang of his door. Harriet cautiously opened hers a crack.

She hauled in the two cases and then shut it again. 'Now what?'

'I need my case in *my* room, dear,' Cathie commented. 'Surely he didn't think we were sharing?'

'I doubt if it crossed his mind.' Harriet was tart. 'Go on. Take it and run over. I'll cover you.' She wasn't too sure what the last phrase entailed, but it certainly seemed appropriate.

'I can't run. It's heavy.'

'Well, drag it then.'

'Should we go to bed, do you think?'

'Well, I'm not going to sit up all night. Lock your door.' Harriet was beginning to feel alarmingly tired. She had driven nearly two hundred miles that day and now, to find her room was next to that of a gunman – actual or potential – it would be surprising if she had not found the situation exhausting. She watched Cathie drag her case across the hall and disappear into her room, then with a sigh she closed her own door and locked it.

The rest of the evening was uneventful. She managed to reach the bathroom safely, then she regained her bedroom where she climbed into bed with a book and her little transistor radio to listen to the news. The news, when it came, was disappointingly lax in reporting any escapes from any prisons anywhere and she turned it off, half relieved, half disappointed, and opened her book. Hercule Poirot was hot on the trail; she began to gnaw her thumbnail avidly, her pages turning more and more quickly as the book neared its climax.

And then she heard it. In the silence of the room she could just make out the sound of a movement next door. She dropped her book on the counterpane and listened intently. Yes, there it was. A scraping and tapping. And then footsteps. A drawer being dragged open – quite distinct, that sound – and a low cough.

She pulled the bedclothes up to her chin and listened as hard as she could. The wind was blowing more strongly now. She could hear the hedgerows rustle and squeak, and the tapping, somewhere, of a twig against the window.

Suddenly she could not bear not to know what was happening. She slipped out of bed, turned off her side-light and tiptoed, shivering in the dark, to the window. She flung back the curtains and peered through. It was pitch black out there, save where the light from a neighbouring window, his window, streamed out across the pale grass.

She waited, hoping to see his shadow, but there was no sign of movement, only the methodical noises from next door. Then the light went out and there was silence. She held her breath.

Distantly she could hear the strange echoing, churring noise of a nightjar somewhere on the marshes. It was a very lonely sound above the endless sighing of the sea. She strained her ears again. There was no sound of bedsprings from next door. Had he gone to bed, or was he still up waiting, and listening, just as she was? Leaving the curtains open she turned towards her own old-fashioned iron-frame and climbed wearily in. She was still very tense and she found herself longing to be able to go and fetch some hot milk. That alas was not possible in someone else's house, even had she plucked up the courage to leave her room again.

Eventually she dozed.

The dog awoke her, barking furiously somewhere the other side of the house. She lay rigidly clutching the bedclothes, her heart pounding uncomfortably as she gazed up at the ceiling. Then, cautiously, she moved her eyes. A large round moon had risen. The pale colourless light flooded through the window illuminating her door and the far wall. Her eyes went without volition to the door-handle. Had it moved? Her hands flew to her mouth as she stared fascinated, hardly daring to breathe.

Then she heard it again. A stealthy movement from next door. He was stirring. She raised herself cautiously on her elbow and groped for her little clock. Half past three. Footsteps trod softly across the floor in the next room and she heard a creak and then a low clatter. He was up. He was walking about.

She put the clock down and lay back on her pillow, tensely listening to every sound. A bar of cloud drifted over the face of the moon and for a moment her eyes closed.

He had picked up the gun and was standing carefully behind his door listening. The dog was silent now and nothing in the house seemed to be awake. He checked that the gun was loaded and then, shouldering his haversack, he opened the door softly and listened again.

The old woman was standing in the hall in a patch of moonlight, waiting for him. It was the blonde, nervous one; the younger of the two. She stood there in her pink flannel nightdress, her hands stretched out as if to bar his way.

Harriet had opened her door a fraction. She put her eye to the crack and with a gasp saw Cathie standing there blandly smiling in her nightdress, her bare feet white in the moonlight. What was she doing? Why didn't she move? Was the silly woman sleepwalking?

She tried to call out as the man stood in his doorway, his face growing ugly with anger, but Cathie didn't seem to see that she was antagonising him, and no sound came to Harriet's dry lips. Her throat was constricted with fear.

Then it happened. The man strode forward. He tried to push Cathie out of his way but she stood firm, gazing at him gently, that irritating foolish smile still on her face. He pushed again and she began to struggle with him, the two figures circling slowly, soundlessly on the rag rug on the polished wood floor.

Then the gun went off. It wasn't a loud bang. Just enough to make Harriet jump, her heart leaping, thudding, into her throat. Then she saw the blood. Cathie was still smiling, but there was blood soaking through her nightdress. Drops fell darkly onto the rug and the polished floor, wet, black pools in the silver moonlight.

Slowly Cathie's hands went to the place and, surprised, she

looked down, and still looking surprised, she sank slowly to her knees. Harriet wanted to scream. She wanted to call out. She wanted to run.

She stood rooted to the spot for a moment, and then, terrified as the man turned to look at her, his face a blank mask, she moved at last, retreating into her bedroom, slamming the door, leaning against it, sweat pouring down her face. The key. Where was the key? Surely there had been a key?

Her fingers fumbled desperately at the lock and at last she managed to turn it. She ran for the chair which stood before the small table and wedged it under the door-handle, then she ran to the window and drew the curtains tight to shut out the cruel moon.

'Cathie!' she sobbed out loud. 'Cathie.'

She heard steps outside her door and she froze. He was listening at her keyhole. She turned to look but the room was pitch black without the moonlight. She dared not move to try and find the light-switch.

She waited for what seemed like hours, hardly daring to breathe, then at last, shaking uncontrollably, she groped her way to the bed and sat down. She dared not open the door to look. But supposing Cathie were still alive? Suppose she needed a doctor? She pictured again that swelling scarlet patch on the flannel nightdress, and miserably she closed her eyes. It had been right over Cathie's heart.

She must have dozed. When she awoke it was daylight. She lay, puzzled for a moment at the intense misery which gripped her whole body, gazing out of the window at the blue sky, light with high puffy clouds. Then she remembered. She dragged herself from the bed and went to the door and listened. The house was silent. She swallowed hard, then, suddenly resolute, began to dress as quickly as she could. She was stiff and her fingers were awkward and cold but she was determined to face whatever had to be faced from the security of her tweed suit. She even ran a brush briefly through her curly white hair.

Then she was ready. She listened carefully as very cautiously she turned the key. It took a lot of courage to open the door but she did it at last and looked out.

The body had gone. The floor was clean. Everything was as it had been the night before when she first went to bed. She breathed a sigh of relief. Mrs Cosby must have found Cathie. Perhaps the ambulance had already taken her away.

Plucking up her courage she went softly down the passage towards the guests' sitting room. A strong incongruous smell of bacon was floating up the passage. She shuddered as she pushed the door of the sitting room open. The same two tables were laid again, one for one, one for two. At the latter sat a figure.

'Hello dear.' Cathie peered round. 'I knocked on your door earlier, but you must have been sound asleep.'

Harriet's mouth fell open.

'Are you all right, dear?' Cathie looked concerned. 'Come and have some cornflakes. This sea air has already made me hungry.'

Harriet groped her way to the table and sat down. Her eyes were fixed on Cathie's bosom which was covered in a pale yellow jumper.

Cathie smiled at her benignly. 'Have some coffee, dear. That nice Mr Danway will be in soon. I was asking Mrs Cosby about him. He's here for the duck shooting, you know. He went out in the early hours this morning. I'm surprised you didn't hear him.' She leaned forward confidentially. 'Do you know, Hattie. It was so ridiculous last night. I dreamed he broke into your room and shot you! It really quite upset me this morning till I realised it was just a dream.' She gave a little giggle as Harriet slumped into her chair. 'I suppose it was the gun that did it. Silly me. Shall we go down on the beach later and look for shells, dear?' she went on happily. 'It's going to be a lovely day.'

With a shaking hand Harriet reached for her napkin, guiltily pushing away the whisper of treacherous disappointment which had touched her at the sight of Cathie's robust form. 'You must have eaten too many sausages last night,' she murmured with something almost approaching her usual asperity. 'Fancy dreaming a stupid dream like that!'

Frost

THE CHAIN-LINK FENCE gleamed red in the light of the rising sun. Looking down at it from her bedroom window across the bare square of earth and rubble which would one day be their garden, Amanda sighed. Turning from the window she sat down on the end of the bed and stared round the room. Small, functional and new, like the garden. So new it still smelled of paint and varnish and the sour tang of sawn deal.

Next door the baby was crying again as it had been on and off all night. The muffled protests and the distant sound of a radio somewhere across the road only served to emphasise the silence in her own house.

'We must live somewhere new; so new no one else has ever lived there before! I don't want a second-hand house! I don't want a house full of other people's dreams and nightmares.' Andrew's sweep of argument carried all before it as it always had and her own dream of an old cottage with a thatched roof and roses round the door crumbled before his enthusiasm, swept away as impractical and romantic and hopeless.

So here they were, newly married, newly moved, practical and down-to-earth and Andrew had left for work, early as usual, leaving her with the long day stretching out before her, empty, soulless and alone.

'You'll soon find a job; make some friends. Go and knock on some doors.' So easy for him. He had done it already and talked cars and sport and TV programmes and the relative qualities of the local pubs. Her knocks had been greeted with vague smiles, barely concealed impatience, screaming children, hurried uncomfortable exchanges in the frantic business of her neighbours' days.

Standing up at last she went to the window again. The sun was up now, the light outdoors harsh and unforgiving. Beyond the chain-link lay all that remained of the old suburban garden in which their small development of 'executive starter homes' had been built. The grey stone mansion had long gone, destroyed, so she had heard, by fire, but something remained to titillate her curiosity for there, beyond the long swaying grasses and the lichen-covered apple trees, she could see the reflection of the sun on glass. Several times she had walked round the neighbouring streets, trying to find the entrance to the garden, but with no success. It seemed to be a lost enclave, an unsold, unremembered plot amongst the neat geometric streets, the small red roofs and the manicured lawns. The lost garden beckoned. It was old; it was romantic; it was the focus of her dreams. One day she knew she would find the entrance and walk there on the old land beneath the new.

She had no premonition that today would be the day, no warning that suddenly the urge would become undeniable. One minute she was standing in her lonely bedroom listening to the baby's wails, the next she was running downstairs, knowing that she had to find what lay beyond the wire.

No one saw her. Glancing behind her at the rows of neat windows, most swathed modestly in ruched nets and fancy frills, she put her foot, without giving herself time to think, on the concrete stanchion which held the high fence in place, grabbed at the top of the wire and vaulted it. In the neat houses behind her, women got their children ready for school; they fed their babies and made their beds and looked for the car keys so they could go to a supermarket too far away to visit on foot. None looked out of the windows. There were no gardens yet to admire. Some had laid neat squares of grass bought by the metre; two had planted small whips of birch and miniature weeping willow. None looked beyond the chain-link fence. Those who did saw nothing but a wilderness of weeds and wondered, if they thought at all, why the plot had not been sold.

Amanda stood for a moment feeling the unexpected iciness of early morning dew soaking into the legs of her jeans. It made her gasp with surprise. Glancing back she saw how high the wire she had vaulted was from this side, with beyond it the blind windows, and she shivered. Ducking through the wet grasses she ran for the apple trees, suddenly afraid of being seen, feeling the catch of bramble and spear thistle, the slippery wetness in her shoes, the cling of burrs in her hair, then she was out of sight of the houses and wrapped in the silence of the garden.

She stopped, trying to steady her breath, willing the beating of her heart to quieten and steady, and at last, as the pounding in her ears subsided, she let the peace and beauty of the garden enfold her and soak into her soul. Walking slowly now, exploring, confident she could not be seen, she found that she was listening to the liquid song of a wren as it scuttled and hid in the ivy which swathed an old grey garden wall. On the top of one of the apple trees a blackbird eyed her suspiciously and then relaxed, ignoring her. Its throat swelled and it began to sing, the sound echoing gloriously round her in a cascade of liquid notes.

Enchanted, she listened without moving, conscious that in the distance she could hear the steady popping sound of ball on racquet from the municipal tennis courts in Celadon Road – surely once part of this same garden. She did not move until the blackbird stopped, flirted its tail and flew away. Then she plunged further into the undergrowth.

She saw the old man before he saw her. A trug laden with flowers on his arm, he moved slowly and silently away from her along the path and out of sight. Frightened and embarrassed she drew back into the shelter of the brambles and watched.

The half ruined, shabby greenhouse stood against a high brick wall. Most of the glass was broken; that which remained was smeared and furry with lichen. On the wooden battens the paint rose in blistered flakes to leave weathered broken frames for the surviving jagged triangles of glass which they clasped. This then had been the glass she had seen from her bedroom window; this the glass which had caught the rising sun. She crept closer, staring in. Where had he got the flowers? She could see the wild remains of an old vine, clinging to the glass; giant nettles, fat hen, avens. A few poppies splashed the only colour through the green; the staging was littered with broken clay pots and rotten splintered seed trays.

At the back door of the house he proffered the basket of blooms. 'The last of the chrysanths, tell her ladyship.'

'Her ladyship wants to see you.' In a flurry of white aprons and uncomfortable self-importance the cook beckoned him in.

He nodded, stamping mud from his boots, pulling his cap from his head. For special occasions she often asked him in, planned the flowers with him, consulted his expertise. She loved flowers, did her ladyship. With a smile he stepped onto the shining oak boards and made his way towards the morning room.

Amanda glanced through the door and then stepped inside the greenhouse. With a frightened squawk a bird flew up from the floor and beat for a moment against the glass before finding a gap and soaring out into the sunlight. She ran a finger over a work bench. The soil was dust under her hand. A rusty tobacco tin rattled as though it were full of nails. Another was full of empty, desiccated seeds. Keeping a wary eye out for the old man she wandered further in, savouring the warmth, the smell of dry earth, the buzz of a bee trapped beneath the glass. Outside the sun moved higher in the sky.

The shadows shortened. The dew evaporated. The day grew hotter.

A strange sweet smell assailed her nostrils. Unpleasant. She sniffed with sudden distaste. It was the smell of decay. Near her hand, as she picked idly over the rubbish on the bench she found a packet of cigarettes, half empty, the cigarettes inside as dry as the dust. She frowned. They must have lain there abandoned for years. Her fingers hovered over them, hesitated and moved away. Inexplicably she felt a shiver tiptoe across her shoulders.

'I'm afraid there can be no hothouse flowers this year, Bates.' She was sitting with her back to the desk, her pen poised, the ink already dry on the nib, turning to him for only a second in her busy day. 'We shall not be firing the boilers.'

'Your ladyship?' He could think of nothing to say.

'That will be all, Bates.'

'But the orchids, your ladyship. The frost —'

'I'm sorry, Bates. There will be no more orchids.' None of his business why; hide her fear and sorrow and rage from the servants at all cost. She could see it all in his face: first the bewilderment; then the realisation; then the sick disbelief. 'That will be all Bates.' She could say nothing else. Beneath the high frill of her silk blouse and the long strings of creamy pearls she too felt sick. In the drawer of the desk only a few inches from her hand the pile of gambling debts burned like a fire. Reginald was in the garden now. Sulking. She could see him if she moved her head slightly. 'I'm sorry, Mama.' That was all he had said. 'I'm sorry, Mama.'

She closed her eyes and took a deep slow breath.

'You may go now, Bates,' she said.

Suddenly she could smell tobacco. Amanda looked round, afraid, expecting to see him there, but she was still alone. The greenhouse grew warmer. She put her hand up to the neck of her blouse uncomfortably and turned back towards the door. A fork and spade were leaning against one another, dug into the earth. Around their handles a trail of bindweed had woven them together.

'She told you then.' Cook felt a twinge of pity for the white-faced old man. He stared at her blankly. 'She let two of the maids go this morning,' she went on as if it would be a comfort.

He shook his head blindly. 'The orchids. They'll die.'

She shrugged. 'They're only flowers.'

He had pale blue eyes, irises as clear as the sky. Unfocused now, they swam with tears. Shocked, she stepped back.

'The frosts are coming. I can smell 'em.' The old man's voice cracked.

She shook her head. 'It's the horses. Mr Williams heard them quarrelling last night. He owes thousands. This wouldn't have happened if his old lordship were still alive.' She shook her head and turned away. No point in telling him the rest, poor old man. It wasn't just the orchids which were going. Half the servants; her ladyship's jewellery; the silver; maybe even the house itself.

Leaving the greenhouse Amanda followed an overgrown track round towards the old kitchen garden. The walls which sheltered the neat beds had nurtured a tropical jungle there. She wandered over the paths and finding a bush of raspberries long grown wild picked some, sucking their sweet juice from her fingers as she remembered she had had no breakfast.

'No!' The shout behind her was full of pain.

She spun round, staring wildly towards the bushes. The birds had stopped singing. She could no longer hear the tennis balls. Nervously she retraced her steps towards the gnarled pine tree which towered over the glasshouse and dodged behind it, looking round. There was no sound of footsteps, no further cry. Her heart was hammering under her ribs and suddenly she was not enjoying herself any more.

She glanced over her shoulder. From here she could not

see the chain-link fence at all. All round her the overgrown shrubs and tall grasses pressed in in a thick wall. She took a deep breath. Backing away from the tree she glanced to her right. A pane of glass in the greenhouse had caught the sun, blinding her. Beyond it lay the stretch of grass which had once been a lawn and beyond that the fence and home.

To her left a shrubbery – leggy, thin-leafed rhododendrons, holly, smoke trees – scrambled over one another towards the light, above them a huge acacia.

Cautiously she made her way back towards the greenhouse. Behind her she could hear a pigeon. The soft coo swelled into the silence and then died again as she saw the old man hobbling towards her. She stood transfixed with embarrassment. There was nowhere to go; nowhere to hide in time. She bit her lip and stood waiting, expecting a tirade of abuse for her trespass.

He walked straight past her. His eyes, the clear pale blue of forget-me-nots, did not move to left or right. With them steadfastly fixed on the greenhouse he hobbled within two feet of her and on down the path. Behind him the air was cold.

There would be a frost that night. The evening was clear. The smoky bonfire spread the scent of burning leaves throughout the garden; the plume of blue rose straight up into the still air as he raked them higher and higher onto the pile. He glanced over his shoulder towards the glasshouse seeing the blooms basking in the warmth through the sparkling panes: creamy petals, tinged with pink – velvet, pampered, exquisite blooms fit for the show tent. There was no breath of wind. A huge moon hung like a wraith in the blue sky, lifting over the trees. By dusk it would be at the zenith and the first ice crystals would start to crisp the grass.

He rubbed his eyes with the sleeve of his jacket, raking harder. Behind the windows of the house mother and son were once more at war. Their voices filled every room now. He had taken her pearls, her diamonds, the silver flatware and sold it for a song. More than that. He had taken her pride.

Below stairs the Williamses waited, shocked and afraid. The others had gone: the last of the maids, the under gardener, his lordship's valet. This morning when Mrs Williams had brought the breakfast tray into the dining room her ladyship had sat there at the head of the table as usual but she had spoken no word; her face was white, almost transparent with exhaustion, the lines beneath her eyes blue-black. Staring in front of her she made no sign, spoke no word of greeting or command and putting down the tray Mrs Williams had crept away and cried.

Staring after the old man Amanda shivered. Perhaps he was blind? But surely he would have sensed her there so close to him on the path? She could see him now, pottering about in the greenhouse, bent, slow moving, deliberate in his movements as he groped amongst the rubbish on the staging.

Nearby the blackbird burst once more into song. With a sudden shock Amanda looked round. When she turned back to the greenhouse the old man was no longer in sight. She bit her lip, conscious of a rash of goose pimples across her skin and, hurrying now, tiptoed back the way she had come.

He banked up the bonfire as it grew dark, put away his tools and stood for a moment staring up at the sky. The first ice from the north was sharp. It would be a hard winter. Shrugging, he walked slowly back towards the greenhouse and went inside. Closing the door he stood for a moment in the soft darkness. The air still carried a trace of heat from the sun but already the chill was building. He lit his lantern and stood it on the staging, waiting for the flame to steady and the shadows to stop their wild jumping. The old wooden chair, where he used to sit to eat his piece and drink the tea one of the maids would bring him stood now beside his untidy workbench. He reached for the packet of cigarettes and drew one out with a shaking hand. The pull on the nicotine was good. It steadied him. Made him feel calm. Sitting there he watched the smoke drift up around his head as the temperature began to drop.

As the leaves began to droop and the brown touch of the frost claimed the first blooms, turning the plants to pulp, he threw down the cigarette end and climbed onto the chair. His long scarf made a gentle noose for the scraggy neck as he hooked the end over the curved nail in the roof support. He gave a wry smile as he pulled it tight. No more than an old turkey cock who must die at last. He shivered. Around him he could hear the plants dying. His own death, he thought, as he kicked away the chair, would be less hard.

Amanda stopped. She turned towards the greenhouse. From somewhere she could smell burning leaves. She frowned. It was an autumnal smell; aromatic and smoky, redolent of cold days and frosty nights. She shuddered again, violently this time, suddenly acutely aware of ice in the still, summer air.

The chain-link fence rose six foot in front of her, a barrier between her and home. The foothold which had hoisted her over was on the far side. For a moment she stood, defeated, aware that her neighbour was watching her from one of the upper windows of her house. With a smile and a shrug Amanda turned back towards the trees to look for something to stand on.

From the bedroom window she could see the reflections on the glass in the evening sunlight. A different angle, a different colour, it was as beautiful as in the morning, but warmer, richer, more textured.

As soon as she had dropped back onto her own square of bare earth and ducked into her house her neighbour had knocked on her door, baby on hip, and smiled conspiratorially. 'I saw you over there. You've got more courage than me. I've wanted to explore that garden since the day we moved in.'

She was, it seemed, a kindred spirit after all. And she knew the story. The fall of the family fortunes, the gambling debts, the frost and then at last the fire that destroyed the house.

'There is no entrance to the garden,' she said as they sat down over a cup of coffee, the baby, quiet at last, playing at their feet. 'My husband has seen the plans of the estate. They sold off all the land bit by bit after the fire – that was sometime between the two World Wars, I think – then the owners moved away. The son, or perhaps it's the grandson, still owns just that last couple of acres, but he never bothered or noticed that there was no access to it. It can't be sold. It can't be entered. It can't be touched by the developers or the council or anyone.' She smiled at Amanda. 'A secret garden – with no one to look after it. Safe. No one to spoil it.' She paused, and added sadly, 'No one to love it.'

'Oh, there's still someone to love it.' Amanda returned the smile and bending down she gave the baby a biscuit. 'The gardener's still there.'

Her new friend's eyebrows shot up. 'You don't mean –?'

Amanda nodded. 'He's still looking after it. He's keeping it safe. And I don't think he would mind if you and I go there from time to time. In fact, I don't think he would even notice.'

It was an irony that she would like to have shared with Andrew but probably never could: the new house in the ancient garden; the dreams and nightmares there beneath the untrodden floor and on the far side of the fence.

The Fairy Child

THE RAIN WAS STREAMING DOWN the office windows as I folded my letter booking the cottage, clipped Peter's cheque to it and pushed them both into the envelope. I looked again at the address. 'Ishmacuild.' The word was a magic spell in itself.

A magic spell. I repeated the phrase out loud, gazing at the orange carpet at my feet, but seeing only silver sand, rippled by wind and tide. Was that why I had chosen the island for our summer holiday; why of all the places in the guide book I had picked a tiny lonely spot like Ishmacuild: because of a magic spell?

'Your turn to choose where we go this summer, Isobel,' Peter had said with a grin. 'Don't choose the Bahamas though, will you? I don't think the family coffers will quite run to that.'

In the five years of our marriage it had worked out that way. He had chosen one year and I the next, each seeing places we might not have dreamed of otherwise, for our tastes were so different. I, the dreamer, seeking lonely places or sites steeped in history, and Peter, the energetic sportsman, choosing lively walking, sailing and exploring holidays. Such an arrangement could have spelled disaster for some marriages, but for ours it was a stimulus and an excitement. We both enjoyed the new efforts we had to make and learned,

61

too, far more about each other than we ever would have done had we reached a dreary compromise each year.

The next time I was in the public library I crossed to the travel shelves and scanned the titles. I knew roughly what I wanted: the Scottish Highlands and Islands. I, with the maiden name of Macdonald, had never been there. My father had always said that our family came from Scotland years ago, and although we'd often talked about it we had never visited it when I was a child. This year, I was determined, I was going to remedy that. I reached down a volume and flipped slowly through the pages, glancing at the breathtaking photographs. There were so many places to choose from, so many lovely things to see. I took the book home and with it another of stories and legends. It was in this second book that I found Ishmacuild:

> Below the picturesque village, deep amongst the rocks, lies the magic fairy pool where countless generations of Macdonald women have gone by moonlight with a gift of gold to ensure the birth to the family of a son and heir. . .

I blinked and read on quickly. That was a very unhappy subject and one I tried to put out of my mind, but somehow over the next few days my thoughts insisted on turning back to that magic pool. After all I was a Macdonald woman, and I desperately wanted a son and heir.

The first two years of our marriage had been intentionally childless. The last three not so. Neither of us had worried at first and we had used the chance we had to go to concerts and theatres and have the kind of holidays our friends with growing families could not afford. But of late I had begun to wonder if anything could be wrong. I had not mentioned it to Peter but once or twice I had seen him glance broodingly into the pram of our baby nephew, and I knew that like me he was thinking about children.

The guide book recommended Ishmacuild for its peace

and silver sands and the beauty of the surrounding mountains. It listed several addresses.

When, tentatively, I suggested the place to Peter he laughed. 'So the famous Macdonald blood is coming to the surface at last.' He dropped a kiss on my forehead. 'It's a lovely idea, Isobel. We'll write for details at once.'

So it was all arranged. On a beautiful June evening we climbed onto the train which was to take us north. My heart should have been singing and my blood tingling with excitement but it wasn't, for something was wrong with Peter.

Peter was usually a cheerful, matter-of-fact person. Tall, strong, broad-shouldered with the clear grey eyes and tanned face of an outdoor man, he was everything a dream husband could possibly be. I could never quite get over my luck in having married him at all. His humour and optimism carried me along on the crest of a wave even when I was feeling a bit down. But now, for two days he had been moody and depressed. He had eaten nothing and snapped at me every time I spoke to him. His face had taken on a sunken grey look which secretly terrified me. I wondered whether to suggest he saw the doctor, never a popular idea with Peter at the best of times, and I wondered with a sinking heart whether I should suggest cancelling the holiday, but in the end, cowardly, I did neither and hoped for the best.

In the sleeping car which normally would have been an exciting adventure to share and enjoy we undressed in total silence. Peter hauled himself into his berth without a word and settled down, his face to the compartment wall. He never even said goodnight.

I lay awake for hours listening to the rhythmical rattling of the wheels over the miles of track, tense and unhappy. The further north we got the more I was filled with a dreadful sense of foreboding, and when at last I fell asleep in the early hours of the morning it was to a restless slumber tormented with formless nightmares.

The grandeur and beauty of the scenery and the excitement of the boat trip out to the island distracted me a little next day, I must admit, from Peter's mood. He seemed to have made up his mind to try and enjoy himself and he smiled and talked and gazed as I did at the scenery unfolding before us on every side. But I could see there was still something very wrong. The strange look haunted his eyes and though his mouth smiled and joked I could see that deep down inside he was in bleak despair. I shivered as, standing by the boat rail, feeling the hot salt wind blow the hair off my face, I turned suddenly and caught him looking at me with such an expression of bewildered resentment and hate it was all I could do not to cry out in horror. It was as if he had become a stranger. I turned back to watching the slippery silver waves and bit back my tears.

The cottage we had rented was tiny; no more than two rooms with a little kitchen and bathroom extension built on at the back. From the sink as I filled the kettle for our first pot of Highland tea I could see a vista of mountain peaks and valleys leading to the horizon and before them the silver sea lochs, glittering ribbons in the dusky twilight. Somewhere down there beyond the horizon lay the magic pool.

The next morning dawned bright. I lay for a long time listening to the shush of the sea in the distance and the weird, eery whistle of the curlew, watching the thin beams of early sunshine edge slowly through the undrawn curtains. Suddenly I realised that Peter was watching me. I turned to him, and leaned over to kiss him, but abruptly he turned his back on me and pulled the pillow over his head. Hurt, I drew back.

'What's wrong, love? Can you tell me?' I whispered, hardly daring to ask the question which had brought such fear into my heart.

'Oh, go to hell,' the muffled words sounded so desperate I didn't know what to do. I climbed out of bed and stood gazing down at him numbly. 'Go on; go away. Leave me alone.' Peter's voice was taking on an angry tone. Quickly, stunned with misery, I grabbed my dress and sandals and fled to the bathroom.

The path from the back door led across an area of heather bent towards the rocks and the loch. I ran quickly, wanting to get as soon as possible out of the sight of the cottage windows. Tears, half of fear, half anger, were running down my cheeks, and all I wanted was to hide my misery on my own by the shore.

I didn't see the small fishing boat, hidden as it was by the rocks, until I was almost on it and by then it was too late to turn back. A young man, tall, with a thatch of midnight-black hair and piercing blue eyes, was learning negligently against the stern pulling a net from the tangle at his feet. His lips were pursed in a soundless whistle. I turned away as soon as I saw him, wanting to be on my own, and headed up the beach but he must have seen me at once. 'It's a grand morning.' His voice, not raised above a half-whisper, arrested me where I stood. Seeing me turn back he gave a broad smile. His teeth were astonishingly white in his tanned face.

'You'll be staying up at the cottage. How are you finding it?' he asked casually, his fingers never ceasing to work through the tangled black mesh.

'Oh fine.' I rubbed the back of my wrist across my eyes, hoping he wouldn't see that I had been crying. 'We only arrived yesterday though. So I haven't seen very much.'

He grinned. 'Well, I'll take you out in the boat any day you want. Do you like the fishing?'

I shook my head, warming to the charm of his infectious smile. 'I'd like to go for a sail though. And one thing, I would like so much . . .' I hesitated, imagining he'd think me such a fool.

'You'd like to visit the fairy pool,' he finished for me. 'Aye, everyone wants to go there. I'll take you whenever you wish. Now, if you like.' He straightened hopefully, but I shook my head. 'I must go back and get some breakfast for my husband now. Perhaps later?'

He shrugged. 'Any time. You'll always find me round the boat if I'm not at sea. My name is Ross by the way. Ross Macdonald.'

'I'm Isobel,' I said. 'Once Macdonald too, now Hemming.'

He held out his hand. 'No doubt we're kin. I saw it in your eyes.' He grinned. 'Now, away to your food, Isobel Macdonald. You must not let your man starve.'

He turned back to his nets and I began to retrace my steps towards the cottage. My encounter with Ross Macdonald had cheered me and when I went back into the kitchen I was humming quietly to myself. I stopped abruptly when I saw Peter sitting at the kitchen table. He was absent-mindedly stirring a cup of coffee.

'There's more in the pot, Isobel,' he murmured and there seemed to be a note of apology in his voice.

The next three days passed quickly and without further incidents. I told Peter about Ross and we went out with him twice on fishing expeditions. I was beginning to like the tall islander very much. He had a calm, gentle sense of humour which did much to ease us over uneasy silences and the awkward angry moods which still came on Peter seemingly for no reason at all.

Then on Wednesday night came the most terrible moment of my life. I had had my bath and was sitting up in bed reading, wondering why Peter was taking so long. On the past two nights he had gone to bed early and had been asleep when I joined him. At last he came, turning out the light, and he stood looking down at me for a long while without speaking. I threw down my book and held out my arms expectantly. He went white and took a step back as though I'd hit him.

'No, Isobel,' he said, quite loudly. 'Never again, my dear. Never; I'm going to divorce you.'

'Peter!' I heard the anguish in my own voice, like the voice of a stranger. 'Peter, what's happened?'

'I don't want to live with you any more. That's what has

happened. There's no more to be said on the matter.' He walked deliberately to his side of the bed.

I flung myself up on my knees and caught hold of him. 'Peter, why? Peter, I love you. Is there someone else?' My eyes were burning with hot tears. 'What's wrong?'

Quite coldly and deliberately he flung me off. One minute I had my arms round him, clinging, the next I was lying on the cold, painted floorboards. He climbed silently into bed and turned his back.

Sobbing wildly I scrambled to my feet, grabbed my jacket from the back of the chair, and flinging it round my shoulders over my nightdress ran out into the translucent warmth of the night.

It was quite easy to pick my way down to the loch for although it was after eleven, it seemed not to get dark at all this far north. My heart was hammering against my ribs with fear and I felt very sick.

All I wanted was to be alone by the gently lapping waters of the loch. Alone to think.

It was almost as though Ross were waiting for me. One moment I was alone, sobbing desperately, and the next he was there beside me. With only the slightest hesitation he put his strong arm round my shoulders and pulled me against him.

'There, there, lassie; it's best to cry. No woman should be afraid of crying, especially one as beautiful as you. Why, your tears are like crystals, here on your cheek.' He raised his finger gently and brushed them aside.

'Oh Ross, what shall I do? Peter wants to divorce me.' I clung to him, thinking only of my husband and the terrible pain in my heart.

'I could see that there was something wrong between you.' Ross nodded, his lips very close to my hair. 'My dear, I'm so very sorry.'

Slowly, clinging to him for reassurance and comfort, I

walked beside Ross down the warm beach. We didn't talk at all after those first few words, then at last when we reached the barrier of fallen rocks which lay across the end of the sand he stopped and turning me to him he kissed me. Behind us an enormous moon was rising slowly from the circling mountains and somewhere on the waters of the loch a lonely night-bird cried.

I hardly know what made me let him do it. The magic of the night, the warmth of the sand, the ache of rejection in my heart which needed so badly to be comforted and stilled. All those things must have helped to enchant me as we sank slowly together to our knees in the moonlight, still kissing, and I let him slide the pale blue silk of my nightdress from my shoulders.

It was dawn when I finally let myself back into the cottage. I felt chilled and the hem of my nightdress was wet with dew, but I felt indescribably reassured and happy. It was as though Ross had imparted to me some of his own quiet strength.

I put on the kettle and groped in the cupboard for the teapot as the first red glow of the sun rose above the mountains.

Peter found me there. He stood for a moment in the doorway looking down at me and I saw with a hideous lurch of pity that he had been crying.

Without a word I pushed a cup towards him and began to pour out.

'Isobel, I'm sorry, darling.' He sounded hoarse and uncertain. 'I've been thinking about it all night. I must tell you the truth.' Nervously he clasped his hands around the cup, staring deep into the steaming liquid. 'I went to see Dr Henderson a week or so before we came here. No.' He held up his hand as immediately I tried to interrupt, full of anxiety. 'No. I'm not ill or anything . . .' He sighed and sipped the scalding tea, trying to find the courage to speak. 'I had to know if it was my fault we have no children, Isobel. I had to know.' He looked at me pleadingly. 'I'm sorry, love.' He seemed unable to go on and I waited, not daring to say a word. I could feel myself beginning to shiver.

'I'm sterile, Isobel. I can never father a baby.' He suddenly managed to find the words and they came out in a rush. Then he sat quite still, not looking at me.

I felt numb.

For a long time we sat in silence, neither looking at the other. I could sense his misery and shame and I wanted to comfort him but part of me was crying out in a shock of disappointment and yearning. Never have a baby. Never hold my own child in my arms. I could not bring myself to believe it. I wanted to argue; to say it couldn't be; to talk about specialists and further tests but one look at his face clamped the words in my throat.

At last I dragged myself from my chair and going round the table to him I dropped a quick kiss on the top of his head. However I felt about babies I still loved him more than life itself and I told him so, kneeling before him on the cold kitchen flags, my hands resting, pleading, on his.

'You can't divorce me because of this, darling. You can't.' My own voice was breaking. 'I won't let you. I love you too much. Babies don't matter so very much; perhaps we might adopt one, but the important thing is we have each other. That's all I care about.'

At last he brought himself to look at me, and I saw the anguish and uncertainty still flickering behind his eyes. 'I'm not a proper man Isobel. I can't be, I . . .'

'I've never had any complaints, have I?' I leaned forward and kissed him firmly on the lips. For a moment he stayed completely still, without responding, and then, almost unbelieving, he returned my kiss. We clung together for a long time as the sunlight slowly crept into the kitchen and then at last we went together into the bedroom.

We lay together, not making love, just lying quietly, for a

long time, in one another's arms until eventually, exhausted by misery and tension, Peter fell asleep.

Never once did I give Ross Macdonald a single thought. What he and I had done together on the warm moonlit beach had belonged to the magic of the Highland night. Save for the sense of calm serenity which he had left with me, our meeting might never have been. It would certainly never happen again. Strangely I felt no guilt, only a happy wonder when I thought of it at all and gratitude that he had comforted and reassured me in the only way that mattered – then.

The rest of our holiday passed in a daze. We were both stunned by the loss we were sure was ours, but our happiness in refinding each other in some way made up for that. We walked and swam and climbed the lower slopes of the mountains and went fishing with Ross. Ross never showed by word or sign that he remembered our encounter and I was grateful for his silence. I knew there was nothing cheap or easy in what we had done and I treasured the memory of it in secret.

But most of all I treasured Peter and our time together. We never mentioned the subject of babies again; at night sometimes after he had gone to sleep I found myself crying quietly into my pillow and my dreams were sad and lonely ones, but during the day I refused to let myself think about it at all. Time enough for that when we had both had the chance to adjust a little.

On the last day of our stay, deeply mysterious, Peter insisted on walking alone into the village three miles away. I guessed it was to buy me a present so I happily kissed him and after watching for a moment as he set off up the white stone road I turned and wandered slowly down to the loch to make my farewells to the mountains alone. Ross was leaning against his boat sorting out the nets very much as I had seen him that first day of the holiday.

'Hello there,' he smiled at me, his blue eyes clear and friendly and somehow understanding.

'It's our last day,' I murmured. And I stood still.

When he held out his hand I took it naturally and we stood for a moment looking at each other. Then gently he let my fingers fall. 'Shall we take a wee walk along the shore?' he said, and I nodded.

When we reached the rocks he led me this time between them. I followed up a steep path winding high into the cliff face and then back down among the rock pools at the corner of the island itself. Finally we came to a deep circular sheltered pool, hung with weed the colour of emeralds and garnets.

'There you are lassie,' he glanced at me and smiled. 'The magic pool of the Macdonalds. Will I leave you while you make your wish?'

I looked down into the opaque shifting water, suddenly overcome with misery and shook my head. 'I've no wish, Ross. No wish now. That is why I didn't ask you to bring us here. To have done so would have been the most tactless thing in the world.'

He looked puzzled. 'I thought you and your man were happy again?'

'We are, Ross.' I held out my hand to him, wanting to feel the comfort of his fingers as I fought back the urge to cry. 'We are happy; but there's no wish. Not now.' As I stretched towards him I felt a slight catch at my wrist. My bracelet had snagged on a corner of rock. With a little cry I tried to grab it as the fine gold links snapped but I missed it and it slid into the deep pool.

'Oh no, my lovely bracelet!' I cried. Ross scrambled over to my side and together we gazed down trying to see beyond our own reflections into the depths of the water, but it was impossible.

'It's bottomless, lassie; it goes right down through the island to the sea bed. That's why it's so magical.' Ross looked up at me. He smiled enigmatically. 'It seems the fairies were determined to have your offering of gold after all. So perhaps they know your wish already . . .'

I felt very sad as I walked back up the beach with him, over-whelmed by the end of the holiday, my beloved bracelet gone and my misery over Peter a blank pall. There seemed to be nothing left to look forward to. Nothing but emptiness.

Ross and I didn't say goodbye. He squeezed my hand when we got back to the boat and bent once again to his nets. I walked slowly back up the beach without looking back.

Peter was waiting for me when I reached the cottage look-ing very pleased with himself. In his hand was a box. I opened it and it contained the most beautiful carved silver brooch. The kind they made locally. In the excitement of putting it on I forgot to mention the loss of my bracelet.

Two months later I knew I was pregnant. Of course Dr Henderson must have known it wasn't Peter's child but he said nothing as he ushered me from his surgery, he just shook my hand and wrote a note for the office to get them to give me a few days off work as I was looking, so he said, so run down.

When Peter came home that night I was sitting on the sofa. He kissed me hello and I pulled him down beside me. 'There's something I've got to tell you, love,' I gulped. I had felt strangely calm waiting for him, but now the moment had come I found my hands were shaking.

He held them tightly and looked into my eyes, frowning. 'What is it, Isobel. What's wrong?'

'I went to see Dr Henderson today.' I swallowed hard and went on in a rush. 'I'm sorry Peter. I'm going to have a baby.' To my horror I could feel the tears welling up suddenly. I tried to blink them away but they spilled over onto my cheeks.

Peter let go of my hands. For a moment he looked so hurt I was stunned. Then he stood up.

'I never guessed there was someone else, Isobel.' He bit

his lip. 'I can't blame you, I suppose. I expect you want a divorce as quickly as possible to marry him?'

'Oh no. No! No!' I flung myself at him. 'Oh Peter darling. There's no one else. There never has been; not like that. It's just that . . .' I stopped.

His arms were round me and I was sobbing into his shirt front.

'It was the fairy pool. I dropped my gold bracelet. It would never have happened otherwise.' I burst into sobs again.

'The magic pool of the Macdonald women?' he murmured into my hair. 'You went and wished and the fairies granted you your heart's desire?' He didn't sound cross, it was almost as if he were smiling.

I glanced up at him through my hair. 'I know it can't really be that. It only happened once – that night you threw me onto the floor. I ran down to the beach and . . .'

He put his fingers on my lips. 'Don't tell me any more, darling.' He dropped a kiss on the top of my head. 'I'd rather think it was the fairies.' He took a step back for a moment and gazed at me steadily. 'This is something we would have had to discuss and think about sometime, Isobel. I know we never mentioned it but there are other things besides adoption when,' he hesitated, 'when there is nothing wrong with the woman. That way she can have a baby herself even when her husband . . .' he stopped and took a deep breath, 'when her husband is like me. Perhaps I would have preferred a more clinical approach,' he grinned, 'but on the other hand perhaps it's nicer to thank the fairies than a doctor.'

Our daughter was born two months ago now, a gorgeous child with eyes the colour of amethyst and a fuzz of soft black hair. Peter was there at the birth and if I ever had any fears that he might reject her they were dispelled when I saw him with her. He adores her and is as proud as any father I've ever seen.

We called her Faye.

Who Done It?

FLAKES OF SNOW blew in through the door with him as Jenkins pushed his way into the warmly lit bar of the Dog and Duck. It was early yet and only old Fred and Mr Denby were in.

'My usual, Sam,' said Jenkins. He was full of importance. Leaning his elbows on the bar he looked sideways at Mr Denby. 'Heard the news, have you?'

'No Jenks, what's that then?' Sam slid the pint glass expertly across the polished counter.

'They found a body up Highfield way.'

'A body?' Mr Denby straightened up sharply and looked at the newcomer for the first time. 'A dead 'un you mean?'

' 'Course I mean.' Jenkins was indignant. He took a long drink at his glass. 'Huddled up under Jeffrey's barn he was, in all the puddles and melting snow up there.'

'Who was it then, Jenks?' Fred spoke for the first time. His hand was shaking slightly as he raised his own glass to his mouth.

'Don't reckon they know yet.' Jenkins drained his beer and waited expectantly, his fingers casually nudging the glass across the bar. 'He was pretty soggy, so they say.'

'He would be.' Mr Denby nodded sagely. 'It's been thawing the last twenty-four hours.'

'Snowing again now, though.' Jenkins nodded towards the dark windows. The glass was as far as it would go without pushing.

Mr Denby noticed at last. 'Same again all round, Sam, please.'

'What do the police say, Jenks?' Fred was lighting his pipe, sucking the flame down into the encrusted bowl.

'They reckon it was murder.'

Fred dropped the match and blew on a burnt finger. 'Murder? What makes them think that?'

'He had a hole in his head, that's what. And blood all over him.'

'Poor chap.' Sam produced three brimming glasses. 'I wonder if it was old Everett. He used to sleep rough in the barn sometimes.'

'No, it wasn't him.' Jenkins clasped his glass happily. 'It was Everett as found the body.'

'Do they reckon he did it?' Mr Denby looked at him sharply.

'Nope. He's got an alibi.'

The four men were silent for a while, listening to the fire hissing round the logs in the hearth, then Fred slammed down his empty glass on the counter and turned for the door.

'Goodnight all,' he called and was gone.

'I think he knows something,' said Jenkins quietly. 'Did you see how his hand was shaking?'

'And he burned hisself on that match.' Mr Denby nodded. 'Do you think we ought to tell Constable Conway?'

'No.' Sam shook his head vehemently. 'If he did it he had good reason. Fred never does anything without a very good reason.'

Fred plodded slowly up the hill. The lights in Constable Conway's cottage were blazing as he went up the slushy path and knocked on the door. Mrs Conway showed him into the parlour where the constable, his blue shirtsleeves rolled up above the elbow, was sitting at the table, eating a large bowl of stew.

Fred sat down opposite the young man and waited until

his host's mouth was empty. 'That body you've got. Know who it was?'

Conway shook his head without speaking and spooned up some more stew.

'Did he have a red shirt and a townified tie?' Fred was twisting his cap round between his fingers on his knee.

Constable Conway choked slightly. 'How do you know that?'

'I seen him before. He was heading up Highfield way. Looking for hammer beams, he said.'

'Hammer beams?' The constable's mouth dropped open. 'What are they when they're at home?'

'Don't rightly know, but Jeffrey's barn's got 'em. He had a camera with him.'

Conway nodded. 'Yes, that was still there. There wasn't no robbery. The chap had quite a bit of money in his wallet.'

'Was it by the door you found him?' The casualness of Fred's question did not fool the constable. He had risen and, buttoning on his tunic was already reaching for his notebook.

'Now see here, Fred. You'd better tell me everything. What do you know about all this?'

'Nothing much. But a few days back I was up that way. I saw one of those great icicles fall over that doorway. Like a sword it was, three or four foot long. That would kill a man if he were standing underneath.'

'I reckon it would.' The constable nodded thoughtfully. 'Could have been that.'

'And the icicle would have melted long since.'

'I reckon it would.'

Fred left the cottage well satisfied.

There was no one left in the village now who would remember the slick fancy architect fella who had seduced and then abandoned Fred's pretty daughter. Only old Mrs Hennessy, and she was blind. And you can't fingerprint a puddle, now can you?

Watch the Wall, My Darling

PART ONE

WITH EACH SMART TAP of her foot on the sun-baked ground the swing arced higher. Above her the dappled shade of the oak tree cooled the air. Mercifully hidden now behind the high yew hedge the garden party was in full swing.

Caroline Hayward grimaced as, throwing back her head at the apogee of the swing's travel, she felt her long heavy hair slip from its combs. Her bonnet had already gone, hanging from its ribbons behind her like an unruly animal. Shaking her head she laughed suddenly, feeling her hair whip across her face. What did it matter how she looked? She was alone at last and for a few precious moments she was free!

'That swing was not designed for adults!'

The deep voice startled her so much she nearly released her hold on the ropes.

Dragging her slippers in the dust to slow her momentum she tried desperately to stop, suddenly acutely aware of the acres of petticoat showing beneath her light, blown skirt. Grabbing at what remained of her dignity as the swing slowed she curbed her first instinct which was to jump to her feet. Instead she smoothed her skirts, taking a deep breath as she saw who had addressed her. Dressed in sober black like all the men present at the bishop's garden party, the Reverend

Charles Dawson, her host's elder son, was standing facing her, his darkly handsome face showing uncompromising disdain; Charles Dawson who had spent the best part of the party surrounded by a cluster of his father's younger women guests.

'You obviously find our party boring, Miss Hayward,' he said with a humourless smile. 'I'm sorry, but I must suggest you find other ways to amuse yourself. That swing was not designed to take someone of your weight.'

'I am not that heavy, Mr Dawson!' Caroline retorted. To her chagrin one of her slippers had fallen off and she was feeling for it desperately with her foot, hidden beneath her full, long skirt.

He allowed himself another tight smile. 'I didn't mean to imply that you were.' He gave a slight bow, his eyes gleaming. 'Nevertheless, the swing was put up for my brother's children, who are aged six and seven respectively. When you have recovered your shoe –' he raised an eyebrow slightly, '– perhaps I can escort you back to the party and fetch you a glass of lemonade.'

She could hear in the still heat of the garden beyond the hedge the deep voices of the sober, assembled clerics, the higher voices of the women, the occasional constrained laugh. She and Mr Dawson were uncompromisingly alone.

No one had noticed when she had slipped away. Her father, the Reverend George Hayward, had been deep in conversation with his bishop, his daughter long forgotten, when she had glanced round the company, many of whom she had known all her life, and experienced her sudden, quite unexpected wave of rebellion.

The violence of the emotion which had swept over her had astonished her. She was overcome with anger and despair. She was still a young woman, wasn't she? She was still reasonably attractive, wasn't she? She was still full of day dreams and of hopes. So why was she here, at her father's side, faithfully accompanying him as ever on parish business, in the role into which she had slipped almost without realising it when her mother had died? Her sisters were married, her brother now lived in London. She alone was left. And it had been expected and accepted by everyone that she would fill her mother's shoes. All thoughts of her marriage seemed to have flown from her father's mind. The few persistent suitors who had called on her slowly slipped away. And no one seemed to have noticed but her.

She glared at Charles Dawson. She had not been one of the young women clustering round him with adoring looks and simpering giggles. No, she had been beside her father listening dutifully as he talked church business with the bishop! Not that she would have talked to Charles anyway, she reminded herself sternly. It was no problem for her to remain immune to his handsome good looks, behaving as he was like an extension of her father in his obvious disapproval of her. She had always detested him for his pompous ways. And he would never, ever, have been one of her suitors. Rich and well connected, he would look far higher than a mere rector's daughter.

The thought made her even more cross. She had never allowed any of the young men who had found their way to the Rectory door in Hancombe to arouse their hopes when they had come calling upon her and now it was too late to change her mind. She was old. She was destined to look after her father for the rest of his life. She was on the shelf. She was twenty-nine years old.

'. . . don't you think so, Miss Hayward?'

With a start she realised Charles Dawson had been speaking to her as he escorted her away from the swing and back towards the party. He was tall, broad-shouldered, and, oh yes, he was good-looking. As he looked down at her she realised she had been staring at him.

'Don't you think so?' he repeated.

'I'm sorry, I didn't catch what you said,' she murmured.

She caught the expression of impatience, quickly hidden, which crossed his face before she looked away.

'I said, that I fear there may be a storm later,' he repeated.

'Yes indeed, the air is heavy.' Now he would think her deaf as well as rude and stupid!

As they emerged through the gap in the hedge she noticed several pairs of eyes speculatively upon them. Her father's were not amongst them, she saw at once with relief, and suddenly she was overcome by an irresistible urge to laugh. Here she was, dishevelled, her hair down and her gown awry, appearing in the company of the most eligible man there, and quite unchaperoned!

As if reading her thoughts Charles Dawson stepped away from her rather too hastily. 'May I suggest, Miss Hayward, that you retire to the house to tidy yourself,' he said curtly, and with a bow he left her. For a moment she stood where she was, aware that she was still being watched closely, then slowly and demurely she began to walk across the grass.

Somehow she managed to reach the ladies' withdrawing room in the palace and there she managed to redo her hair and replace her bonnet. Outwardly she was docile and smiling. Inwardly, her moment of amusement gone, she was seething with resentment and anger. Of all the pompous, sarcastic men why did it have to be Charles Dawson who had followed her? He would tell his father what he had caught her doing and no doubt they would smile about it together over the port that evening, and then the bishop would tell her father! And her father would not find it amusing. He would be very, very angry. Oh, the humiliation of it all!

Leaving the shelter of the palace at last she ventured back onto the lawn and, in spite of herself, she found herself looking for Charles. She saw him at once, talking to a group of elderly ladies, and to her chagrin he looked up and caught her eye. For a moment she felt his gaze sweep up and down her body, as if checking her appearance, then infinitesimally he smiled.

Anger erupted in her once more and riding home beside her father in the carriage later she could feel her resentment still seething. But to her relief it appeared that nothing had been said to him about her escapade for he was in high good humour as they trotted through the leafy lanes back to Hancombe, nestling in its fold of the Downs.

'Tomorrow, Caroline, you and I shall visit the cottage up the Neck,' he was saying, sure as always of her obedience and her time. 'I should like to take baskets of food to Widow Moffat and the Eldron family. Poor things, it is two years since Sam worked . . .' He broke off suddenly. 'Caroline, are you listening to me?'

Guiltily Caroline turned to him. Her gaze had been fixed on the crest of the Downs where the golden haze of the afternoon had settled in a shimmering blur on the woods.

'Of course, Papa. I shall prepare the baskets myself.'

The shadows were running up the valleys between the hills, turning the green of the fields to soft purple beneath the haze. She could smell the rich drift of honeysuckle and roses from the hedgerows on either side of the lane. There was a beauty and a poignancy in the air which soothed her and at the same time unsettled her strangely.

She longed to be alone, away from her father's strident demands, but it was hours before she was able to escape to the privacy of her bedroom. With relief she closed the door at last behind the maid, Polly, and, drawing her loose wrapper over her nightgown she went to the window and leaned out, staring down at the dusk-shadowed garden. She still felt tense and unsettled; lonely.

It was very hot; the coming darkness was bringing no relief from the heat. If anything it was hotter now. Her mind turned back to the party and the cool freedom of the swing. If Charles Dawson hadn't found her she could have remained there all afternoon, with the breeze combing its untidy fingers through her hair. Unbidden, a picture of her host's son floated before her eyes; his tall, stern features, the arrogant smile, the quirked eyebrow when he saw that she had lost her shoe. Almost she had thought he was laughing at her, but then she realised that he must have despised her for being such a hoyden. His own white shirt and silk cravat had been immaculate; not a hair of his head nor his beard was out of place. No doubt he had never sat on a swing in his life.

Slopping some water from the ewer into the flowered basin on her washstand she bathed her face and neck. Then she lay down on the bed. There was no point in thinking about Charles Dawson; no point in thinking about men at all. Lighting her bedside candle she picked up a book and allowed it to fall open.

It was several weeks now since her sister, with a finger to her lips, and a stern warning not to tell their father, had given her the leather-covered volume of Lord Byron's works and from the day she had first opened it it had become her most treasured possession. Her favourite poem was *To Caroline*.

'Thinkst thou I saw thy beauteous eyes . . .'

She shivered as she read the impassioned words, words she knew by heart she had repeated them so often in the lonely darkness of her room. If only they had been addressed to her.

'Caroline!'

The abruptness with which her door flew open startled her so much she dropped the book. It slid to the floor with a crash. Her father, still fully dressed, stood silhouetted in the doorway, the candles on the table in the passage behind him streaming in the sudden draught. 'Caroline, where are my drops? I've been calling you!' His voice, usually so strong, dropped to a whine.

Caroline got up wearily, her feet bare on the cool boards. 'They are in your dressing room, Papa.'

'What were you reading?' His voice rapidly regaining its strength, her father approached the bed and, stooping, picked up her book, staring in curiosity at the gold letters on the spine.

Slowly the colour drained from his face. He held the book out towards her and shook it. 'Where did you get this . . . this obscenity?' he hissed. His voice was tight with anger.

Caroline had gone white. 'Please give it back, Papa. It is mine –'

'No!' He was beside himself with fury. 'This goes on the fire where it belongs. I don't believe – I cannot believe that you knew what you were reading! That a daughter of mine should dream of opening such a book –'

'Papa –'

'Enough!' His voice was strident, his need for medicine forgotten.

Caroline clenched her fists. 'Papa, I am a grown woman, old enough to decide what to read for myself.'

'No woman under any circumstances should be permitted to read anything that . . . that monster of depravity has written, Caroline.' He turned away. 'I would never have allowed your mother to do so, and I shall not allow you to do so, either.' At the door he stopped and looked over his shoulder. 'We shall talk of this again tomorrow,' he said ominously, and he closed the door.

For several moments Caroline stood still. Fury and indignation vied with sorrow for her beloved book and fear of what her father would do to punish her, grown woman or not. For a moment she blinked back humiliating tears, then galvanised into action by the same streak of rebellion that had driven her to seek refuge from the party earlier she began once more to get dressed.

How dare he!

He dared because he was her father and he knew best.

But he didn't know best! He had never read Lord Byron's work, of that she could be almost certain. He, like so many others, was reacting to the unnamed scandals to which her sister with a whisper had hinted. Terrible scandals. What they were she could not guess. And she did not care. Nothing anyone said about him made his poetry less beautiful. Caroline felt the heat of the night caress her languid body as she eased her wrap more loosely around her shoulders. The air had became almost unbearably humid. She pinned her long hair back off her neck in a heavy looped knot and still barefoot, let herself silently out of the room.

The Rectory was in darkness. She padded down the broad staircase and hesitated for a moment at the bottom outside her father's study door. All was silent within and she could see no light beneath it. He must have gone to bed. Turning she pushed through the door which led to the kitchens at the back of the house. The fire in the range was not damped down as it should have been. It was burning brightly. Peering in she could make out the blackened edge of the binding of her book in the heart of the coals. He had been as good as his word. With a sob she slammed the range door shut.

The key to the garden door was missing from its hook. For several seconds she stared at the empty place in the long line of keys, then again she rattled the door. It was locked fast.

With a sob of anger and frustration she turned and made her way to the front hall. The Rectory was completely silent save for the slow ticking of the grandfather clock in the hall. Cautiously she opened the door into the vestibule and putting her hand on the front door knob she turned it. That door too was locked. She was trapped in the dark, silent house.

Back in her room it was hours before she slept.

At breakfast her father was quick to tell her her fate. He had obviously spent at least part of the night thinking of a suitable punishment for his errant daughter.

'You have behaved like an irresponsible child, Caroline.' He put his hand to his forehead dramatically. 'Yet I cannot believe you knew what you were doing. If I did . . .' he paused, shaking his head sadly, 'I don't know what punishment would be sufficient, but as it is, I put your sin down to ignorance rather than the intention of knowingly reading such . . . such filth. Each evening from now on, child, you will read and then learn a passage from the Bible which I shall mark for you, to cleanse and purify your mind.'

Spooning some devilled kidneys onto his plate as he spoke he never looked at her face, never saw the anger and indignation in her eyes. Already he had moved on, to talk of their parish visits, of the Sunday school picnic she was to organise, and of the garden party the day before. It never crossed his mind that she might defy him.

Still seething with anger, she was putting on her bonnet, ready for the first of those parish visits when Charles Dawson was shown unexpectedly into the morning room.

'Mr Hayward. Miss Hayward. Forgive me. I see that you are about to go out!'

Caroline felt her mouth go dry. So this was it. He was going to tell her father himself about her unladylike behaviour at the party and that would seal her fate. Her father would be convinced of her utter depravity! She felt Charles's eyes on her, and defiantly she raised her own to meet them.

'Thank you for your hospitality yesterday,' she murmured. 'My father and I enjoyed our visit to the palace so much.'

'Did you indeed, Miss Hayward?' His tone was lightly mocking. 'I'm so pleased. It would have been so easy for one such as yourself to become bored.'

'Indeed not . . .' Caroline replied, flustered, but already her father was interrupting.

'Oh come, sir, my daughter enjoyed every moment of it, as I did. I have of course already written to your mother to thank her for her hospitality – Charles.' He hesitated slightly before using the younger man's first name. 'Her parties are renowned throughout the county, you know.'

'Indeed they are.' Charles bowed and Caroline caught the slightest quirk of his eyebrow. 'I shall however tell her that you enjoyed yourselves. Particularly you, Miss Hayward. I am sure she will ask you again.'

Was he deliberately taunting her? Trying to keep her intense embarrassment hidden, Caroline glanced at him angrily from beneath her lashes, but his face was bland as he turned back to her father.

'Forgive me calling so early, Mr Hayward, but I had to be in the area on business and I felt I must call in to say good morning.' He smiled. 'It did worry me that Miss Hayward did not seem to be herself yesterday.'

Both men looked at Caroline.

Her father frowned. 'She seemed all right to me.'

Caroline clenched her fists. 'Of course I was all right, Papa. I can't think what Mr Dawson means.'

He was enjoying himself hugely. She was sure of it now.

'You looked pale, Miss Hayward. Several people remarked upon it,' he went on solicitously.

'Did they indeed. How kind of them to comment.' She could feel herself growing more cross and agitated by the second. 'If so, it must have been because of the heat.'

'Indeed it must.' He bowed assent with a smile. 'And it is going to be hot again today. Already the hills are covered in heat haze. I suspect that storm is not too far away.' He smiled again. 'However, I must not delay you any longer.' He turned towards the door and snapped his fingers at Polly who was waiting in the hall. As she brought him his hat and cane he turned back and held out his hand to Caroline.

'Miss Hayward.' He bowed slightly over her fingers. 'How nice to see you again, Mr Hayward.' Then he had taken his hat from Polly and with another bow he had gone.

George looked after him with a frown. 'Charming young man. Such style. And showing such concern to come and ask after your health.' He sighed. 'A pity you could not have married someone like him, my girl, while you had the chance.' He shook his head. 'A great pity. And now it is too late. You won't marry now, I don't suppose.' Unaware of the cruelty of his remark he reached for his own hat.

'I have not looked for anyone to marry, Papa, since Mama died,' Caroline put in softly. 'It is my duty to look after you.'

'Quite so.' The rector picked up his gloves, either not hearing or deliberately ignoring the wistfulness of her tone. 'Young Dawson is likely to marry Marianne Rixby, I hear.'

Caroline was occupied with tying the ribbons of her bonnet, facing the mirror in the hall. For a moment she saw her face reflected in the glass – clearly showing still the traces of angry colour. As she watched the colour faded. Then she saw Polly's eyes were fixed on her face too. Bleakly she smiled. 'Shall we go out, Papa? Polly has already put the baskets in the trap.'

It was a long day and she was exhausted when they returned home. Her father had lost no opportunity of lecturing her about her reading habits and reproaching her about the potential husbands she had apparently thrown away through her selfishness and her arrogance. As the afternoon grew more and more hot and uncomfortable she found herself biting her lip in an effort not to scream. Desperately she wanted to get away.

The haze was pearly now over the Downs. The lanes shimmered with heat and the pony's coat was black with sweat beneath the harness as they drove slowly back towards the Rectory. She was dreading the evening. They had guests for dinner, amongst them Archdeacon Joseph Rixby and his wife and daughter, and she would be expected to play the radiant hostess yet again. There would be no escape.

Her room was cool as she changed into a green silk gown and looped her dark hair gracefully around her pale face. She longed to send a message to her father that she had a headache and could not come down to dinner, but her sense of duty prevailed as usual. She must be there as hostess to his guests. She must ignore his jibes and his sudden spite and be gracious to them.

Wearily she went downstairs into the drawing room. With relief she saw that the double doors into the garden stood open and the fragrance of the night drifted into the room. Calmly she greeted their guests at her father's side, looking with more than usual interest at Marianne Rixby as the girl arrived, beautiful and sylph-like in a gown of white lace at her parents' side. So this was the woman Charles Dawson had chosen to marry. She raised her eyes to Marianne's, forcing herself to smile a welcome as she took the girl's hand

and was astonished to find herself greeted with a look of undisguised venom.

She took a step back. Behind them Polly was moving around the room with a tray of glasses, and already the Rixbys had drifted off with her father to talk by the window. 'I saw you yesterday,' Marianne hissed at her. Her mouth was fixed in a narrow smile. 'What were you doing with Charles?'

'Doing?' Caroline frowned uncomfortably. 'I wasn't doing anything.'

'No? Coming out of the shrubbery, with your hair down and your dress all disordered?' Marianne's eyes spat fire. 'Did you think no one would notice?'

'I ... I had been feeling unwell,' Caroline stammered, aware that her father's gaze was fixed on her suddenly from across the room. 'Mr Dawson ... Charles ... was kind enough to lend me his arm, that was all.'

'All?' Marianne's whisper turned into a small shriek. 'And how, pray, did your hair come down?'

'I had been sitting on the swing,' Caroline replied wearily. 'I thought the cool air might help my head.'

'And did it?' The other girl's voice was full of malice.

'A little.' Caroline's composure was returning. 'Your fiancé is a compassionate man, Marianne. He saw my distress and offered to help me, that is all.'

'Not her fiancé, Caroline, not yet.' Sarah Rixby's ears had picked up the end of the conversation and she sailed over to her daughter's side. 'Though we are expecting dear Charles to speak to her father at any moment, are we not, my darling?' From the rector's elbow the archdeacon inclined his head towards his wife and went on with his conversation. 'Dear Marianne,' Sarah continued, 'it will be such an excellent match, do you not think?'

'Indeed,' Caroline nodded, malicious in her turn. 'A very excellent match indeed.' She wondered briefly if Marianne had ever been subjected to the man's sarcasm and insufferable snobbery. She thought not.

The candles burned low over the dinner table as the evening grew even hotter. The ladies' faces glowed with heat and it was with relief that after they had withdrawn, the gentlemen retired into the gardens with their cigars and their glasses of port. And it was still comparatively early when they called for the carriages, all now aware that the long-promised storm was finally on its way.

By the time she had returned to her bedroom Caroline's head was splitting with pain. She sent Polly away as soon as the girl had brought up her hot water, not even allowing her to stay and help her undress, then, kicking off her shoes she threw herself onto her bed. Beside her a moth beat its way suicidally around her candle; beyond the open windows the night was humid and very still as if waiting with baited breath for the storm to break.

She must have dozed for a while. She awoke suddenly aware that the moth had dropped, its wings singed, to the floor beneath her bedside table. The candle had burned low. Her bedroom was shadowy as she made her way at last to the ewer and, dipping a corner of the towel into the rapidly cooling water, she bathed her forehead to try and ease the pain. It was then for the first time she noticed her book-case. It was completely empty. She gasped. Throwing herself down on her knees in front of it she ran her fingers over the hollow shelves. During dinner someone had come upstairs and removed every single book. No, not every book. Her Bible still lay there on the top shelf. Inside it was tucked a sheet of paper with a passage noted in her father's neat hand. Glancing at it furiously she saw that he expected her to read and learn by heart twenty-five verses by next morning!

'Papa!' Her fury and anguish were for a moment over-whelming. She was paralysed by the sheer frustration and anger which swept over her.

She climbed to her feet and paced up and down the floor several times before she stopped in front of the window to stare out at the night. The garden lay there cool and inviting, a haven of calm. Her headache, she realised, had miraculously disappeared.

It was then that her rebellion boiled over. Still wearing her evening gown she slipped her shoes on once more, and opened the door. The landing was dark.

Picking up her bedside candle Caroline crept downstairs and into the kitchen. The door into the garden was locked once more. This time she was not to be deflected. She had to get out. She crept into the dining room, still warm with the smells of food and hot wax from the candles, and found to her relief that the windows into the garden had only been latched. There was no key. Pushing them open she stepped out onto the moss-covered terrace.

She knew where she must go. Tiptoeing towards the gate she let herself out and began to walk swiftly up the lane. No one saw her. The windows of the Rectory were all in shadow.

The night was strangely airless. Above her the sky was sewn with stars and a quarter-moon hung hazily above the Downs, but to the south the night was thick and brooding and she thought she heard a distant rumble of thunder.

Buoyed up by her fury and her frustration she walked fast, holding her skirts clear of the dry ruts in the lane, and turned up the path towards the church. Behind it the hillside led up steeply to the ruins of the old castle, the place she went to sometimes to be alone, when she had to escape the claustrophobic atmosphere of the Rectory. The villagers seldom went there, and never at night, or so she had heard. They thought it was haunted. She herself had only ever been there during the day.

The lychgate into the churchyard squeaked as she pushed it open and she glanced behind her in spite of herself. But the lane was empty in the faint moonlight beyond the ancient yews. Reassured, she shut the gate and made her way over the dew-wet grass, threading her way between the mossy, moon-shadowed tombstones. On the far horizon lightning flickered faintly, but she ignored it.

The church was in darkness. She glanced at it warily, for the first time feeling a little nervous. The building looked somehow larger and unfamiliar, the well-known shapes and corners of the walls irregular, menacing. She bit her lip, for a moment wavering, then the thought of her empty bookcase and the string of verses from the New Testament, together with the memory of the tortured burnt remains of her poetry book simmering in the heart of the range returned and with it her anger and indignation. Gathering her skirts she began to run on towards the second gate.

The hillside was steep and shadowed. She could hear herself panting as she scrambled up the winding path, groping blindly where the shadows made it totally dark. She could smell the night-scented stock in the cottage gardens in the village below and the newly scythed grass in the churchyard. The smell of smoke hung on the air and she wondered bitterly if it was from the Rectory chimney.

She was panting when she finally reached the top of the hill and emerged from the wooded path into the clearing which held the castle ruins. Up here the moonlight was clear. She could see the black shadows of the crumbling walls hard across the grass. She stopped right in the middle of what had once been a courtyard and stared southwards at the sleeping countryside. Again the sky was lit by the flicker of summer lightning, and this time a low menacing rumble of thunder followed it. She ignored it. Panting slightly she walked across to a low, ruined wall and hitching herself onto it she started reciting the little litany she always repeated when she came up here. 'Papa relies on me. I have to obey him. He means well and I have to look after him. That is my duty . . .'

Duty, her soul was screaming, her duty! To suppress all her hopes and dreams; to give up all thoughts of having her own mind, all thoughts of any independence, all thoughts of a home of her own in order to look after a bigoted selfish old man? Yes . . . Yes . . . I am his daughter. It is my duty . . . Besides, I love him.

So often she had fought this battle within herself, up here, in the ruined castle, where long ago battles had raged. Each time her better self had won. She had firmly suppressed the rebellion, allowed the peace of the countryside to soothe her and returned to the Rectory, meekly ready to take up her duties once more as a dutiful daughter. But this time . . . this time she wondered whether she could ever bring herself to go back.

She sat there for a long time as the moon hazed and disappeared behind the clouds, watching the storm draw closer as it moved steadily inland from the sea.

The sound of a stone falling was very loud in the silence. She stared round into the darkness, forgetting her father and the troubles at the Rectory, as her mind flew nervously back to thoughts of ghosts.

In spite of herself she couldn't help remembering cook telling her once of the headless man who was supposed to run across the courtyard and disappear into the thickness of the wall and she shivered. The lightning flickered again, throwing the castle ramparts into eery relief and out of the corner of her eye she thought she saw something move. Her heart hammering, she slipped off the wall and crouched close to it. It was stupid to think about ghosts. No one of any education and sense believed in ghosts! What she had heard was a piece of masonry falling; the movement was a trick of the eldritch lightning. The thunder growled once more and she took a deep breath. She should return to the Rectory now, before the rain came.

As she stepped away from the loose rubble of the wall she heard from somewhere quite close the sound of a low laugh. For a moment her terror was so great she thought she would die, then relief flooded through her and she heard herself sigh. What she had heard was no ghost. It must have been one of the village lads, up here courting. Almost trembling with relief she frowned at the unexpected, miserable wave of loneliness and envy which fleetingly seized her as instinctively she moved back into the shadows again. Whoever he was he had come up here to be alone with his girl. It would embarrass them enormously to think they were being spied on by the rector's daughter.

Gathering up her skirts she had started to creep silently around the side of the wall when the sound of more subdued laughter pulled her up short. It was male laughter, strident for all it was guarded, and it came from several throats. Frowning, she glanced over her shoulder towards the sound, and was in time to see the flare of a flame. For a second it illumined a face as it was sucked down into the bowl of a pipe, then all was dark again. On the leaves overhead the first raindrops began to patter down.

Caroline flattened herself against the wall, suddenly afraid again. The face she had seen was no familiar village lad. It had been that of a stranger and there had been something furtive about his action – the fleeting way he had glanced round over his shoulder into the darkness. Whatever he and his companions were doing, they did not want to be seen doing it; and she did not want to see them.

Cautiously she stepped back, holding her breath, her heart thumping with fear. The path back down the hillside seemed a thousand miles away. Away from the trees the rain was harder. She could feel the drops cold on her head and shoulders. Praying that the lightning would not betray her she picked up her skirts again and ran towards the outer wall. Reaching it safely, she pressed herself against the wet stones, listening as she peered round. They did not appear to have seen her. Breathing a quick prayer of gratitude she stepped carefully towards the steps and flattened herself back as a brighter than ever flash of lightning tore across the sky. It was enough to show her that some dozen men were standing inside the ruined walls about twenty yards from her. A second flash showed her they were intent on piling some boxes beneath the rubble in the old castle moat.

'Smugglers,' she breathed to herself with a shiver of real

fear. She had so often heard her father talking about the men who avoided the excise by bringing in brandy, wine and tobacco all along the lonely Sussex shore and how they cheated the government and the people of the country. It was a favourite theme of his. These men had obviously met a boat down in the estuary, collected a load of some sort of contraband, and were hiding it up here in the castle. Suddenly she was seething with indignation, her fear completely swamped by her anger. All she wanted to do was to get back down the hill so that she could alert the authorities and they would be caught.

As she watched the storm surged on overhead. It was raining hard now and she was becoming drenched. Her hair pulled loose from its knot and hung down on her shoulders. Her thin dress and petticoats were soaked, the silk clinging to her body like a second skin. As each shaft of lightning tore the black sky open she cowered back against the wall. She was not afraid of storms, they exhilarated her, but the speed and power with which this one had finally driven inland from the coast was awesome. Another green flash split the night sky and as suddenly as it had come her anger and indignation had gone and she felt the excitement of the night. Her anger had been her father's, not her own. To her amazement she realised that she envied these men. They were free, able to sail on the wild sea, ride their shaggy ponies through the storms. Like all men, they were their own masters. What they were doing was exciting and dangerous. What did it matter if the revenue men lost a few guineas? Was that so very dreadful?

In that second, as she watched them, her heart beating with excitement, distracted by her romantic dreams, one of the men saw her in the next flash of lightning which lit up the sky.

She saw him turn towards her, saw his hand raised to point at her, then his warning cry was lost in the crash of thunder which followed.

Her exhilaration vanished and was replaced by icy panic.

Abandoning all caution she turned and fled towards the gap in the wall. Her wet skirts tangled between her legs; her hair whipped across her eyes and her thin shoes slipped on the wet grass. Her heart pumping with fear, she ran blindly to the left, her hands outstretched to feel the wall. Another flash of lightning betrayed her. In the long suspended moment of white light they all saw her now. Dropping their loads the men were after her. She heard their angry shouts as she dodged around the end of the wall and across the strip of old cobbled courtyard.

She did not stand a chance. They cut her off in seconds and when the next flash of lightning illumined the scene she was surrounded. She pressed herself back against the wall, trying to catch her breath, feeling the cold, wet stone against her shoulders. Her head high she looked defiantly at the men. One of them had produced a lantern, and he held it up towards her.

'Miss Hayward?' The astonishment in his voice as he recognised the rector's daughter was genuine.

Dazzled by the lantern light held so close to her face Caroline could see nothing of the men behind it. She was shaking with cold and fear.

'You know her?' A harsh voice queried near her, clear above the rumbling thunder.

'Aye, I know her. It's Miss Hayward – rector's daughter.' So one man at least came from the village. Blinded by the lantern, Caroline felt a desperate rush of hope. 'What are you doing up here, girl? Surely you know better than to come here at night?' His voice was hard with anger.

The first man swore obscenely. 'I don't care who she is. She'll talk. She'll have to be disposed of.'

'She'll betray us, Jake.' A third voice rose above the whispers of the men around her. 'There's too much at stake to let her go, you know that . . .'

'No!' Her voice sounded shrill and unsteady to her own ears as she stared frantically around. 'No, I won't betray you,

I promise. I'll say nothing. Please, let me go.' She could sense their fear and anger mirroring her own as the lantern hissed and smoked in the blinding rain.

'She'll get us all hanged!' The angry words were fierce and uncompromising. 'Better get rid of her. Take no risks.'

'Aye!' The voices of the men around her were raised in agreement.

'No –'

Her cry of terror was cut off as the man Jake turned on the first speaker and roared at him, 'Would you turn us into murderers, Bill Sawyer? Is that your game? This woman will not betray us. I'll vouch for her. She's been good to me and mine.'

Jake Forrester. Caroline recognised his voice now. His wife had been ill for most of the summer, and Caroline had day after day taken her food and medicines from the Rectory. Pushing the others aside Jake stood in front of her. 'Will you promise you'll tell no one of what you've seen here tonight?'

'I promise.' Her mouth was dry. The faces around her were hostile, shadowed in the lamplight, streaming with rain. 'I won't tell anyone. I'm . . . I'm on your side. I swear it.'

The excitement was gone. There was fear and suspicion all around her. She could feel them considering, weighing up the risks. Even Jake looked grim. They surrounded her, hemming her in. She was trapped. If they decided she could not be trusted there would be no escape. She bit her lip, feeling the cold rain trickling down her neck, soaking into the bodice of her gown.

'Go on, girl. Get back to the village, quickly now,' Jake said softly. 'You keep quiet and no harm will come to you or yours. But if you ever betray us by so much as a hint . . .'

The threat was obvious. She shivered. Without a word she turned and made her way towards the steps. The men parted. Blindly she walked between them, hardly daring to breathe, feeling their eyes following her. Somehow she forced herself not to run. With as much dignity as she could she walked across the wet grass and stones and out of the light of the flickering lanterns into the deep shadows of the trees.

Once she was out of their sight she began to run, her feet finding the way by instinct in the dark as she hurled herself down the slippery path towards the churchyard. Scrabbling with the latch of the gate she pulled it open and slipped through, her breath catching in her throat. A flicker of lightning, more distant now, lit up the churchyard as she made her way between the tombstones and down towards the road to the village. The rain was stopping.

As she let herself out of the lychgate into the lane she could feel her heart thudding beneath her ribs; she was gasping for breath, her wet hair falling across her eyes, blinding her so that she didn't see the tall hidden figure until it was too late.

She screamed as the hand reached out in the darkness and seized her wrist. Struggling frantically she was swung forcibly to face her captor and felt her arms gripped by fingers of steel.

'Don't make a sound!' The command was hissed at her viciously. Below them on the road she could hear now the sound of horses' hooves. A troop of horsemen were riding along the road from the direction of the village. So Jake and his friends were betrayed. Even if she screamed again they would not hear her, up in the castle ruins. And they would think it was she who had betrayed them. She struggled desperately to free herself. Somehow she had to warn them.

As if he read her thoughts her captor released her arm and clamped his hand across her mouth. With a little moan of despair she kicked out at him and she heard him swear quietly under his breath as her foot met his shin but he did not release her. He held her in silence as the horseman passed close below them. It seemed like an eternity before the riders disappeared into the distance and the sound of the hooves on the track faded into silence. A desultory flicker of lightning pierced the yew branches overhead. For a moment their faces were lit. The man's expression was grim as he looked down at her and at last, abruptly, he let her go.

'Miss Hayward!'

It was the Reverend Charles Dawson.

PART TWO

Beneath the dripping branches of the yew trees Caroline stood rigid with shock. She could still feel the burning imprint of Charles Dawson's hands on her body through the wet silk of her dress and the bruises from his merciless grip over her mouth. He stared down at her for a full minute in the faint moonlight, then his voice cut through the silence. 'What in God's name are you doing here?'

'I was going for a walk and I got caught by the storm.' She was unhappily aware of the way the thin material of her dress was clinging to her, making her feel vulnerable and almost naked under his glare.

'You were going for a walk!' He sounded incredulous. 'Another of your sudden whims, no doubt – this insatiable desire for your own company.' He sounded furiously angry.

'That's right.' She was defiant. 'As far as I know there is no law against it, sir, as there undoubtedly is against laying violent hands on someone as you have!' She steadied her voice with difficulty, fighting off sudden stupid tears of shock. How dare he! He was accusing her, trying to make her feel guilty, when she had simply been walking alone, minding her own business, in the churchyard of her father's church.

She was praying that the men in the castle would remain silent up there above them as she straightened her shoulders and looked as imperiously as she could at her captor. Behind them another cloud shrouded the moon. 'What exactly are *you* doing here, Mr Dawson?' She tried to see his face and failed. All she could see was the faint gleam of his eyes.

'That's my business.'

Caroline retreated a couple of steps and felt her shoes sink into the leaf mould at the side of the path. She could feel her small store of courage evaporating fast. 'In that case, there seems no further reason for me to stay here in the wet,' she said defiantly, keeping her voice as steady as she could. 'I think I should like to go home now.'

'I'm sure you would.' His voice was strangely soft. 'But first I think we have to find out just what you've seen on this midnight walk of yours.'

'I've seen nothing.' She had spoken too quickly, she knew it, and her voice was too high.

'Nothing?'

'It's dark. I was getting some air and when the storm came I sheltered beneath the lychgate –' She broke off. In the silence of the churchyard behind them she heard clearly the sound of light, running footsteps. Her heart almost stopped beating with fear. Somehow she had to distract him; somehow she had to get him away.

'Please, will you take me home?' Until she spoke she didn't realise that there would be so much fear in her voice. She put her hand out and felt her fingers touch the rough linen of his shirt. He wasn't wearing a jacket, she realised suddenly. Behind them the footsteps drew closer.

'Please –'

But he had heard them. He caught her wrist and pulled her out of the streaming moonlight into the deep shadows once more. 'Don't make a sound.'

'But –'

'Quiet, I said!' His fingers bit into her wrist. Near them the footsteps drew to a halt and they could hear someone breathing heavily. Then, clear in the silence of the night, came a low cautious whistle.

Swearing under his breath Charles Dawson stepped out into the moonlit churchyard, dragging Caroline with him.

Jake Forrester stood clearly visible in the pale light.

'I thought you'd gone, girl.' He was staring beyond Charles towards her.

'You knew she was here?' Charles's voice was hard-edged.

Caroline looked from one man to the other uncomprehendingly.

'She was up at the castle, but I reckoned she could hold her tongue –'

'Hold her tongue?' Charles snapped. 'She had arranged to meet the patrol! If I hadn't stopped her she would have sent them straight up to take you all where you stood.'

'No! That's not true,' Caroline cried. 'I didn't know they were coming – I didn't know who they were.' She swung round to face Charles. 'I don't understand any of this. What are you doing here?' With dawning comprehension a slow feeling of dread was beginning to creep over her. Feebly she tried to pull her wrist free of his grasp.

He was looking at her thoughtfully.

'Whoever it was who rode by just now, I wasn't going to meet them, I swear it,' she cried again. 'You must believe me, I didn't know they were coming. And even if I did I would not have betrayed –' She was going to say, 'you.' She fell silent, trying to come to terms with what was happening. She couldn't bring herself to believe that Charles Dawson, the suave, tight-lipped son of the bishop of Larchester, was in league with the smugglers. It was impossible. But his next words confirmed that that was indeed exactly what he was.

'Come on.' He addressed Jake. 'Back to the other men. The roads are alive with soldiers tonight. We must disperse quickly.' Already he was striding back towards the castle, dragging her with him.

'No.' Caroline pulled away from him. 'Please, let me go home.'

The two men looked at her. 'She'll not talk, sir,' Jake said quietly.

Charles looked down at her, his face hard. 'There is too much at stake.'

'There is nothing at stake, sir!' Caroline retorted, goaded into fury by his expression. 'I have given my word. That should be enough for you. I shall not betray you. Whatever your motives are in doing this it is not my concern. Now, please let me go!' She wrenched her wrist free of his grasp.

He frowned. 'Men's lives are at risk . . .'

'I am well aware of that, Mr Dawson,' she snapped. 'I can guess what you were doing, though why you should be involved in this I cannot even begin to imagine –'

'Then don't,' he said curtly. He hesitated for a moment then he stepped away from her. 'Go, then, Miss Hayward. Go back to your bed. But I shall expect you to keep silence. If you don't . . .'

'If I don't?' His threatening tone enraged her.

'If you don't it will not only be these men and myself who suffer,' he replied softly. 'Because you and your father will find yourselves implicated as well.'

'What do you mean?' she flared. 'That's not possible. We had nothing to do with any of this!'

He smiled. 'You need find out, Miss Hayward, only if you betray us.' He turned away and began walking fast through the churchyard towards the gate. Jake hesitated for a moment, then he followed him.

Caroline closed her eyes and took a deep breath. Her knees felt shaky and her mouth was dry with fear as she retraced her steps towards the Rectory. She was beginning to shiver. Her soaking dress clung to her and her shoes squelched uncomfortably in the mud. Softly she opened the gate and slipped into the garden. Avoiding the raked gravel of the driveway she tiptoed across the wet grass and round to the back of the house. The French window still stood slightly ajar. With relief she pulled it open and slipped through the curtains.

The candelabra on the sideboard had been fitted with fresh candles. Her father was sitting at the head of the table, swathed in his dressing gown. His Bible lay open on the table before him, the pages golden in the flickering candlelight.

'I have been waiting for you.' His eyes travelled up her wet form and she saw the lines on his brow deepen. 'I am sure you have an explanation for your absence.' He got up heavily and walking past her, he reached up to shoot the bolts on the windows. He closed the heavy curtains then he turned to face her once more. 'I am waiting.'

Caroline shrugged. 'I went for a walk in the gardens, Papa. When the storm came I thought I would shelter rather than try and run back.'

'Your shelter was obviously sadly inadequate.' He was staring down at the carpet where the sodden hem of her dress was seeping into a puddle round her feet.

'The rain was very heavy.'

He sighed. 'Indeed it was. Would it be too much to wonder why you felt the need to walk in the garden in the early hours of the morning just as a storm was breaking?'

'I had a headache, Papa, and I couldn't sleep. I thought the air might help it.'

'And did it?'

'Yes.'

'Then I suggest that you go back to bed before you catch cold.' He blew the candles out one by one, leaving a single flame burning in the candlestick by the door. 'We will talk more of this tomorrow. I do not like the thought of my daughter wandering alone, even in the gardens, at night. It is most unseemly.'

'I am sorry, Papa.' Gritting her teeth, she lowered her eyes. 'But there seemed nothing wrong in it, to me –'

There was mud all over her skirt – distinctive, chalky mud from the hillside, mud which could not possibly have come from the manicured beds and lawns of the Rectory garden. With a quick glance at her father Caroline clutched at the sodden green silk, trying to hide the tell-tale smears.

'Forgive me, but I am very cold. I think I shall do as you say, and go to bed.'

'Would you like a glass of ratafia to warm you?' As she reached the door, he stopped her, his voice unexpectedly gentle.

She shook her head. 'Thank you, no, Papa.' She took the candle from him and turned away.

As she fled up the stairs, the shadows leaping round her, she was uncomfortably aware of his eyes following her in the soft lamplight from the table in the hall, and of the streaks of dirt left by her swirling skirts.

There were dark rings under her eyes when she confronted her father over the breakfast table next morning. Her hair was tightly knotted at the back of her neck, her dress neat and irreproachable.

'I have not learned the Bible passage, Papa.' She met his eyes defiantly. 'There has not been time.' She held her breath, waiting for the outburst she knew would come, but to her surprise her father merely shook his head. 'Tonight, then, tonight. You are none the worse for your soaking?'

'None the worse, thank you, Papa.'

Her father was helping himself from a dish of eggs beneath one of the silver covers on the sideboard. 'I thank the Lord you were not tempted to stray beyond the garden last night,' he went on, not turning. 'The smugglers were out. My verger was here at eight. He said the excise men failed to catch them.' He sighed as he sat down. 'These rogues must be caught. They killed a man down on the foreshore last night.'

'No!' Caroline's distraught cry made him look up.

He frowned. 'I am afraid so. But don't distress yourself. They will be caught.'

All night her brain had been whirling with the events at the castle and in the churchyard. Each time she had closed her eyes she had seen Charles Dawson's tall figure – wet through, wild, dressed in shirt and breeches, his hair tousled by the storm, his eyes alight with anger. And her body had remembered the hard touch of his fingers with a strangely disturbing glow of shame.

She shivered imperceptibly again now at the thought.

'Is it known where they come from?' she asked cautiously as she sat down.

'Local,' he replied. 'It would surprise me if some of them didn't come from this village. The rogues! They deserve to hang!' He frowned at his daughter. 'Do you not wish to eat?'

She shook her head. 'I'm not hungry, Papa.'

'I trust you are not sickening for something. Take some hot chocolate at least. I am going into Larchester later this morning to consult with my fellow magistrates. There must be something more we can do to catch these men. It is a scandal that they are still free!'

Caroline watched her father ride away an hour later with mixed feelings. Half of her was relieved that he was so distracted by his anger against the smugglers that he had forgotten his indignation at her; the other half was eaten up with anxiety over what was to happen about the smugglers. How could Charles Dawson be involved with them? How could he, a man of God, be a thief and a murderer?

Miserably she paced the floor of the morning room, oblivious to the beauty of the day outside. Still his image rose before her eyes. The anger and hardness in the man, his determination, his ruthlessness. If Jake had not been there to restrain him, what would he have done to her? Her mind shied away from the answer to that question. But the truth remained. He or his men had killed that night. And if they had killed once, why should they not have killed again?

Suddenly making up her mind she ran for her bonnet and taking her basket, loaded with jars and packets, on her arm she let herself out of the Rectory. The lane was already drying in the hot sun, the muddy ruts hardening beneath chalky crusts as the hedgerows steamed, glittering with raindrops.

Jake Forrester's cottage was at the far end of the village, a tiny run-down hovel. She hesitated only a second before she knocked at the door. It was several moments before it opened.

Mrs Forrester peered out, blinking in the sunlight. She was

a thin, stooped young woman, her heavily pregnant figure obvious beneath her threadbare gown and flimsy shawl. 'Why, Miss Hayward!'

'How are you, Susan?' Caroline groped in her basket for her jars of calves' foot jelly, her honey and her loaves of fresh baked bread from Polly's oven. 'I thought I would come and see how you are. Is your cough still bad?' She followed a flustered Susan Forrester into the cottage and peered round the small dark room. It was empty. She could feel the chill striking off the walls. 'How is your husband, Susan? Is he here?'

Susan shrugged. 'Jake's all right, Miss. He's gone over the hills today and tomorrow to help with some droving.' She sat down heavily. 'I don't like him going so far and leaving me so long, but we need the extra, with another baby on the way.'

Another baby. Caroline had noticed the empty cradle by the window. Three babies had been born in this house in the last three years and all had been dead within six months. She felt a clutch of pity at her heart. 'He's a good man, your Jake.'

'Aye.' The woman's thin face broke into a smile. Then as swiftly as it came it vanished and Caroline saw fear and worry in the woman's eyes.

'What is it, Susan?'

'Nothing.' She made a big effort to smile again. 'I worry about the baby.'

'It will be all right this time, Susan. There's been no disease in the village this summer –'

'Not yet!' Susan could not keep the bitterness from her voice. 'Squire Randall said he'd improve the cottages, but he hasn't done it. He said he'd see we'd have the thatch patched; look at the damp in here after last night's rain.' She was racked with coughing again as she pointed to the glistening marks on the mud walls. 'And new wood for the door. They even talked about some kind of drains in the village once,

105

but nothing ever came of it. Dr Styles says we'll never be free of the fever until they sort the drains.'

Caroline bit her lip. 'I'll talk to Papa again. I'm sure Mr Randall will listen to him.'

'He'll listen. And he'll promise. He'll promise the world. But he'll do nothing.' Susan put her hand to her belly defensively. 'You see if I'm not right. If anything's to be done it must be done by ourselves. My Jake's promised he'll do the roof, somehow. He's got some pennies saved, he reckons.' She smiled tolerantly, obviously not really believing it. 'Maybe that'll do to keep the place water tight this winter and keep the baby warm.'

Caroline frowned. 'I'll do all I can. I promise.'

'I know you will try.' Susan smiled wearily. 'You've been good to me.'

But not good enough. Caroline frowned as she walked slowly away from the damp cottage, still cold, even on such a warm day. It was not right that women such as Susan Forrester, who worked so hard and asked so little in return, should suffer so in the loss of her babies. Did Susan know Jake had turned to smuggling? She thought not. And could she really blame him for it, if it brought some money into that penniless household? Wouldn't she have done the same thing in his shoes?

Her thoughts were interrupted by the sound of hooves in the village street and she looked up to see Marianne Rixby and her brother, Stephen, trotting towards her. They drew to a halt beside her. Stephen raised his hat. 'It's a very hot day to be walking, Miss Caroline.'

Caroline smiled. 'I wasn't going far.' She eyed Marianne cautiously. The girl's riding habit looked cool and elegant, her hat on her bright curls throwing a delicate shade across her face. And she couldn't help making a comparison between this spoiled, cosseted young woman with her rich, elegant clothes and slim, daintily gloved hands and Susan in her threadbare home-spun. It was an uncomfortable thought.

She bit back a wry smile. What would Marianne think if she knew her precious Charles was out at midnight after the dinner party last night with a gang of smugglers; what would she say if she knew that, for a moment or two, admittedly in anger, he had been holding Caroline pressed close to his chest!

At the thought she felt the heat rise again in her cheeks. She put her hand to her face. 'Perhaps I should go back to the Rectory. I hope we shall see you again soon.'

'Indeed you shall.' Marianne simpered prettily. 'Charles has asked to speak to Papa this evening. When he has done so and we announce our engagement we shall have a party, and you shall be invited, dear Caro.'

Dear Caro! Caro! Caroline seethed as she walked on her way. Marianne had never, ever, called her that before. She swung her empty basket onto her other arm. No doubt Marianne would be less happy when she had sampled Mr Charles Dawson's vicious temper and found out what a hypocrite and a liar he really was!

The rector returned in time for luncheon very pleased with himself. 'Someone on the quay has talked. We know who their ringleader is!'

'You know?' Caroline stared at him, white-faced.

He nodded smugly. 'Not only do we know, but we know they've planned another landing tonight. The devils! They thought that would fool us – going out two nights running. How wrong they are! We'll catch them red-handed and we'll hang every one of them.'

'Papa –'

'No, Caroline. I know how soft your heart is. But they must be punished.' He turned as Polly knocked on the door to announce the meal. 'Come, my dear, let us eat, then you can learn your Bible passages this afternoon while you rest.'

He couldn't know about Charles. If he had learned that a man of the cloth, and the bishop's son, was involved in the smuggling surely he would not be so calm? Surely he could

107

not keep something as terrible and shocking as that to himself? She glanced at him warily. He couldn't know the truth. He couldn't.

Later, in her room, Caroline stood looking out of the window at the garden. The heat of the afternoon lay like a gauze curtain on the countryside, making it shimmer like gossamer. Her Bible lay open near her on her desk but she had not looked at it.

Her mind was far away.

Jake Forrester, hanging on the gallows. Susan and her baby, due any day. And Charles Dawson. Would he be caught too? Would he hang? Or did he wait at a safe distance, his own cover still intact, directing these men to their doom?

Why? Why did he do it?

She paced back and forth a couple of times, the image of Susan and her pale, strained face, her hacking cough, constantly before her. When she had mentioned the cottage to her father at luncheon he had frowned. 'I'll speak to Joe Randall again about those hovels,' he had said. 'They are a disgrace to the parish. It wouldn't have happened in his father's day. He looked after his workers.'

And with that she had had to be content.

Twice more she paced up and down the room. She had to do something. She couldn't let Jake be caught. His companions might have killed a man, and they should be punished, but would more deaths solve anything? Weren't they all men driven to crime by poverty and despair? All except Charles Dawson, who had no such excuse. She was desperately angry. How dare he! How dare he send these men to their deaths?

Almost without realising she had done it she had slipped out of her muslin gown and reached for her riding habit. She would ride to see him. However much she detested him, she had to speak to him and force him somehow to call back his men; to warn them of the trap. She had to save Jake for Susan.

She paused outside her father's bedroom door and listened for a moment as she tiptoed down the stairs. Sure enough she could hear the faint sound of snoring. He had retired to rest in the heat of the afternoon.

The groom was asleep too, on a heap of hay. It was several minutes before he could bestir himself enough to saddle Caroline's pretty bay mare, Star, and lead her out of her cool shadowy box into the blinding sunlight of the stableyard. He offered to ride with her – part of his duties if she rode out alone – but with little enthusiasm and was obviously relieved when she turned down his offer.

Charles Dawson's parish was some five miles away through narrow lanes and across trackways over the Downs. It seemed a long way in the heat. Time and again she slowed the sweating horse, letting her walk in the dappled shadows beneath the trees which bordered the lanes. There was plenty of time. The raid would not take place till after dark, but he had to have time to send messages to his men. The closer she got, the more slowly she rode. Her anger had evaporated slightly in the heat and she had to admit that she was a little apprehensive. She was not looking forward to meeting Charles Dawson again.

The Rectory at Pengate was a large Georgian house, set between two graceful cedar trees. As Caroline rode up the long drive she saw the curtains in the main rooms were drawn against the sun and her heart sank. It had not crossed her mind that he might be out. Dismounting, she pulled the bell and waited, Star's rein looped around her arm. Her heart was thumping painfully now, and she found she was having to hold tight to her courage before it oozed away completely.

It was several minutes before the door opened and she found herself confronting the tall figure of Charles Dawson's butler. The rector, she was informed, was indeed out.

'He can't be!' she cried out in dismay. 'He must be here.'

'I am sorry, Miss. He is not expected to return until tomorrow!' James Kennet was eyeing her crumpled habit and the dishevelled wisps of hair flying from beneath her hat. He frowned.

'Then where is he? He was going to the Rixbys' this evening, but surely not already?' She knew she sounded desperate.

'I am sorry, Miss.' He tightened his lips in disapproval. 'I do not know where he is.'

And with that she had to be content. Disconsolately Caroline turned the mare's head back towards home.

The afternoon had grown hotter. The baked mud in the lanes was like stone; the air, as the horse left the shade of the deep lanes for the open downland, was stifling.

But she was not going to be defeated that easily. She would have to go to the Rixbys' and lie in wait for him. That was the only choice she had left. She had no idea how late he would be – perhaps too late – but what else could she do? She was not going to give up. Not yet. Kicking the reluctant Star into a canter before she could change her mind and cravenly seek the cool shadows of her curtained bedroom she took the road that led towards the archdeacon's house in the cathedral precinct.

The roads were busy and a pall of dust lay over the city of Larchester as she threaded her way through the streets praying she would not meet anyone she knew, trying to decide how to go about reaching Charles before he got to the Rixbys. Now that she was nearly there, the practicalities of the situation faced her squarely. She was in Larchester, unchaperoned, looking for an unmarried gentleman whom she was, to all intents and purposes, about to accuse of murder! She bit her lip. So what! It had to be done. Jake had to be saved.

She halted her mare in the shade of some trees near the cathedral. Charles was expected in the evening. That was all she knew. Early or late? She had no way of knowing. He might have cancelled his visit or be there already for all she knew. At the latter thought she kicked Star on. If he was already there she had to find a way of speaking to him now.

Star solved the problem for her. As they walked towards the precinct Caroline realised that the mare had begun to limp painfully. Slipping from the saddle she ran gentle fingers down the sweating pastern – then slowly she coaxed her forward.

'I am so sorry to intrude,' she said to Mrs Rixby. 'I couldn't think what to do when she went lame, then I thought I could ask your groom as you were so close.'

In the stables Star had been fed and watered and bedded down in deep straw to rest the sprained tendon. Caroline had been ushered into the huge, cool drawing room and given lemonade and a fan and already she knew that the archdeacon would be returning in an hour and his wife had been unable to resist telling her that Charles Dawson was calling on him at six.

At six. Surreptitiously Caroline glanced at the clock on the mantelpiece. She had over an hour to wait and she had gathered swiftly that her presence, if not exactly unwelcome, was certainly not timely.

'Our groom shall drive you home, my dear, as soon as you have drunk your lemonade,' her hostess said firmly as Caroline sipped from her glass. 'Your horse can remain here until she is better.'

Caroline smiled, her brain working like lightning. Above all she didn't want to be escorted off the premises. Somehow she had to make them let her leave alone. She put down her glass. 'Thank you, but I can go home with our verger. He drove into town this morning and I can easily get a lift with him.' She jumped to her feet. 'There is no need to trouble your groom. But I'll just say goodbye to Star . . .'

She smiled at Mrs Rixby's haughtily raised eyebrow, said a firm goodbye and made her way, alone, back into the stable-yard. To her relief the groom was nowhere to be seen. It took only a few seconds to slip into an empty stall and sit down on some straw bales in the deep shadows, out of sight.

She heard the cathedral clock strike the quarter, then half past. Twice she heard footsteps nearby and once a horse rode into the yard at a trot. Creeping to the half door, her heart in her mouth, she peered over, but it was a stranger.

She did not let herself think what would happen if Charles went straight up to the front door. Instead she concentrated every bit of her mind on praying that he would ride into the yard and that she could catch his eye before he shouted for the groom. If not she – and Jake and all the others – were lost. What Charles would say when he saw her here, of all places, she did not dare to think at all.

It was nearly a quarter past six when a sturdy black cob turned into the yard and stopped. The groom was at its head before Caroline could reach the door. Heart in mouth she watched as Charles, a tall figure in immaculate coat and trousers, strode towards the house without once glancing in her direction. It was the groom who saw her.

'Oy! What are you doing in there? Come out of there!' His voice echoed round the stableyard as he caught a glimpse of her white face peering over the half door.

Charles stopped dead and looked round. Paralysed with fright and embarrassment, for a moment Caroline did not move.

'Why, Miss, I'm sorry.' It was the groom who recognised her first. 'What are you doing in there? Your mare is over here.' He seemed bewildered.

'Miss Hayward?' Charles strode towards her. He pulled open the stable door, his face full of suspicion.

'I . . . I had to see you,' she stammered. 'I couldn't think what to do . . .'

For a moment he stared thoughtfully down at her. Then he turned to the groom. 'You may see to my horse. I shall look after Miss Hayward.'

'I . . . I heard you were coming to ask for Marianne's hand this evening . . .' she floundered on. 'I went to your house, but you had already left.'

'I see. You couldn't bear to think of me wedded to another.'

The sarcasm of his tone belied the sudden amused gleam in his eye.

Caroline went scarlet. 'It's not that at all!' She exclaimed indignantly. 'I had to warn you –' she put her hand to her lips and as she glanced over her shoulder, her voice dropped to a whisper. 'Oh, please, don't you see? I had to find you. My father says you have been betrayed. The excise men will be waiting tonight on the coast. Your men will all be taken –'

He cut her short in mid-sentence with a sharp gesture of his hand. Behind them the archdeacon had appeared. He was staring at Caroline in astonishment.

Charles forestalled his questions. 'You will have to forgive me, archdeacon. Miss Hayward has brought me an urgent message. She has met with someone from my parish who needs my services. It seems to be a matter of life or death. Would you forgive me if I return to see them at once? Perhaps we could discuss our business tomorrow?' He smiled.

The archdeacon's brow had furrowed sharply. He looked far from pleased. 'If you feel you must, then of course, I cannot prevent you.'

'Quite so.' Charles's answering smile did not quite reach his eyes as he beckoned his horse forward once more. He turned back to Caroline. 'Is there more to your message?'

She nodded, aware suddenly of eyes watching them from the windows of the drawing room beyond the rose garden to the north of the stableyard.

'Then please excuse us, archdeacon.' Charles turned to their host.

At his imperious tone Joseph Rixby's expression froze. He was looking extremely angry. 'I won't detain either of you,' was all he said however and with a stiff bow he turned away.

'Well?' Charles turned back to Caroline, his horse's rein in his hand.

'They know. They know who leads them,' she whispered.

113

'They know?' he looked at her in astonishment. Then his face darkened. 'And was it your father who told them, I wonder?'

'I didn't tell him,' she flared. 'I don't break my word.'

She turned away sharply, aware suddenly that there were pieces of straw clinging to her skirt. She wondered if the archdeacon had noticed them and knew immediately that he had. 'I don't know how they found out, or even if they are right in what they think. Papa didn't tell me who it is they suspect. All I know is that you must hurry. You have to. I just pray you are in time to save Jake and the others. It's them I care about.'

'I don't doubt it.' He paused. 'Who else knows about this?'

'I don't know. The authorities. Papa came into Larchester this morning to meet the other magistrates –'

'And they told him I was involved?'

'I suppose so.'

'So, why am I still free? Why were the soldiers not waiting for me here?'

'Perhaps because they want to trap you all together. I don't know. Oh, please hurry. You must warn them . . .'

'If I am being watched I must avoid them – how did you get here?' He spoke sharply.

'On my mare. But she's lame.'

'Then we'll borrow one for you. Here, boy.' He shouted behind him into the yard. 'Saddle Miss Marianne's mare quickly –'

'But you can't – what will the Rixbys say?'

'Nothing if they think I want to marry their daughter.' He spoke with strange bitterness suddenly. 'You shall ride beside me. If they are looking for a man alone or a group of men they certainly won't stop a woman and a clergyman.'

'You mean I'm to come with you to warn your men?'

'Why not? It was Jake Forrester you were worried about wasn't it?'

'Yes, but –'

'Then you can help me save him.'

He turned as the groom led an elegant grey horse out of one of the boxes. There was a glint of silver as some coins changed hands. 'No word of this loan, my friend,' Charles winked at him. 'We'll have the horse back by dawn. I doubt if Miss Marianne will want it tonight. If she does you'll have to think of an excuse and find her another mount.'

Charles turned and with scant ceremony swung Caroline up onto the side saddle. The groom was grinning as they turned and rode out of the stableyard. Behind them the curtains in the archdeaconry twitched and fell into place. In the drawing room Marianne subsided into tears.

Charles set a fast pace south and the grey mare, fresh from her stable, kept up with ease. He glanced at the horse approvingly. 'She makes a good ride, I'll wager,' he shouted above the drumming of their hooves.

Caroline turned and glanced over her shoulder. To her relief the road behind them was empty. She had half expected to see the glint of the sun on bayonets and the glow of red coats. With an effort she reined in the excited horse. 'You don't need me now. We're not being followed. I must go back,' she called.

'Why? Don't you like the sound of our adventure?' He slowed down beside her and patted the neck of his sweating mount. 'I would have thought that a woman who walked through churchyards and visited haunted castles at night would enjoy such an excursion.'

She coloured. 'It's not that. But Papa will worry. He may even suspect –'

'That you consort with criminals?'

'Don't be silly.' Her retort was sharp. 'But I am not supposed to leave the house alone. He doesn't know where I am –'

'He will within the hour.' He laughed grimly. 'Do you think the Rixbys won't send after you to find out what you were doing in their stableyard? Your reputation may well be

115

ruined when the world hears you rode off with me.' His expression was unrepentant.

'It may well be when the world knows you are a smuggler and a murderer, sir,' she retorted tartly.

Slowly he reined in his horse. 'I am not a murderer, Caroline. Nor are any of my boys out there. They are all good men, like Jake Forrester. The man who died last night was killed by one of his own comrades in the skirmish. None of my men had firearms. It was a tragic mistake, but not of our doing.'

'Not of your doing?' The wave of relief that flowed over her at his words did not stop her turning on him. 'Being a smuggler is a usual and acceptable second occupation for a country rector I suppose?'

'No.' He urged his horse on once more.

'Then why do you do it?' They were riding side by side now, their horses striding shoulder to shoulder in the narrow lane. 'Why?'

'I have good reasons.' He kicked his mount into a trot. 'Come, we must get on. We pass close to Hancombe soon. You can go home, if you wish. I'll go on over the Downs.'

'No!' Suddenly the thought of returning to the claustrophobic atmosphere of the Rectory was unbearable. Besides, she sensed a challenge in his words. 'I'll go with you. As you say, they are not looking for a woman.'

For a moment he looked at her closely, then he gave a tight smile. 'You know what you are risking?'

She nodded.

'Then you are very brave.'

Before she could think of an answer he had pushed his horse forward into a gallop and she found herself kicking the grey frantically to keep up with him.

They did not stop again until they could see the sea below them – a ribbon of brilliant blue, gilded and coloured by the westering sun. Charles was breathing hard as he slipped from his horse. 'It's early yet. The boys won't gather till dark.

There will be plenty of time to warn them then. The ship comes in with the high tide in the early morning. And the soldiery won't gather till late if I know them. A night spent getting drunk in Larchester to keep their courage up is more to their taste than a cold beach at dawn and by then we'll have signalled the *Marie Blanche* to return to France with her cargo untouched, and my boys will all be tucked up in their beds.' He turned to where she still sat on the high side saddle. 'You must go back now, before your father calls out a search party. Tell him the bishop's son asked you to do an errand for him.' He gave a ghost of a smile. 'If he questions it, send him to me. I'll pacify him. It's better if you go. There's no more for you to do here. I'll be better alone.'

She looked down at him. He still appeared immaculate, scarcely a hair out of place beneath his hat, every inch the elegant churchman, escorting his lady to a Sunday picnic. Only his eyes didn't fit. They were silver in the tanned face – alive, excited, seeing danger ahead, and, she realised suddenly, enjoying it.

'You didn't tell me why you do this,' she said quietly.

'No, and I'm not going to.' He smiled. 'Take care of the horse, Caroline, or we'll have the Rixbys after us. This will take some explaining tomorrow, I fear!' He did not look the slightest bit afraid. 'I will see to its return in the morning.'

'It was a matter of life and death, didn't we say?' she murmured. She didn't want to go. To ride alone through the dusk and go back to her stifling room and learn a passage from the Bible . . . it was unthinkable. Impulsively she pulled off her bonnet and shook her head, feeling her hair slipping from its combs. 'Will I see you again?' She meant: to get their story straight.

He grinned. 'Undoubtedly. You must come to our next garden party.' He was loosening his horse's girth, tethering it beneath the trees.

'Goodbye, then.' In spite of herself she felt strangely desolate.

He looked up at her again. Then he swept off his hat and bowed. 'My thanks, Miss Hayward.'

She gathered up her reins. 'Would you really have implicated Papa if I had betrayed you?'

He laughed. 'Indeed I would.'

'How?'

'I'd have told them about the four kegs of brandy hidden in your hayloft! Goodbye, Miss Hayward.'

He brought his hand down on her horse's rump with a smack and it leaped forward. Almost unseated, Caroline struggled for control. When she had at last brought the mare back to a halt and turned round he had gone.

She set off slowly with her back to the setting sun, following the lanes as best she could. She wasn't familiar with the country here and the horse was tired, so she did not want to take any short cuts.

It was two miles further on at the village of Ewangate that she saw the militia, a huge crowd of men and horses gathered outside an inn. There was no doubt as to their mood and there was no doubt that most of them were, if not local, then at least men brought in from along the coast. The women in the cottages were huddled defensively on the green, talking in low voices together, and their menfolk were eyeing the strangers with obvious hostility as the soldiers drank their ale and talked and laughed. Caroline felt herself grow cold; they were here already, and so close. Charles was wrong. They were not from the barracks in Larchester. They were men from the coast, men who knew the sea, men who, in spite of the ale, were far from too drunk to know what they were doing.

She slowed the mare, aware that every eye was upon her as she made her way up the village street. It was too late to turn back. She could only go on, conscious that an obviously well dressed young woman on a valuable horse, completely unescorted, would be noted and remembered by every single person who saw her.

Cursing her stupidity in riding so carelessly into the village she rode on, looking neither to right nor left, keeping her eyes fixed on the bend in the road ahead.

'So, where are you off to, my beauty? Why not stop and have a drink with us instead, eh?' She froze with horror as a gnarled hand clamped suddenly onto her horse's bridle, making the animal sidestep nervously. 'Too proud to look at the likes of us, are you?'

She found herself staring down at an unpleasantly scarred face with blackened teeth exposed in a leer.

'Leave her, man.' As if in answer to her prayer an officer had appeared from inside the inn. He saluted. 'I'm sorry. Captain Warrender, ma'am, at your service. Take no notice of these ruffians.'

Caroline gave him an uncertain smile. 'It seems strange to have an army gathered here, Captain. Are you looking for a war?'

Her remark was greeted by a growl of laughter from the men who had crowded around her.

'As good as. We fight the free traders, ma'am. There's bounty in it for these fellows, and the satisfaction of knowing that we aid the law.'

'Free traders?' Caroline stared at him.

'Smugglers, my beauty.' The man who had halted her horse grinned at her. 'A hotbed of them, this coast.' There was another growl of laughter which, Caroline suspected, meant that many of the men present could be found amongst the smugglers themselves from time to time.

'Smugglers?' she echoed. 'Are you going to catch them?'

'We are indeed.' The officer grinned. 'Down at Windell's Cove. We've left men on every approach to the coast and we'll be in position there ourselves before dark, and when the devils come we'll be waiting for them.'

She swallowed. 'I'm glad I shan't be there, then. Good evening to you, Captain.'

She rode on, aware that every eye in the village was fixed

on her back as her horse walked past the last cottage and into the leafy lane.

Somehow she had to get back to Charles. She had to warn him. He wasn't expecting this! Every one of those men had been armed to the teeth. She had seen the cudgels and staves, the knives and swords, and she had seen a pile of muskets outside the door of the inn.

Dragging the horse's head round as soon as she was out of sight of the village she skirted back across the fields, heading as fast as she could urge the tired animal towards the clifftop where she had left Charles. But where was it? Desperately she tried to remember the way. Shadows were lengthening now and the lanes were darker. Already the militia would be moving out. She glanced round but everything looked the same in the monochrone light. There were no landmarks. Her heart was hammering with fear as she pushed the horse on, threading her way through the trees, expecting at any moment to hear them behind her.

It seemed a long time before at last she had retraced her steps and found the clump of trees where, to her relief, she saw Charles's horse, grazing peacefully in the shadows. It looked up enquiringly as she rode up, then went on with its eating. She slid from her saddle and tethered the mare beside it, leaving her detested bonnet dangling by its ribbon from the pommel, then she turned towards the cliff.

'Charles?' Her whisper was lost in the taunting cry of a lone, circling gull. There was no sign of him. Hesitantly she stood on the cliff's edge, looking down at the cove beneath. It seemed deserted. The sea was calm and gentle, the dark gilded water running in gentle ripples up the sand.

'Charles, where are you?' She looked round desperately, pushing her hair out of her eyes. The place was deserted.

Biting her lip she looked at the narrow sheep track which wound its way down the cliff, almost sheer as it zigzagged between rocks and clumps of grass and clustered flowers. The sun was dropping now into the sea. A dazzling sunpath lay across the water, touching the wet sand. Slowly gathering the skirt of her habit in one hand she began to descend the path.

Charles was waiting behind an outcrop of rock at the base of the cliff.

'I hope you have a good reason for coming back.' His tall figure threw a long shadow across the sand behind them.

'I saw the militia – not two miles away.' Her words tumbled over each other in her rush to tell him. 'There were dozens of them, all armed, and they will be here before dark.' She was out of breath after her climb. 'They have blocked all the main roads. They mean to trap you.'

Charles let out an oath.

Caroline gave a rueful smile in spite of herself. 'That was the smuggler, not the rector speaking, I take it,' she said wryly.

He glared at her, then, unexpectedly he laughed. 'I fear it was. My apologies.' For a moment he was silent, considering the situation. 'It appears I am doubly in your debt. I would have sat here waiting for the trap to close. I have sent word to the men, and I pray the message will get through in spite of your road blocks, but a few of them may not get the warning in time.'

'How did you send word?' She stared at him. 'There was no one here.'

'Oh, but there was.' He was leaning against the rock, watching the clouds entwining themselves around the sun, changing it from gold to crimson as they dragged it down into the sea. 'I have a system which usually works. The two men here will each have told two more, and they in turn two more, on through the villages. As long as no link breaks they will all be warned.'

'And if the link breaks?' She was watching his face, fascinated, as the westering light threw the planes of his cheekbones and his nose into silhouette.

'That was why I stayed. In case.'

'And you would have stayed here all night?'

He nodded. 'All night, if need be.'

'You care about those men.'

'They are my brothers.'

'Of course.' She was silent for a while. 'I still don't understand why you do it.'

'For the money.' He seated himself on a slab of rock. 'What other reason could there be?'

In spite of herself she was disappointed. 'But you don't need the money –'

'They do.' His mouth hardened. 'You want to know why I do it, Miss Hayward? I'll tell you. Those men, every one of them, are ground into poverty by the way this country operates. And the two things working men have to alleviate their pain and their poverty, alcohol and tobacco, are taxed to a price where few can afford them and the taxes are frittered away by an administration that is uncaring and incompetent. I come from a class, Miss Hayward, which could help men like your Jake Forrester. But we don't. We watch them die. We watch them die in their babyhood and their childhood, in their teens and in their twenties of disease and deprivation. These men are old before the age of thirty. Well, I decided to do something about it. By exploiting one of the local pastimes.' He gave the ghost of a grin. 'I redirect some of that money to where it should go. To the poor. To the sick. To the deserving.'

'Like Robin Hood,' she said softly.

He laughed. 'Perhaps.'

'Besides which, you enjoy the excitement.' She had suddenly discovered that she liked Charles Dawson after all.

'I won't deny it. It beats spending the evening writing sermons.'

'No doubt you have already written your sermon for this week.'

'Of course.' He was mocking. 'How are we going to get you home, Caroline?' he went on softly. 'You can't ride in the dark.'

'I know.' She liked the way he used her name. Sometimes the acerbic Miss Hayward, sometimes the soft, almost caressing Caroline. 'I don't know the way through the countryside, and the roads are blocked.'

He frowned. 'It was unforgivable of me to bring you down here. Did your father have no idea at all that you were going out? He really will be worried now that it is dark.'

She laughed nervously. 'I was supposed to be in my room learning a passage from the Bible as punishment for my waywardness.'

'Indeed?' He raised an eyebrow. 'May I ask what dreadful deed you could possibly have perpetrated to incur such a punishment?'

She grimaced. It seemed so long ago since her father had burst into her room and snatched away her book. 'I was reading Lord Byron's poems.'

His crack of laughter was quickly smothered. 'My poor Caroline. So your soul is damned to perdition. Poor George Gordon. Is he still thought to be an ogre, then?'

'Not by me. I loved his book. But Papa put it on the fire.'

'One day I'll give you another copy, and you shall read it to your heart's content –' He broke off as the sound of a rock falling resounded above the gentle sighing of the sea. Silently he stood up and putting his arm around her shoulders he pulled her into the deep shadows of the tumbled rocks.

Straining her eyes towards the far side of the little cove Caroline felt suddenly very afraid. There were men out there with muskets ready to shoot on sight. If she and Charles weren't killed they could be captured and quite possibly hanged. What was she, after all, if not a willing accomplice of the leader of the smugglers?

She closed her eyes and took a deep breath, very aware of Charles's strong arm around her shoulder, of his tall figure so close beside her, comforting her, giving her a quite spurious sense of security. Then his lips were at her ear, almost touching.

123

'Up the cliff. Quietly,' he breathed. Taking her hand he turned and began to tiptoe back towards the path.

Behind them as the cove fell into darkness it remained empty. If there was anyone there they were hidden in the shadows, out of sight.

The horses were where they had left them. There was a quiet whicker of greeting from Charles's cob, then intense silence in the wood. It was as if the whole world were holding its breath. Soundlessly Charles untied the horses and helped Caroline onto her saddle. Just for a moment he went on holding her hand. 'You're a brave woman, Caroline Hayward.' Leaning down towards him she saw him glance up at her. He reached up and gently touched his finger to her lips. Then he had vanished into the darkness and she heard the rustle of hooves as he led his cob ahead of her.

She was about to turn her exhausted mare after him when the night exploded into noise. By the livid light of the powder flashes from a dozen muskets she saw the ring of armed men who surrounded the wood and she knew that they were trapped.

PART THREE

As the muskets exploded around them Charles span round. 'Get back!' he shouted. 'Get back into the woods. I'll head them off!' Leaping onto his horse he rode straight at the line of armed men.

Fighting to calm the panicking mare Caroline managed to pull her back into the darkness. Throwing herself from the saddle she dragged the horse deep into a thicket and tied it there with shaking hands before creeping back towards the edge of the wood.

Flares had been lit now and it took her only a moment to see that Charles had failed in his attempt to ride through the line of men. They had dragged him from his horse and as she watched he was overpowered and she saw them binding his arms behind his back.

Her mouth was dry with terror as she clung to the powdery trunk of the tree round which she was peering. In the flickering light of the flares she saw Charles, blood streaming from a wound in his forehead, dragged between two men back to his horse and pushed up onto the saddle. Already the ranks were closing round him. In the smoky light she saw the face of the officer who had spoken to her earlier.

'Half a dozen of you come with me,' he shouted. 'We'll take this fine gentleman back to where he can do no more harm. The rest of you, search the wood for the other horse. See if there is anyone hiding in those trees. Then wait at the cove.'

With a gasp of fear Caroline shrank back into the shadows.

'The other horse was mine.' She heard Charles's voice clearly above the shouting. 'And my men are far away, my friend, all forewarned about your trap. There will be no one there for you to find.'

'No?' She saw Captain Warrender look up at him and smile. 'I think we'll check anyway.'

With a little sob of fear she turned back into the wood, pushing her way through the undergrowth, feeling the branches and leaves whipping across her face. She groped her way frantically back to the mare and tearing free the rein somehow managed to scramble back into the saddle. Get away! She had to get away.

She turned her horse's head away from the flares and the shouting of the men and, blinded by tears, urged the animal up a soft ride at a canter, praying the horse could see better than she in the darkness beneath the trees.

It was a long time before she reined in and tried to listen for sounds of pursuit. There was nothing behind her. She had crossed meadow and downland in her wild flight and now she was in the forest. The trees around her were still.

Only an owl in the distance broke the silence. They had not followed her.

Go back.

She swallowed, trying to gather her wits.

Find out where they are taking him.

Go home, another part of her mind was screaming. *Go home and hide. Forget him. He brought it on himself.*

Go on. Follow him. After all, he was caught because he wanted to save you.

She leaned forward and rested her forehead wearily on the mare's sweating neck. It was the truth. He had ridden at the men in order to distract them from her. Had he ridden the other way, into the darkness, he might have got away.

She straightened and took a deep breath. She would go after him.

Turning the tired horse she began to retrace her steps, her ears and eyes straining for the least sight or sound of another rider in the darkness, but the meadows and woods were empty in the thin moonlight. She carefully skirted behind the cove, not daring to go near the cliffs where the soldiers were presumably hiding. Instead she headed west, making for the main road. Reaching the crest of the hill she stopped and cautiously surveyed the road ahead as the moon fought its way out of the haze and swam free, bathing the landscape in clear silver light.

She could see them clearly, half a dozen riders clustered tightly together – at that distance she could not make out which one was Charles. To her relief she realised that they were riding slowly now, making it easier for her to follow them safely.

It was half an hour before they reached the outskirts of the market town and port of Lakamouth and ten minutes after that before the militia escorted their prisoner into the castle. Reining in the mare at the foot of Market Street Caroline saw them disappear beneath the gatehouse arch and the heavy doors swing shut behind them.

Immediately she turned away. Now that Charles was out of sight she felt abandoned and alone. Up till that moment she had concentrated on keeping him in view and on not being seen herself. Now the sleeping city frightened her. She glanced sideways down the narrow streets where the moonlight never reached and she shivered. Somewhere she heard the sound of running feet and nearby a cat yowled.

What was she to do? She had no money, and anyway would never dare approach an inn at this time of night, and she was so vulnerable: a woman, alone, with nothing but her horse for protection. And the horse was exhausted. It would never carry her back to Larchester.

She took a deep breath and turned back towards the road. In the open countryside at least she felt safer, free from the spying eyes which seemed to her to be watching her from every street corner and alleyway.

In the end she found a barn on the outskirts of a village. Leading the horse inside she thankfully helped herself to hay and water from the trough for the horse, and curled up herself in a pile of sharp-scented straw, too exhausted to care where she was or who found her.

It was full daylight when she awoke, stiff and hungry. The mare was munching contentedly at the wisps of hay and sunlight streamed in through the huge open doors, evaporating the dew on the fields. Wearily climbing to her feet and dusting the straw from her habit she looked around. There was no sign of anyone about. Relieved, she splashed her face with water from the trough, tried vainly to smooth back her tangled hair – her bonnet had been lost long ago in the wood – and set about resaddling the mare.

It was still very early when at last she reached home and to her relief the roads were comparatively empty, for wherever she passed people she was painfully aware of their amused stares.

She went, not to the rectory, but to the Forresters' cottage. Susan was outside with two buckets of water she had drawn from the pump in the street. She straightened and stared at Caroline in astonishment as she threw herself wearily from her horse.

'Susan, where's Jake?'

'He's inside. He came home last night after all –'

She broke off as Caroline thrust the mare's rein into her hand and pushed past her into the cottage. Jake was lacing his boots. He straightened in astonishment at the sight of her.

'They've captured Charles – Mr Dawson,' Caroline began, with a glance over her shoulder to make sure Susan had not followed her in. 'They've taken him to Lakamouth Castle.'

'Dear Lord!' Jake stared at her. 'But I thought everyone got away. He warned us hisself –'

'He stayed to protect me!' Caroline cried in despair. 'We have to help him. What can we do?'

Jake sat down heavily on one of the two wooden chairs. 'As to that –' He scratched his head. 'Lakamouth, you say? Why so far? Why didn't they bring him back to Larchester?'

'I don't know.' She shrugged impatiently. 'Maybe the militia are based there.'

'Ay, that's more than likely.' He paused thoughtfully. 'Leave it to me. I'll talk to the others and see what they think is to be done. Your father's been looking for you.' He seemed to notice at last the state she was in. 'You'd best get back home –'

'But you'll send me a message? I must know what you're going to do.'

Jake shook his head. 'It's best you leave it to us now, Miss –'

'No! Don't you see?' She caught his arm. 'Jake, if it hadn't been for me he would have got away. I owe it to him to help him.'

For a moment he said nothing. Then he nodded. 'All right,' he said, 'I'll send you word.'

Leaving the mare in the rectory stable with strict instructions that she be rubbed down and fed and watered Caroline crept towards the kitchen door and pushed it open. Polly and the cook were seated at the table shelling peas.

'Miss Caroline!' Polly jumped to her feet. 'Dear Lord! Look at the state of you! Where have you been?'

'Where is my father?' Caroline collapsed onto a chair.

'He's ridden over to Pengate again. Such a to do there's been. Archdeacon rode over last night and demanded to know why you'd taken Miss Marianne's pony. Then when we couldn't find you anywhere and he told your Papa you'd gone with Mr Dawson your father went straight over there, and oh my dear, the servants there said they hadn't seen hide nor hair of either of you. Mr Hayward was all for scouring the country. And now, look at you! Did you have a fall?'

Caroline closed her eyes with a little prayer of gratitude. Of course, that was the perfect alibi. 'Yes. I fell. I'm sorry I frightened everyone. I must have knocked myself out. I felt too dizzy to ride so I stayed in a barn somewhere until morning.'

The two women threw up their hands in horror.

'But where was Reverend Dawson to let you ride home alone?' Cook was frowning at her closely.

'He had to stay behind. I wanted to get home. It wasn't his fault. I should have stayed with him, but I knew Papa would worry – and now I've made things so much worse.'

To her relief she was able to wash and change and eat something before Mr Hayward, summoned by the groom, returned to the rectory. His anger was only slightly mitigated by his concern when he heard that Caroline had fallen from the borrowed horse. Peremptorily he sent for the doctor, who examined her closely and professed himself surprised by the absence of bruises, before ordering her to bed for the rest of the day. She went gladly, relieved to escape her father's furious questioning which was leading her deeper and deeper into a tissue of lies.

Her room was cool and quiet. The house was silent. She

lay back in the bed, staring at the open window where the curtains stirred gently in the breeze. What was happening to Charles? Would he be tried? Surely he could not be hanged? She closed her eyes miserably, her fists clenched so that her nails cut into the palms of her hands. She couldn't stop thinking about him and unhappily she realised that she had come to admire Charles Dawson far more than she should.

Messages had been sent to the Archdeaconry and to the Rectory at Pengate confirming the safety of horse and rider and one had been received back from Kennet, Charles's butler, saying Mr Dawson had been detained – Caroline blanched at the word – and would not be home for several days. Who had sent that message, she wondered?

All day she waited for news – from Jake, or from her father – with the revelation that Charles Dawson had been arrested but nothing happened.

Then, on her supper tray she found a note:

Are you willing to help? If so, be at the Forresters' cottage at dawn. That was all. There was no signature. She stared at it. It was written in an educated hand on a sheet of heavy, good quality notepaper. Holding it over the empty fireplace she watched it burn, letting the last pieces of ash flutter down into the cold grave. Her heart was thumping nervously.

She barely slept. Long before dawn she was up and dressed in her freshly pressed habit, her hair bound up in a net. Holding her boots in her hand she crept down the stairs into the cold grey of the dew-soaked garden. It hadn't crossed her mind not to go.

She walked swiftly down the village street, flitting like a shadow past the rows of cottages until she reached the Forresters' at the end of the street. It was silent and in darkness.

Nervously she raised her hand to the door, but it opened before she knocked. There were several men inside. Of Susan there was no sign.

'I knew you'd come.' Nervously Jake produced a chair. Seated on the only other chair in the room was James Kennet,

Charles Dawson's butler. So, he knew all about it. Suddenly she realised who must have written the note. He half rose in acknowledgement of her presence then he subsided again. She could feel him eyeing her closely.

'Mr Charles and I had a plan worked out in the event of this ever happening, Miss Hayward,' he said formally. 'At the moment our luck holds. They are still holding him at Lakamouth but we have found out that they intend to transfer him to Larchester for the assizes. I hardly need tell you the scandal that would ensue once he was recognised. It is imperative that we rescue him before he is discovered, never mind before he comes to trial!'

'And how do we do that?' Caroline found that her mouth had gone dry.'

'Bribery, Miss Hayward.' He sighed. 'There is no garrison proper at Lakamouth, which should make things easier. The prison there is, so I gather, guarded by a very poor sort of person. With luck we should be able to spring him with no trouble.' His mouth turned down at the edges wryly at his use of what he obviously thought was the correct cant term.

'How much money will you need?' Caroline's heart sank as she glanced around the room. So this was why they wanted her. But she had nothing of her own.

Kennet smiled. He had obviously read her thoughts. 'It depends how much you can get. You'll have to go to the bishop.'

'The bishop?' Caroline stared at him. 'You mean he knows?'

'No, of course he doesn't know.' The man's voice was scornful. 'But Mr Charles left this letter.'

Caroline unfolded the paper he handed her. 'Father, I have urgent need of several hundred guineas for a cause which would I know, gladden your heart. Please, would you entrust the money to the bearer of this letter. I shall explain to you as soon as I may. Your affectionate son, Charles.' She looked up. 'He was expecting this to happen!'

'We all knew that it might.'

'But why do you want *me* to go to the bishop?'

'You are a more respectable messenger even than I, Miss Hayward.' Kennet allowed himself the ghost of a smile. 'You could wheedle more out of him. We'll need as much as we can get, and quickly.'

It was still only ten o'clock when James Kennet drove Caroline in the Pengate rectory chaise to the door of the Bishop's Palace in the close at Larchester. She had been released from her bedroom into Mr Kennet's charge by her father only when he knew that she carried a message from Mr Dawson to the bishop. Only half an hour after that she had left, having been regaled with a thimble-sized glass of sherry, a hearty handshake from the bishop, a bag of gold coins and a large, scuffed soft leather wallet stuffed with notes issued by the Larchester and Lakamouth Bank.

She had changed into her prettiest sprigged muslin dress and tied her best bonnet over her gleaming curls for the visit, and the bishop, his eyes twinkling, had been openly appreciative of his attractive visitor.

'Charles in a scrape again, is he?' he had roared at her as he filled her glass, having read the letter. 'No, don't bother to deny it. That boy was always in trouble. No different now he's grown. I just hope he's all right.' He had eyed her closely. 'A friend of Charles's, are you?'

'I hope so, my lord.' Caroline could feel herself blushing.

'Hayward's daughter, eh?' He seemed to be trying to place her. 'Good, very good.' And with that she was ushered out once more by the bishop's attentive chaplain.

They drove out on the Lakamouth road, the money lying in Caroline's lap.

'The others will be there to meet us in case we need any help,' James Kennet said after a long silence. 'They'll have seen to it that there's a boat ready to take him off on the afternoon tide.'

'And if they don't release him?' Caroline glanced at the man's profile.

'Then we'll have to think of something else. But I don't think we'll have any bother. Half those men are smugglers themselves. They join the militia for the bounty. If your money's better, then they'll take it.' He flicked the reins.

They put up the horses and chaise at the Angel Inn. Jake and three companions were waiting for them there, lounging around in the stableyard.

'We've signalled the *Marie Blanche*. She's standing off to take him to France.' Jake grinned contentedly. 'All we've got to do now is use a bit of gentle persuasion up at the castle.'

They all looked at Caroline.

'Oh no. Not me!' She stared at the five men in turn, horrified.

'Who better?' Jake grinned. 'Let your hair down and let them see your eyes red from crying. The sight of you would soften the hardest heart. Mr Kennet will go with you.'

She glanced round wildly. 'But I can't!'

'Of course you can. It's his only chance.'

For a moment she was tempted to turn and run, then her courage returned. Hadn't she wanted excitement? Hadn't she resented the boredom of life in the rectory? Well, her prayers had been answered. She had found herself an adventure. Besides, it was for Charles, and for him she realised suddenly, she was prepared to risk anything. Slowly she nodded. 'All right, I'll do it.'

'Good girl.' Kennet's slightly patronising, and certainly disrespectful accolade left her glowing with pride.

The whiteness of her cheeks was real however as she walked shakily under the great gatehouse arch and paused, her face hidden by her lowered veil, as Kennet asked the way. She followed him past the guards, across the rounded, slippery cobbles towards the far side of the courtyard.

The officer in charge of the prisoners was lounging at a desk in a small room inside the Edward Tower. He stood up as Caroline entered, hastily buttoning his tunic. 'Madam?' He glanced from Caroline to James Kennet and back suspiciously.

For a moment Caroline was struck dumb. She didn't have any idea what to do or say. She was no actress and she was very frightened. She looked up at the man piteously and unexpectedly and, perfectly genuinely, burst into tears.

It cost them every penny they had with them as well as the gold locket Caroline wore around her neck, but at last they found themselves making their way down long dank passages to the cells with a signed release form from the captain of the guard folded into Caroline's reticule.

Charles was sitting at a rough wooden table in a small cell. His jacket was torn and the cut above his eye had, before it crusted over, bled copiously into his shirt, but he was not, as she had feared, in chains.

Nor was he pleased to see her. 'What in God's name are you doing here? I was sure you had got clean away!'

Taken aback, it was a moment before she replied. 'We've come to release you. I would have thought you'd be pleased,' she said tartly. 'You are free.'

'Cost your father a pretty penny, too, Mr Charles.' Behind her, Kennet winked. 'We thought Miss Caroline could wheedle a bit more out of him than I could. And she did. Are you ready, sir?' He lifted Charles's torn jacket from the back of the chair and held it out to him.

'You fools!' Charles put on the jacket with a grimace. 'Do you want her implicated? Do you want me identified? How long do you think it will be before someone recognises her? Already they have her bonnet!'

The guards had taunted him with it that morning – crushed and sodden with dew as it had been when they found it trodden into the hoofprint in the muddy wood.

'All they know,' said Caroline, her dignity hiding her hurt at his ingratitude, 'is that there is a lady in your life who cares enough for you to pay her every last penny to get you out of here. Who is there to recognise me anyway? Besides, I have my veil.' She turned and walked out of the cell.

Charles frowned. 'Caroline, I'm sorry. I didn't mean to –'
But she had gone.

With a glance at one another the two men followed her, and uneasily they retraced their steps back towards the courtyard. They were almost there when the door of the guardroom opened and a man stepped out. He stood barring their way.

'So, what is this? A rescue party?' His eyes ranged from one to the other, then came back to Caroline and his expression sharpened. 'Don't I know you?'

'I don't think so.' She kept her voice as low as she could. She had recognised him at once. It was Captain Warrender, the officer whom she had met the day before as he and his men mustered at the roadside. She wished the flimsy veil over her bonnet were thicker. Feeling his sharp eyes on her she lowered her head. But it was too late.

'I know who you are! The girl on that blood mare at Ewangate yesterday. By God! You were one of them! It was you who warned them –'

'This gentleman has his release, Captain.' Kennet stepped forward. 'It was all a case of mistaken identity. 'You must be mixing this lady up with someone else.' He reached behind him and firmly gestured Charles and Caroline on. 'If you wish we can check with your superior officer.'

Caroline felt Charles take her arm. They were moving on past the guard post. In another moment they would be outside.

'Wait –' the captain called. His cry was broken off as Kennet brought the edge of his hand down sharply on the back of his neck and he crumpled to the floor. Dragging him back into the empty room Kennet locked the door on him and pocketed the key. 'Hurry,' he breathed.

They walked as fast as they could without attracting attention across the cobbled courtyard towards the gatehouse, through it and out into the street. Threading their way swiftly back towards the Angel, they were, almost at once, lost in the crowd of horses and carriages and milling townspeople.

'The boat's waiting at the harbour steps.' Jake met them at the stable entrance with the horse and chaise. Within seconds Kennet had dived into the box beneath the seat and produced a shirt and coat from the change of clothes he had hidden there. He helped Charles strip off his bloodstained garments, wrapped them in a bundle and stowed them away. For a moment Caroline found herself staring at Charles's broad chest and muscular shoulders and she felt a strange twist of longing deep inside her. Then he was being thrust into fresh clothes. He saw her staring and gave a tight smile. 'I'm sorry. No sight for a lady. You should have turned away.'

She blushed. 'I'm . . . I'm sorry. Please. We must hurry.'

'Indeed we must.' Kennet was beside her again. 'Let me help you up, Miss, and here, if you'd remove your bonnet. I thought we might have need of disguises.' He had dived once more into the box and produced this time a crimson shawl. 'If you wrap this round your hair, Miss. Now you look quite different. See?' He pushed her bonnet out of sight beside the bloodstained shirt.

Moments later she found herself wedged between Kennet and his master in the two-seater vehicle. With a wave to Jake and his companions they were driving away from the inn.

Caroline was very conscious of the pressure of Charles's thigh against her own, his shoulder next to hers. 'I haven't thanked you yet,' she said. 'You saved me by riding at those men.'

'I did no more than you did for us,' he said curtly. He glanced behind them, through the small window in the hood of the chaise. 'You have put yourself in more danger coming here. That was foolish.'

'She was very brave, Mr Charles,' Kennet put in on her right. There was a hint of reproof in his voice.

'I don't doubt her bravery. I merely deplore her headstrong urge to rush into danger,' Charles retorted. Abruptly his face lightened into a smile. 'Not that I would have her any other way now I come to think about it. I must like obstreperous women!' He glanced down at her with a teasing grin. 'One of these days I'll come back for you, if you're not careful, and enroll you amongst my followers.'

Caroline didn't answer. Already they had reached the harbour. Kennet drove to the water's edge and stopped at the top of a flight of steps. A small rowing boat waited below. The man at the oars glanced up and raised his hand.

'The *Lucy* out there will take you out to the *Marie Blanche*. Good luck Mr Charles.' Kennet leaned forward slightly.

Charles leapt down. 'Thank you. Both of you.' He inclined a slight bow to Caroline. Then almost as an afterthought he reached up and taking her hand kissed it lightly. 'Take her home, James, and tell her father to keep her out of mischief.'

That was all. He did not look back. They watched as the small boat rowed out to the fishing boat anchored in the middle of the harbour. Already its sails were lifting.

'Where will they go?' Caroline asked sadly.

'They'll meet with a Frenchman in the Channel.' For a moment the butler sat still, staring after his master. 'Mr Charles will go to ground for a while in France while we see which way the land lies here. There will be a hue and cry for him when they find he's been released in error.' He grinned complacently. 'Nowhere along the coast will be safe while they look for him.' He shook the reins. 'No time to hang around for you, either, Miss. I must get you home. Once you're there, you'll be safe.'

She did not let herself look back and in seconds the chaise had swung back into the network of busy streets.

Her father was waiting for her in his study. 'I expected you back long since.' He frowned. Then he went on more eagerly, 'You saw the bishop?'

She smiled wearily: 'The bishop was very hospitable, Papa. I was able to carry out Charles – that is, Mr Dawson's – instructions.'

'And when are we to see Mr Dawson home?' He was watching her closely.

She shrugged. 'I don't know, Papa. No doubt he will contact his father when he returns.'

The rector was obviously dying to ask more, but something about his daughter's bleak expression stopped him short. He walked over to the window and stared out at the sunlit garden. 'The archdeacon's groom came over this afternoon and collected Marianne's mare. He says you can go and fetch Star tomorrow,' he said quietly. He turned and looked at his daughter. 'I understand Marianne is rather upset.'

'I'm sorry,' Caroline replied listlessly. 'I shall go and see her, of course.'

He sighed. 'I think you should. And now, perhaps you should go up and rest before dinner. It will give you the chance to catch up with learning the Bible passages I gave you.' He sat down at his desk and pulled a book towards him. When he did not look up again she understood that the interview was closed.

Marianne was tearful. 'But where did you go? *Where?*'

Caroline shrugged. 'I've told you. All I did was ride into the countryside with him. Somewhere outside his parish – I don't know where.'

'But why? Why you?'

'Because I brought him the message.' Patiently Caroline repeated once again the story she had decided to tell. It was after all, so near the truth.

'He hasn't come back, you know,' Marianne went on miserably. 'He said he would talk to Papa the next day. But he didn't.'

'I am sure he intended to. I am sure he will as soon as he can.' Caroline stood up wearily. 'I don't know any more than I've told you, Marianne. He didn't confide in me.' That last at least was true.

* * *

The Rectory was intolerable. Her days were as meaningless as before, boring, filled with the chores of everyday life – interspersed with learning the interminable verses her father set her. Firmly she suppressed her rebellious desire to escape. She had to help her father. But even he could not stop her dreams. And dream she did of her few stolen hours with the handsome rector of Pengate.

She couldn't stop thinking about him. Those last few words to her in the chaise: had he meant them? Had he meant he would come back? She lived again and again his quick kiss on her hand and the disturbing sight of him, naked to the waist, his muscular body so close to hers as he changed his clothes. Where was he? Had he reached France safely or had his ship been intercepted by an excise cutter in the Channel? She didn't even know that. Her father had spoken of the abortive raid with fury, and later he had mentioned that the ringleader had been caught and then allowed to escape. He gave no sign that he knew who the man in question was. Soon even those few mentions stopped and the smugglers were not spoken of again. Once she had gone furtively to the stable to see if any kegs were hidden there. If there ever had been, they were there no longer.

Caroline's only moments of real pleasure were her visits to Susan Forrester, whose tiny new daughter had, to her astonishment and pleasure, been christened Caroline. She knew Jake had no news; the smuggling had come to an end. No repairs had been started on the cottage.

Then came the invitation to the bishop's Michaelmas party. The reception rooms at the palace were as usual crowded. At her father's side Caroline stood looking around, still listless, her face pale and strained. She had not wanted to come. Almost at once she saw the Rixbys on the far side of the room and her heart sank. Marianne no longer bothered to hide her hostility to Caroline, or the fact that she blamed her for what she took to be Charles's jilting of her. She replied to Caroline's tentative smile with a scowl and a toss of her head, then she turned back to the young man at her side.

'Young Lord Wentworth.' Mr Hayward had noticed the direction of his daughter's gaze. 'It seems Miss Rixby is no longer pining for her lover's memory.' He noted his daughter's heightened colour with a sad nod. Just as he had suspected. The silly child imagined herself in love with Dawson. He sighed. How providential that the bishop's elder son had absented himself from his parish – for his health, the story from the palace went – and a curate left in charge at Pengate. George Hayward bowed absent-mindedly to a colleague. When he turned back, Caroline had gone.

The gardens were deserted. Her shoes crunched on the carpet of golden leaves as she made her way along the yew hedge and through into the garden beyond. There were leaves on the grass beneath the swing; leaves had drifted onto its seat in the still afternoon. She stood for a moment, her hand lightly caressing the rope. The only sound came from a robin sitting on a trellis nearby, trilling its song into the clear autumn air.

'I hope you remember that you are too heavy for that swing.'

For a moment she thought she had imagined the voice. She spun round. Charles was standing near the hedge watching her. He was dressed once more in sober black, his hair neatly brushed, his shoes spotless. He gave a slight bow. 'So, you still hate parties, Miss Hayward.'

'What are you doing here?' She took a tentative step towards him. To her annoyance she found she was trembling.

'I followed you. I guessed you'd come here.'

'I meant what are you doing back in England?'

'I am attending my father's party.'

'But it's not safe –'

'I had to come back, Caroline. I couldn't leave my parishioners forever.' He paused. 'I have something for you. Kennet told me you gave your locket as part of my ransom.

140

I can't replace it, of course, but I should like you to have this instead.' He reached into his pocket and produced a pendant on a thin gold chain. He held it out to her. 'Please. I should like you to have it.'

'I can't.' Caroline stared at the dainty thing lying in his palm. It was a wisp of filigree gold and pearls. 'I can't accept a gift from you. It wouldn't be right.'

'It's not a gift, Caroline, it's to replace the one you lost. Please. It's the least I can do. I owe you my life.'

She looked at him uncertainly. 'You know I shouldn't take it.'

He smiled. 'But you never do things you should, do you? Did you learn your passage from the Bible?' There was a teasing light in his eyes.

She nodded ruefully. 'There was no escape.'

'So, now you are the dutiful daughter of the Rectory once more? No more galloping round the countryside at night with criminals?'

She shook her head. 'I fear I am quite reformed.'

He must not guess how much it hurt her to smile and spar with him like this; how much she longed for him to touch her.

'Poor Caroline.' He took her hand and tipping the pendant into it closed her fingers over it. 'So, make this one last gesture of rebellion. Take my gift, with my thanks. I must go back to the house.' He gave her a long searching look and for a moment she thought he was going to say something else, but he turned away.

She waited at least ten minutes before she followed him.

She found her father where she had left him. This time he was busily engaged in conversation with the archdeacon.

'Papa! There you are.' Both men stared at her interruption and she saw her father frown.

Marianne, she noticed, was talking to Lord Wentworth again. Her fingers closed more tightly over the pendant in her hand and she slipped it regretfully into her pocket. She would never be able to wear it, of course. Her father would see it at once and ask her where it had come from. Already he had enquired where her mother's locket was.

'You look so pretty, Caroline, my dear,' the archdeacon said valiantly, eyeing her flushed cheeks. 'How are you?'

'Well, thank you.' Her smile froze as Charles appeared beside her father. He gave a slight bow. 'Miss Hayward, gentlemen. How nice to see you here.'

George Hayward gave him a searching look. 'I didn't realise you were back, young man.'

Charles smiled. 'Only yesterday. I decided my parish could not do without me another moment.'

'And did you have a good holiday?' the rector persisted.

'Hardly a holiday, sir,' Charles said cryptically.

'Last time we met you were going to come and see me, Charles,' the archdeacon put in forcefully. 'About my daughter, as I recollect.'

There was a moment's silence. Caroline's eyes were fixed on Charles's face. For a moment he seemed taken aback at the archdeacon's questions but he recovered himself fast.

'Indeed I was, sir. Perhaps I could come and see you one day next week? Then, maybe, I can explain my circumstances more fully.'

'I think you should.' The archdeacon's face relaxed slightly. 'And now George, there are things you and I must discuss.' He took Caroline's father's arm, leaving her standing awkwardly, facing Charles.

There was a moment's silence.

'Are you going to ask for Marianne's hand?' She knew it was none of her business. The moment the words were out of her mouth she could have bitten off her tongue.

He glanced over his shoulder. 'It seems I may have implied that I will.'

Somehow she made herself smile. 'And will you tell her of your alternative career?'

'I doubt it.' He smiled. 'I fear that career is over. I shall, however, have to think of other ways to help those who need money.' He hesitated. 'Caroline –'

'I'm sure you will have a strenuous helper in Marianne.' She stepped away from him, unable to hide her unhappiness for another moment. 'Forgive me, but there is someone I must speak to.'

She fled after the archdeacon and her father.

How could she have been so foolish as to dream for even a moment that one day he would think of her as anything other than useful at a moment when he needed help? He had not seen her as a woman – or if he had it was only because being a woman made her a nuisance. The pendant meant nothing. It had been exactly as he had said, a replacement for the one lost; nothing more.

She found that she was staring at the archdeacon. He smiled. 'You look a little distrait, my dear. Can I fetch you some lemonade?' She saw his eyes searching her face curiously. 'Has someone upset you?'

'Indeed, no.' She smiled desperately. Charles had followed her. She felt his presence as a sudden tingle down her spine.

'Your daughter, archdeacon, seems much taken up with Lord Wentworth,' Charles said thoughtfully. 'I wonder if she would have time for me now.'

The archdeacon's nose became a trifle more puce. 'If you are implying –'

'I am implying nothing, sir.' Charles gave an elaborate shrug. 'It was merely an observation.' Behind them they all heard clearly Marianne's throaty giggle and saw her coquettishly tap Lord Wentworth's arm with her fan. She had not given the Rector of Pengate a second glance and not once had she acknowledged his presence in the room.

The archdeacon frowned. 'My daughter is very young, Charles –' He broke off as Caroline gave a horrified gasp.

Barely ten paces away from them, standing talking to the Mayor of Larchester, was Captain Warrender of the Lakamouth Militia. Before she could move he turned and saw her. His mouth dropped open and she realised at once that he had recognised her.

'What is it?' Charles stared at her ashen face.

Already the man was thrusting through the crowded guests towards her.

'Oh God! Hurry!' Not stopping to think, Caroline grabbed Charles's hand. To the astonishment of the archdeacon and the other guests around them she turned and fled, pushing her way through the room with Charles close behind her.

In the hall she stared round wildly. 'Hide!' she gasped. 'We've got to hide!'

'My father's study!' Charles threw open the door opposite them and pushed her inside. Closing it behind them he locked it. Then he turned to her. 'Who was it?'

'The captain of the militia. He recognised me!'

'And why, may I ask, should the captain of the militia recognise you, Miss Hayward?' The bishop's deep voice made them both swing round in alarm. Charles's father was seated at his desk near the window, having taken a few minutes' break from his guests.

Charles closed his eyes and took a deep breath. 'Father, I'm afraid I have to do some explaining . . .'

Behind them the door-handle turned and rattled. They all saw the wooden panels give as someone thrust against it from the other side. The bishop stared at the door over his gold-rimmed spectacles. 'May I suggest you both go into my chapel, my children, and pray that you can think up a good explanation for all this, while I see who is so anxiously waiting at my door.' The bishop stood up slowly.

Charles took Caroline's hand and dived towards a door half hidden by a curtain in the corner of the room. Inside, the bishop's tiny private chapel was dark, lit only by the small lamp hanging over the altar. Charles pulled the door closed softly. He turned to Caroline and raised a finger to his lips warningly. Silently they waited in the semi-darkness. There was no sound from the bishop's study. Caroline sat down heavily on one of the four chairs. She found she was shaking violently.

Going on one knee beside her, Charles took her hands in his. Neither of them dared speak. They stayed like that for a long time, clinging together in the shadowy silence, then at last the door opened.

They followed the bishop sheepishly back into his study and stood side by side before him as he sat down at his desk once more.

'I have told Captain Warrender that he was mistaken in thinking any guest of mine could have been involved in a gaol break,' he raised his eyebrow painfully, 'and an attack on an officer in the Royal Militia,' he said at last. 'The captain has apologised and left the palace. Charles, would you be kind enough to tell me exactly what has been going on. From the beginning, if you please.'

Charles did so.

Caroline listened. His voice did not waver once as he told his father the whole story, and not once did the bishop's face betray his feelings as he heard it.

When Charles had finished there was a long silence.

'You realise that your motives, however altruistic some of them may have been, cannot excuse your behaviour,' the bishop said at last.

Charles grimaced. 'I realise that, Father.' He looked for a moment like a chastened small boy.

'I could not allow you to remain in your parish, even if it were safe for you to do so.'

Charles blenched.

'And what of Miss Hayward?' the bishop went on relentlessly. 'She is in as much danger as you. She could be recognised anywhere. Quite apart from which it appears to me that she had been quite unpardonably compromised. Do you realise what you have done to this young woman, Charles?' He sighed wearily.

'I can at least put that right,' Charles said with an unrepentant grin, 'if I marry her.' He paused. 'And that could be my penance too, perhaps, to marry a rector's daughter?' He looked at his father hopefully.

Caroline's face burned miserably. 'I wouldn't marry you if you were the last man on earth,' she replied angrily. This wasn't how she had dreamed of him; this wasn't how she wanted it to happen. She turned to the bishop. 'Your son is already engaged, my lord. And I assure you, I do not feel myself compromised.'

The bishop looked at her thoughtfully. Then he turned to Charles. 'Do you think the Rixbys would have you as a son-in-law once they knew you were gaol bait?'

Charles laughed grimly. 'I doubt it. But the matter is resolved I think by Marianne herself. She has found more glamorous amusement than me! I am sure I shall find the Rixbys no longer hope for a proposal from me.' He turned to Caroline. 'I meant it you know. I was extraordinarily attracted to you from the first moment I saw you on the swing. Up till then I'd always thought you beautiful, but too quiet.' He grinned. 'Then later I found you were quite different from the average rector's daughter and I fell hopelessly in love. Given all the time in the world I should have pursued you with total single-mindedness and spoken to your father without delay. But as things are I must tell you now, without preamble, that I am absolutely certain that you are the woman I want for my wife.'

'As a penance!' Caroline retorted.

The bishop let out a snort of laughter.

'Some penance! Can't you see that he is in love with you, my dear? And I don't blame him. I would be myself if I were twenty years younger.' He stood up and came round the desk. 'Poor Miss Hayward. So public a proposal. And by such a reprobate. If he weren't my son I should advise you not to have him.'

He put his arm around her shoulders. 'I'm afraid deviousness runs in the family, my dear. You don't stand a chance against Charles and me together. You must accept. If you love him that is. You can leave the archdeacon to me. From what I saw earlier Marianne won't break her heart over Charles. And I think I can persuade your father to give his consent. I have been debating the replacement of poor old Canon Peters and it seems to me your father might be a very able successor to him.' He smiled. There was a moment's silence.

'I won't make you learn passages from the Bible,' Charles murmured in her ear. 'And you can have a new bonnet and your very own copy of Lord Byron's works.'

Caroline smiled in spite of herself. 'With promises like that, I confess I am tempted. I'll think about it.'

'Good.' The bishop nodded approval. 'But now to the other problem. You cannot go back to Pengate, Charles. Quite apart from any other consideration that man was no fool. He will lie in wait outside the close to check for himself that the young lady he saw really is someone else, and in so doing he is bound to see you. You will have to stay here, both of you, until we can think of a plan to get you away.' He frowned.

'In the meantime, you could marry us, father?' Charles took Caroline's hand.

The bishop looked at them thoughtfully. 'I think that would be a little premature, Charles. Ladies like months to plan things like weddings.'

'Not this one, father.' Charles smiled. 'This one is a rebel. There is nothing she would like more than a secret wedding in the cathedral at dead of night, followed by a honeymoon aboard the *Marie Blanche* on the way to France. Am I not right?' he appealed to Caroline.

She laughed. 'I'm afraid Charles knows me too well already, my lord,' she said. 'I do find that idea appealing.'

'And your day will be made if you are pursued by armed soldiers with warrants for your arrest, no doubt,' the bishop said dryly. 'I would rather your honeymoon were spent quietly in London while I find you a suitably quiet parish somewhere far from the sea!'

'Oh, Father –'

'That is my decision, Charles.' For the first time the bishop looked angry. 'And now, you may take Caroline into the garden for a while, while I speak to her father.'

Charles seated himself on the swing and gently pushed at the ground. He smiled up at her. 'You can wear the pendant now.'

She took it from her pocket. 'Would you mind a new parish?'

He shook his head. 'I have to remember that my father is also my bishop. I must obey him. Besides, it's a challenge! Think what we could do in a new parish together.'

She smiled. 'You could become a highwayman.'

'With you for my Moll?' He laughed. 'What a pair we should make. I can see life will never be dull with you!' He grew serious again. 'And what if I reformed and settled down to a life of hard work? Would that dismay you?'

She looked up at him soberly. 'If life grows dull, Charles,' she said, 'I can always ask Captain Warrender to tea!'

OBE

It was the fault of the books of course. She knew they said that the technique would work but she hadn't actually believed it. Not deep in her heart of hearts.

The thing was that she loved the theory. Who wouldn't? It was pure fantasy. And she loved the whole scenario that went with it all. The exercises, the meditation (an excuse to sit for twenty minutes twice a day without moving and feel self-righteously good, not guilty, about it), the props: the oil burner, the candle, the chunk of amethyst and best of all the feeling which she knew was probably wrong, not in the spirit of the thing at all, that she had a secret and one which would, if Desmond found out about it, shock him to the roots of his hair.

She had never joined in as much as she should with the parish work but it was becoming commonplace for vicars' wives these days to have a job (in her case boring secretarial) so the ladies of the parish had been given free rein to follow their inclinations for supporting good causes and she kept out of the way as much as she could.

This evening, for example, she had intended to go to the W.I. meeting. That was why she hadn't gone with Desmond to the school nativity play. The trouble was as soon as the door closed behind him she experienced such an incredible feeling of release. Poor darling Desmond. If only he wasn't so – so – Pi!

When they had married he had been a market gardener. Not garden centre material; not even really the specialist nursery type. But that might have come. With her pushing and her energy it really might have come. Instead he had suddenly got God. Badly. Within five years he was an ordained priest, the market garden and house had gone and they were living in an inner, well not city exactly but definitely urban environment, in a small modern church-owned cottage which gloried in the name of Rectory. She still wasn't quite sure why she hadn't left him. No, that wasn't true. She knew exactly why. She still loved him. Adored him actually. And he still adored her. Obviously. Otherwise how did she manage to entice him to do the things she still managed to entice him to do under the cover of the ecclesiastical duvet?

It was all his fault actually because he had given her the idea in the first place. After a particularly exciting interlude which had left him with watering eyes and distinctly out of breath, as he lay triumphantly on top of her, her wrists firmly held to the pillow where they could do no more harm (if that was what you called it), he had whispered the word. Witch.

Lying still, looking up at him with misleading docility Serena smiled.

The word appealed to her. It did not conjure up pictures of old crones and broomsticks and untimely bonfires. Not the way Desmond said it. Oh no. It had definitely been intended as a compliment.

It was as she was choosing a book for Desmond's father's birthday ('golf or gardening: they're safe') that she saw the book on Wicca. That's what they called witchcraft these days. She sidled nearer the table on which it was displayed. *New Age/Religion/Popular Psychology* it said on the sign hanging over the display and she flipped the book open. The photograph thus exposed (the right word, she thought, with a gasp and then an audible, half embarrassed, giggle) was of a woman, stark naked except for a beautiful necklace, facing an equally naked man who had no necklace, but whose wrists appeared to be tied together.

For a long moment she stared. She did, she had to admit, feel quite aroused. She glanced up and saw two tables away, thank the dear Lord with his back to her, Stan Eversley, a churchwarden from their parish. She slammed the book shut and wondered in sudden embarrassment whether this was a hot flush. Something exceedingly uncomfortable was certainly sweeping up her body and colouring her cheeks an unseemly hue.

'Mrs Perkins? I thought it was you.' He had seen her then. The hot flush was swiftly followed by a cold douche of dread. She picked up the nearest golfing book (had the assistant classified it under New Age/Religion or had a careless customer put it down in the wrong place?) and she left the shop with her innocent purchase, smartly wrapped, under her arm.

She didn't buy any books on Wicca of course. Of course not. Even though it did seem to have more scope for, well, fun, than the C of E. What she did buy was a book on personal development. Later. When no one she knew was in the bookshop. And even then she told the assistant it was for her nephew. Then she bought another, on yoga and one on meditation, both recommended by the first.

She drew the line at incense. Desmond, a low church man if ever there was one, would freak out at the first whiff, but aromatherapy oils were all the rage and – she studied a book on this subject as well – could with a judicious choice of oil be used in meditational settings. The amethyst cluster was actually being used to decorate a shelf in one of the local hand-made pottery shops. It wasn't for sale, but she knew by now that if a crystal calls you and wants to live with you, you cannot argue with it. Luckily the shop assistant had read the same books and knew this as well so a mutually satisfactory deal was struck and the amethyst too was presumably ecstatically happy.

There weren't often occasions when she could light her

beautiful ceramic oil burner and her candle and lay the crystal near them. She needed to be sure not only that Desmond was out but also that no one else knew that she was in. (The parishioners, even though they knew she worked, still felt they had a right to every second of time she was at home.)

Guiltily putting on the answerphone and switching off the lights she crept upstairs to the cupboard euphemistically called the sewing room (not by her, as she told anyone who would be interested) and closing the door behind her she stood still for a moment to centre herself.

It was growing increasingly easy to slip into the meditative mood. She was, she thought, quite good at it, although she wasn't sure how one judged such things. Certainly she was learning how to go more and more deeply into whatever it was that made her tick.

The first time she had what her book called an OBE (out of body experience to those of you who are unrehearsed in these matters – forget the Order of the British Empire) she nearly died of fright. One moment she was sitting cross-legged on the floor, her eyes shut, her mind alert but free, her hands upturned on her knees, the next she was up in the corner of the ceiling looking down. With a yelp of fear she tumbled back into herself, scrambled to her feet, tore open the door, ran down the stairs and into the kitchen for a very unalternative caffeine fix. Her hands were shaking so much she couldn't get the lid off the Gold Blend. For the first time in her life she wished she smoked. That would give her something to do to settle her nerves. She had actually been there, on the ceiling. Not imagining it. Not dreaming it. Not wishful thinking it. Actually. For real. Genuinely.

When Desmond came home she was curled up on the sofa watching an old tape of *Taggart*. He glanced at the screen, gave a slight grimace aimed in equal parts at the gory corpse in close-up and the unintelligible Glaswegian dissertation on methods of slicing through the jugular, and he dropped a kiss on top of her head.

'My roots need touching up, don't they?'

Serena didn't take her eyes off the green-clad figure in charge of the scalpel.

'Do they?' He squinted down. 'They look all right to me.'

It was amazing how much she had noticed in that split second of altered viewpoint: the greying roots and an unacceptably prominent, some might say slightly conked nose she had never noticed – never before seen from that angle, the spiders' webs festooning the light bulb and lamp shade and the worn patch on the carpet just inside the door which was barely noticeable from ground – or normal eye – level.

It was two days before she meditated again and of course she couldn't do it properly. She was too tense, and let's face it, too afraid.

A week later though it happened again and this time she found she could move around the ceiling. Two days after that she discovered that, unbelievably, she could fly through walls.

Practising sometimes twice a day she became proficient at manoeuvring. In fact all she had to do was think herself somewhere and there she was.

It was while she was skimming around Desmond's study that the thought of him transported her abruptly to where he was, sitting uncomfortably in the Eversleys' sitting room, a cup of coffee balanced precariously on his knees, a crumb from a lately-consumed biscuit stuck provocatively – or so thought his wife – to the corner of his lower lip. Oh Des. It would look so silly to anyone else. He would be mortified if he knew. Opposite him Jean Eversley was sitting on the sofa, her hands laced around her knees, her eyes glued to the crumb. Every now and then she brushed self-consciously at her own lips. He frowned, puzzled by her action, failed to imitate her body language, and ploughed on with what he was saying.

'Jean, my dear. I appreciate your confiding in me, I really do. I just wish there was something I could do to help.'

Serena thought herself onto the arm of the chair next to

him. Cautiously she reached out a finger to touch his lip.
Desmond frowned. He shivered visibly and looked round.
'I'm sorry, Jean. Someone must have stepped on my grave.'
The crumb was still in place.

Serena felt herself smile. She didn't dare try and touch him
again. She still wasn't that good at this manoeuvre which was
rather advanced. The technicalities were still a little vague and
she wasn't convinced she might not suddenly materialise in
person. In fact she wasn't convinced that Jean Eversley
couldn't see her, for the woman's eyes had grown suddenly
huge and her normally florid complexion had paled.

She had thought she was invisible – had been to herself
when she hovered in front of a selection of mirrors at home,
and was, obviously, to Desmond or he would have reacted
to the vision of his wife floating neatly onto the arm of the
chair in which he was sitting and arranging herself with provocatively crossed legs right there in the churchwarden's
overheated sitting room – but her worst suspicions about
Jean were confirmed a moment later when the woman's voice,
a creaky, whispered, shadow of its former strident self suddenly said, 'Can you see it?'

'It?' Desmond frowned. Vaguely locating the area on which
she was focusing he stared straight at Serena. 'See what?'

Serena breathed a sigh of relief.

'It. The ghost!'

Desmond shook his head sternly. 'Oh come now, my dear
Jean. You're overwrought.' Standing up he put a fatherly arm
around the woman's shoulder. To her relief Serena saw the
crumb, dislodged by this sudden activity, release its hold on
his lip and fall harmlessly out of sight onto the carpet. 'It's
the thought of Stan playing you up, that's all. You're upset.
Once things have settled down again you'll realise there are
no such things as ghosts.'

'What about the holy ghost?' Jean was trembling visibly
but not too shaken to be perverse. Serena scowled. How
typical of the woman.

Desmond however handled it brilliantly. He gave a deep, world-weary sigh. 'That is not the same sort of ghost, Jean.' He smiled. 'As I'm sure you very well know . . .'

He was about to get boring.

Serena thought herself home.

When he got there himself by more orthodox methods (1987 Vauxhall) half an hour later, she was making biscuits.

'So, do I gather Stan Eversley is having another affair?' She smiled at him innocently.

'How on earth did you know that?' Desmond seemed genuinely shocked. After all Jean had only just found out.

'Village gossip.' Deftly Serena put the baking tray into the oven. 'The old hypocrite! How does he think he'll get away with it?'

Desmond threw himself down in a chair and pulling the teapot towards him he shook it experimentally to see if there was any tea left. 'He always does. Jean will forgive him. She adores that silly old man.'

Of course she had to be very firm with herself. Spying on parishioners was definitely not on. Nor was spying on Desmond. Not once she had checked that his relationship with the beautiful and frustrated Dawn Freeling really was the spiritual and healing challenge he said it was. But it was oh so tempting.

When Don French rang up to say he couldn't come to the vestry meeting because he had a migraine she couldn't resist running upstairs, locking herself in the loo and popping over to his house to see what he was really up to. Just to give some support and spread a healing thought or two, you understand. She found him in the sitting room, his feet propped up on the coffee table, sharing lager and a take-away curry with Joseph Porter, the tearaway brother of the Methodist minister. They were glued to a video of *Seven*. Apoplectic with rage she almost lost control. Luckily the sweeping gesture designed to hurl the already emptied, crushed, cans of Holsten to the floor had no effect at all other than to make her spin round and round in circles. But she saw Don give a shiver. He edged away from the table and put down his fork. 'Joe.' He had gone pale. 'Did you feel that?'

'Wha'?' Joe, the son of an Oxford scholar, was glotally disadvantaged at the best of times. After a chicken vindaloo he was virtually incoherent.

'Cold. Rather unpleasant.'

Thanks a bunch! Serena was fuming, but back in control.

'Na.' Joe lurched forward to grope with a wayward hand for his can.

With slit-eyed concentration Serena honed in on him. Putting her own hand firmly round his wrist she pulled.

Joe let out a scream. Curry and lager flew in all directions. He leaped to his feet, vaulted the back of the sofa and cowered behind it as Serena positioned herself next to Don and whispered, with gratifying effect, the one word 'Rectory'.

When she walked back downstairs to where Desmond and Stan and the others were holding their meeting the phone was ringing. Desmond returned from answering it with a smile. 'Don is feeling a bit better. He thought he would come over after all,' he said.

She knew she had to stop doing it. Her conscience was troubling her more and more and besides that, her character was changing and Des had noticed. She was becoming a know-all – she knew for example exactly when Stan Eversley had stopped dallying and returned to Jean's bed – and she was becoming insufferable. She had all these private jokes. She was like those poor souls one saw walking down the street chuckling to themselves at some hilarious unshared secret. Maybe this was what they were laughing at. Maybe they could all do it: leap from their bodies and whiz around the world. She had tried that as a change from the affairs of the parish. World travel. She would watch a programme on the TV about some distant, exotic and above all expensive place and then she would pop over there for a quick look. And no danger of malaria or funny tummy.

But secrets become burdens. There was no one to share her experiences with; her close friends had dropped away or become hostages to the Royal Mail when she and Des had moved to the parish – so far from where they lived before – and she had made only acquaintances since then. Not once did she meet some other out-of-body soul and only seldom did people see her and when they did they were nearly always afraid.

Except once. In France. She was standing gazing at the most beautiful waterfall she had ever seen, in a lush, narrow, deserted valley high in the Franche Comté when she heard footsteps near her. The man who stood there was tall and devastatingly good-looking in a particularly French way. Only a little out of breath after the climb, he sat down on some rocks to recover as he stared down at the rainbow arc of water. She studied him with interest, made brazen by her invisibility. He was definitely a dish.

'So, *madame*, what do you think of the view, eh? Is it not beautiful?' He had not looked directly at her, but who else could he be speaking to? It had to be her. There was no one else there.

Startled out of politeness, she grimaced, ignoring this question. 'Can you see me?'

'But of course.' He smiled.

As well he might. It was hot at home now summer had come and she had retreated to the sewing room wearing only knickers and bra – for which small mercy she gave a quick prayer of thanks, she had so nearly succumbed to the urge to walk around the house naked!

Embarrassed, she tried to resist the urge to wrap her arms protectively and disguisingly around her chest, and failed. She could feel herself blushing.

'Are you really here, properly?' It was a dumb question, but she was feeling severely rattled.

'We are both here properly, *madame*.'

She laughed. 'Not necessarily.'

He turned and looked at her at last. He had the most beautiful eyes. They ran swiftly and a little too professionally over her body, and then returned to do it again, slowly. Caressingly. She could feel her blush spreading.

Casually he stood up and walked to the edge of the chasm, staring down at the falls. The sound of water was deafening around them. 'So, are you suggesting that we are, or should be, improper?'

She could hear the laughter in his voice above the roar.

'No, I am asking if you are a ghost.' It sounded crazy, but it was a crazy situation.

He let out a huge guffaw of laughter. 'I am if you are.'

'I'm not a ghost!' She was shocked.

'No?' He turned to face her, his eyes sparkling with humour. 'But I think you may be a wraith, perhaps. Do you know the difference?'

She shook her head.

'Ah.' He reached between the rocks to pick one of the delicate bell-shaped flowers which grew there and stood looking down at it. 'I think it is a matter of relativity.' He chuckled. 'We must come here again to discuss it.' He paused. She saw his glance run quickly over her again and Serena was agonisingly aware of her faded, non-glamorous elastic, well past its sell-by date – the kind of thing no French woman would be seen dead in – probably no Frenchwoman *was* seen dead in. He did not seem to notice. She saw his tongue run fleetingly across his lips as, smiling benignly, he stepped forward and ran his finger over her shoulder, lightly, causing only the slightest frisson, nudging one of the offending straps out of the way.

His touch was only too real. But she was supposed to be out of her body. So what was her body doing here? It should be at home waiting for her. And it should not be showing or feeling the slightest interest in the presence of another man, however attractive. She did, after all, still adore Des.

Serena bit her lip. She knew it was time to go.

Before she lost all sense of reality.

And shame.

He was standing very close to her now. Smiling, he handed her the flowers.

And that was it. The next moment she was sitting cross-legged on the sewing room floor.

Her first thought was, 'Bother!' or a word to that effect. Her second was, 'I must buy some new underwear; how could I ever let Des see me like this,' her third was, perversely, 'I wish I could tell him all about it!'

But Desmond, she knew, would not understand.

He would probably have her certified.

He would probably have her burned at the stake.

Better to keep it a secret. Just between herself.

And the Frenchman.

Looking down she found she was still holding the spray of flowers he had given her and she wondered what they were. Perhaps he would know. She could always return to collect some more. But perhaps not. It wouldn't be fair to Des!

Smiling, she stook up and, still wearing only her underwear, she wandered slowly downstairs.

The Gift of Music

THE TENNIS BALL hung for a second in the sky, dazzling white against the blue, and then with a smashing hit Kim had driven it across the net.

'Ser-*vice*!' The note of admiration in Fel's voice was genuine. 'How come you didn't do that last time, honey?'

She laughed. 'Don't think I wasn't trying to!'

She crossed the court and held her ball against the racquet ready to serve again. In front of her the ground was almost bare of grass. Each time a ball hit little spits of dust shot up. It was uncomfortably hot. She thought with longing of the cool porch and the iced lemonade, made with real lemons, waiting in the kitchen, and distracted by the thought served a double fault.

'Deuce!' Fel called. 'Come on, I thought you were going to beat me.'

'I can't.' She threw down the racquet, rubbing the palms of her hands against her short skirt. 'Come on. I want a drink. I'll race you up to the house!'

She vaulted the net, laughing, as he collected up the balls. She knew it irritated him to leave the game unfinished and she liked teasing him by doing it. Fel was a meticulous man: that was part of his charm, but just occasionally he had to be shown that life could be unpredictable, as unpredictable as it had been for her when, in London, she had met the young

American lawyer and within months had married him and found herself living in New York.

They ran up the green lawn to the house and threw themselves down on two long chairs on the porch. 'Well, who's getting the drinks?' Kim asked. She pushed her dark hair out of her eyes and glanced across at him.

He groaned. 'I'm having second thoughts about marrying you, woman. Marry in haste, repent at leisure. At this rate I shan't have any leisure to repent!' Levering himself up again he stood looking down at her. From above, her small neat head with its pointed chin and long-lashed hazel eyes looked strangely vulnerable and childlike. He reached out to touch her, just for a second, protectively, unable to stop himself and she smiled up at him, reaching out with her hand in his.

Somewhere deep in the house the phone rang. Fel listened, distracted by it, then it stopped.

'Ma must have answered,' he murmured.

It had been a risk bringing Kim up to Connecticut to meet Ma. That was why he had waited until they were safely married. He glanced over his shoulder towards the shadowy door. His mother was a strong personality. She liked to interfere, to run her children's lives. His sister had escaped, and he had learned to negotiate from a safe distance. But Kim. Would Kim be able to cope with her?

He grinned down at her again. 'Ma likes you, honey. We did the right thing coming straight here to tell her ourselves that we've got married.'

'I like her too.' Kim stared dreamily across the rose bed towards the two great chestnuts which almost hid the next door house. 'She's nothing like I expected.'

He grinned. 'Nothing like me, you mean. That's because I took after Pa. You'd have liked him, Kim. He was a terrific guy. My sister Penny is more like Ma.'

Kim glanced up. Yes, there it was again, the troubled, preoccupied look she had noticed whenever he mentioned his sister. She wondered now if it was the moment to ask him about her, but already he was changing the subject. He released her fingers gently from his and went to lean on the verandah railing. He seemed to have forgotten about the lemonade.

'I told Ma about you last night, Kim. I mean about your wanting to go to the music school.' He frowned, scraping at the flaking paint with his finger nail. 'She wasn't too keen on that idea. She reckoned a wife ought to stay home and look after her husband.' He tried to lighten the remark with a laugh.

'Just as you do!' she flashed. 'What a coincidence! And I suppose she reckons that a wife should be kept barefoot in the kitchen. What is it? *Kinder, Küchen, Kirche.* That would be right up her street, I'll bet. Straight from the old country. How archaic!'

She swung her legs down and sat sideways on the chair, her face tight with anger and disappointment.

'Calm down, Kim. She said nothing of the sort.' Bracing himself against the railing, Fel looked at her. 'Listen sweetheart. Of course I'd like you at home looking after me. What man wouldn't? And I'd like kids – soon. I want a family and I've never made a secret of that. But you've never made a secret of the fact that you want to give up work to go back to school and train to be a professional singer. Okay. I knew the score when I met you and I asked you to marry me, knowing what you wanted.'

She levered herself from the low chair and came to stand beside him, picking a cluster of rosebuds from the climber which circled the pillar and sniffing at them. 'So why keep bringing the subject up? You make me feel a selfish louse.'

'Kim!' He put his hands on her shoulders and pulled her to face him. 'That's nonsense and you know it. It wasn't me who brought it up. It was Ma. It's natural she should care. She wants grandchildren.'

'She's got grandchildren, Fel.'

He stared at her. 'What do you mean?' Imperceptibly his grip tightened on her shoulders.

Astonished she saw there was anger in his face. 'You told me that your sister had kids – when I first met you.'

'I did?' He dropped his hands and stared at her for a moment. Then he reached into his hip pocket for a cigarette pack. 'I'd forgotten that,' he murmured. 'Did I tell you about her?'

'What about her?' She tried not to sound too eager. He had in fact told her practically nothing. But again he fell silent. He shook out the match and dropped it into the roses below. 'I'll get the lemonade,' he said briskly and he strode into the house leaving Kim staring after him, nonplussed.

She heard the tap of May Bernstein's heels on the polished floor of the dining room inside the shuttered windows. The windows were open inside the shutters, leaving the room beyond comparatively cool in the dim light. It crossed Kim's mind briefly that the woman had been eavesdropping but she shrugged. What if she had? She had to know the truth – that Kim wanted a career. And what business was it of hers anyway? Fel's yes. May Bernstein's – never.

She held the already drooping roses to her chin and sniffed them sadly. What if she did have to choose? Career or marriage? Which would it be?

She knew she could sing. Professor Bertolini had himself suggested she take lessons both from himself and at the music college. But what if after that she failed? No one could guarantee success. Would it not be better to choose marriage to the man she loved and who would give her a home and security and love?

It wasn't the fact of her working Fel hated. She worked now. It was more than that. He knew that music could become a rival if she were good; it could take over her whole life. And it was that which might threaten their marriage.

'And I am good.' To her embarrassment she found she had spoken out loud. She listened, but there was no sound from behind the shutters and then she heard Fel's voice from the depths of the house. 'Is that you, Ma? Come and have a glass of your lemonade. We're on the porch.'

They came together, their footsteps echoing on the polished wood floors and Kim heard May Bernstein's rather petulant voice quite clearly, echoing a little as they crossed out of the kitchen into the hall.

'That was Penny on the phone. Imagine! Suddenly she wants to know me again after all these years. And why? Because she wants help with those kids! And I told her. I can't have them. I can't Fel, can I? At my age? What would I do with two kids?'

'Ma, you'd love them.' Fel sounded distinctly uneasy.

'So? And they'd kill me! Why the hell can't *his* family take them? That's what I say!'

The screen door clattered open as Fel pushed through with the tray. On it were three tall frosted glasses and a jug of lemonade.

May Bernstein was behind him. She was a short, stout woman with hair unnaturally dark for someone her age, aggressively waved. Her face had heavy features which lightened into charm only when she smiled.

She smiled when she saw Kim. 'My dear, but it's so hot. I'm glad you stopped playing tennis. Have a drink. Fel, give the girl a drink, she's wilting.'

Fel had already poured out a glass. Tiny pieces of lemon pith floated in the cloudy liquid.

Kim took it gratefully and began to sip, the ice balls banging against her lips.

'What does Kim think I should do?' May asked suddenly. She sat down heavily on a chair and held out her hand to Fel for a glass.

'I haven't told her,' he said unhappily. 'I didn't want to burden her with family problems.'

'And isn't she family now?' May looked indignantly at Kim. 'You want to know, don't you?'

164

Kim nodded, dying of curiosity.

'Well, I'll tell you. My daughter left her beautiful home the first chance she got to go and live with a no good, weak-kneed drop-out of a man. Not marry mind you. Just live. And he's paid her back by going off and leaving her, dumping his two kids on her. That's all. And now she comes crawling home and she wants me to take the kids.'

Kim looked bewildered. 'You mean they're not hers?'

'That's right.' May's lips tightened imperceptibly. 'Their mother was a black girl.'

'And she can't have them?'

'She's dead, Kim,' Fel interrupted gently. 'The story is terribly complicated, but if Ma insists on dragging you in you may as well get it right.' He shot his mother a challenging look. 'Penny met Brad years and years ago, before she left here actually, and they had something really good going for quite a long time. Then things went a bit wrong. She went to Europe to work for a couple of years and when she came back she found he had married Val and they already had two babies. But she was very ill and the younger child was barely two when she died. She had no family to help and Brad turned back to Penny and of course she took on all three of them. But he started going to pieces. It was hell for Penny. All she heard about was his lovely dead wife and how he missed her. He never seemed to realise how much Penny loved him and how much he hurt her by talking about someone else all the time. Anyway, to cut a long story short he began to leave her – and the kids – for longer and longer intervals. He didn't seem to be able to bear the kids near him – I suppose they reminded him too much of Valentine. Then about six months ago he left. And he left a note saying that Penny could keep the children or put them in a home, he didn't much care.'

'But that's awful!' Kim stared from one to the other, appalled.

May opened her mouth to say something, but Fel got in

first. 'It sure is. Penny is at her wits' end. She's got a chance to go back to her old job and she's due to go abroad again soon; she loves the kids but she can't afford them or look after them on her own.'

'But can't the law make him –'

'She doesn't know where he is. Of course they could track him down, but meanwhile what happens to those two mites?'

'And she wants *me* to have them!' May tipped the last of her lemonade down her throat.

'Can't you?' Kim couldn't stop herself glancing at the big garden, thinking of the empty, echoing house behind them.

'Nope. I'm not sentimental and I'm not well. You can't hand over two children to someone, like two puppies and say, "Here, you have these, I don't want them any more." '

Kim bit her lip. 'How old are they?'

'Four and five.' Fel's voice was abrupt. 'Hadn't you better go and take a shower and change, Kim? If we're going to eat before we leave we'll have to hurry.'

She glanced from mother to son and nodded slowly. Fel's face was dark with disapproval and his mother's had become stubborn and malicious as her gaze came to rest on Kim's face.

With a sudden shiver Kim set down her glass. 'I'll see you later, when I've changed,' she said, and she turned and went into the house.

The water was like ice cold needles on her skin. She stood under it for several minutes feeling it beating on her closed eyelids, dragging her hair back from her forehead and cascading across her shoulders. Why doesn't Fel try to persuade his mother to take them, she thought as she reached for the soap. God, I hope he doesn't feel we ought to offer.

The thought was still with her later as they drove back through the evening traffic towards the city. She glanced sideways at his face. He was humming gently with the car radio apparently concentrating on the traffic.

'Does Penny want Brad back?' she asked suddenly, as they drew up at a red light.

'Do you mean does she still love him?'

Kim nodded.

'I think she does. But she must know it would never work even if he did come back. He's changed a hell of a lot.'

'You knew him?'

'Oh yes. I introduced them.'

Kim stared at him. 'Then for God's sake, don't you feel a bit responsible?'

'Why should I? People must work out their own destinies.' He shrugged.

'Not people of four years old, Fel!' To her surprise she found her face was flushed with heat.

'No.' Fel's voice dropped sadly. 'And they're lovely little kids.'

'You've met them?'

'Yep. I've known them since they were born. I kept in touch with Brad when Penny went away and I met his wife, Valentine. She was a lovely person. They knew she had cancer when they married. That's why I could never forgive him for letting her have babies. They both knew she wouldn't be there to look after them. Oh hell, Kim, the whole thing was a mess. She wanted children because that way she felt she could live on through them and of course he wouldn't refuse her anything. I've never told Ma this. As she says, she hasn't an ounce of sentiment. She wouldn't even try to understand. Valentine was a jazz singer. She sang like an angel and she told me once that she was sure that her talent would survive in her kids –'

His voice cracked as he spoke and Kim looked at him sharply. He was staring straight ahead, his knuckles white on the steering wheel.

She was silent for a moment.

She understood. She knew how Valentine had felt. She would have felt the same and suddenly she knew what her own choice would have to be if it ever came to it. And the winner would not be Fel. She closed her eyes tight and rested her head against the back of the seat.

'How long will Penny be abroad?'

'Three months.' The car crawled into a long line of traffic and stopped. From somewhere ahead the sound of music drifted above the murmur of idling engines.

'Three months isn't so very long.' Kim heard herself murmuring the words as Fel wound down the side window to rest his elbow. He gave no sign that he had heard.

It was late by the time they climbed the stairs to their door. Wearily Kim put her bags down and went straight through to the kitchen, groping in the icebox for a can of frozen orange.

'Come on, Kim, don't keep on brooding about it.' Fel followed her in.

'I'm not brooding.' She scowled at him and went to the kettle.

'There's nothing we can do, Kim. We can't have them here.' He gestured back towards the rest of their domain. Three tiny rooms.

'We could.'

He stared at her. 'Kim, darling. We can't afford it. You'd have to quit your job to look after them and we need your salary for a while. And anyway,' he added triumphantly, 'what about your singing career?'

'What about Valentine's?' Kim echoed in a sad, tight little voice.

'Oh God!' Fel hit his forehead with his clenched fist. 'I should never have told you that bit. Val is dead, honey. There's nothing we can do for her now. If the kids can sing – well, they'll sing. It makes no difference who looks after them.'

Kim gave him a withering look. 'I know you don't believe that, Fel, so don't say it. And I still think your mother should be the one to help. Why don't you try to persuade her? You could you know.'

'Kim, forget my mother. Leave her right out of this, honey.' Fel frowned grimly. 'I am not prepared even to try. I don't even want to see my mother again for a bit.'

Kim stared at him. Then she picked up her glass of orange and walked through into the bedroom. By the time he followed her she was asleep.

The next morning after Fel had gone she called her office and told them she was sick. Then she sat for ten minutes with a cup of black coffee beside her, staring at the telephone. On her knee lay Fel's address book. She had found the number under P – he had simply written Pen.

Taking a deep breath she dialled. The girl who answered had a pleasant throaty voice.

'Kim?' she queried. 'You mean Fel's new wife?'

'Yes, how are you?'

'Distracted! Did he tell you what's happening?'

'Yes, Do you have to go?'

'I can't get out of it. Hey, Kim, why don't we get together? I'm dying to meet you.'

Penny's home turned out to be a large untidy apartment on the West Side. Kim was distinctly nervous as she rang the bell but Penny soon made her forget that. She greeted her with a hug. She was a tall, big-boned girl, very like Fel but several years older, her long honey-blonde hair tied back in a pony tail which brushed heavily across her shoulders every time she moved. Kim liked her immediately.

'Excuse the chaos,' Penny said cheerfully, waving her arm around the room. 'The kids had a party yesterday and I was so dead after it I left the lot to clear up today. Come on through and we'll get some coffee.'

'Where are the kids?' Kim asked.

'School. At least Tad is. And Betsy Hen goes to baby school now, mornings.'

'Betsy Hen?' Kim giggled.

'Elizabeth Henrietta. She's the cutest little madam you've ever seen. On Lord, Kim, what am I going to do?'

Penny sat down on a stool and put her elbows on the breakfast bar.

'I love those kids as if they were mine and most of the time I can cope. I've a lovely woman who will come in and take care of them when I'm on an assignment – I'm a journalist, I suppose Fel told you? She's taking half the money she should as it is. But she can't do it for three months. No one could.'

'Can you keep the flat on?' Kim asked curiously.

Penny nodded. 'Their father put it in my name before he went, bless him. It's the only security he left us – but it was a lot. No, it's not the accommodation that is the problem, it's money. I've got to find the money to pay Annabel to come and take care of them.' Penny reached for a bag of coffee beans and poured some into the grinder.

'I was with your mother at the weekend when you rang,' Kim said. 'She thought you wanted her to take the children. That's why she said she couldn't help.'

'Oh she could help all right. With one hand tied behind her.' Penny pressed the button on the grinder viciously. 'There are two reasons why she won't help. One is they're half black. Oh yes, you've no idea how bigoted she is. And the other is to spite me. She wants to pay me back for walking out on her all those years ago. If she doesn't get her way with someone she'll hold it against them for the rest of their lives. Never cross my mother, Kim. Never.' She was pouring hot water into the jug.

Kim closed her eyes and sniffed appreciatively. 'Why did you leave home, Penny?'

Penny glanced up. 'Didn't Fel tell you?'

Kim shook her head.

'Because I wanted out. As I expect you've discovered for yourself, my mother is a self-centred, domineering busybody. She had my life planned out for me to the last second and my wanting to be a writer did not even figure in her calculations. I was to marry – a man of her choice would you believe – and raise her grandchildren for her and go to whist drives with her and plan little trips to town with her. I knew that she was clever enough to make it all happen too, so I fled before she had the chance. Since then she hasn't wanted to know me. I was a fool to ring her yesterday, but she's loaded and she has that big house, and hell – it was worth a try!'

Kim bit her lip. 'Fel said Valentine wanted them to sing,' she said quietly after a moment.

Penny smiled. 'I reckon they will too. Here, have some sugar.'

'I'm going to start training as an opera singer this winter.' Kim spooned some of the dark molasses sugar into her mug and stirred it thoughtfully. 'So I know how much the gift of music can mean.' Pride and sympathy and longing were all there, in her face.

Penny was watching her closely. 'I know you want to help, honey. But you can't. You concentrate on your own career and become a great success, right? My problem is something I've got to work out myself. Perhaps I'll quit my job and try to get another that doesn't need me to travel so much.'

'But that's so silly. Your mother has got to help,' Kim cried. 'It would all be so easy for her. She's so rich. Do you think if I tried to explain to her how much you love them – or Fel? Fel could speak to her.'

Penny shook her head. 'She's like a brick wall, Kim. Don't bother. And don't get involved for God's sake or you'll end up getting hurt too.'

But Kim did bother. She took the train that afternoon and rang May from the station to come and collect her.

May was delighted to see her. She drove her back to the house chatting amiably and ensconced her in a chair on the porch. But when Kim mentioned the reason for her visit her lips tightened.

'They are nothing to do with us, Kim,' she said primly. 'They must have some relatives who would take them. Some of *her* relatives I mean; their own people.' She flicked delicately at an invisible speck of dust on her silk shirt.

'You know they haven't.' Kim shook her head. 'Ma – you did say I could call you Ma?' She smiled pleadingly. 'I went to see Penny this morning. Have you been to her place?'

'It's not hers, dear. It belongs to that man.'

'It's her home,' Kim persisted gently. 'He's given it to her and the kids. It's such a happy place; it's full of love. I think you'd enjoy it there. And Penny would so like to see you. She misses you, you know.'

She was increasingly certain that Penny misjudged her mother. Underneath May Bernstein was as sentimental as anyone else. It was just a case of managing her right.

'Penny misses me?' May looked astonished. But Kim saw the little touch of colour that had risen in the heavily made up face. 'Did she say so?'

Kim crossed her fingers. Then she nodded.

'She was such a self-sufficient child,' May complained suddenly. 'She never needed me. It was Fel who demanded attention all the time. Penny has always gone her own way. She couldn't wait to get out of here and into the world on her own. It hurt her poor dear father so much when she left.'

'She was sorry too,' Kim said gently. 'She wanted to come back, but she was too proud. It's her love of the children which has given her the courage to swallow her pride and cry for help.' She was playing the sentimental bit as hard as she could, but she was sure she had read May Bernstein right. Behind the immaculate clothes and make-up, the money and the whist drives there was a very lonely woman begging for love from her children.

Behind them the house felt very empty.

May reached for the bourbon bottle which stood on a tray

on the table in the corner of the porch. She poured herself a hefty measure, then, on second thoughts she offered Kim some too.

Kim shook her head. She took a deep breath. 'I met the two children just before I left. They came home at lunchtime. They worship Penny, Ma, they really do.'

She couldn't put the thought of the two small faces out of her mind. They had inherited their real mother's dark skin and her curly hair, but there could be no mistake about who their mother was now. They had thrown themselves at Penny, burying their faces in her mane of blonde hair, talking nineteen to the dozen about what they had both done that morning. Then, shyly, they had kissed Kim too and she had lost her heart to them. It was then she had decided to go to her mother-in-law for help.

'I know Penny finds it hard to talk about her feelings,' Kim went on slowly. This was she decided an inspiration. 'For all she's a brilliant journalist, she's holding a lot of herself inside. And she's afraid of being hurt, afraid you'd reject her after all this time. But she needs you so much, Ma. She wants you to help her. She loves those two kids as though they were her own. And she desperately wants you to love them too, to tell her she's right to give them a home and security. To come and see them. They haven't got a grandma except for you.' She was putting every ounce of emotion she possessed into her plea.

May sat down heavily on a wicker chair. 'Penny thinks I'd reject her?' she repeated slowly. 'But she was so aggressive on the phone. She sounded as if she's become a real hard bitch.' She tightened her lips at the memory.

'That was fear,' Kim put in quickly. 'She was on the defensive. She expected you to say no.'

'And I did, eh?' There was a wan smile round the older woman's eyes.

Kim walked over to the tray and poured herself a glass of lemonade. The heavy cloud which had overcast the morning was thinning and a patch of pale sunshine shone down on the lawn.

'So you think I should go and see her?' May said suddenly into the silence.

Kim turned, her face bright with hope. 'Would you? Of course it's terribly untidy and everything but –'

'Penny has always been untidy. Her bedroom used to be a pigsty.' May put down her glass. 'Did this man leave any money at all to support his kids?'

Kim surreptitiously crossed her fingers again. This time it wasn't for a lie. It was for luck. 'Not a penny. Just the apartment. Penny's finding it quite difficult I think. But she's managing.'

'And you say she loves them?'

Kim nodded, holding her breath.

With a groan May levered herself up out of the chair. 'And you love them too? Why for God's sake? You don't even know them. All right. Tell me. How do I know she wouldn't slam the door in my face if I went there?'

'She wouldn't.'

'If she had the money could she find someone to take care of the kids? I wouldn't have them here. I meant what I said.'

'She's got someone. She just can't afford to pay her any more – and certainly not for three months.'

'Does Fel know you're here, Kim?' May turned suddenly and concentrated her stare on Kim's face.

Kim swallowed. She shook her head. 'He didn't want me to interfere.'

May grinned maliciously. 'And Penny?'

'No she doesn't know either.'

'I thought not. Come on. You're going to have to get back if you want that train. I'm going to write to Penny tomorrow.'

Kim felt her heart leap with happiness.

Putting down her glass she gave one last look out towards the tennis court. Already she could picture Tad and Betsy Hen playing out there; and then, running up to the house as she had done yesterday, into the music room. Perhaps they would be allowed to practise on that beautiful Bechstein with all the photos on it.

How wrong Fel and Penny had been. May was as sentimental and soft underneath as the next person. And so easy to manage.

She jumped as she felt a hand on her shoulder.

'I'm making some conditions for all this, Kim,' May said quietly. There was a strange harshness to her face. 'I'll help Penny with as much money as she needs, not only now, but to bring up those brats and give them a decent education. But only if she promises never to bring them here. I don't want to see them. Or her for that matter, as long as she's living like that. And you'll have to promise me something too.'

Kim's heart sank. 'Of course, Ma. You know I will. Anything.'

May's eyes were as green as the sea and she stared up into her daughter-in-law's face. 'You give up all ideas of having a singing career, okay. I want you and Fel to move in here. I mentioned it to him yesterday and he said you would never agree. Now that's not right, is it dear? You and I, we'd get on just fine. And I want you to stay home and look after my son and give me grandchildren. Unless you agree there's no deal. Those kids can rot for all I care.'

And she turned away and put her tumbler back on the tray, the gold charms of her bracelet clanking heavily against the glass.

Island Shadows

THE SUN REFLECTED on the tidal mud, turning it to molten silver. Blinded by the glare, Jill reached up onto her head for her dark glasses, extricating them from a wind-blown tangle of hair, and lowered them onto her nose. Ahead of her, the golden retriever trotted eagerly, nose up, pointing, plumed tail jaunty. She could smell it too now: coffee and something fried; uncomfortably powerful smells, activating pre-breakfast taste buds with painful precision. 'Collie, come here.' She had noticed the dog's quickening pace too late. 'Collie!'

But already the retriever had vanished round the low, wood-topped promontory and she was alone on the shore.

Reluctantly, lead in hand, she jogged after the dog, cursing it roundly under her breath. Wretched animal! Disobedient! Stupid! Idiot! Greedy! Her shoes slipped in the muddy sand and her breath caught in her throat, assailed by the icy wind. A small fishing boat chugged up the centre of the estuary, the engine sounding unnaturally loud above the wind and the sharp slap of the tide on the shore. For a moment she heard the distant piping of a bird, then the sound vanished, torn and shredded like the clouds.

Around the headland the cliff had collapsed and the woods, autumn leaves already nearly gone, dropped towards the water, giving a comparatively sheltered mooring. Several boats were still anchored there, and one, near the shore, had run a plank from its deck down to the sand. She was just in time to see her dog trotting purposefully up the plank, tail still waving, to disappear into the boat.

It was fairly large – an old wooden barge, two-masted with black, tarred cabin and brass-rimmed portholes. Smoke was coming from a chimney in the roof of the cabin, and whisked dancing into the sky.

She stopped in despair, waiting for the tirades of abuse which she knew must inevitably follow Collie's illegal boarding.

None came. The boat lay quiet, its reflection broken and jagged in the slapping water, festoons of brown weed floating round it like a streaming, frothy skirt.

'Collie!'

Her call was not as loud as it might have been. There was still a chance she could extricate the dog without their visit being discovered.

'Collie, come here.'

The gang plank was bleached and dry, split by sun and wind and water. It led up at a steep angle. The dog must have jumped without hesitation down into the waist of the ship. She bit her lip. 'Collie drat you! Come back!'

She was conscious suddenly that she could hear music from the boat – faint, distorted by the wind, hardly audible – the chanting of monks. Plainsong. Unaccountably the sound reassured her.

The tide was coming in. She stared at the end of the plank. It was stirring, carving elliptical patterns in the muddy sand around it as it worked loose, easing up and down. The boat itself, she realised suddenly, was beginning to stir. It had been firmly aground but now, soon, it would be afloat.

'Collie!' She shouted properly this time and almost at once she saw a head appearing over the far side of the cabin roof. A man's head.

She bit her lip, embarrassed and suddenly shy, rooted to the spot as he came to the side and looked down.

'The mutt eating my breakfast is yours, I take it.' The

177

voice was deep, musical, surprisingly unangry considering the content of his words. He was very tanned, with short grizzled hair and piercing light-blue eyes. The faded denim shirt he wore was threadbare and torn and covered in paint stains.

'I'm afraid so. I'm so sorry. She didn't hear me call.'

He still hadn't smiled. Looking down at her intently he didn't even speak for several seconds and she stepped back, feeling the intrusion of that intense gaze as an almost physical assault. Then at last his face lightened slightly. 'You had better come and collect her.'

'Thank you.' She hesitated. The plank was narrow and steep and her tatty trainers already muddy and slippery. She put her hand on the cold overlapping boards of the boat's side and reluctantly put one foot on the plank. Above her he was watching.

'It feels a bit wobbly.' She found herself saying it apologetically, conscious of her own inadequacies rather than the short-comings of the gangplank.

'Take a deep breath and run,' he advised. He had folded his arms to watch.

'Couldn't you just send Collie down?' She gave a small laugh – a deprecating shrug.

He sighed. 'I doubt she'll come.'

She had realised by now that he was enjoying the situation and the realisation spurred her at last into action. Four quick steps and she too had jumped down onto the deck to stand next to him. He hadn't moved. His arms still folded, he had made no attempt to steady her as she arrived.

'This way.' He turned towards the steps which led beneath a hatch into the main cabin. For the second time she hesitated.

She had only ever really trusted one man. Their relationship had encircled and empowered her. It had given her all she needed in her life to be strong and secure and in her own eyes, a reflection of his, attractive. Then one day she had returned home unsuspecting, happy, confident in a future extending into contented companionable old age, to find a note. The enchanted circle had been no more than a smoke ring, puffed into non-existence by another who had sneaked in beneath her lack of suspicion. The certainties of life had no more substance than a house of cards and she found herself a naïve, worthless nonentity in her own eyes.

Only Collie sustained her, lying patiently across her knees, a six-stone teddy bear, with a warm flannel tongue to lick away the tears. Months passed. To outsiders she was herself again. Only the dog knew the nights of self-questioning and despair, the emptiness inside her and the shattering of trust. Blithely certain that she had got over 'it' he had called her a couple of times to check – big deal – that she was all right. He did not know or care that never again would she believe or trust another human being.

And another human being was staring at her now, standing on the steps which led down into his lair and in that lair was the only friend she had left in the world.

'Collie!'

Her cry was suddenly desperate.

He raised an eyebrow. 'Why, when the dog is patently a goldie do you call it Collie?' His tone implied a conversational level suitable for a three-year-old.

She smiled at last and he saw the thin pale face with its halo of dark straight hair and deep grey eyes spark for a moment into animation.

'She's called Colleen.'

'I see. An Irish dog. I should say that explained everything.' The humour, if it was there at all was so tart and spare as to be all but indiscernible. He turned and disappeared into the cabin.

She waited, conscious of the cold breeze lifting the weight of her hair on her neck, the shift of the tide and the loosening of the plank in its contact with the solid earth, although lashed this end, she noted, to the rail.

Seconds turned to minutes. The silence was unnerving. The tape which had still been playing when she first set foot on the deck had stopped and not been replaced.

At last she could bear it no longer. First one foot on the ladder then another, her knuckles white on the companion-way rail.

The first thing she saw was Collie, traitor that she was, lying at the man's feet. He was standing in front of an easel beside a large glass window, let into the stern. Even from where she was standing she could see that he had been painting the birds. The rich colours of the shelduck and oystercatcher leapt from the canvas, vibrant and astonishingly real.

'Coffee?' He nodded towards the table where amongst a debris of paints and brushes and unwashed cups and saucers she could see a red enamelled coffee pot. She wanted to, but good sense prevailed. 'I don't suppose I have time. The tide seems to be coming in.'

He smiled. 'Another time then.'

And that was that. She slipped the leash onto Collie's collar, thanked, apologised, stammered, blushed and left. She doubted if he had heard any of it. He was still standing by his easel, his hands thrust deep into the pockets of his old jeans, his eyes fixed on the middle distance where the tide race and wind met to hurl white horses across the mouth of the estuary and out towards the island.

She went back of course. Not the next day, nor the next, but on Monday when the sun broke through the heavy cloud and brought an icy wind in from the Arctic she put on her jacket and scarf and, keeping Collie on the lead this time, went for a tramp down the beach.

The boat was there, but even from the distance she could see it was empty. It looked abandoned. There was no smoke at the narrow chimney and no dinghy bobbed from the stern. The gangplank had gone. She stood for a while, staring at it wistfully. It looked lonely now. At the weekend the other yachts had gone. Winter was coming fast and they had no doubt retreated to their safe marinas to await the coming of spring. Only the one boat remained, dark on the water. As the tide swung her gently to the mooring ropes she could see the name now. *Araminta*.

Without knowing why, she sighed. She turned away, head down into the wind, the dog's lead round her wrist, and plodded on, feeling the coldness of the wind now on her face, realising the evening would soon be there. She must turn back. Go home to the empty flat where she no longer bothered any more even to put flowers.

'Just to the end of the groyne, Coll,' she addressed the dog firmly. Collie looked back and wagged her tail. 'Then we'll go back and make hot buttered toast and get disgustingly fat, the two of us.'

The dog beamed. It had an uncanny knack of understanding when food was being discussed. Together they traced the edge of the tide, kicking and sniffing respectively at bits of driftwood and weed, then as one they turned and began to walk back.

He was trudging down the shore, laden with backpack and two shopping bags, his head down into the wind as hers had been. It was Collie who recognised him first. The lurch with which she set off to meet him dragged the lead out of Jill's hand.

He looked up and for a moment she thought she saw a smile flicker round his eyes. 'Well. The collie from hell.'

'Hello.' She found it was quite easy to smile after all. 'I thought you must have packed up and gone away for the winter, with the rest.'

'Wimps and townies.' He hauled the pack off his back and dumped it on the ground with his other bundles. The small tender, she noticed now, was drawn up well above the water line under the stark branches of the trees. He caught the painter and hauled the dinghy down towards the water. 'Do you want to go out to the island tomorrow?'

'The island?' Startled by the invitation, she stared past him out into the estuary.

He had begun to pack his things into the little boat, tucking the bags under the thwart. 'I'm going to take some photos. The forecast is good. Cold and bright. Should be calm. The mutt can come if she can sit very still.'

'You mean we'd go out in that?' Jill couldn't hide her horror as she stared down at the tiny boat.

He smiled properly this time. 'It floats.'

'Maybe not, with me and Collie in it.'

'Weigh more than twenty stone between you?' He raised a laconic eyebrow.

'Of course not!'

Her indignation pleased him. He nodded. 'Thought it unlikely. No problem then. I'm leaving about eleven. That way we can use the tide and minimise the effort.' He smiled again. 'Come if you want to. Don't if you don't.'

With that he turned his back, catching hold of the edge of the boat and dragging it down into the water. In seconds he had vaulted into it and slotted the oars into the rowlocks. He did not say goodbye.

Jill watched him for a moment – disconcerted to find he was facing her as he rowed towards the *Araminta*. He nodded, once, but that was all.

She turned away, knowing she wouldn't have the courage to go.

She was there at ten to eleven, dressed in jeans, a thick sweater and jacket, her hair tied up in a blue silk scarf, a thermos and some sandwiches in a haversack on her shoulder. Collie was excited, leaping about ahead of her, and Jill had serious reservations about taking the dog. Supposing they capsized out in the deep water? In this weather they would drown in seconds.

He was waiting for her with the boat, his arms folded, his eyes once again on the distance. Turning as the dog bounded up to him he gave that tight half smile she was beginning to recognise. 'I'm glad you came.'

His camera and drawing things were packed in a waterproof

bag, tightly wedged in the bow. Her haversack joined them and she followed, with Collie, grinning delightedly, at her feet. The boat seemed very low in the water with its load, but he rowed easily, heading confidently out into the waves.

'You haven't told me your name.' She had to raise her voice over the wind and water.

'Roger.'

She could see that was all she was going to get. 'I'm Jill.'

They didn't talk. Her hand firmly clamped round Colleen's collar Jill sat staring out at the water, revelling in the wind and the emptiness around her. To her astonishment she found her apprehension had vanished; she suspected that her own grin was as big as Collie's as she stared at the dog which sat motionless, ears streaming in the wind.

They beached in a small shingle cove, ringed with stunted pine trees, pulling the boat up above the tide while Collie gambolled happily round them.

She sat on a pile of stones and tried not to watch him as he unpacked his camera. The quick sure movements of his slim fingers as he slotted the lenses back into place, the powerful wrists, the intense concentration in the face fascinated her. He was the antithesis of Justin, who had smothered her with his shambling good humour, who had infuriated her with his vagueness and captivated her with his charm.

Looking away at last she stared out towards the sea, her eyes narrowed against the breeze. The island was strangely sheltered. The air seemed almost balmy. The trees, evergreen and resinous, had a spring-like quality which she found strangely relaxing.

It was Colleen, pressing nervously against her legs, who alerted her to the figure standing in the trees. Accustomed to the dog's unfailing sociability Jill frowned. She glanced at Roger but he was preoccupied with his camera, squatting on the shingle, rummaging in a waterproof bag containing his rolls of film. Collie pressed closer. The distinctive line of hackles on her back rose and she whimpered.

183

Jill put a warning hand on her collar. 'It's not our island, girl,' she whispered. 'Other people are allowed to be here.'

Roger heard her. He glanced up. 'Have you seen something?'

'There's someone standing watching us. In the trees.'

He raised an eyebrow. 'I thought there might be. He's probably from the monastery. Just ignore him.'

'Monastery!' Jill echoed. She couldn't resist a quick glance. The figure was still there, unmoving, and now she realised the slight oddness was due to the uncanny stillness of the man, who watched, arms folded, his silhouette made unusual by the habit, knotted at the waist. That was why Collie was growling softly in her throat. She had never seen a monk before.

'Should we be here?' She asked Roger at last as he straightened and slung the camera round his neck.

'We won't go near their end of the island.' He smiled that sudden revelatory smile which he dispensed so rarely. 'Come, we'll go down to the rocks.'

There were flocks of birds there, paddling along the tide line, probing the stones and mud with their bills. Jill put Collie on the lead and took her for a long walk along the top of the low sand cliffs while Roger set up his hide.

The monk was standing now at the edge of the cliff staring across the estuary towards the mainland. Jill froze, her hand tightening on the lead. She needn't have worried. Collie had dropped, head on paws, hackles raised in a crest all down her back. It was the same man, she was almost certain – or did they all look the same in that dark heavy robe?

He did not turn or acknowledge in any way that he knew she was there, and afraid that her presence might in some way compromise vows of silence and seclusion she crept away.

They walked in the pine wood, keeping a wary eye out for any further members of the brotherhood, and then eventually made their way back to the boat. There they sat in a patch of sheltered sunshine and shared sandwiches and Jill drank coffee and poured some water into a plastic bowl for Collie. Without being told she knew Roger would have lost all sense of time once he had crawled into that tiny hide out on the rocks. It was strange how soon the birds seemed to have forgotten the man who had disappeared inside it. Unconcerned they made their way up to and round it, plodding over the flat rocks and through the wet sand.

The sun began to drop in the west and Jill felt a shiver of cold. The shadows of the trees crept long and black across the beach. She was beginning to get worried about the darkening strip of water over which they had to row when at last she saw him emerge from the hide, dismantle it, roll it up and walk back towards her, accompanied by the alarm calls of the birds on which he had been spying.

'We saved you a sandwich.'

'Thanks.' He took it and ate ravenously.

'Did you get good pictures?'

He nodded. 'The best. The light was perfect.' He accepted a mug of coffee and absent-mindedly he patted Collie. In the distance a bell had started to toll.

'Is that for the monks?' Jill saw the dog's hackles rising again.

'Compline.' He shivered. 'Come on. We'd better load up. I don't want to be on the water in the dark with no lights.'

'I didn't realise there was still a monastery on the island,' she said half-way back across the water. She was sitting, her arms tightly wound round Collie's neck against the cold. Shivering she buried her face in the dog's thick ruff. 'I think I remember hearing that there was a ruin there.'

'There is.' He was rowing fast. 'One of Henry the Eighth's ruins. Beautiful.'

'So they rebuilt some of it?' She was peering over his shoulder now, looking out into the darkness. The water had a strange oily intensity in the distance. It was sinister; forbidding.

He didn't answer. He was pulling harder on the oars and

she felt a sudden frisson of nervousness. Supposing they became lost out here in the cold and dark?

He read her thoughts at once. 'Don't worry. We're nearly there. I'm not going to risk losing my cameras.'

'Thanks!' Her indignation was real.

He smiled.

On the beach she helped him pull up the boat and unload his equipment. It was almost full dark now. The water behind them gleamed with an eerie luminosity and already a sheaf of stars was bright in the heavens. He looked up.

'There'll be a frost tonight. You'd better get home.'

For a moment she was hurt. She had thought he would ask her into the boat – offer her dinner. But why should he? They were barely acquaintances. She nodded. 'You're right. It's a walk to the village. Perhaps I'll see you again?'

He smiled. 'Knock on the side of the boat when you're passing, and I'll provide some breakfast for you and the dog.'

She waited three days. Then he cooked them bacon and toast with free range eggs from the farm on the cliff and real coffee, perked on the black stove in the galley. He showed her the photos and she was astounded by their professionalism. It was as she was looking through his sketches of shelduck that he asked the question.

'Where's your husband?'

She looked down at her hand. She had taken the wedding ring off the day she found out that he had gone to someone else, but the tell-tale circle of pale skin on the tanned finger betrayed her.

'He left me.'

'Did you love him?' His voice was strangely hard. She glanced at him and saw he was staring out of the window towards the island.

'Yes.'

'And you still love him.'

'Yes.' She shook her head. 'I'm trying not to.'

'Don't!' He swung round and she was astonished at the

sudden intensity of pain in his face. 'Never try and deny love. However much it hurts, it is better than emptiness.'

He walked across the cabin and back, with quick restless steps, as though unable to contain his sudden emotion. He swung back to her. 'I'm going to the island again this afternoon. Do you want to come? Only for a couple of hours. I need a few more pictures; not birds this time – just general views of water and trees. Collie would like it.'

At the sound of her name Collie sat up, ears pricked.

Why not? There was nothing to return home for. No washing or ironing or cooking. As yet no job to fill the lonely hours.

'Okay. I'd like to.'

She let him wander off alone again, sensing that he needed no company; that she and Collie would interrupt his concentration. Instead she went once more down to the rocks and then up to the cliff where the monk had stood. It was almost no surprise when she sensed Collie cringing behind her and turned to find the monk standing near her. He was staring out again towards the sea. 'I'm sorry. I didn't hear you.' She backed away, embarrassed, the dog winding around her knees.

She was about to walk away when he slowly turned towards her. His face was shadowed in the cowl he had pulled over his head and his arms were folded. For several seconds he stood looking at her, then he took a step forward. Disengaging his arms from his long sleeves he reached out to a bush growing out of a crack in the rocks. He broke off a spray of leaves and held it out to her.

She put out her hand, and when he didn't move closer she took a step towards him. Collie whimpered. She took another step and accepted the sprig from his fingers. Their hands did not touch.

'Thank you.' She smiled. She could not see his face and she felt a strange nervousness tightening across her chest. He gave a small half bow and turning away he began to walk slowly back towards the trees. In only a few seconds he had vanished into the shadows.

Jill looked down at the sprig in her hand. It was rosemary. She looked round, surprised. How could a rosemary bush survive out here on the cold, exposed cliff? She walked over to the spot where he had picked it. All she could see was gorse, clinging in the crevices with sparse grass and brambles.

Thoughtfully she walked back to the boat.

The sun was setting when Roger returned. It blazed crimson across the water, from a sky laced with black and green.

'There'll be a storm tomorrow.' Roger narrowed his eyes, looking at the sun path.

'The monk gave me this.' Jill held the rosemary out to him. 'The same one, I think, that we saw last time.'

Roger looked at it for a moment. He made no attempt to touch it. He was silent for several seconds then he took a deep breath. 'There is something I have to tell you.' He walked down to the water's edge.

'I'd rather you didn't.' Somehow she knew this was something that was going to spoil whatever thin thread of friendship was developing between them. He frowned. For a moment he said nothing but as they stood where they were in silence, she could feel the distance stretch and spin out, pulling them apart before they had ever properly drawn together.

'I'm a murderer.' He didn't face her. Almost, the words were lost in the wind.

She didn't believe him. For a moment. Her disbelief made her laugh – a high, hard, insincere sound which rang emptily in the silence around them.

He turned then. 'You don't believe me? I find it hard myself. I did something out of love – the greatest love possible. I killed a woman – the woman I loved – to save her from pain so great it was driving her to despair.' He took a deep breath, finding the strength to go on. 'She had cancer, you see. It was inoperable. There was nothing anyone could do. At the end,' he hesitated, staring blindly at the ground, 'at the end, she knew what I was doing and she blessed me for it. I saw it in her eyes.'

He turned again and walked away from Jill along the edge of the tide, staring out at the sinking sun. 'In this country such an act is called murder. The police are looking for me. If they find me, I shall go to prison.'

'Roger.' She didn't know what to say. For a moment she didn't move. It was Collie who went after him; Collie who pressed herself against him, giving comfort.

He put his hand on the dog's head, gently. Then he turned back. 'I don't know why I told you. Because I was in danger of growing fond of you, I suppose. I couldn't do that to you, and I couldn't do that to her.' He looked at her for a moment. 'Are you going to give me away?'

She shook her head. 'You know I'm not.'

He nodded. 'I wanted you to come out here to the island. This is a special place; very special. I used to come here as a boy. I used to see the monks too, then.' He turned away from the sea and began to walk back up the beach. 'Come on. We must get going. It's growing dark.'

They did not talk on the way back. Not until they reached the mainland. 'If your man comes home, forgive him, Jill. If he doesn't, forgive him anyway. Hate and bitterness are corrosive. Her husband ran away with someone else and she let her anger and misery eat her up. When we found each other it was already too late.' He gave a strange, strangled sob. 'Who knows, if one believes in these things, perhaps we will have another chance in another life. Perhaps not.' He gave another of his deep, painful sighs. 'Come into the boat a minute. I've something for you.'

It was a painting of the estuary, with the island in the foreground. Amongst the trees she could see the ruined Gothic arch of the old abbey.

'It's beautiful, Roger. Thank you.' She reached up and gave him a kiss on the cheek. 'They won't find you here, will they.'

He shrugged. 'I hope not. I am not prepared to go to prison.' The way he said it had a finality which made her shiver. 'Come again in a few days.' He looked down at her fondly. Then, squatting, he took Collie's head between his hands. 'And you, mutt, look after your mistress. Don't go introducing her to any more strange men.'

She walked up the shore in the dark, turning at the headland to look back at the *Araminta*, a silhouette against the stars, lit only by the glowing light from two portholes. In two steps she was round the headland and out of sight.

She went back the following Saturday. It was no surprise to find the *Araminta* gone. She stood forlornly on the beach, staring out to sea. 'Where do you think he went, Collie?' There was no need of a lead today. There were no people or dogs on the rain-lashed sand, and no boats in the fairway.

It was not until April that she returned to the island. Justin had phoned and suggested hopefully that for old times' sake, maybe, they could go out for a picnic somewhere. If Collie had been a child he would have access, he pleaded, and it wasn't as if he were still with anyone else. The someone else had been a mistake, a disaster, a moment of madness he would regret for the rest of his life. When he arrived, he told her remorsefully that he had been an unforgivable fool and touched her hand and the voice she heard in her head was Roger's. 'If your man comes, forgive him, Jill.'

She took Justin into the flat and showed him the new picture over the fireplace. 'I want to go there.'

'The island? I used to go there as a boy.' Roger's words too. 'It's a wonderful, magic place.'

So they hired a boat and he rowed across, dog in the bows, Jill with the picnic in the stern. The day was beautiful, bright, tossing wind and small slapping waves, and they explored the island from end to end. He showed her the monastery ruins, the beautiful abbey church with its towering broken arch, the weed-filled herb gardens, the crumbling walls, the filled-in, useless well. There was no modern part of it, nowhere habitable at all.

She stood for a long time on the grass-floored nave of the old church, listening, half expecting to hear the plainsong in the wind, or the call of the bell. There was nothing except the carolling of a blackbird in the thicket. There were no monks there now; there hadn't been for four hundred years. Somehow it was no surprise.

Collie gambolled around, carefree and plainly happy. For a while Jill wondered if she should tell Justin what had happened. He had changed. He was more thoughtful; more mature. It was obvious that he too had been unhappy. It would be easy to confide. She thought better of it though. The monks belonged to her and to Roger and to the distant past of the island on which they stood.

And Justin himself? Well, maybe Justin belonged in her future. Forgiveness, with Roger's silent prompting and that of her own heart, was easy. Trust might be more difficult. She would have to see.

There was only one moment when her resolve not to talk about Roger and the monks wavered. As the evening drew on and they returned to the boat Collie, leaping ahead over the sand, stopped dead. Her hackles rose and she backed away from the boat, whimpering.

'What's wrong with her?' Justin, puzzled, released Jill's hand and went on ahead. There was nothing wrong that they could see. Only, on the thwart where Jill had been sitting, a small posy of rosemary.

A Test of Love

'MUM, YOU CAN'T MEAN IT!' I gazed at my mother aghast. 'I don't believe you. It's not true.'

She sat down and put her hand to her head wearily. 'I'm sorry, Holly, I've been trying to decide for three days whether or not to tell you. I don't want you to be hurt.'

'Well, I am!' I rounded on her. 'I'm very hurt. That you could believe such rotten malicious gossip. I thought you liked Mick.'

She sighed and looked up at me, shrugging her shoulders. 'I did. I do, Holly, I like him very much, but now . . .'

I had been able to see from the moment I walked in that there was something wrong. My mother was young and pretty and she and I had always been more like friends than mother and daughter. Sometimes I called her Carol instead of Mum, and we would giggle and she would borrow some of my clothes to wear. I knew men found her very attractive and most of the time I wasn't jealous because I was so happy with Mick.

Now as I looked down at her sitting in the kitchen at the battered old table I noticed for the first time the lines round her eyes and at the corner of her mouth. In her glossy hair there were several streaks of grey. And I was glad. Suddenly I felt really bitchy.

'You're just saying that because you're jealous,' I blazed at her. 'You're always been jealous of Mick and me, watching us, envying us. I've seen you.'

I flung the shopping basket I was carrying down onto the table, shot her a look of real hatred and turned for the stairs. Once in my bedroom I flung myself down on the bed and burst into a storm of tears.

The trouble was that for all my indignation, deep in my heart I was pretty sure that what she said was right. And I couldn't bear it.

My mother had just told me, quietly and matter-of-factly, that Mick, the man I loved more than anyone or anything in the whole world, had been in prison and that he had left his home town and come to live near us because he was in trouble again.

Gradually my sobs grew less violent and eventually I just lay there thinking about him, sniffing miserably into my pillow. I was numb with shock and unhappiness.

I had met Mick three months before at the end of term dance at the college where I was studying. From the very first I had known he was the man for me. He wasn't particularly tall or good-looking but he had something very special: a kind of style which made me feel a million dollars. Soon I was going out with him practically every day, but deep down, I just had to admit it now, I had had from the start a niggling doubt about him. He refused to talk about his past at all, or about Warpington which, he had once let slip by mistake, was his home town. He told me nothing about his family or friends. 'It's now that matters, Hol,' he would say if I pressed him. 'Now and us. I want to forget there was ever a time when I didn't know you.'

Being not entirely naïve I had wondered briefly whether perhaps he had run away from a wife and family or something, but I had put the thought out of my head straightaway. Mick would never deceive me. Of that I was sure.

There was a timid knock at the door and Mum came in. She was carrying a cup of tea.

'Holly, darling. I had to tell you. If I hadn't someone else would have.' She sat down on the bed.

I turned and looked at her, sniffing into my tissues. She seemed so tired. I felt very remorseful suddenly.

'I'm sorry I shouted,' I whispered. 'I didn't mean it.'

She smiled and reached for my hand. 'I know, love.'

'You don't know for sure it's true.' I looked at her desperately. 'Do you? Who told you?'

'Shirley Rhodes told me, Holly. Her aunt knows Mick's grandmother, who he used to live with. I'm afraid there's no doubt.'

I flung myself back on the bed and gazed up at the ceiling. 'What did he do?' I asked tonelessly.

'He went to prison for receiving stolen goods, Holly. He ran an antique shop in Warpington and I gather he bought several lots of jewellery and valuable furniture from various thefts and then passed them on.'

'And now he's in trouble for doing it again?'

My mother shrugged. 'She didn't know but there had been another wave of burglaries around the area and apparently the police questioned him straightaway. His grandmother said he left home without a word the same night. She hasn't heard from him since.'

'He kept the shop on then, after he came out of prison? What happened to it?'

Mum shook her head. Then she stood up and went to the window, looking out at the grey evening. Rain streaked the glass.

'I'm not going to ask you not to see him again, or anything like that. I know how much you love him, Holly. But please, promise you'll be careful. Don't get mixed up in anything.'

I could feel my stomach turning over sickeningly. At that moment I never wanted to see Mick again. I was heartbroken. I felt as though he had actually hit me. I had trusted him, loved him, secretly I had dreamed of marrying him and now – this. I could feel the sobs welling up inside me once more.

Turning from the window Mum glanced down at me, then she went softly to the door. 'Come down when you feel better,' she whispered, and she left me on my own.

Mick was supposed to be picking me up the next evening for a party. All day I tried to pluck up the courage to ring and tell him not to come, but each time I went to the phone there was someone in the box. I did not have the determination to wait. And I don't think I really wanted to put him off. That was too easy and too final. I had to be quite, quite sure. I had to see him just once more.

So when the time came for him to arrive I was at home, waiting miserably for him. I had not bothered to change.

Mum refused to go out. 'I'll be in the kitchen, Holly,' she said firmly. 'I won't appear unless you need me.' I think she had visions of Mick, suddenly revealed in his true colours, a furious gangster, pulling a gun on me, or at least a knuckle-duster.

Perhaps I did too, a little. I was shaking with fear, certainly, when I opened the door to him.

Mick took one look at me and put his arms out to me in concern. 'Holly, darling. Aren't you well? What's the matter?'

'Everything's the matter, Mick.' I led him into the sitting room and closed the door. I was terribly conscious of Mum across the hall probably listening for all she was worth in the kitchen.

'I know everything.' I looked at him sadly. 'I know the truth.'

He flushed and looked terribly guilty and my heart sank. I had prayed he would deny everything. I had hoped desperately that there was another Mick Woodfield somewhere. I had made every excuse possible for him. I had expected him to laugh or bluster, or just lie his way out. I couldn't bear that he just calmly admitted it.

He came and sat beside me. 'I don't know who told you Holly, but I doubt if you know the truth.'

'It was your grandmother. She told a friend of Carol's. That's how I know. Your own grandmother.'

I looked at him defiantly. To my surprise he grinned, obviously relieved!

'In that case Holly darling, I'm sure you've got it wrong. What do you know?' He reached for my hand, but I snatched it away.

'I know that you've been in prison. You were a fence for stolen jewellery and furniture through your shop, and now you've . . .' I could feel tears flooding my eyes. 'You've done it again and you're . . .' I could not go on. Suddenly I was crying openly.

He smiled gently and persisted in feeling for my hand. 'I'm on the run?' he finished for me. 'Is that what she told you?'

Softly he brushed the tears off my cheek. 'I'll tell you the truth, Hol. I was done for receiving, although I was innocent, as it happens. I should have known the things were stolen, or at least been suspicious. My shop hadn't been open long and I was so keen to make a go of it. I was pleased when I was offered the stuff. They more or less implied they wanted to help me because I was new. And green,' he added bitterly. He looked at me, pleading. 'Of course it was my job to find out whether it was okay. All the articles had been listed and descriptions circulated by the police but I hadn't bothered to look at the lists the police gave me. I was stupid and careless. I was given a short suspended sentence. I never went to prison.'

I could feel the relief welling up inside me. I raised my eyes to his. 'And now?' I whispered, hardly daring to believe him. 'Why did you run away this time?'

He flushed again. 'Yes, you're right. I did run away. Of that I am guilty, Holly. The first robbery there was the police were on to me like a ton of bricks. It suddenly dawned on me. From now on I shall be suspect, however innocent I am.

They will always be there checking on me till I begin to feel like a criminal. And I hardly dared buy anything for the shop after that. It was as though I had lost my nerve. I closed it. I gave the key to an agent to sell it for me, and I came through here to find an ordinary job.'

'But why didn't you tell your grandmother?' I stared hard at him, trying to read his mind, desperately wanting to believe what he said.

He grinned. 'My grandmother, Holly darling, is a wicked old lady. She loves to shock people. She told all the neighbours about my long prison sentence as though she were proud of my record and whenever she met a stranger she played up my activities until I sounded like one of the great train robbers.'

'But that was unkind. And stupid.' I was indignant.

'To me, yes,' he smiled fondly. 'But she didn't mean it that way, Holly. It was excitement for her; fame, in a way. She's very old, that was why I moved in with her, to keep an eye on her – not that she needed it, and she doesn't quite realise the significance of it all. I'm sure when I left she told most of the neighbours I'd fled to the greenwood, an outlaw like Robin Hood. She knows jolly well where I am and why I left.' He grinned again. I could see he was very fond of the old lady but she must have been exasperating to live with. I could see that too.

'Oh Mick, darling.' I threw myself into his arms suddenly. 'I was as bad as her. I believed such terrible things of you. I even let Carol hide in the kitchen to save me if you were violent.'

Mick roared with laughter. 'And she's there now?'

I nodded and giggled feebly. 'It was silly, wasn't it?' I was so relieved he had taken it as a joke. It suddenly dawned on me that he could have been very angry indeed at me for believing gossip about him. I had nearly wrecked our relationship completely. I closed my eyes and breathed a silent prayer of gratitude that I had not made that phone call from college.

As though he could read my thoughts Mick suddenly held me away from him at arm's length and gazed sternly down at me. 'You know I ought to be very angry with you, Holly. You shouldn't have decided you knew the truth about me on the strength of a little gossip. You didn't have much faith, did you?' Then he relented a little and I saw the old twinkle come back into his eyes. He planted a kiss in my hair. 'But thanks for giving me the chance to tell my side of the story. If I'd been in your shoes I'd probably never have wanted to see me again.' He kissed me again.

'I love you, Mick.'

There was a sudden burst of music from the radio in the kitchen and the clink of china. We jumped apart and then laughed.

'Carol is as relieved as we are,' Mick said quietly. 'I think we'll forgive her eavesdropping just this once, shall we, as she was there as a bodyguard!' He drew me to him again. 'After all, let's face it, I have got a record now, there's no getting away from it. And I should have told you about it.' He looked down at me, suddenly solemn. 'Does it make any difference? Would you rather we finished now you know?' He gazed at me so seriously that I felt my blood run cold. I couldn't bear the thought of losing him. Not now.

'Oh no, Mick, no, no.' I buried my face in his jacket. 'I love you so much. I think even if it had all been true I would still love you.' I suddenly realised that was true, and paused, as serious as he was. I don't think I had realised just how much I had loved him before.

'I think,' I said quietly, after a moment, 'I must always have had a secret longing to be a Maid Marion.'

We were still in each other's arms when Mum knocked rather too loudly on the door and brought in a tray. There were three glasses on it, and the bottle of sparkling wine Uncle Bill had given her at Christmas. We had been saving it for a special occasion.

'I think,' she said, handing the bottle to Mick to open,

'we'd better drink to you both and then we can decide on a date to summon Friar Tuck to perform the ceremony.'

'Carol!' Mick was laughing again. 'You were still listening?'

'Of course I was you silly boy.' Mum smiled at him, quite unabashed. 'How else would I have known the right moment to come in?'

How else indeed!

Witchcraft for Today

I HAD ALWAYS LIKED Sarah's kitchen. It wasn't fitted; every woman's dream of beautiful bleached oak fitments, hob and eye-level, spit-in-your-eye grill, Provençal crockery, Le Creuset casseroles did not feature at all. Instead it was a room, just like any other, a living, eating room, in which she happened to cook. The antique Welsh dresser and waxed oak table were kitchen equipment I suppose – although both were habitually lost under a drift of books and papers and magazines. And cats. There were cats everywhere. A litter of kittens which had somehow never been given away, had stayed around, much to their mother's disgust, until they grew into fat, sleek, contented moggies who only now and then remembered their kittenhood and rioted as a pack round the dresser shelves, scattering willow pattern, two-year-old invitations and even older bills which were then retrieved and carefully returned to their previous positions in the dust.

Sarah was my best friend. We had known one another since school and the relationship, sometimes close, sometimes distanced by the exigencies of husbands and jobs, had remained easy and relaxed. It was, I thought, a real pleasure for us both when destiny brought us to live within fifteen miles of one another. Our house was a pretty terraced cottage in a street of eighteenth-century symmetry in a small East Anglian town. Hers was a rambling farmhouse in a scattered village, once pretty, now blighted with the dreadful post-war housing for which Britain will be drummed out of the Pantheon of the Arts forever when the final great judge hands out prizes for architecture.

My first visit was a revelation.

'Sarah!' I kissed her on the cheek and gave her a hug.

'Belinda!' She kissed me back, her lips not quite touching my face and, drawing me into the kitchen, she ensconced me in an old armchair which was covered in an embroidered shawl. Judging by the state of my skirt later the entire family of cats had been sleeping there only minutes before.

She made coffee – thick, real, stomach-churningly delicious – in a heavy earthenware jug and produced some home-made biscuits. Then she pulled up her own chair near me. There was only one cat in the room at the time. A beautifully marked silver tabby, it sat on the back of the Aga staring at us with disconcerting intensity.

'Donald has left me.'

The baldness of her statement took me aback. She said it without any visible emotion, without a tremor in her voice, though now I noticed for the first time the dark circles under her eyes, the transparent unhappiness.

'When? Why?'

My response shocked even me by its crass inappropriateness, but my surprise was absolute. Their marriage had always struck me as being absolutely sound – one of the great love affairs of the kind which would endure until they were both in their nineties.

'When? On the seventh of May.' She smiled. 'About six in the evening to be exact. And why? Why do they ever go? They dress it up and justify it in every way possible, but when it comes down to it I suppose it is fear. Fear of growing old. Fear of responsibility. Fear of death. He is desperately trying to retrieve his youth.'

'There's someone else?' I asked it in a whisper.

She smiled. 'The younger model. Of course. And apparently she looks like me. Even sounds like me on the phone. I suppose I should be flattered that he wants a repeat prescription. He can't have hated our lives together so much if he wants to travel the same road again. It's her energy he wants, of course. He needs it to restore his own.' She crumbled a biscuit on her plate and stirred the crumbs into the shape of a star with a fingertip.

I didn't know what to say. If Keith ever left me I would die, and we are far less close in some ways, I had always thought, than Sarah and Don.

'Are you going to get divorced?' I knew as soon as I said it that it was probably the wrong thing to ask, but what do you say?

She shook her head thoughtfully. Standing up she went to look out of the window. Behind her the kitchen felt safe, warm, comfortable. I could smell our lunch cooking in the Aga. There was a bottle of Harvey's Amontillado on the dresser with two crystal sherry glasses, next to an old stuffed teddy bear. A vase of pinks and lavender vied with garlic and oregano to scent the air.

I jumped as a soft, delicate-pawed cat plumped into my lap and sat facing me, huge green eyes fixed on mine.

'I'm going to get him back.' She turned, and leaning against a fridge almost invisible beneath a cluster of magnetised posters and postcards, she scrutinised my face. Her gaze was for a moment uncomfortable, too intense, like the cat's. It invaded my space and filled it and I was shocked by the emotions which reeled around me. Pain, fear, longing, jealousy. They spun like living things in the room, circling, prowling, sucking energy from the air.

'Sarah –' My protest sounded strangled in my own ears and I actually put a hand up to my face as if to ward off something physical. The cat leaped off my knee and vanished through the cat flap.

She smiled suddenly and the atmosphere changed abruptly. 'Sorry.'

For a moment I thought she was going to say something else, but she changed her mind and reached instead for the sherry. Pouring two glasses she handed me one. I hadn't finished my coffee, but I put down my cup without comment and took the glass instead.

'Do you believe in magic?' She asked the question with such elaborate casualness that I felt myself stiffen. A shiver of goose pimples spread across my back. Somehow I knew we weren't talking Paul Daniels here.

'Do *you*?' I replied in a whisper.

She appeared to consider for a long moment then she nodded.

I should perhaps say, here, that Sarah had somewhat unruly grey hair, gardener's hands and the kind of gentle attractiveness you might expect from a grandmother of three – which she is. In spite of the bunches of herbs hanging in fragrant profusion from the ceiling beams – herbs at which I now glanced slightly apprehensively – she has never for an instant reminded me of a witch.

'What are you going to do?' I asked at last. My mouth had gone dry. I drank my sherry with unladylike haste and held my glass out towards her. She topped it up without seeming to pay any attention to what she was doing. All her concentration was elsewhere.

'Oh, I've already done it,' she replied.

I could feel my eyes rounding like marbles in their sockets and I found myself staring at the teddy bear on the dresser. The central seam up its stomach and chest had come unravelled and some of its stuffing was showing.

My hysterical train of thought was interrupted by a shout of laughter from Sarah who had evidently followed both my gaze and my train of thought. 'Oh, Belinda! Not that. Not Pooh!' She swooped on the bear and hugged it to her. 'He's here for running repairs, not as a moppet! Do you think I would stick a pin in *him*?'

There was something about her intonation which I did not

like. It implied volumes. 'So what do you stick pins in?' I asked dryly.

'No pins.' She turned to the Aga. The casserole inside was Le Creuset after all. Withdrawing it she lifted the lid and stirred the contents. Then, the casserole back in the slow oven, she put a heavy pan of water on a hot-plate.

'It's not difficult, you know. Magic. Once you've got over the initial distaste. One thinks of it as bad. Evil. I kept reminding myself that I was a member of the PCC.' She gave a small giggle. 'But all it is really is the controlled manipulation of events. You need little more than focused attention to achieve your goal.'

'You must need more than that,' I protested. 'Otherwise everyone's dreams and curses and hopes and fears would manifest all over the place all the time.'

She sat down, leaned back in her chair and reached for her own sherry glass, savouring the drink sip by sip.

'Who is to say they don't,' she replied quietly.

My mouth dropped open. 'Well, clearly they don't,' I said. I sounded, I suspect, a little bit cheated and that was how it felt. Surely it couldn't be that easy. If it was she would look happier, younger, triumphant! And I – well, my dreams and regrets are not part of this particular story.

'Have you any idea, Belinda, just how little of our brain we use?' She squinted at me sideways over the sherry.

I had heard that one often before. Nodding sagely I reached for the bottle. She didn't seem to notice.

'A fraction of its power. Not intellect. Sheer power.' She gave me that look again. 'Focused, it is capable of becoming a laser.'

I didn't altogether like the implications of all this. 'Are you saying,' I put in doubtfully, 'that magic is a way of focusing the brain?'

'Exactly!' She nodded vehemently. 'And if you can do it properly, you can do *anything*!'

'I suppose it's a bit like prayer,' I went on, hopefully trying for normality as I gazed into the depths of my glass.

'No.' She shook her head vehemently. 'No. No. No! Prayer is a plea. It is part of a one-sided bargain. Our side. It is a submissive thing, a begging thing. We grovel before our god and ask him to work everything out and then give us what we want. Magic is a command. We demand that the forces out there comply with our wishes. We are in control.'

There was a long silence. I didn't dare meet her eye. When at last I looked up she was staring at me fixedly. The expression on her face was quizzical.

'So, what have you done?' I wasn't sure I actually wanted to know.

'She is going to be sent abroad any day now.'

I didn't have to ask who 'she' was. 'How?'

She shrugged. 'I haven't worked out all the details. I don't have to. All I know is that it will happen.'

'And then Donald will come back to you.'

She looked at me enigmatically. 'He'll come back anyway. When I'm good and ready.'

That last bit was bravado. Even I could see that. It was obvious just how much she still loved the man. I stared out of the window for a minute. Would I want Keith back if he had gone off with someone else? I didn't think so. After all, how would I ever be able to trust him again? But perhaps she had already thought of that. Perhaps she had fixed that side of things as well.

As we sat down to lunch I found myself eyeing the plate she had set in front of me with some suspicion. She spotted it, of course, and let out a hoot of laughter. ' "Eye of newt, and toe of frog, wool of bat and tongue of dog," ' she quoted mischievously. 'Belinda, you are a fool. What do you think I'd want to turn you into?'

What indeed!

In fact, after that the conversation took a decided turn for the normal. We swapped family news (other than marital) and gossip and happily tried to cap each other's stories of our respective children's brilliant achievements. I put my suspicions aside and enjoyed her culinary expertise and the second jug of rich coffee which succeeded it and we did not mention Donald again until I was digging in my handbag for my car keys.

'Let me know how things go,' I said meaningfully, the way one does.

She beamed at me. 'I'll ring you when there's news,' she said.

She rang me four days later.

'You know the little project I mentioned,' she said with elaborate casualness. 'It appears Sandra has been offered the job of a lifetime in New York.'

I didn't really know quite what to say. In the event, I said, 'And she's taking it, I suppose?'

'Of course.' Sarah sounded rather modest under the circumstances. 'She realised that he was only playing with her. She was far too young and unsophisticated for him. She thought he would marry her once he'd divorced me. Apparently she was under the impression the divorce was only a matter of formality. Imagine it!'

'Imagine!' I echoed rather feebly. 'So, what happens next?'

I had to wait two weeks to find out. Although it was really her turn to come to me I accepted Sarah's invitation to lunch with alacrity. I had by now learned what the sign against the evil eye (the one they are always talking about in historical novels) is all about and how to do it!

I knew something had happened as soon as she opened the door. It wasn't just that she seemed to have lost about a stone and gone blonde instead of grey. It was something else. She was sparkling – even glowing – with happiness.

We didn't waste time with coffee or sherry. There was a bottle of Moët in the fridge.

'I suppose I needn't ask,' I said as I caught the froth in one of her cut-glass flutes. 'Donald has come home.'

She poured two glasses carefully and handed me one. Only

then did she shake her head. 'I'm arranging for Donald to go to New York too,' she said.

I stared at her. I didn't even bother to ask her what she meant by 'arranging'.

'But –' was all I managed to say. A large black cat was eyeing me from the dresser.

She giggled. 'I wasn't entirely frank with you last time, Belinda, because I wasn't completely sure it would work.' She sipped airily.

I waited in silence. I know a pause for effect when I see one.

Sure enough when she felt she had whetted my appetite sufficiently she put down her glass. She had, I noticed suddenly, taken off her wedding ring.

'I had been reading about Thought Forms,' she said. 'In another of those wonderful New Age books.' So, that was where she had got it all from. 'And, well, I thought maybe I might try and create one.'

'A Thought Form?' I was completely at sea.

She nodded. 'You visualise something. And you visualise it so hard and so often and so well that it sort of becomes real. It really happens.' Suddenly she was blushing.

'Sarah –?' It took a minute, but at last I had caught on. 'You don't mean . . . ?'

She nodded. 'I couldn't be sure Donald would come back,' she said, being, I thought, deliberately disingenuous. 'So I thought I would toy with a few ideas.'

With the emphasis on the 'toy', I thought. I continued staring at her, waiting to see what would happen. I had by now noticed that the kitchen table was set for three.

She picked up her glass and took another sip. 'Not too young,' she said dreamily. Okay, so not a toy boy, I revised hastily. 'But younger than Donald.' Poor old Donald. 'Tall. Handsome. Well off. A widower, I thought, but well over his bereavement.'

My God! Every woman's fantasy man. I waited, breathless.

'I used to visualise him and all the things we could do together.' For the first time she looked evasive. Even downright shifty. 'Things Donald and I haven't done for years.' She gave an embarrassed little laugh. 'It helped me so much, the day dreaming, the planning. It was like concocting the perfect recipe. Altering a detail here, giving a little tweak to the design there . . .'

A little tweak? All right. So my mind was boggling. Isn't yours?

She put her head on one side. 'I suppose, with my conscious mind, I didn't really believe that it would work but obviously I was doing all the right things.'

Obviously.

'But what about Donald?' I said at last.

She shrugged. 'I thought I would love Donald for the rest of my life. He thought so too. He thought he could come back any time he wanted and I would be here waiting for him with open arms. He was the one who spoiled it. It's always the men who spoil things.' She looked sad for a moment. 'Never mind. Even if Sandra doesn't want him there are loads of hungry women in New York who will.'

'And you?' I said.

'I am going to live in Tuscany,' she replied. 'With Antonio.' She stood up. 'Belinda, I want you to meet my Thought Form.'

He must have been waiting in the hall for his cue. The door opened and in he came. Everything that the recipe had specified. Tall. Handsome. Rich (well, he certainly looked it). Charming. Forty-something at a guess. As he took my hand and kissed it my first thought was, poor, poor Donald. But it was, after all, his own fault. My second was: can I learn how to conjure the spell?

The Poet

SALLY COULD HEAR the thunder of the waves on the beach through the open window and her heart beat with suppressed excitement. Hastily she finished unpacking, throwing the last of her clothes into the drawer. In the bottom of the suitcase lay her volume of Keats's poems. She took it out and looked at the faded limp cover. The dreaded A levels were over. For the whole glorious summer she could forget school and work, but still, with all its underlinings and pencilled notes she had wanted to bring this book. Keats knew exactly what it was like to be in love, to ache with feelings, and to dream.

She gave the book a little hug and put it on the bedside table. Time enough for reading when the great white moon was shining on the beach, and something – excitement, fear, her own beating heart? – kept her awake, watching the brilliant colourless light making a pool on the pattern of the rag carpet.

'Are you ready, Sal?' She could hear her brothers calling from the living room of the holiday bungalow.

'Come on Sal.' Her father added his voice. 'We're going shopping.'

She ran out to the car, tossing back her long hair. It was three miles to the village and each year that they had come to Farmingley-on-Sea the daily drive to the shop and post office had been a ritual for the whole family.

They did the shopping together, working their way through

the long list and then went on to buy some postcards. Three doors beyond the post office was Shore Cottage. Sally hugged herself with excitement as she looked at the neat white front door and the hollyhocks in the garden. He was due to arrive tomorrow.

For nearly ten months Sally had been writing to Nick Hamlen. He had published a poem in her favourite magazine and she had written to say how much she liked it. He had replied and she had written back. And so it had gone on. He wrote amusing, sensitive and understanding letters, and she had fallen slowly in love with this unseen man; her very own poet. Once she had asked for his photograph but he had ignored her request and she had not liked to mention it again.

Then, a few weeks back she had told him that they would soon be off to Farmingley for their annual two weeks by the sea.

'Surprise, surprise,' came the reply. 'You'll never guess where my dad and I are booked for a week!' He had not actually suggested that they meet but Sally read the letter over a hundred times and gloated, and dreamily planned their first encounter.

She knew Nick had left school the year before. He was a trainee reporter on his local paper. He had had several poems published in magazines and papers and was collecting enough of them to make up a little book. Sally pictured him as tall and thin and a little pale. He would be immensely attractive, perhaps a little like Keats, and she thought perhaps he too would cough a little now and then, discreetly, into his handkerchief, ill and exhausted from long hours at his desk. That, she was sure, was why his father was bringing him to the bracing sea air: for his health.

That night she sat cross-legged on her bed and read the *Ode to a Nightingale* softly to herself. She could hear the waves on the beach and smell the salt and the seaweed and the cool night air, and her window became a magic casement, opening on the foam of perilous seas in faery lands forlorn.

She waited three days – agonising wasteful days – praying Nick would come over. Then, unable to bear it any longer she took the chance while her brothers were in the shop to go to Shore Cottage herself. She stood for a moment outside, her hands sticky with nerves, trying to steel herself to go up the short path and ring the doorbell. Then she managed to do it at last. The door was opened by a middle-aged man with a pleasant face. He smiled down at her rather vaguely.

'Could I see Nick, please?' she enquired in a small voice.

'He's gone for a walk on the beach,' the man, presumably Nick's father, explained. 'I doubt if he'll be back before midday.'

The beach!

Sally fled back to the others in a ferment of impatience to get home, but her mother who was sitting in the kitchen poring over a new recipe book said there had been no visitors. Sally muttered something about a quick walk before lunch and ran out of the sandy front garden across the path and onto the dunes.

From the top of a great shoulder of sand, named Ben Nevis by her younger brother, she scanned the deserted beach. It was a grey unsummery day and the waves were being whipped into angry horses which leaped skywards and lost themselves far out at sea beneath the murky clouds.

A long way off she could see a lone figure walking slowly along the tideline. He stooped slightly and she could see his hands clasped loosely behind him. Every now and again a heavily crashing wave running up the beach further than the others would come up over his shoes, but he didn't turn aside. It had to be Nick.

She ran down the shifting dune, kicking the sand from her sandals, and fled towards him across the empty beach, her hair flying behind her in the cold wind.

He heard her coming and turned and waited. She had pictured this moment so often. He would hold out his arms as she, his life and his inspiration, came to him through a golden mist.

He didn't. He stood watching her, his shoulders rigid. He wore glasses and his face, with a stubborn upturned nose, was freckled. Sally stopped, breathless, a few feet from him and looked at him in blank disbelief. He was short, about the same height as she was, and his sandy hair stood up from his head even in the wind, in an unromantic bush. His mouth was too big and his eyes were small and rather close together beneath the heavy horn rims.

'I'm sorry,' she muttered, blushing. 'I thought you were . . . *are you*, Nick Hamlen?'

He nodded, looking rather puzzled. 'I don't think I know . . . ?' Then his face cleared and he grinned merrily. 'Why, you must be Sally.' Spontaneously he held out both his hands to her.

Involuntarily she took a step back. He had a nice smile, but he was so unlike her imaginary picture of him. Surely no poet could look like this? She knew she should smile back; she knew she ought to shake his hand, talk politely and smile. Don't show him your shattered dream, she heard a voice inside her head. Don't be rude and unkind.

Tears came to her eyes, and she shook her head blindly. 'It's the wind,' she said, brushing her arm across her eyes.

'I know, it's wild today. Superb.' He stood looking exultantly out to sea without speaking for a moment. Then he grinned at her again. 'It's good to see you, Sally, after all this time. You never told me you were so pretty.'

He said it matter-of-factly. Not like a boy chatting her up. He said it as though it were the simple truth.

Sally felt herself blushing again. But she couldn't help thinking: so he never bothered to imagine me as pretty. He has probably never bothered to think about me at all. She suspected now that he had probably never even been going to look her up. Bleak with disappointment she stood silently beside him watching the sea and wondering what to say.

He turned to her again suddenly. 'How did the exams go? I nearly forgot to ask.'

'All right.'

'You're not worried about the results? I was when I took my A levels. I nearly died of nerves.'

She looked at him astonished. He did not look as though he had a nerve in his body.

Suddenly he looked at his watch. 'I've got to get back, Sally. It'll take me half an hour or so to walk back to the village and Dad will be expecting me.'

She felt snubbed. But at the same time she was glad. Obviously he had not wanted to meet her. Their letters had been fun, but no more. His lovely romantic descriptions and his lively libellous passages about his employers: that was just the way he wrote. He himself was nothing like that. The Nick Hamlen of her dreams did not exist. This young man was totally unromantic, she was sure. Probably he was very practical. He looked as though he had never had a cough in his life and he was not even good-looking. She wished she hadn't come.

With a shy, sad little smile at him, she turned away to walk back up to the dunes.

'Sally!' He was still watching her. 'Will you be on the beach this evening?' His ginger hair was being blown ludicrously forward across his head and he kept brushing it back with his hand.

'I don't know, it depends.' Their words were being whipped away by the wind. 'It might rain.'

'It won't.' He grinned, and turning began to walk fast along the beach away from her.

He was right. The wind had blown itself out by early afternoon and slowly the clouds began to lift. By tea-time a watery sun had broken through. Sally sat for a long while after the meal, in her bedroom, looking through Nick's letters. Then she lay back on her bed, her arm across her eyes.

She had made up her mind not to go and meet him. Her

213

dream was shattered, and now she supposed he wouldn't even bother to write to her again. What was the point?

She ignored her father and the boys when they called her to go for an evening swim and lay, overwhelmingly sad and depressed, looking up at the ceiling with its cracked, crumbling plaster.

She must have fallen asleep at last for her mother woke her, knocking on the door of her room. 'Sally, there's a young man here asking for you.'

She scrambled to her feet, horrified. She had never dreamed he would come to the house.

He was standing grinning in the living room, one hand behind his back. He looked taller indoors and his smile was full of charm.

'Hi!' he said. 'You weren't there so I thought I'd come and collect you. Come and watch the sunset.' He seemed quite unabashed by her mother who was standing there looking at him.

'Go on, Sally dear,' she said. 'Some fresh air will chase your headache away.' With a smile of encouragement she disappeared into the kitchen.

'I've brought something for you,' Nick whispered.

Sally smiled uncertainly.

'Come on outside,' he went on. 'It's turned into the most beautiful evening.'

She followed him through the tamarisks, across the dunes and down onto the beach and still he hadn't given whatever it was to her. Together they walked away from the evening bathers, up to the west towards the rocks. The setting sun was staining the sea red and gold.

He stopped suddenly and looked at her with a shy grin. 'I hope you won't think I'm foolish, Sally, but I've written you a poem.' He held out his hand at last. In it was a piece of crumpled paper.

She stared at him. 'A poem. For me?'

'I know I don't look the part, Sally. Everyone tells me that.

They laugh if I tell them I write poetry, so I don't tell people any more. That's why I was so pleased when you wrote to me. You seemed to understand. I didn't want you to meet me because I knew you'd take one look at me and run.' He shuffled his feet in the sand. Then he looked up again, laughing at himself. 'Go on. Read it.'

She took the paper and read silently for a few moments, the light wind gently stirring her hair. Then she looked up at him, her eyes wide. 'It's beautiful, Nick. It's the most beautiful thing I've ever read. Thank you.'

He grinned happily. 'Will you come for a picnic tomorrow?' he asked suddenly.

Looking up at him she noticed for the first time what beautiful deep blue eyes he had, set beneath thick dark lashes. 'Try and stop me, Nick,' she said quietly.

The Toy Soldier

FOR THE FIRST TIME since they had arrived the house was completely empty. The removal van had gone and Joe had levered himself into Sue's small Fiat and driven down the road to the post office/general store to find some tins of food.

She was standing in the middle of the kitchen. Slowly she ran her hand across the cooker. It was rusty, disgustingly greasy and the enamel was chipped. It wasn't her cooker. Her cooker, her hob and oven, her beautiful fitted kitchen, belonged to the building society now, together with their house and garden. Joe's car had gone too, three days after he had had the letter. The letter which had destroyed their lives with that one word: redundant.

She sniffed and turned quickly towards the window, determined not to cry. Self pity would not help. They were lucky. Joe had found another job at once and a job which came with a cottage. It was little more than glorified care-taking really, looking after his uncle's house and supervising the running of the farm while he was away abroad for a year. The trouble was it was the sort of job where one isn't sure, as Joe kept repeating to himself endlessly, whether one has been done a huge favour, granted charity which could be withheld at any moment, or whether it was oneself that was doing the favour, working for less than the going rate, grateful for a house of less than acceptable condition and tied to both, as the donor fully intends, by guilt and gratitude.

Sue glanced round the room. Most of their furniture was being stored in the next door barn. They had brought in only enough to live. She touched one of the cardboard packing boxes. Her heavy iron saucepans, her wooden bowls, even the bunches of dried herbs, packed carefully, newspaper wrapped on the top. All she had to do was put them on the shelves and hang them up and it would feel like home. She smiled ruefully. Tinned spaghetti in one of her beautiful French dishes. It didn't seem right, somehow.

She moved towards the back door. A shabby curtain hung across the glass on a piece of wire, the angular blue and green pattern a busy cacophony of design. She screwed up her face in disgust. Turning the key she pulled open the door and caught her breath at the sight beyond.

The unkempt garden was separated by a skimpy thorn and beech hedge from a field that had been newly ploughed. The dark expanse of earth stretched so far it seemed to curve with the horizon beyond her sight, but above it the sky blazed with the setting sun. She stood and stared, forgetting the squalid kitchen behind her.

Crimson.

Magenta.

Ruby.

Opal.

Emerald.

Sapphire.

She tasted the words, breathless with delight.

In their suburban, tree-lined avenue she had never properly seen the sunset, never imagined a sky so vast and empty and – her mind groped for the word – pure.

'Isn't it stunning.' Joe was suddenly behind her.

She jumped. She hadn't heard him come back. Narrowing her eyes against the glare she found herself suddenly near to tears. 'It's the most beautiful thing I've ever seen. Better even than Cornwall.' It was the greatest praise she could bestow.

Behind them the shabby kitchen was growing dark. Putting his arm around her shoulders Joe pulled her against him fondly. 'Almost makes it all worthwhile,' he whispered. There was a hint of pleading in his voice which made her heart turn over with sadness.

'Almost,' she echoed. She was surprised her own whisper sounded almost cheerful.

They watched the sky turn at last to a pale aquamarine. One single star appeared low on the horizon.

'I've bought some grub,' he said after a long silence. 'And a bottle of plonk.'

'Oh, Joe, we can't aff — ' her words of reproach were cut off as she felt his fingers tighten on her arm.

'We can afford it. This is our first night in our new home, for God's sake. Surely we can stretch to a £1.99 bottle of wine!'

She swallowed. 'Of course we can. To wet the house's head.' She turned to him. A stupid phrase to use under the circumstances, but it had slipped out before she could bite it back. She reached for the light switch and clicked on the naked bulb which hung starkly on its cord in the middle of the room. Immediately the sky dimmed and with a sigh Joe shut the door.

'So.' He looked round the room bleakly. 'Where are the glasses?'

'In a box, I expect.' She stared round hopelessly at the closed cupboards. 'I wonder if there are any here we could use.' She stooped and pulling open a warped door beneath the draining board, looked inside.

A child's toy sat there in lone splendour on the shelf. A colourful plastic soldier, Instead of legs it had a rounded base so that when it was pushed it rocked sideways and stood upright again.

She lifted it out and stood it on the window sill. As she moved it, it gave out a soft musical chime.

'At least it's bright,' she said.

'Sue –'

'Let's look in these.' She pulled open the top cupboards now. They were empty. Bending over the cardboard boxes stacked in the floor under the small table she found some crockery at last, wrapped in newspaper, and carefully she extricated a couple of cups. 'These will do.'

'Sue, we have to talk about it.' Jim was staring helplessly at her exhausted face. 'You didn't have to give up work. I'm sure you can still keep the job. You can have the car. Your career matters.'

'My career existed fifty miles from here, Joe. My career couldn't, it seems, support us. Your career folds so we have to come to this Godforsaken place to give you a job and mine has to go.' She clenched her lips, her fists, and stared up at the ceiling in despair. Damn. Damn. Damn. She had to keep her bitterness inside! 'I'm sorry, love.' She turned to him and forced a smile. There was genuine regret in her voice, and sadness. 'Don't take any notice. This job is perfect for you. You are going to be really happy here, I know it. And so will I be, once I've found my feet.'

Once.

How?

She sniffed. 'I don't suppose we'll be able to find the corkscrew,' she said.

Joe came up behind her. Putting his arms around her he rested his chin thoughtfully on the top of her head, inhaling the smell of her hair: shampoo and dust and the sweet scent of her skin. 'No problem,' he said. 'You are presupposing a wine posh enough to have a cork. This is a screw-top bottle.'

And suddenly they were laughing. Putting down the cups she threw her arms around him and hugged him. Behind them somewhere in the garden an owl hooted.

She was down first in the morning. In spite of the worry she had been so exhausted she had slept like a log. Pulling her heavy sweater down over her hips with a shiver she unbolted the back door and peered a little apprehensively out into the darkness. It was only just growing light. The rank, weed-strewn garden smelled fresh and clean and she could see a few daffodils near her, their petals almost luminous beneath the cold sparkle of the dark.

She took another deep breath, savouring it, feeling the oxygen pumping round her body, then she closed the door and turned to face her lacklustre, grease-encrusted kitchen. On the window sill the toy soldier rocked gently back and forth, his big plastic grin cheerful against the peeling wood.

'What have you got to smile about?' she asked him out loud as she filled the kettle. Then she frowned. She walked across to the toy and pushed him with her finger. He was heavy. The weighted base needed a firm push to make him rock. A gentle chime rang out as slowly he rocked to a standstill.

The door. Of course. The door had caused the draught. Giving him a final push she reached into the packing case on the floor for cereal bowls and headed for the food boxes to find some cornflakes.

By midday she had scrubbed the kitchen, lined the shelves with clean paper and filled the cupboards, threaded a pair of old curtains onto the wire which served as a curtain rail and hung up an oil painting of scarlet nasturtiums which Joe's nephew had painted for them last Christmas. She had left the toy soldier on the window sill. He was bright and cheerful and she liked his smile. Some child must be missing him terribly, she thought as she caught herself glancing at him yet again. Or had they merely outgrown him and abandoned him to a lonely life of imprisonment in the cupboard waiting to see if he was going to be passed on to another child or merely thrown away?

Leaving the kitchen she started on the low-ceilinged, beamed living room, vacuuming, unrolling rugs over the worn patches on the carpet and unpacking the few cherished ornaments and books they had decided to bring with them. She looked in despair at the two armchairs, their covers torn and stained, and the sofa which seemed at some point to have been pulled off a bonfire. It had scorch marks all down one arm (on closer inspection she found several cigarette stubs down behind the cushions). Luckily for whoever had lived here before, the coarse old horsehair had smouldered and gone out. Wrinkling her nose she humped all the cushions outside onto the small front lawn. When Joe found her she was beating the dust out of them, her fists white on the handle of her broom. He watched for several seconds, then he called her. 'Hey, what did he do?'

She stopped, pushing the hair out of her eyes with the back of her arm. 'Joe! What are you doing home?'

He shrugged apologetically. 'I suppose I could have taken sandwiches . . .'

Her hand flew to her mouth. 'Oh Joe, I forgot. I'm sorry.' It was his first day at work. His first lunch break. Before, he had gone to the office, catching the ten past eight train and not returning until five fifty-seven, out of sight, out of mind while she immersed herself in her career, her life, her whole existence, as an advertising executive in their local market town. Today she had prepared nothing for him.

They shared a can of tomato soup and a cheese sandwich then, dropping a kiss on her head he went back to the farm office. She sat on at the kitchen table over a cup of instant coffee, too depressed and tired to move as she planned vaguely to swop all the furniture for some of their own from the barn. Nicely furnished, the old cottage would actually be very attractive. Behind her the sun moved round at last to the kitchen window and flooded into the room. On the sill the soldier smiled silently into space.

Finishing the coffee she forced herself to stand up at last, went to the phone and dialled.

'Robert? It's Sue. I know this is a long shot, but is there

any chance I could have my job back?' After all she could always commute. She disguised the urgency of her request with a small deprecating laugh but her knuckles were white on the receiver. She listened intently to the mellow even tones the other end, hearing the laughter, the rattle of keyboards, the sound of other phones ringing in the background, the sound of a large office in action – her world – and at last she nodded. 'Oh well. I knew it was a long shot. Keep me in mind, won't you, if she doesn't stay the course.'

She put down the phone and found that she was shaking. Slowly she walked back towards the kitchen and stood in the doorway, staring at the sun-filled room. More coffee? That, of course, would make her feel worse; jumpy; sick. It was only a job. There would be others; other things she could do. Something she could do from deep country. Perhaps she could go freelance? On the window sill the little soldier rocked back and forth, chiming cheerfully. As she watched the rocking slowed and ceased. The window behind him was open a crack. The curtains stirred a little in the draught. She smiled. For a moment she had thought . . . but that was silly. Reaching for her rubber gloves she went back to her scrubbing.

When Joe came back that evening she had a small fire lit in the narrow black grate, and a casserole simmering on the cooker. The rooms were fairly straight and she had found enough early spring flowers in the wild garden to deck the house.

They had saved enough of the screw-topped wine to have a glass each while the potatoes were cooking.

'If you really don't need the car I thought I might drive into town on Monday and see if there are any temp jobs going locally,' she said as she sat down near the fire. The cottage was cold now it was dark. She did not look up. She was staring at the burning fir cones she had thrown onto the flames.

'I see.' He sounded bleak; she was rubbing in his failure,

adding to his guilt. 'Are you sure that is what you want?'

She nodded. 'Just for a few months – to keep me occupied. And it would help to tide us over.' She straightened up. 'We're lucky to have this place, Joe, and we'd survive here even if I didn't work. It was brilliant of you to land this job' – the sop to his ego at last – 'but,' she hesitated, 'I'd go mad, here, on my own. I'd be better working.'

He sat down, rolling his glass between his palms. He looked defeated. 'Perhaps you're right.'

'I know I'm right.' She came to sit on the floor at his feet, leaning against his knees. 'We'll make a fortune yet, Joe, you see if we don't,' she said softly. 'You see if we don't.'

She awoke suddenly. The cottage was silent. Beside her Joe was sleeping flat on his back, breathing steadily, one arm thrown up across the pillow, the other hanging down to the floor.

She lay still, staring up at the ceiling. A half moon hung outside the window, throwing a wash of pale light across the floor. Then she heard it. From downstairs – a gentle chiming sound. She waited, her eyes on the moon, listening drowsily, then slowly she sat up. Glancing at Joe's sleeping face she pushed her feet into her slippers and padded towards the door.

Opening it silently she stood on the landing and listened. There it was again. The quiet musical chime. She ran down the stairs and tiptoed across the cold boards to the kitchen door. Quietly she pushed it open.

The kitchen was completely silent. Moonlight shone through the thin curtain casting a bluish glow into the darkness. On the sill she could see the silhouette of the little soldier. The toy sat unmoving, staring at her with large unblinking eyes.

She stood for several minutes waiting, watching the plump plastic outline, then with a sigh she turned and closing the door quietly behind her she went back upstairs. When she reached the top she was smiling. A dream; that's what it was. A charming, silly dream.

'Are you all right?' Joe was awake as she slid back into bed.

She nodded. 'Very all right.' To her surprise she found that she meant it.

'Good.' He moved towards her and gently he began to remove her nightdress. What with all the stress and worry it had been weeks since they had made love.

All the next day she found that when she walked into the kitchen her eyes went first to the window where the little soldier sat on his sunny sill. Each time he stared back, his eyes bland and expressionless, his eyelashes black cowlicks against his brow, his red plastic cap set at a jaunty angle.

After lunch she wedged open the back door and set to work on the flower bed just outside, pulling up the rampant weeds, exposing the poor smothered daffodils and finding to her delight lavender and marjoram and a clump of newly shooting chives. Every now and then she straightened her back and stood staring out across the field. Behind her the toy stared solemnly inwards, his back to the garden, his stance rigid, immobile as the curtain danced gaily around him in the afternoon breeze.

When Joe came home at dusk he had a box of groceries in the back of the car. Included was another bottle of screwtop. 'To think I used to worry about vintages,' he said cheerfully as he undid the bottle and slopped some into the two glasses she had put ready on the table.

'Joe.' She turned to stir the pan on the stove. 'Who lived here before us, do you know?' Her hand tightened on the wooden spoon. *Please, don't let it have been a child who died.* She closed her eyes for a moment, then she turned and took her glass.

'Funnily enough I was talking about it to one of the farm workers in the office today,' Joe said. He opened the back door and stood staring out at the sky. A band of black cloud bisected the colour of today's sunset which was a stormy scarlet damask. 'The same couple lived here for forty years. They stayed on a few months after he retired, and then went off to live with their daughter down on the south coast somewhere.'

'Forty years!' Sue echoed. 'Perhaps he belonged to their grandchildren then.'

'Who?' Joe shut the door. Taking the lid off he peered in and sniffed appreciatively.

'My soldier,' she said.

'Him?' Joe pushed the toy and watched as it rocked to and fro, the chime ringing around the room. 'Must have done. How long will supper be?'

That night she awoke again. She lay in the dark, her ears straining as in the distance she heard a rumble of thunder. Joe lay on his side, his head cushioned on his arm. They had made love again that night and she was glowing with happiness. It had never been quite so good when they were both exhausted after work. A flicker of lightning showed outside the window. Smiling to herself she snuggled down under the covers, feeling Joe's warm heaviness comforting beside her.

The chime was so quiet she barely heard it. Her eyes flew open again and she held her breath. Beside her Joe groaned and turned over.

For a moment she was tempted to wake him, then slowly she pushed back the covers and stood up. As she reached the foot of the stairs she heard it again – quietly plaintive as if the toy were rocking to and fro slowly, pushed by a methodical hand.

The kitchen door was shut. She turned the knob as silently as she could and eased open the door. She was groping for the light switch when a flicker of lightning illuminated the kitchen and she saw the toy on its sill clearly outlined against the window. There was no sign of movement. Not now, but she had the distinct impression that the expression in the soldier's usually bland eyes was one of guilt.

Clicking on the light she went over to him and after a second's hesitation she picked him up.

'What on earth are you doing?' Joe's voice was so unexpected in the silence she nearly dropped the toy.

Putting it down hurriedly she turned to face him. 'I'm sorry. Did I wake you? I couldn't sleep because of the storm.'

'Are you sure it was the storm? You're not still worried are you?' Avoiding her eye Joe went over to the kettle and plugged it in. 'We're not so badly off, you know, Sue. We have a roof and enough money to live. I know it's not what we're used to, but things could be worse. In fact you know,' he paused, and then went on, still not looking at her, 'now that you're not working, or not full-time, wouldn't this be the perfect time to think about starting a family –'

'No, Joe!' She cut him off firmly.

'Please, Sue, can't we at least discuss it?'

'No, Joe. We've discussed it a thousand times. You know I don't want a baby. I don't want children! You know it!' She swung to face him. 'I need a job, Joe. I need people. I'd go mad stuck at home with a baby, I know I would.'

'Lots of people do both, Sue. They work as well!' He took down two mugs from the shelf.

'No, Joe. I'm sorry.'

He nodded sadly. 'I know. I know. I just hoped.' He looked down at the empty mugs. 'I suppose with us both losing our jobs' (I didn't lose mine, Sue thought, anguished, I gave it up, for you) 'and the house going and everything, suddenly my priorities have changed. I've stopped being acquisitive.' He gave an apologetic shrug. 'It's as if money doesn't matter any more. We lost so much, but we still have what is important. We have each other; we have a home, however small. Any home is enough as long as you are there. That's important. That sunset the other night. That was important. And when I saw you standing there with that child's toy –' He shook his head and when he spoke again it was very quietly. 'For me, that was important too.'

There was a short silence. She looked up at last and he smiled. 'Sorry. Deep stuff. Philosophy lecture over.'

She grinned uncomfortably. 'You were being a bit pompous.' Taking the mugs out of his hands she put them on the table, then she threw her arms round his neck and held him close.

It was later – much later as she fell asleep – that she heard the chime of the little soldier again. This time she didn't go down.

'I cleared these cupboards out myself, my dear.' Julia Somerskill, from the end cottage, was staring at the toy soldier, perplexed. 'They were empty. And there's been no one else here since. No one at all.'

'So, where could he have come from?' Sue leaned forward and filled up the other woman's coffee mug. Joe had needed the car after all this morning, so she had not been able to drive in to see the job agencies.

Julia shrugged. 'There weren't any toys in the cottage. There haven't been any kids here for about thirty years.'

'None that died?' Sue bit her lip, wondering why that uncomfortable thought kept surfacing.

'Good Lord, no, my dear. They're a healthy bunch round here. It's the good air. Besides,' Julia reached for the toy, 'this is modern.' She shook it and the cheerful chime rang round the kitchen. 'I suggest you keep it for your little one.'

'I haven't got any children,' Sue put in quickly.

'No, but you're expecting, aren't you?' Julia reached across and spooned some sugar into her coffee. 'I can always tell.'

'I bloody hope not!' Sue was shocked out of politeness. She grimaced shame-facedly. 'Sorry, that slipped out. No, I'm not expecting and don't intend to be.'

Julia smiled comfortably, not in the least put out by the outburst. 'Maybe. Maybe not. You've already had a job, haven't you.' Did she sound a little bit pitying? 'Perhaps you never got round to thinking about kids.'

'Oh we thought about them. I just don't want them.' Sue scowled.

'And your Joe. Does he feel the same way?' The gentle voice was probing.

Sue shook her head. It was none of the woman's business, but she might as well know the score.

'This house is very special,' Julia said quietly after a moment's silence. 'To you it probably seems small and shabby and not very nice, but there is something about it. It's over three hundred years old you know, under the linoleum and the patches,' she grinned. 'And people in the village have always regarded it as a wishing house. If you spend a night under the roof and wish, you can make your dreams come true.'

Sue's mouth fell open. 'You're joking. There's no such thing!'

'Maybe, maybe not.' Julia, a small twinkle in her eye, gave a mysterious shake of her head. 'Children are a powerful dream.'

'My husband's, not mine.'

Julia met her eye. For a stranger she seemed to have assumed an air of unexpected authority. 'And you think his dreams are less potent than yours? You need to beware, my dear, lest his dreams are the stronger.' She smiled.

Sue stared at her. 'But we've agreed.'

'Then that's all right then.' Brushing biscuit crumbs from her skirt Julia stood up. 'I must go, my dear. Thank you for the coffee, that was nice. I'll see you soon.'

She was not pregnant! She would know if she were pregnant. She could not have been so careless. Sue put her hand to her stomach nervously as from the living room window she watched her visitor walk away up the lane.

When Joe came home she was still worried. 'She sounded like the village wise woman,' she said, surprised how much Julia's comments had unsettled her. 'I know it's silly, but it was as though she knew something.'

'Don't brood on it, Sue.'

'You don't think she could be right?' She couldn't hide the horror in her voice.

He shrugged. 'I doubt it,' he sighed. 'It would be a miracle if you were.'

She stared at him. The woman was right. Why should Joe's dreams be less powerful than hers?

They did not discuss it again, nor did she feel like making love that night and when she heard the little soldier's chime she turned over and pulled the pillow over her head.

She wasn't pregnant. Cursing the stupidity which had allowed her to turn her back on the job agency and instead, when at last she got hold of the car, to waste precious money on the kit from Boots, she binned the offending items and went out to hide her relief in the garden, ripping out nettles and dead thistles until it began to grow dark.

Pulling her boots off on the back doorstep, she went inside and hung up her jacket, automatically turning to switch on the kettle. It was not until she went to the shelf for the tea caddy that she noticed that the soldier was gone.

She stared at the spot by the window where he normally stood. It was empty. Turning round slowly on her heel she scanned every work surface and shelf. Then she opened every cupboard. He had been there when she went out, she was absolutely sure of it.

'Joe?' The second she heard his step in the hall she ran out to meet him. 'What have you done with my soldier?'

Joe shook his head. 'What do you mean? Nothing.'

'But you must have. He's gone.'

She searched the house from top to bottom, but there was no trace of him, and that night as she lay in bed the long dark hours, brightened by the moonlight flooding into the cottage windows, were completely silent.

* * *

She tried two temporary jobs and hated them both. When the second came to an end she did not go back to the agency. Instead she went to the garden centre and bought boxes of bedding plants, comforting herself that she and Joe could always forego the fearsome screw-top if they were really short that month. Joe was pleased, the more so when his uncle flew in from Nairobi and, far from warning Joe that his job might come to a premature end, asked him instead to agree to a five-year stay. 'He's offered us the tenancy of the farmhouse too.' Joe took her out to dinner on the strength of the payrise which accompanied all this largesse.

Sue shook her head. 'Let him rent it to someone else. I'd like to stay where we are.' In her head she had called it the cottage of dreams, though her own had not come true, and neither, as far as she knew, had Joe's.

Until now with the proper job.

He nodded. 'I hoped you'd say that. It's all those plants you've put in the garden. Awful waste if we moved again.'

'Joe.' She looked up at him, and put her hand over his as it rested on the table. 'Tell me what you want most in the whole world.'

He smiled. 'You really want to know?'

She nodded.

'To stay in this job. I love it. I really do. And to stay in the cottage with you – the new happy you.' His smiled broadened. 'I don't know if you've noticed, but you grin a lot these days, and I've even heard you singing over the washing-up.'

'Never!'

'Have so.' He turned his palm over and squeezed her fingers. 'Stay happy, Sue.'

'And that's all you want?' She glanced suspiciously into his face.

'For now.' He winked. 'You are happy, aren't you?'

She thought for a moment and then she nodded. 'I suppose I am.'

'What about the job?'

'I didn't like the jobs.'

'I meant your real job. The one you gave up for me.'

'I don't miss it so much now.' She looked down at her plate. 'In fact I think I'm quite glad to see the back of it. I didn't realise at the time how tired and stressed and hyped up it made me. And you're right I had a whole set of priorities which no longer seem to be valid. Even though I didn't want it for myself and I was always measuring myself against what other people had, what they did. Celie and Jane and Liz – with their children and their Volvos and their dogs and school runs. And Janet and Martina with their high-powered jobs and their mobile phones. They all seemed so much more competent and fulfilled than me. Now, none of that is important any more.'

'Perhaps you've proved to yourself that you are competent and fulfilled as well,' Joe said slowly.

'Perhaps I have.'

'So, do you feel properly settled in now?' Julia was walking her dog up the lane as Sue, puffing, was mowing the front lawn. 'I heard you were going to stay.'

Sue nodded. She walked over to the gate and leaned on it, twiddling her fingers at the old spaniel which sat down with relief to rest while they talked.

'And have your husband's dreams come true yet?' Julia grinned mischievously.

Sue laughed. 'Not all of them certainly.'

'It's only a matter of time.' Bending to fondle her dog's ears Julia shook her head.

'Silly woman,' Sue muttered to herself as she went back into the cottage. Going through into the kitchen she was about to wash her hands under the tap when a small sound caught her attention. Spinning round she stared at the window sill. The toy soldier was back in place, and he was rocking gently.

231

Shocked, Sue stood quite still. 'Where have you been?' she asked out loud.

The bland face beamed at her silently.

'I suppose you think you can just come and go as you wish?' Sue turned back, crossly, to the tap and finished washing her hands. Silence.

'And I suppose you think you've won? You and Joe between you. You think I'm going to provide you with hordes of screaming children to play with and spend the rest of my life vegetating in the country.' Reaching for the towel she turned round. 'Well?'

The hat seemed at a jauntier angle than before; the red-painted mouth more cheeky, the black eyelashes curved like birds' wings on the white plastic face. As she stood and watched the toy began slowly to rock again. And at last she heard again his cheerful chime.

To Adam a Son

PICKING UP THE handful of letters from the mat I threw them on the table while I fetched myself another cup of coffee. Paul, my two-year-old son, was playing happily in one of the kitchen cupboards, unloading saucepans all over the floor. Sitting down, I sorted through the post. Two were bills, two circulars, one a business note and one . . . I stared at the envelope in disbelief. It was Adam's handwriting, there was no mistaking the sharp black italics on the white paper. *Ms Claire Sutcliffe*, it said. I snorted at the 'Ms'. How like him!

I had heard nothing of Adam for over two years and now, this, out of the blue. Still not opening the letter I turned to look at Paul. He had Adam's black hair, his blue eyes, his smile, his charm.

I had tried so hard not to think about the old days that it was a shock now to find it all coming so vividly back to me.

Adam had known me since I was a child and from the time that I was about seventeen, he was years older, we had become more and more inseparable. Then there had been that terrible car crash which left me with a twisted leg and a limp for life and Adam with recurring headaches. We had never been lovers but I think there had always been an understanding that one day we would marry. I had treasured the hope, and planned secretly for the day that I would move into Adam's beautiful house as his wife. He was an important man in our town and his wife would have to be a superb hostess. I used to practise my cooking on all our unsuspecting guests with this in mind. How I longed to entertain in his elegant drawing room.

After the crash however it all changed. Although we still saw each other just as often it became increasingly clear that I would no longer be considered as a potential wife. It dawned on me eventually that a woman with a limp did not fit Adam's plan. I just could not really believe this of him, but no sooner had the idea crossed my mind than it began to torment me. At the first opportunity I challenged him with it. How badly I chose my moment! He had one of his headaches, and, as he had been doing more and more regularly, he had been drinking heavily. We had a dreadful row and I screamed at him, did he not think he owed it to me to marry me now; after all, the crash had been his fault.

I had never mentioned to him before that I knew or cared whose fault it had been – I didn't – but obviously I had struck a very exposed nerve. I remember it so clearly. He went white, even his lips, and then he hit me, hard, across the face. Gasping with shock I paused only a second before hitting him back and it was a matter of moments before we were rolling on the floor exchanging punches like two spoiled children. I suppose technically it would be correct to say he raped me. His anger turned to a passion before which I was helpless and then back to anger, and when eventually he had slammed out of the door, leaving me lying practically naked and terrified on the floor, it had been a long time before I could get up and dress myself and creep wearily home through the dark.

The next morning I left town, nursing my bruises and an unbelievable fury. I even contemplated going to the police, but my pride stopped me in time.

It was comparatively easy to pack up the flat where I had lived since my parents died, and make the journey to London.

I stayed quietly in a hotel for a while, living on my savings while I got my breath back, so to speak; then I found myself a flat and a new job.

Two months later I knew I was pregnant. A chance in a million but that's the kind of luck I had. I had been brought up a Catholic and although I never went to church now, I had enough beliefs left to know that I could never contemplate abortion. It took me nearly two months more to make the decision to go back and see Adam.

I don't really know what I had in mind; or whether I was even going to tell him about the baby. I think I hoped that when we were facing one another again I would know instinctively what to do.

Choosing a time when I felt fairly certain he would be home I drove my hired car up to his house. I felt really sick and frightened as I stood on the doorstep ringing the bell, and while I waited I turned to look at the bleak windswept garden with one or two rain-blackened roses still clinging to the bushes.

Eventually I heard footsteps. Adam's younger brother Colin opened the door.

'Claire!' He was plainly astonished to see me.

'Hello Colin.' I smiled brightly. 'Is Adam home by any chance?'

'Not yet.' He looked slightly puzzled. 'They've only been gone four days.'

'They?'

I must have looked a little bewildered for Colin suddenly invited me in. Leading the way into the living room – where it had all happened four months before – he poured me a glass of wine.

'We looked for you everywhere, Claire. Where on earth did you go? Why did you leave so suddenly?'

'Adam knew,' I said briefly.

Colin looked even more puzzled. 'But he said . . .' He stopped suddenly, obviously deciding not to pursue the subject and it was then, after taking a sip of wine himself, that he dropped his bombshell.

'Adam got married last week, Claire. He and Alison are away on their honeymoon.'

I remember the beautiful cut glass falling harmlessly from my fingers onto the soft white carpet, and the pale gold stain as the wine lay for a moment in a pool before it soaked away into the deep pile.

Then Colin was pushing my head between my knees and gradually the room stopped swimming.

After a fainting exhibition like that I could hardly pretend I didn't care, but I don't think Colin guessed the real reason for my weakness. I was fairly certain my pregnancy didn't show yet, and anyway I had dressed to make absolutely sure that it would not on this occasion!

Eventually I got away, without leaving any address, and I returned to London to work out my problem alone.

I was extraordinarily lucky really. I still had some savings left, and some money my parents had left me. I had a really super little flat, not too expensive, and found that my landlord would not mind a baby, and my job – I was a designer – was very easily changed so that I could work at home. I became a freelance, fitting out my bedroom as a studio. The tiny box room became the nursery and I spent many happy hours decorating it.

Paul arrived at last and I was thrilled to bits with him. It was the happiest moment of my life when I took him home and laid him for the first time in the little wicker crib.

Strangely enough I very seldom thought about the lack of a man in my life at all. Or perhaps it would be more truthful to say I never allowed myself to think. Sometimes in the evenings when I was tired and depressed I would lie on my bed and abandon myself to tears of frustration and loneliness, but as time went by and Paul grew older I had less and less time to myself for self pity. He became more active during the day and so I had to work at night, sometimes going on till one or two in the morning to get it all done. Then there was no time for tears. I would be asleep almost before my head touched the pillow.

The people I worked for were tremendously kind and all very sociable, so I was not really lonely, I suppose. Occasionally I had to take Paul into one of the offices with me if Mrs Martin next door could not have him for an hour or two and he was always spoiled outrageously.

I wore only trousers or long skirts now, so my twisted leg never showed, and I think my limp became far less noticeable as time went by. My hair had grown very thick and lustrous during my pregnancy and I was very lucky, it stayed that way. I grew it long and although I shouldn't say so, I think I became much more attractive over those two years, certainly more self-sufficient, more confident.

I made a point of never thinking about Adam and Alison, although once, at the dentist's, I saw a picture of them in one of the society magazines. I tore out the page when I thought no one was looking and kept it for months on the kitchen dresser. Then one day it got torn and I threw it away without a thought.

And now, here I was beginning to tremble as I looked down at Adam's letter in my hand. Slowly I tore it open and extracted the single sheet of paper. *Dear Claire*, I read. *I wonder if I could come and see you next Wednesday evening. I'll be there about nine if you agree. Adam.*

How on earth had he found my address? I gazed down at the two lines of neat writing, trying to see so much more than he had written. Of course, I couldn't guess what he wanted after all this time, but I knew a moment of crazy, idiotic hope.

The next few days passed in a whirl of uncertainty. I longed for Wednesday and yet I dreaded it even more. I was puzzled too about what to do about Paul. Did Adam know about him or should I try and hide all traces of him?

In the end I tidied all the toys out of sight into his bedroom, folded the pushchair which usually sat in the hall and put it under my bed in the studio and swept the bathroom clear of baby powder, potty and toy boats. Paul practically never woke up at night so I was fairly sure there would be no sounds from the nursery.

I was carefully dressed and made up long before nine and rapidly feeling more and more sick. I tried to get on with some work to kill the time but I got very little done.

The doorbell rang at three minutes past nine and I walked very slowly to answer it.

'Hello Claire.' Adam stood for a moment smiling before he moved to step forward. I was staggered by his appearance. He had aged about ten years. His hair had begun to go grey and his eyes were sunken and dull. There were premature lines around his mouth and nose and as he came into the living room I saw that he stooped slightly.

I was acutely conscious suddenly of his gaze on me too. That at least had lost none of its intensity. I was relieved that I had taken so much trouble to look nice; casual but elegant clothes, immaculate hair and nails.

I was about to pour two glasses of whisky – I had bought a bottle specially – but he stopped me with a raised hand.

'I'm sorry, Claire. Could I have coffee? I'm on the wagon these days.'

I put the bottle down, surprised. 'You don't drink any more?'

'I had too many warnings, Claire. Too many times when . . . well, when I didn't know what I was doing.' He glanced at me sideways and in spite of myself I felt a blush coming to my cheeks.

'Okay. I'll put the kettle on.' I screwed the top back on the bottle.

I had just whisked a small yellow car out of sight into a drawer when I realised Adam had followed me into the kitchen. I don't think he saw.

'Tell me,' I said as I filled the kettle, 'how did you get my address?'

He grinned wryly. 'There are ways of finding people if one has to.'

'And did you have to?'

As there was no immediate reply I turned to face him. He was frowning vaguely.

'You look very beautiful, Claire. You've changed a lot.'

'You mean I wasn't beautiful before?' I raised my eyebrow archly.

He smiled. 'Of course you were. I wouldn't have loved you otherwise.' He hesitated. 'But now you're . . .' he paused, 'you're quite lovely.' He seemed lost for words and I was suddenly embarrassed. I busied myself making the coffee and Adam carried the tray back into the living room. I knew he was studying me carefully as I walked in front of him – my limp had almost gone now – but he made no comment.

We sat stiffly opposite each other in silence, cautiously sipping the hot coffee. I kept a weather ear open towards the small bedroom, but there was no sound.

'You didn't tell me how you found me, Adam,' I prompted at last.

'There are firms which specialise in that sort of thing.'

'You mean a private detective?' I was scandalised. 'You haven't had me watched!'

'No, no.' He laughed at the rising note of horror in my voice. 'Only traced, Claire, not watched.'

Even so, he must have been told about Paul. I felt myself growing cold.

'Why have you come, Adam? I think you had better tell me.'

He leaned forward to the low table and put down his coffee cup.

'My divorce came through last week.' He said it so quietly, so flatly, I did not for a moment understand. He went on, 'You knew I was married? Well we separated five months after the wedding. The whole thing was a disaster from the start. I never should have married Alison.'

'Then why did you?' I kept my voice deliberately low.

'I suppose it was . . .' he fumbled for words and then with a wry smile at me he went on, 'it was on the rebound really. The night you and I parted was so terrible. I came to find you the next morning but you had gone. I searched everywhere.'

'But not with a private detective?' There was a touch of sarcasm in my voice but he ignored it.

'No, I didn't think of that then. When I couldn't find you I got very angry. Alison seemed to be everything I wanted in a woman; she was beautiful, sophisticated, intelligent . . .'

'And she didn't limp.' I could have bitten out my tongue after I had said it.

'Claire, Claire, you're wrong.' His voice was anguished. 'It wasn't your limp, my darling. As if that mattered. I thought that perhaps I would never be able to marry – not anyone – because of *my* injuries, injuries I didn't tell you about, not yours.' He glanced at me. 'I thought I was going to die, Claire.'

I was stunned into silence.

'Then soon after you disappeared I determined to marry Alison to prove to myself I didn't care, however long I had. To prove that all I wanted was a beautiful hostess just like you said.' He paused a moment. 'You had your revenge for what I did to you, Claire. We were miserable.'

We sat in silence for several minutes. Then he went on. 'They operated on my head. It wasn't as I feared.' He mustered a smile. 'Once they put all the bits back together I was as good as new.' He glanced at me again. 'I still love you Claire. I always did. Will you give me another chance?'

I was not the type to fling myself on his neck crying, but for a moment that is what I wanted to do. The flood of relief which swept over me brought home suddenly just how much worry and unhappiness I had had over the past two and a half years. And just how much I still loved him. I glanced up, fighting the pricking behind my eyelids, but he held up his hand.

'Claire, there is something else I must tell you.'

I waited, panic-stricken suddenly by the worried, sad look which had returned to his face.

'I have a little daughter. She was born after Alison left me, and my loving wife sent her back to me with her compliments. I have custody now. She has a nanny, but she needs a mother.' He looked at me pleadingly.

I couldn't help a little half-smothered smile. 'There is something, in that case, which I must tell you too. I have a little son, and he has no nanny but he badly needs a father.'

Adam stared at me, a smile slowly breaking across his weary features, and held out his arms. 'They told me you'd been seen regularly with a little boy, but I couldn't be sure he was yours.'

'Ours, Adam,' I corrected him gently and then I did go to him.

We were married three weeks later. Juliette, Adam's daughter, was a delightful little thing, only a few months younger than Paul, and the poor baby, who had known only a swiftly changing succession of nannies, clung to me eagerly from the start. Paul was a little disgruntled at first, at having to share his mummy with two new people, but this was more than made up for by the thrill of having two new playmates – Adam being especially popular.

I live in that beautiful house now, and I am learning to be a hostess, not that the idea appeals as much as it did before. I prefer to be alone with my family.

Writer

HIS MOTHER HAD called him Oliver after the boy in the film who had been one of Fagin's gang. He hadn't seen the film, but he knew the story. Oliver ended up being rescued by a nice rich family and living happily ever after.

Nolly, his mates called him. Only his mum in the whole world called him Oliver and then only when she was angry. And she had been angry this evening, angrier than she had been for a long time.

The lift had been out of order for a start and she had had to carry the shopping up the nine floors, heart thumping, face and body shining with sweat. Instead she would like to have stood looking at the graffiti on the inside of the lift doors, trying to hold her breath against the smell, but grateful not to have to face the echoing stairs.

The note was the last straw. *Nolly has a good imagination*, Mrs Peters had said. *When I get stories they are first class. But this is the third homework this week he has not handed in.*

'How many times have I told you, you silly little tyke!' Sheila Garnet stared at her son helplessly. 'What have I got to say to make you understand? If you want to get out of this dump, you've got to get your exams!'

Then, disconcertingly, she had burst into tears.

Nolly was dumbfounded. His mother never cried. She was tough and cheerful even when he could see nothing to be cheerful about.

He had no brothers or sisters, no dad, no grandmother or grandfather. The few times he had made tentative enquiries about these missing pieces of the jigsaw of his life she had frozen him off. 'We've got each other; that's enough,' she said firmly.

And, mostly, she was right.

He was a sturdy boy, strong for his twelve years though not yet very tall, his hair carroty, his face covered in freckles, his eyes a brilliant green, the colouring, though he would never know it, of a certain handsome squaddie in the Argylls who had been posted to Sheila's town a year before he was born and she had left for London. Also from that squaddie came his stubborn chin, his flashpoint temper and his incurably romantic soul.

He saw nothing wrong at all in the high-rise block in east London where he and his mother lived – and for one good reason. He never really saw it. He lived in a dream world, populated with imaginary friends. This evening however his mother's tears had catapulted him for a while into the present. Consumed with guilt and remorse he quietly began to put away her shopping for her in one of the small chipboard kitchen cupboards, carefully folding the carriers to use again, and then he reached for the kettle and put it under the tap. The pipes banged a little as the water ran and he was conscious suddenly of the smell from the rubbish can under the sink. Every day his mum made the trek down to the bins in the windy street below. Perhaps he ought to offer to help her. Carrying the mug of tea into the small living room of the flat which doubled as her bedroom – the other room she had given to him – he put it down on the coffee table in front of her. The coffee table was one of the things Uncle David had helped them get – taking them in his car to Texas and then putting it together for them. He wasn't a real uncle of course, he hadn't any of those, just the husband of one of Mum's friends. And he hardly came over any more.

He sat down next to her on a sofa that was blue and brown

and red in sort of squiggly patterns. There was a cigarette burn on the arm though his mum never smoked.

'Sorry.' His voice came out quiet and on this occasion genuinely contrite. 'I'll do the next one. The one tonight. Honest.'

She looked up at him. Her eyes were a brilliant blue and he loved them for their real beauty but at this moment they swam behind a screen of tears. The dam, which had been in place, firmly, for years, was beginning to crack.

'Please, Nolly. Do it. You could do so well.' She shrugged helplessly.

It was easy to slip away of course. He did it every night. After their tea she would sit down to watch *Neighbours* or *Home and Away* and after only a few minutes she would be asleep. Sometimes she didn't wake until it was really late and time for her to go out again, which was really boring, but although he was now beginning to realise a little just how exhausting his mother's life was with her two jobs, the shopping, the stairs and everything, mostly he didn't think about her at all. Checking that she didn't react when he stood between her and the screen he quietly slipped out of the front door, pushing the key on its piece of string back through the letter box after him. One flight down, running fast, he remembered the rubbish. For a second he hesitated, then shrugging he ran on. He'd do it for her tomorrow.

His favourite place at the moment was behind the train sheds at the end of Alma Road. If he ducked through the broken rusty wire fence and ran lightly over the railway sleepers he found himself in a piece of wasteland hidden completely from the road. Shoulder high with rose bay and buddleia the place had a special smell, a feel of its own. It was a quiet, hidden paradise. He had never seen anyone else there and he was careful not to tell any of his mates. This was special. It was a secret world and he didn't want it spoiled.

In a rusty old box hidden in the dry rank grass he had secreted a couple of books. Sitting down on the grass cross-legged he didn't touch them for a bit. Instead he stared round. On the far side of the no man's land in which he sat was a car dump. Rank upon rank the car bodies rose in the air, some flattened, some just tossed and abandoned like old dead leaves. Decaying and uniform in their rust they had a strange appeal for the boy. Each one, once, had been shiny and new. Each one had been cleaned and polished and loved. So when had things started to go wrong? Had their engines broken down? Had they been torn and flattened in some horrendous motorway pile-up (and was there blood still to be seen by a discerning eye?). Sometimes he would slide through yet more rusty wire and wander amongst the heaps of corpses, once or twice irresistibly drawn to touch, one small almost gentle hand stroking the disintegrating metal, not breathing, daring the great heap to fall. Never once had he been seen; never once reprimanded. This was a part of his secret kingdom.

Tonight, though, on this beautiful warm evening, he had come to sit and read. His mates would call him a suck if they knew so he did it in secret. The books he had nicked from the library.

One was on butterflies and moths. He wouldn't think where the butterflies here in his secret place came from but here they were on his little piece of paradise. Cabbage white and tortoiseshell and red admiral and even occasionally a beautiful peacock on the blue sugary plumes of the buddleia. The other book was on birds. Not the birds he saw here – sparrows and pigeons and starlings mostly with an occasional brave blackbird – but the birds of the sea and shore: gulls and waders and divers. Birds that would paddle on the sand's edge and probe the mud with their long bills; birds that would soar across highland lochs and plunge into the icy water to emerge with fish clutched in their cruel talons.

He had seen them on the telly of course, but mostly Mum wouldn't watch the natural history programmes. She would if he asked especially, of course, because it was educational, but he knew she thought they were cruel because they showed animals eating each other and she would rather be watching her soaps or a nice comedy to make her laugh and he'd feel guilty even as his stomach turned over with the excitement of seeing the wild beautiful places in front of him. *EastEnders* was too much like home, thank you very much.

Turning a page he ran his hand gently over the photograph of the osprey, absorbed, empathetic, feeling the wind in the great wings, the uprush of the cold water, seeing with those black gold-rimmed eyes the unsuspecting salmon gently cruising in the dim, peaty depths.

The librarian watched Oliver as he came in. Slouching casually, the scruffy haversack on his shoulder bulging with torn exercise books, his school tie hanging round his neck like a halter, one trainer lace dragging, he looked like most of his class-mates. She wasn't sure what had first caught her eye – the flaming red hair perhaps – but it was his behaviour which set him apart. To begin with he would joke and push and be a complete pain like the others, disrupting the silence, bringing as they did some undefinable sense of threat to the older users of the library. Then quietly he would slip away from the crowd round the book stacks to the natural history section or to the travel books.

When she saw the first book vanish into the haversack she knew she ought to jump on him but something stopped her. Instead she went to see what he had taken. And she wondered why he had not borrowed it openly. The answer was not hard to work out. To borrow a book was to set yourself apart. One or two boys had tried it but the jeers of their friends were cruel and the books were unceremoniously dumped back on one of the reading tables. She sighed, and wearily she stood up and moved away from her desk. Soon the security marking of the books would be finished. He had to be sorted before that.

'Excuse me.' Her hand on his shoulder was light. Startled green eyes looked up at her, first frightened then defiant then hostile. The last expression assumed by the small face was one of blank insolence. This one stuck.

'You were going to check that book out properly?' She smiled at him, careful to be non-threatening.

'Yea.' The universal and sometimes she thought the only word they all knew.

'There's a new bird book over there, on the acquisitions stand. You might like to borrow that too.' She moved casually between him and the other boys. 'Take a look.'

He glared at her suspiciously. 'Okay.' He sounded casual too now; in another age he might have put his hands in his pockets and started whistling.

'You have got your library card?'

'Yea.' He was uncomfortable. She had held him too long.

'Good. You can take them both out.'

'Might.'

'Tell your mates it's for an extra project. A punishment. Make you look well 'ard.' She winked conspiratorially and turned away.

When she got back to her desk her fingers were crossed.

The library was crowded. It wasn't possible to watch him all the time and she didn't see him leave. But when she passed the acquisitions shelf later the bird book had gone.

Jodie and Squill had seen him borrow the books and they had jeered and given him grief as he knew they would but he had taken the library woman's advice. 'It's for Mr Brent. Extra. Mega punishment.' He glared defiantly and to his surprise they accepted it. Just like that. No more hassle; she obviously knew a thing or two that library woman. He had glanced back at her as he pushed his way out of the heavy doors and in the gaze was the smallest hint of respect.

He didn't open the new book until he was ensconced in

his special place. Unwrapping the piece of gum he had jobbed off Squill he tucked it in the corner of his mouth and pulled the book onto his knee.

The glossy paper smelled cool and exotic, of grass and cream and brandy. He wasn't sure what cream and brandy smelled like, but he thought it would be like that, sort of hot and cold at the same time; peppery and smooth.

The book was nothing but pictures, hundreds of wonderful pictures of exotic colourful birds, flying and swimming and preening and eating against a background of brilliant skies and seas and jungles. He sat transfixed, turning each page slowly, relishing the crisp noise they made as they brushed his T-shirt, hearing in his head the crash of waves on the sand, the wind in the trees and the eerie call of the birds in the night.

He took the book home with him when it grew too dark outside to see. Fishing the key out of the letter box he let himself in and looked round. His mum had already left for work and the flat was empty. He went into the kitchen and looked in the cupboard. She had left him a can of beans and half a loaf of bread for his tea. Putting the book down on the work surface he opened the can and put the pan of beans on the gas ring. He toasted four slices of bread, slopped the beans over them and carried his plate through to eat in front of the TV. He flipped through the channels. All talk; newsy things about politics and stuff. No animals. No birds. No travel. No adventure. He frowned. Best of all he would like to have watched a film – Indiana Jones sort of stuff with jungle and exotic places and birds and animals and himself as the star.

He glanced at the kitchen door. From where he sat, his mouth smeared with sauce from the beans, he could see the book sitting on the side. The bloke who took those pictures must have travelled by boat and train and plane and jeep. He had visited all those places, like the birds.

Putting down the empty plate, he drew his legs up under

him on the sofa. 'Slinging the Pentax round my shoulders I climbed down from the cockpit and put my feet onto the burning sand,' he said to himself out loud. 'Around me I could hear the cicadas and in the distance the cry of an eagle. The shadow of the bird swept over me and for one second came between me and the cruel sun.' He paused, his head on one side and grinned. That had sounded real good. Just like a film.

Pushing himself off the sofa he went to the chest of drawers beside the divan his mum used for a bed and rummaged through the top drawer. Amongst all the women's stuff he found a ballpoint pen that worked. He knew there ought to be something to write with in his bag but there wasn't. But there were his exercise books. Turning one upside down he opened it and was confronted with the most exciting and frightening thing a writer can see. A clean (only slightly creased) page. He looked at it for a long time, almost paralysed by the thought of what he was about to do, then slowly, sitting at the table in front of the window, he began to write.

Outside the undrawn curtains the panoramic view of the lights of London lay like a carpet of sparkling stars. He did not see them. 'I could see the zig zag marks the snake had left in the sand. The heat was burning through my trainers – ' he paused and looked up for a moment. A small smile touched the corners of his mouth. He had written himself a Pentax, why not some Reeboks? Crossing out the word trainers he wrote in the change, a small frown between his eyes, his tongue protruding from between his teeth as, on tiptoe, he crept from the sand into the edge of the forest, conscious of the flash of birds' wings high in the branches over his head. From somewhere in the distance, a half echo on the wind, he heard the sound of jungle drums. The small hairs stood up on the thin brown arms of the boy sitting at the table on the ninth floor of the tower block and he felt the skin on the back of his neck prickle with fear. Somewhere on the periphery of his concentration he heard the beat of music from the flat below him. He took no notice. His exercise book filled, he put it to one side and took another – on the front it said, 'French', but it was almost empty apart from a few one word answers, in columns, all marked with crosses. 'Raising the camera I squinted through the view finder and pressed the shutter. The click was very loud in the silence of the forest and I waited, holding my breath in case the head hunters had heard. They hadn't. They continued sharpening their spears as though nothing had happened. On the branch next to my shoulder a huge hairy spider began to move towards me, spinning a silken thread between its clawed legs.' He stopped. The images in his head were so powerful he wondered how he could ever find enough words to describe them, to keep up with the urgency of the story that was suddenly pouring out of him. Looking up he saw the reflection of his own face in the dark square of window. If he looked beyond it, beyond the light hanging from the centre of the ceiling, he could see the stars and the winking lights of a plane flying west towards Heathrow. Who knows, perhaps it had flown in from Rio or Buenos Aires. Exhausted, he put down his pen and stretched his fingers, then he picked it up again. 'I couldn't stay. Carefully I backed away into the shadow of the jungle, checking with my thumb the sharpness of my machetty – machety – masheti –' he couldn't spell it and cross and frustrated he scribbled over the word and wrote in 'knife'.

When his mother arrived home just before six she found him at the table fast asleep, his head cushioned on his arms. Exhausted herself after a night cleaning offices in the City her tired face relaxed into a smile. It had not been a bad night. The girls had remembered and clubbed together and bought her a box of chocs for her birthday and there was a strong rumour going round that there was a small payrise in the pipeline. She rested her hand for a moment on her son's head, wondering if she should wake him, then she caught sight of the exercise book beneath his arm, the page covered in his quick careless writing. Pulling it out carefully she closed it without looking at it and nodded. So the little tyke had decided to finish his project essay after all. That was the best present of all. Putting the box of chocolates down in front of his sleeping head she glanced once out of the window at the glorious dawn sky. A flock of seagulls flew across the window, their wings pink in the light of the rising sun. She smiled. Not such a bad old world, perhaps, after all.

The Fate of the Phoenix

*This story, although complete in itself, was writ-
ten as a short modern-day sequel to an incident
in my novel* Child of the Phoenix. *There the
first part of the story of the jewel is told against
a thirteenth-century background of love and
passion, betrayal and treachery, emotions which
echo through time, to be heard today by any who
will listen.*

THE OLD MAN watched the golden cascade of the girl's hair
as she lowered her head over her sketchbook and he heard
her pencil scratch the paper. Outside, through the window,
he could see her boyfriend's car. The old man examined the
lines of the sleek Porsche. It lacked style in his eyes. It was
aggressive and spurious, like the eighties age which spawned
it, though the young man himself looked pleasant. He glanced
at the girl again. It was as discreet as a widow's veil, this long
hair of hers.

She had written asking if she could sketch the treasures in
his collection, her enthusiasm and the freshness of her words
leaping off the page at him. 'I heard so much about your
things from Grandmama. She thought you might show them
to me.'

Grandmama. The word echoed with mustiness and age. How could his beautiful Julia be a grandmama? If only he had married her when she had danced through his life, laughing. But he had been so wrapped in his studies he could not picture Julia Grant in his life of academe and so he had lost her. He could imagine her voice now, teasing, laughing with this golden child: 'See if the old buzzard is still alive. See if he is still in love with his stones and fossils.'

'I'm glad you decided to come.' He smiled. 'You are very different from your grandmother. I often wondered if she was still alive.'

'Of course she's still alive.' She giggled. 'She told me you were lovers.'

Ridiculous, but he was blushing. 'Not what you would call lovers,' he corrected gently, 'and it was a long time ago. I'm surprised she still remembers me. She was so lively, and I was such a fusty old bird, even then.'

The girl smiled. 'She loved you, you know. Poor old Grandpa knew he was always second best.'

To cover his embarrassment he stood up, gripping his stick. He looked past her to the young man. 'Let me show you something, Giles, while Vicky finishes her sketches.' He led the way up the staircase to the gallery where he kept more of his treasures. In the doorway he realised Vicky had followed them and he saw their astonishment. It pleased him enormously when people were impressed by the collection.

'It's like a museum,' Vicky whispered.

'I've always been a collector.' He led the way across the floor. 'Julia thought I was quite mad.'

He lifted the lid on a glass-topped case and stared down at the display of car badges. 'All over eighty years old,' he said proudly. He saw Giles bend closer and he smiled.

'Mr Fraser.' Vicky was examining a selection of carved stones. 'Grandmama said to ask you what became of the phoenix.'

'The phoenix?' He stared at her. Then slowly he nodded. 'So she did remember.'

'She said you promised to put it back where you found it.'

'I agreed to do it with her.' He shook his head. 'And I meant to, but she never came back; later I heard she had married; I lost interest in it after that and in the end I stored it away.'

'Can I see it?' There was a catch of excitement in Vicky's throat. 'You must see this, Giles. It is the most wonderful story.'

She could hear her grandmother's voice in her head now: 'John Fraser was an amateur archaeologist even then, and he and I had been going out for ages when I pestered him into letting me go on one of his excavating trips. I thought a few weeks camping in Scotland might finally persuade him to ask me to marry him. It was not just going to be me and John, of course. There would be archaeologists, labourers to do the digging and two other women who were going to share my tent, so it was all going to be very proper and I would be chaperoned. Don't laugh, Vicky! It was important then. We went to this old castle in the hills. I can see now why John found it so romantic and exciting, but then I was nothing but a silly little flapper, and I found it boring. I wanted to drive and picnic, I wasn't interested in exploring ruins. It was such a desolate place. And John thought it was wonderful. He used to tell me to listen but all I could hear was the silence of the mountains and moors, broken only by the sound of sheep and eagles.' She smiled wryly at Vicky's rapt expression.

'Anyway, the novelty of tents and uncomfortable camp beds soon wore off. As did the charm of the hot evenings. I was eaten raw by midges. John laughed at me and told me to wear a veil over my hat like the others. And something with long sleeves. He thought I would get used to it. But I didn't.

'Then, one evening when it was so sultry even I could feel the atmosphere of the place John told me about a siege hundreds of years before when everyone was killed or hanged and the women who were captured were put in cages.' She shivered. 'I didn't want to hear about it. We had a gramophone and some records back at the tents and I wanted to go and dance on the shingle at the river's edge but instead I sat smoking furiously to keep the insects at bay and waited while he finished some work. I was looking forward to the walk back across the fields with him. It was almost dark inside the castle walls and the others had all gone when John called me to him. He was in what used to be the chapel.' Vicky felt the hairs on the backs of her arms stirring. 'John had been working near a pile of stones and suddenly as we stood there a part of the wall fell in. We stood looking down at the rubble guiltily, you know, like children who had broken something – and it was then that I saw the shine of metal.'

There was another pause and Vicky found herself holding her breath. 'Was it treasure?' she whispered at last.

Julia nodded. 'It was an enamelled pendant. John picked it up and I remember the awe in his face as he asked me if I realised what we had found. I didn't of course. After the initial excitement I was disappointed. It was dirty and crudely designed. Some sort of bird on a nest. I could see that much. We decided to wash it so we climbed down the ravine behind the castle. It was spooky and I was afraid, as if I knew we shouldn't have touched it.' She fell silent. Vicky watched her. 'He shook it in the peaty water,' Julia went on after a moment. 'We saw the dirt dissolve and it began to glitter. It was gold and enamelled. It was a phoenix. Even I could see that.'

Her eyes seemed to be fixed on the far distance. Vicky waited patiently.

Julia shook her head at last. 'We decided to keep it a secret. It was very naughty. John was racked by guilt, but we wrapped it in my scarf and hid it in my tent. It was strange –' She stopped. Her voice had softened, and Vicky saw a wistful smile on her face.

'Strange in what way?' she urged.

'Well, that night a storm broke and we had to run for our tents, rescuing the gramophone and the chairs. We were all laughing and singing. For the first time it was almost as good as I had dreamed it would be.' She fell silent again, thinking back. 'John grabbed me and I felt his lips on mine. It was magical. Romantic. Wonderful. He had never done anything like it before. Then the moment was over and he had gone, leaving me at the entrance to my tent.

'As I got undressed I was walking on air. Then I found myself wondering about the pendant which was under my pillow. I climbed onto my camp bed and suddenly I found I was shivering in spite of the heat. The rain was drumming down on the canvas and the thunder rolling round the hills. It was all very dramatic. I can remember it so clearly. But it was all over. By next morning the excavation was awash. It was decided to abandon the dig for that year. Within two days I was back in London.' She sighed. 'To cut a long story short I decided to wear the pendant to a dance a week later. We cleaned it properly and John bought me a gold chain to hang it on.'

'And what happened next?' Penny breathed.

'I was sitting in my bedroom, getting ready. I picked the pendant up from my dressing table and put it on. It may seem strange, but I hadn't tried it on before. I think I was superstitious about it. It slipped down inside the lace at the top of my petticoat between my breasts. It was very cold.' There was a long pause. 'It was then I felt the hand.'

'The hand?' Vicky stared.

Julia nodded. She grimaced. 'I thought it was my imagination. I could feel this hand stroking my shoulder. Then it moved down my breast. It was gentle, seductive, like nothing I had ever felt before. It touched my nipple – then it stopped. Suddenly I could feel rage – anger – all round me. It was terrifying. And before I knew what had happened the phoenix had been wrenched from my neck. The chain broke, and the pendant flew across the room.' She smiled at the look of horror on her granddaughter's face. 'I was so frightened. I was hysterical. Mother and Papa came up and John ran up after them. And there I was in my petticoat.' She laughed. 'I think I was incoherent. I told them the pendant had been snatched off and I said it was jinxed and I refused to touch it again. It belonged to someone else. It wasn't mine. I had no right to be wearing it. John picked it up as though it were red hot and wrapped it in his hanky and tucked it into his breast pocket. He wasn't afraid.'

'Did you ever find out who it belonged to?' Vicky whispered.

Her grandmother shook her head. 'No. I was in such a state I refused to go out with John that night. It was stupid but I was afraid. I couldn't compete with it, you see. He refused to part with it. I knew we shouldn't have taken it. We had done something terribly wrong. I begged him to go back to Scotland and put it back where he had found it, but he wanted to find out about it. Where it was made. Who it belonged to. Things like that. It was so like him. He cared more for things than for people. I told him I would only go out with him again if we took it back. He refused. I met your grandfather shortly after that. I never saw John again.'

The story still fresh in her mind, Vicky turned to the old man. 'Do you still have the phoenix here?' she asked in a whisper.

He nodded. Leaning heavily on his walking stick he made his way to the far side of the room. There in a locked china cabinet were several pieces of old silver. Amongst them lay the phoenix. Some of the enamels were chipped, and one or two small stones were missing, but still it seemed to glow with inner fire. They stood staring down at it in awe. Then at last Vicky spoke.

'May I touch it?'

John gave a harsh, short laugh. 'Want to see if the same thing happens to you, eh?'

'No!' she cried. Then again, 'No. I just want to see it more closely.'

John reached into his pocket and produced a bunch of small keys. Unerringly he selected the right one and slipped it into the lock.

The phoenix was icy in her hands. It lay staring up at her unwinkingly from tiny red eyes. 'Did you ever find out who it belonged to?' she asked at last, awed.

'No. It was an impossible task. I assumed it belonged to one of the ladies of the castle. It was almost certainly made in Scotland, probably medieval.' He shrugged. 'I don't suppose we'll ever know more than that.'

'Was it lost in the siege, do you think?'

'Ah. So Julia remembered about the siege did she? She hated that castle. She said it was spooky.' He paused, his eyes going back to the jewel in Vicky's hand. 'The castle was rebuilt several times and it could have come from any period. The bird is a crude representation, which makes me think it is quite early, although the enamelling is very fine. What is unusual, is the subject. A phoenix. That is not something which features very much in medieval lore and it's not Celtic. It must have been made for a special reason.'

'And for a special person.' Vicky smiled. Her fingers closed over the pendant. The enamel still felt cold. It was unyielding; spiky. 'You should have taken it back.'

John shrugged. 'I suppose so. It's all so long ago now. I'd forgotten it, to be honest. And I don't think anyone ever missed it. The castle is one of those busy repointed, carefully preserved things now. Heritage.' He made the word sound like an expletive. 'How can people feel the atmosphere of these places when they are sterilised like that? No room is left for the imagination.'

Vicky smiled. 'Not everyone can arrange to go and excavate a romantic ruin, Mr Fraser. Not everyone can be there to see it in the moonlight.'

He sniffed. 'I suppose not. But the fact remains. I couldn't return it now, if I wanted to. There won't be a blade of grass long enough to cover it; nowhere to put it; nowhere to hide it.'

'It should go back to the castle. Your grandmother was right.' For a moment Giles couldn't believe the words had issued from his own mouth.

'It should?' Vicky stared at him. It was a romantic notion.

'Of course it should. We could take it.' The idea was growing on him as he thought about it. 'I'm sure we would find somewhere to put it. It would be right for you to do it, Vicky, if your grandmother was the one to find it.'

John was looking at him closely. 'Others have said the same, over the years. We shouldn't have taken it. It was wrong. Sometimes, when I've been in here I've thought there was someone watching – someone who resents me for touching it.' He laughed, embarrassed. 'I don't usually have much of an imagination when it comes to ghosts and things, but when I look at that phoenix . . .' He glanced at Vicky. 'Would you take it back? You're not afraid of it?'

'Afraid?' Vicky looked at him in astonishment. 'Why should I be afraid?' She glanced from one man to the other. They were both looking down at the pendant in Giles's hand.

They wrapped it in a handkerchief which Vicky put in her canvas shoulder bag. It seemed strange to none of them that John should trust two strangers with something so obviously valuable. Then they picnicked together on the terrace of John's house looking across the gardens.

'Have you met her grandmother?' John asked Giles at last, watching as Vicky took her sketchbook down to the lake. He began to light his pipe for the umpteenth time.

Giles shook his head.

'I wonder why she sent you.' John sucked the flame of his match hard into the bowl of the pipe and watched in satisfaction as the small nugget of tobacco glowed. 'I never married, you know. I wonder if she knew that.'

Giles shrugged.

'You really will put it back?'

'Scouts' honour!' Giles grinned. 'Of course,' he paused, leaning back in his chair, 'once it's gone back, there would be nothing to prevent you ringing Julia. After all, Vicky's grandfather died years ago.'

For a moment John stared at him, then his face broke into a smile. 'You know, I think I might do just that,' he said.

'You're going to put it on, aren't you,' Giles said that evening as they sat in the semi-darkness of the living room of her London flat. They still had not moved in together. He had a place near the Temple, she the first floor of a little Victorian house in Wandsworth. He worked at Lincoln's Inn, she in a solicitor's office in Fulham.

He leaned forward and topped up her glass with white wine, the phoenix between them on the coffee table. 'It seems a shame to take it back. It must be valuable – quite apart from its historical importance.'

Vicky looked up sharply. 'We must take it back. We promised.'

Giles put down the wine bottle and scooped the phoenix into his palm. 'What do you think it was? A ceremonial thing? It must be heraldic, I suppose?'

Vicky shook her head. 'It was a lover's gift.'

Smiling, Giles put it down again. 'You old romantic. Well, it's a lovely excuse for a weekend north of the border. Do you think you can get this Friday afternoon off?'

'I'll try.' Her eyes were shining. 'Giles, how will we hide it if the castle is all touristy? I'd hate it to be found by some uncaring person who would just steal it . . .'

'We'll think of something.' Giles tossed back his wine. 'Listen, I'm going back to my flat tonight. I've got some briefs to study and an early start. I'll call you tomorrow and we'll liaise about Scotland,' and he gathered her into his arms.

She watched him drive away from the window, then she went to the phone.

'Grandma, I've got something to tell you . . .'

The conversation took over an hour. It wasn't until much later, when she had bathed and put on her nightdress, that the temptation proved too strong.

Sitting on the edge of her bed, with the moonlight flooding through the undrawn curtains, she stared down at the pendant in her hands. She had taken a fine gold chain from a drawer and threaded it through the loop, feeling the gold links slide through her fingers. Gently she touched the bird's head with her little finger, then slowly she raised the chain and fastened it around her neck.

The pendant was heavy, just as her grandmother had said. It slid down between her breasts and nestled there, coldly. She held her breath, staring at the open window. Outside, the traffic noise was muted behind the high wall, and she could smell the honeysuckle which climbed the trellis at the back of the house.

Impulsively she stood up and walked over to the window, leaning with her elbows on the sill. Her hand went to the pendant and she stroked it. It was still cold against her skin. Heavy. Unresponsive. Alien. She shivered as a stray breeze from the garden whispered across her breasts.

The touch when it came was so gentle, so slight she didn't recognise it as a touch at all. A slight pressure on her shoulder beneath the lace, the barest caress along her collar bone, the tiptoeing of two fingers across her throat and down towards the mound of her breasts.

She closed her eyes. Her mouth had gone dry with fear; she couldn't move. Her breathing was jerky, her hands suddenly slippery with perspiration as they fell away from the pendant and hung limply at her sides. She could feel him now behind her, a presence so close she could have leaned back a little against him and drawn his arms around her. The fear was going; her body was responding. She wanted to turn; she wanted to raise her lips. . .

The blast of anger was so sudden she threw her arms across her face as if to shield herself from a physical blow. With a sob she staggered back from the window as the pendant was torn from her neck. The chain disintegrated as the phoenix flew into the corner of the room and skittered under the chest of drawers. With a whimper of fear Vicky ran to the door and dragged it open. She fled down the passage into the living room and, slamming the door behind her she locked it. She was shaking violently.

'I'm sorry,' she murmured out loud. 'I shouldn't have put it on.' Her cheeks were wet with tears. 'We'll take it back, I promise.'

She fell asleep at last on the sofa as dawn was breaking. In the garden a blackbird was singing, the notes clear and cold. Under the chest of drawers the phoenix lay on the dusty boards, a short length of golden chain beside it.

It was Saturday afternoon when the Porsche at last threaded its way the last few miles through the mountains. Giles glanced at Vicky. She was pale and tired and for the last hour she had been growing increasingly tense.

He reached across and put his hand over hers. 'What's wrong?'

'How do we know we're doing the right thing? How can we be sure that's what he . . . she . . . it . . . wants?'

Giles shrugged. He removed his hand from hers to change gear as the car purred up towards the top of the pass. 'You were the one who was so sure. If it isn't then he, she or it will have to tell us. Anyway, I thought you said it was a he. Definitely a he.' He smiled. 'It seems to me that he is well able to make his feelings clear.' She had told him what had happened. When he went back to the flat on Friday to collect her, the pendant was still lying on the floor; she hadn't dared to touch it. Picking it up he had glanced round, nervously, waiting for something to happen. Nothing had. Wrapping it in tissue paper he packed it into a small box and put it in his pocket.

They paid their entrance fee, bought a guide book and began the walk across the field towards the grey stone ruins of the castle. The pendant was in Giles's pocket.

'There are a lot of people about,' Vicky said nervously as she followed him through the gate.

He nodded. He had already spotted the triple windows high in the stone wall. 'Look, that must be where they found it. In what used to be the chapel.' He took her hand. Side by side they stood gazing up at the broken stone; at the remnants of once beautiful decoration. 'It must have been wonderful, excavating this. Can you imagine it? All wild and broken and covered with grass, and camping out here in the storm.' His hand had gone to his pocket. His fingers curled around the pendant.

'There's nowhere to put it, Giles.' She looked round desperately. The restoration was immaculate. Short grass, gravel, newly mortared stone.

Giles was staring up at the windows again. They affected him strangely. Such grace and beauty; such a striving towards the sublime in a castle built for war. And they had survived, where the great curtain walls had fallen. 'I wonder what really happened,' he said. He moved forward and rested his hand on the cold granite of a door jamb. 'Did she lose it? Was it stolen from her? Perhaps she was buried here in the chapel and the phoenix was buried with her.'

'It doesn't seem right to bury a phoenix,' Vicky said softly. 'A phoenix should die in the fire and then be reborn.'

'You're right.' Suddenly Giles was businesslike. 'We can't hide it here. Not with all these people. We'll come back tonight, when the castle is closed.'

'How?' Vicky's eyes were enormous with doubt and disbelief and excitement.

'We'll climb over the fence. I have a feeling that whoever he was, he will show us what to do.'

There was a full moon. The broad strath and the distant mountains were silvered and silent as they climbed the fence and dropped into the field. Grazing sheep looked up startled as, hand in hand, they crept towards the castle.

Vicky's shoes were soaked with dew as, half exhilarated, half terrified, she followed Giles towards the gate. Beyond it, within the ruined walls black pools of shadow contrasted sharply with the clear moonlight.

'I'll give you a leg up,' Giles whispered. He bent so she could stand on his knee and vault across the padlocked gate. Following her he caught her hand again and they stood still.

'Can't you see the headlines?' Vicky breathed in his ear. 'Barrister arrested for breaking into Highland ruin for rendez-vous with ghost.'

Giles smiled. He gave a quick glance over his shoulder. 'No one is going to get arrested. We're not doing any harm. Come on.'

He led the way between what remained of the gatehouse towers, then, keeping to the grass they crept towards the site of the chapel.

Inside the walls the air was icy cold; the shadows were thick. Vicky clutched Giles's arm. 'I'm scared.'

He stopped, looking up at the windows. 'So am I.'

'Have you got it?'

'Of course.' He touched the pendant in his inner pocket, then he reached for his torch.

'Could we bury it under the grass?' she whispered.

'I was wondering that.' He had brought a penknife. He could cut a turf and replace it so no one could see.

Slowly he walked towards the wall and ran his hands across the stone. It was cold and unyielding.

Behind him Vicky stood in the moonlight, staring round.

Was he here, the jealous owner of the phoenix? Was she, the woman to whom he had given it?

'Where are you?' Her lips framed the words. 'What do you want us to do with it?' She shivered, remembering the touch of the unseen man's hands on her body.

'Can you smell burning?' Giles whispered suddenly.

She could smell it too now. Not the gentle, autumn smell of woodsmoke. This was acrid. Unpleasant. The smell of dead fire, dowsed by water, and it was inside the walls.

Giles was peering into the shadows, directing the torch towards the corner. 'Look. There's a stair in the thickness of the stone. How odd. I don't remember noticing that before.' He tiptoed towards it and stood, his hand on the newel post, staring up into the darkness. Then he began to climb.

Wordlessly Vicky followed him up the tight spiral. It was pitch dark. They had to feel their way upward, following the narrow torch beam.

Ahead of Vicky Giles climbed steadily. She could hear his heavy breathing. Abruptly he stopped. She heard a gasp.

'What is it?' Behind him on the narrow stairway she could see nothing. The skin was prickling on the back of her neck.

'Look.' He stepped through a doorway and suddenly the stair above her was empty.

'Giles. Wait!' She sped up the last few steps.

The staircase led into a dark upper chamber. The smell of burning was unpleasantly strong up here and the floor was thick with debris. The pale beam of light from Giles's torch showed fallen masonry and burned timbers, tumbled on stone. At the far end the three lancet windows rose up, close above them now, against the starlight. The torch beam picked out the details of the ravaged chapel – the breached, gaping walls, the collapsed roof open to the stars, the broken, exploded floor tiles, and beneath the windows a black gaping hole. Picking his way across the rubble Giles flashed the torch inside. 'There's something here.' He reached down.

'Be careful.' On her knees beside him, Vicky peered into the hole.

'There's a little box down here. It's half burned.' Lifting it out he put it on the floor. 'It must have been beautifully carved. You can just see the remnants of the decoration. What is it? Wood? Bone?'

'It's ivory.' Awed, Vicky picked up the box. The lid was warped and twisted but she managed to prise it off. It was empty.

Their eyes met. Around them the shadows shifted. Beyond the windows in the moonlight an owl hooted. Taking the phoenix from his pocket Giles handed it to her. It was the first time she had touched it since it had been snatched from around her neck. Reverently she laid the pendant in the box. 'It will be safe there,' she said quietly. She smiled. 'He must have loved her so much.'

Putting back the lid, she gave the box to Giles, and he reached down and wedged it into the hole. Then carefully he began to fill it with rubble. On the top he balanced some of the broken tiles.

They stood for a moment in silence. 'I hope you're together, wherever you are.' Giles's quiet words hung for a moment in the air before he turned towards the stairway.

The moon was setting and the shadows had moved and thickened. On the grass below the lancet windows they stopped and stared upwards, but deep in the blackness of the wall there was no sign of the place where they had been.

'Come on. I'm freezing.' Giles reached for her hand. In his inside pocket was a small velvet box. In it was a locket, but suddenly the moment did not seem right. The shadows were too sad. Tomorrow, in the sunshine, he would bring her back and tell her he loved her and give it to her. Tomorrow, when, he knew, there would be no sign of the burnt chapel; no staircase in the wall. When grass and ruins would be as stark and neat as when they had first seen them earlier that afternoon.

When the Chestnut Blossoms Fall

A Trilogy

THE MISTRESS

IT WAS WINTER OUTSIDE. The restaurant was dimly lighted and they saw each other's faces over the saucered candles as pale blurs, half dazzled against the flock wallpaper and the crowded, faded Victorian prints. A waiter hovered, a less substantial figure even than they, in the shadows with his coffee pot and the world-weary stoop to his shoulders.

'More coffee, Tina?' Derek smiled gently and she smiled back, hoping that he wasn't going to reach into his pocket for his glasses to read the bill, a gesture which made him prematurely old.

She shook her head. 'Let's have it at my place, shall we?'

The spell was broken completely when he glanced at his watch. At once she felt a surge of resentment; always the watch came between them; always the time limit; the barrier, the gate through which he passed out of her life and back into someone else's.

He had turned to the waiter. 'No more coffee, thank you. The bill.'

The man bowed – the bill was already made up – and Derek fumbled for his glasses.

'There's just time to come back, Tina, I'd like that.' He

turned to her with a quick smile which never failed to win her back from her agonised depressions. Then he took her coat from the waiter, and helped her on with it, so his hands were already round her shoulders as they went out through the door and into the wet road and it was natural to stay like that as they trod the shiny reflections of the pavement lamps into muddy opacity and lowered their faces before the cold of the slanting rain.

She had left the fire on in her flat. Either way it helped – if he felt he had to go back to his wife it made the loneliness more bearable for Tina; if he didn't, if he came back with her, it made the place inviting and homelike – his second home. She glanced up at him with a quick surge of warm happiness. This time he was there.

She threw off her coat and ran to the kitchen to find two cups, two saucers, two glasses for two people.

'What would you like with the coffee, Derek?' she called. He had lowered himself, by the fire, into the chair which she always thought of as his own.

'Scotch if there's any left. You know, Tina, we must do something about this room. Would you like me to buy you a new carpet? It might cheer it up a bit.'

She stopped, frozen in her tracks. He thought her room cheerless. He didn't like it. Her hand shook a little as she began pouring again and her voice was guarded as she answered. 'That would be nice. I should like that.'

At once he seemed aware of what was wrong, and he levered himself out of the chair and came to lean in the doorway of the kitchen, watching as she fixed the coffee. He took the Scotch from her hand. 'I love the room, Tina. As it is. It's comfortable. A haven, you know that. I just thought some more colour might cheer it up for you when I'm not here . . .'

So he did know how she felt. Of course; he was sensitive and that was why she loved him. One of the reasons. He was sensitive, warm, friendly, everything that that cow of a wife of his did not understand or appreciate.

Tina had never told him about the grey, aching evenings when he was not there. Or of the long empty nights; of the nervy solitary breakfast table when occasionally she would forget her promise to him to give up smoking and grab a cigarette with her black coffee instead of toast. She only told him about happy things, funny things, things which would bind him to her. She turned and smiled up at him. 'You are a darling, Derek.' She slipped her arms around his neck. A little of his Scotch spilled on her shoulder as she returned the hug and, smiling, he nuzzled it, pretending to lick where it had soaked darkly into the wool of her dress.

'God, I wish I could stay tonight!' Suddenly he was holding her in earnest. He felt blindly for the worktop behind her and, clumsily, set down the glass.

'Why don't you?' she whispered. She knew he would shake his head. He would probably glance at his wrist over her shoulder and hurriedly calculate the time it would take to drive home.

'Oh Derek!' She pushed him away exasperated. 'Ask her for a divorce. I can't go on like this. I want you so much and it's not as though she loves you – you've told me that.'

He had picked up his glass again, agitated as always when she touched on forbidden territory.

'No. I said she doesn't understand me, Tina, that's different. She does love me, my dear. That's the problem. That is why I can't hurt her. She loves me very much.'

'You can't hurt her and yet you hurt me every day!' She hated herself for saying it. She pushed past him and threw herself down on her knees before the fire in the dim light of the table lamp. 'And she hurts *you*,' she couldn't resist adding over her shoulder as he remained in the kitchen doorway. 'She knows how much you want a family, yet she refuses to give you any children. I should have thought that alone was grounds for divorce.'

'Perhaps.' He shook his head slowly as he came back to his chair. 'It's too soon, Tina. Perhaps eventually . . . I don't know.' He shrugged helplessly and sat there, gazing at the gently hissing flames in the elements.

'And I want children so much,' she went on piteously, half to herself. 'Life is so terribly unfair.'

He didn't answer. His eyes were still fixed on the fire. Perhaps he hadn't even heard her.

'Would you divorce her if I had a baby?' She looked up suddenly. 'You know, Derek, I think she would understand, if you told her that.' But he was still looking blankly at the columns of blue flame, his eyes vacant, not listening.

'Did you hear what I said?'

Visibly pulling himself together with an effort he focused on her again and smiled. 'I am sorry I was miles away. What did you say?' His face was haggard in the soft light.

She scrambled to her feet, her eyes shining from the idea which had at that moment been born, but her voice was gentle as she stood before him, gazing down into his eyes. 'You're tired.'

He nodded and slowly stood up. 'Perhaps I had better go. It's late and it's a long drive.'

For once she did not try to stop him. She clung to him for the last, treasured, kiss of the night and then stood watching as he walked down the echoing hall outside the flat door. At the corner by the lift he stopped and turned for a second as he always did, then he was gone.

She closed the door and leaned with her back against it. Shutting her eyes she could feel her heart hammering inside her rib cage as, taking a deep breath, she went into the bedroom. She kept her contraceptive pills in the top drawer of the chest of drawers under the window. There were three packets there. It took as many minutes to carry them out to the rubbish bin.

As she clanged the lid shut on them she could feel her hands trembling and she was wiping her palms nervously on her dress as she walked back into the flat. She had made her decision; there was no going back. She picked up Derek's bottle and poured herself a large drink. It was the first time she had ever done that alone.

Derek had promised to take her to the country at the weekend. It was bitterly cold and she sat beside him in the car hugging herself, smiling with excitement beneath her woollen hat.

'What's up? You look as though you've come into a fortune.'

She grinned happily at him. 'I'm just happy, that's all. Look at the frost on the trees, Derek. It's so beautiful after being in town; one forgets.' For once she did not even care that he lived in the country; that his house was probably decorated with hoarfrost even on weekdays and that his wife could see the snow on the boughs of their apple tree from her kitchen window.

They parked at the edge of the beechwoods and began slowly to walk through them, their shoes sinking into thawing leaf mould around ice-rimmed puddles, glancing up at the soaring silver trunks of the trees and the azure sky beyond. They held hands, his gloves leather, hers wool, and the smoke of their breath singled as they laughed. She wanted to run, but she was afraid to because he might remember he was so much older than she and pant and grow red in the face and say he was too old for that sort of thing and spoil it all.

They had tea in a little restaurant in front of a blazing log fire, asking for second helpings of scones and clotted cream and Derek looked at her and smiled. 'It wouldn't do you any harm to put on a little weight, sweetheart. You're as thin as a bean pole.'

And she smiled back, and almost told him what she had done, but didn't quite dare.

They seldom discussed Derek's wife after that. Janet receded in importance as Tina's happiness grew. She didn't care any more what Janet did or thought. She had stopped worrying about her and thought only of what would happen when at last she could tell Derek that she was going to have his baby. She had no doubts about what he would do. She was utterly happy.

He bought the new carpet for her flat. It was deep red and over it there was a soft shaggy hearth rug for her to sit on because it was her favourite place – on her knees before the fire, reading or talking, or listening to music.

Months passed. Spring slowly began to shade the trees and take the edge off the coldness of the mornings. Anxiously now, she counted off the weeks, waiting, hoping, each time again disappointed.

Derek seemed more relaxed and happy to see her happy, and he brought her more and more presents – but he came less often to see her.

There was always a busy time at his office in the spring, she remembered from last year, or thought she did. The excuses he gave his wife of working late, of seminars and conferences, were now true, as he assured her, for these few months. Tina missed him dreadfully, but still, there were the afternoons. One day a week he managed to slip away for a couple of hours. They would stay in her flat, turning their backs on the glory of the spring outside, lying close in her shady bedroom, both too conscious of the alarm they had to set to remind them when their time was up.

She had almost given up hope when at last it happened. A month stretched out to five weeks – six – seven. Breathless with excitement she waited, counting the days, wondering when she dared tell him.

At last she could wait no longer. He was surprised when she greeted him at the door of her flat, fully dressed; for the past weeks she had worn a kimono or a negligée, playing the part of his mistress to woo him. He smiled, pleased to see her excited, and he accepted the drink she had ready. The windows were wide open and they could hear the steady roar of traffic below, though all they could see was the foaming beauty of the horse chestnuts on the pavements.

'You look very smart today,' he said, glancing at her bright skirt and fashionable sandals. 'Do you want to go out somewhere?'

She shook her head. She had grown her hair long to please him and it swung heavily round her shoulders. He longed to take a handful and feel the weight of it in his palm. He turned away and took a sip of his drink.

'I've something to tell you, Derek. I hope you're going to be pleased.' She hesitated. Not until that moment had it crossed her mind that he might be anything but happy at what she had done. She swallowed and glanced down at the floor. The sun was shining in through the leaves outside, throwing a moving fretwork of patterns on the rich pile of the carpet. Derek's carpet.

'What is it, Tina?' He was watching her, amused at her sudden confusion. Not guessing.

She looked up and took a deep breath. 'I am going to have your baby.'

There was a long hush in the room. Even outside the road was empty for a moment as the traffic was halted by some distant red light. Then the deep throbbing roar of a bus passed, the high red roof brushing beneath the branches, shaking the tree so some of the blossom fell.

'Are you absolutely sure?' He sounded appalled.

Shaken, she looked away. 'Well, I'm nearly sure. I haven't had a test or anything, but . . .'

'Then you must.' All at once he was solicitous. Not for the first time he reminded her of her father. 'Once we know we'll be able to decide what to do.'

'But, Derek! Surely there's nothing to decide.' She could feel a strange coldness gripping her stomach as she looked at his face. 'Your wife will give you a divorce at once if she knows about the baby. You know she will. Then we can get married and –'

273

'*No!*'

He set down his glass and walked over to the window, looking down at the street below. 'I am sorry, Tina. Perhaps I haven't made myself clear. As you hadn't mentioned it for so long I thought you had decided to accept the situation. There can be no question of a divorce.'

'But you wanted a baby. You told me you wanted a baby.'

'I want my wife's baby, Tina.' His voice was gentle. 'I'm sorry, my dear, if you misunderstood the situation, but I really don't see how you could have. I've made no secret of the fact that I wanted a family.'

'That's why I wanted to get pregnant.' Her voice was small.

He swung round on her. 'You mean you did it deliberately?'

She nodded.

'Christ!' He hit his forehead with the flat of his hand. 'Oh, Tina, I am so sorry. But it cannot be. Not like that. You must get rid of it. I know it's hard, but . . . there's nothing else to do.'

'No, Derek.' She spoke quietly, suddenly calm. 'Your wife has everything. You; a proper home; your name. This baby is all I have of yours. I don't care how hard it is, but it's happened, and I shall keep it.'

'You can't, Tina!'

'Try and stop me!' She was angry now and very bitter. 'It's my decision, Derek.'

'Then it would be the end of us, Tina. I am not prepared to run a second family behind Janet's back.'

'Oh no,' she held back her tears with difficulty. 'Yet you were quite prepared to run a mistress for two years.'

She turned away from the sunny room and from him and ran into the bedroom, slamming the door behind her.

Left alone he groped for his cigarettes and shook one out of the packet, his hands trembling. Then he stood looking down out of the window, watching the cars go by. It was nearly four. In five minutes he would have to go back to the office.

He glanced towards the bedroom which was quite silent; he had dreaded the sound of sobbing. With a sigh he stubbed the scarcely smoked cigarette out in the ashtray and quietly he let himself out of the flat.

Tina heard the front door close as she lay on her bed. She wasn't crying. She felt too shocked and disappointed for that; too numb perhaps to register what had happened. It was a long time before she got up. She kicked off her sandals and wandered listlessly back into the sitting room. The sun had sunk behind the roofs opposite and the room was in shadow now. She could hear a blackbird whistling from the trees, its song clear over the roar of traffic.

She sat down at the table and drew a piece of paper towards her slowly. She had never written to Derek before; it had been part of their understanding.

'My Darling Derek,' she wrote, her hand shaking a little as she thought out what she was going to say to him. 'I am so sorry that I misunderstood what you wanted. I truly thought that it would make you happy. Please forgive me. We have had such a lovely two years together – and I love you so much. I could not bear it to end like this. I want very badly to keep the baby, but I promise I will make no claims on you now or in the future. Just love us a little, and keep in touch. You will have my love always, Tina.'

Slowly she read it through, then she folded it into the envelope and addressed it to his home. She thought for a moment and then wrote *Private*, on the top of the envelope.

She ran to the box with the letter before she could change her mind, and then slowly walked back to the flat.

It was very hard to sleep that night. She lay tossing and turning on the bed in a turmoil of indecision and misery. Each time she dozed off she thought she heard Derek's voice but then as her eyes flew open in the dark she knew she was alone and that he had left her. 'But I have the baby,' she thought, hugging herself. His baby. The pillow was hot. She turned it over and beat it desperately with her fists. Her eyes were sore. They wanted sleep as much as she. She got up and wandered into the kitchen where the tiles were cool beneath her feet and she poured herself a glass of milk.

She began to shiver as she sipped the cold milk. For the first time Derek had shown her, without a shadow of doubt, that if it came to choosing between Janet and herself, he would stay with Janet, whatever happened.

'He's a coward,' she whispered furiously at the half-lowered blind across the dark window. 'A coward and a liar.' She did not let herself think she might have been wrong.

Strangely, she fell asleep almost at once when she got back into bed, and slept for a few hours, dreamlessly. When she woke it was just beginning to get light. The street was quiet except for the tentative notes of one or two of the first birds in the dawn. She wondered for a moment what had awakened her. Then she knew. The familiar aching pain in the small of her back. The knotted cramp in her stomach. 'Oh no.' She leaped out of bed. 'Please God, no.' Trembling she switched on the bedside lamp and pulled back the blanket. There on the sheet was the small tell-tale patch of blood. There was no baby. There never had been.

THE MAN

It was winter. The garden lay beneath a crisp layer of frost, grey-green and unreal in the glittering sun as Derek made his way to the breakfast table. His wife, already seated, pouring out the coffee, glanced up with a smile. 'Hello you. You're going to be late again if you're not careful.'

'What about you, then?'

'Me, too.'

He went by car, she, hating the traffic, by train. They were both silent for a while, then she looked up. 'Is it tonight that you're working late again? I might stay up in town and do some shopping; perhaps even go to a show.'

He frowned, a little shamed by her tolerance. 'Janet, I hate leaving you on your own so often, I really do.' He meant it.

He reached for the toast rack. A piece of toast fell on the cloth in a shower of crumbs and he laughed a little uneasily. 'I'm lucky you understand. Not many men have high-powered business women for wives.' He intended it as a compliment, but at once she frowned.

'Don't let's go into that now, Derek, for goodness' sake. I'm fed up with hearing how high-powered I am. You know damn well it's just a job, same as thousands of other women do.'

'I know, I know.' Irritated, he dug the knife into the butter dish. 'It's just that thousands of other women manage to combine careers with families these days.' He pushed his chair back abruptly, so that it caught on the rush matting on the kitchen floor and nearly fell sideways.

'I don't happen to like children, Derek.' Her voice was energetically patient. 'For God's sake, do we have to discuss it every day? I love my job. I made it quite clear before we married how I felt; I didn't deceive you in any way; I've been telling you every day for the last eight bloody years! How many more times must I tell you?'

'You don't have to tell me at all. Please, let's not quarrel.' He went to put his arm round her, dropping a kiss on her head. 'I'm sorry. I never mean to bring the subject up.' He laughed uneasily. 'I must be feeling old again; seeking the immortality of sons, or something.'

Was it that? After all, Janet was only thirty-two and there was plenty of time for her, but he, well, he was nearly twice her age. He frowned as he opened the garage doors and slowly backed down the drive, watching the clouds of exhaust wreathing back over the car, enveloping him in a personal, isolating fog. He backed cautiously into the road and swung round towards London. Or was it that he was jealous of Janet's independence? It irked him a little, he had to admit, that she could afford to go off and buy things, big things, for the house for instance, without having to ask him for money. He had always liked the idea – it seemed romantic and cosy, of couples, young couples, putting their heads together to discuss things; working out budgets, agonising and saving and choosing, together. It must bring them close.

He swore as he reached the level crossing. The barrier was falling and that meant that he would have to wait for at least three commuter trains in quick succession. He drummed his fingers on the steering wheel impatiently. Then he thought of Tina.

With her he was the one who did the buying without consultation. He produced the goods for her flat with beneficence, feeling big because of it although he knew she would like to go out and choose with him sometimes; but he shied away from the idea. That would be too near the bone. Too much like setting up home together. It would admit to a permanence he denied.

He often cross-examined himself guiltily about Tina and he always came to the same conclusion. He was fond of her of course. He found her attractive and her home a refuge and a convenient pied-à-terre in London, but when he was not with her he liked to think that she probably ceased to exist; or rather that she became someone quite different; someone confident, poised, invulnerable and whole.

His conscience would never quite face the idea that she lived and loved for him alone. Once or twice he had taken the idea out, so to speak, examined it cursorily, and put it away again as being too uncomfortable to peruse further.

Two trains flashed by in opposite directions, their windows crossing like the flicks of a camera shutter, each hiding and revealing a microcosm of life behind the condensation, and then the barrier arm slowly began to rise. Derek checked his watch as he carefully pressed down the accelerator pedal. Late again.

* * *

278

He was due to meet Tina at six. It was a cold evening. Wet. The sleet, frosty and clean in the country, was unpleasant and depressing in London and he sighed a little, almost wishing he could go straight home to relax by the ash-whitened logs which Janet always kept burning in the evenings, regardless of the extra work it gave her.

Then he saw Tina, early as she always was, waiting in the foyer of his offices, sheltering from the cold, and his heart gave a little lift. Her dark hair was streaked blue-black by the rain, and swung loosely on her shoulders, still disarrayed by the scarf she had torn off as she came in.

'Hello Tina. Have I kept you waiting?' When her eyes met his he knew why he let it go on like this. He could never cease to be haunted by the clear grey honesty and the uncomplicated worship he saw there. And she made him feel young.

She put on the sodden scarf again, and turned up her coat collar, then he pushed the circular door for her, watching benevolently as like a child she half ran, her hand on the glass, until she was ejected breathless onto the front steps. She turned to him and laughed happily, watching as he followed.

Later, after the film, they both had *soupe du jour*. It was thick and hot and full of leeks. She always put salt in her soup regardless and it irritated him slightly that she didn't taste it first, but he said nothing. It was her evening. 'Did you enjoy the film?' he asked, watching as a strand of her hair strayed for a moment across her nose. She blew it off, suddenly gamine. 'I loved the bit where he chased after everyone in the car. That was really exciting!'

'Do you think I should drive like that?' He smiled tolerantly, reaching out to brush her hand quickly with his own.

She looked wistful. 'No one could drive like that in a staid saloon like yours, Derek! I wish you had a sports car!'

'Oh I'm too old for that! I had one when I was twenty.' He laughed a little wryly, not minding the joke against himself, but she, who was twenty, looked stricken. Once more he wished she would acknowledge the difference in their ages

279

and laugh about it as Janet did, instead of constantly pretending it didn't exist.

'We must plan our day in the country, my dear,' he went on easily, reassuring her. 'I rather thought Burnham Beeches might be nice. What do you think?'

Janet had told him only a week ago about her conference and he had been hurt and angry. It was bad enough that her work encroached in the evenings sometimes, but to deprive him of a whole weekend! It had been to get his own back on Janet that he had rung Tina and the excitement and happiness in her voice when he suggested spending the two days together had soothed him a little, restoring his self-confidence.

The waiter had begun to hover again and he sighed. He wanted to linger. 'More coffee, Tina?' He smiled to hide his irritation.

She shook her head, and glancing at the waiter she leaned forward to whisper conspiratorially, 'Let's have it at my place.'

Surreptitiously he glanced at his watch. It wasn't all that late. Perhaps he could stay for half an hour before driving home through the rain. Hunting for his glasses he turned to the waiter and beckoned for the bill.

He loved the way she left the fire and the side-lamp switched on in her flat. Once or twice at the beginning he had reproached her for her extravagance but she had been so hurt that it had dawned on him she did it for him and he had been very touched. It didn't cross his mind it might cheer her too, should she have to return alone.

He sat down in the chair by the fire, relaxing, and glanced round the room while she was in the kitchen, making the coffee. It was comfortable and happy, if a little threadbare. He closed his eyes and gave a deep sigh of contentment. If only he could do something about it – buy her something new perhaps. He squinted down at the worn carpet and had an idea. For a moment she looked crestfallen when he suggested it and he was taken aback; he went into the kitchen and helped himself to the Scotch she had poured him. 'I love the room, Tina,' he murmured awkwardly. 'I thought it might cheer you up when I'm not there, that's all . . .'

She turned and flung herself into his arms, spilling his drink. Putting down his glass, he drew her close to him, feeling the accustomed longing as he smelled the fragrance of her hair. He glanced cautiously at his watch behind her head and swore soundlessly. There was no time.

At the surreptitious movement of his hand which freed the watch from his sleeve he felt her body tense. She knew what he was thinking and she resented it. She pushed him away. He could see the tears welling in her eyes. He knew what was coming and he braced himself, picking up his glass. It was weeks since she had mentioned Janet and divorce and all the unhappy, unmentionable things which would throw him into a panic and force him to realise how the situation could not be allowed to go on. Once, in a foolish unforgivable moment of self-pity he had mentioned the fact that Janet refused to give him any children and she had seized on the fact and nursed it and now, every so often, she would bring it up and throw it at him, imagining it to be a lever against her rival.

She pushed past him, still sobbing, and flung herself on her knees near the fire. He shook himself wearily. What was she saying? Something about Janet understanding. How naïve could she get?

Then she was getting to her feet again, her mood inexplicably gone as fast as it had come. She smiled gently, her face serene. 'You're tired.' She kissed him as he nodded.

'Perhaps I had better go, Tina. It is late and it's a long drive.'

They kissed goodbye and he left her, walking slowly down the long carpeted corridor towards the lifts.

Janet was asleep when he crept up to the darkened bedroom. He undressed quietly in the bathroom, and stood for a while looking at himself in the steamy mirror. His face was strained taut into lines which grooved his cheeks and furrowed his forehead with weariness and worry. He frowned and the lines deepened.

'You're working too hard, Derek.' Janet's voice from the darkened landing made him jump. She appeared in the doorway and smiled. 'Poor darling. I wish you would take a day or two off and let up for a bit. Shall I get you a hot drink?'

Still looking in the mirror he saw her, pretty and feminine, in the lacy negligée he had bought her, her immaculate hair touselled and softened from the pillow, and his own face, in front of hers in the glass, visibly relaxing and lighting before his eyes at the sight of her. He turned.

'Darling.'

'What is it?'

'Do you have to go away this weekend?' He had forgotten Burnham woods.

'You know I must.'

He sat on the edge of the bath, his shoulders slumped, and she came to him, taking his head in her arms and cradling it on her breast.

'I am going to work less afterwards, though, Derek. I've been thinking about it for a while, and there is quite a bit I can delegate.' She smiled and dropped a kiss on his head. 'I've been ignoring my husband shamefully.'

He glanced up at her. Her eyes were bright and her face relaxed and pretty. He quite suddenly wanted her very badly. He stood up slowly and took her into his arms.

He would give Tina this one last treat. Then he must tell her that it had to end. Almost he dreaded picking her up on Saturday, but when it came the time passed in a haze of happiness. She did not once mention Janet, or the possibility of divorce; nor did she say anything which made him feel old. They laughed and joked together in the sun-bright frost and watched their breath mingle in clouds of whiteness and

Derek forgot that he had meant to end it. A few more meetings could do no harm and they gave her such pleasure. Each time as the weeks passed, when his conscience pained him, he would buy her a present; less often now something for the flat; things like flowers and chocolates which required less thought.

Slowly he began to realise that there was something about his wife which was different and it pleased him immensely. They no longer bickered and after a while he realised it was because she was not on the defensive any more. It was as though she had relaxed, accepted something, he was not quite sure what, which she had been fighting for a long time. Puzzled, but pleased, anxious not to endanger their new-found happiness together, he found it surprisingly easy to leave the office earlier now, and as the frosts relaxed their hold and the countryside began to stir he would look forward to the long slow drive through the rush-hour towards home.

He took to snatching a couple of hours in the afternoon every now and again to see Tina. She too had changed. She had grown more composed, more self-reliant; almost preoccupied now. And she radiated a new inner happiness which he hated to endanger, but he knew he had to tell her sometime. It was unfair to her to let her go on loving him. A little he hoped that she had found someone else and that that was the reason for her happiness. He hated the idea, but at the same time he wanted, in a cowardly way, for it to be true. Then he need never tell her.

It was a relief on this last day, when he had nerved himself for the final break, that she had opened the door to him fully dressed. He had not said as much to her, but it had shocked him slightly that over the past weeks of their afternoon meetings she had met him undressed at the door like a whore, too blatantly waiting for him to make love to her. He grinned at her now, relieved. Perhaps today she was going to give him his marching orders and save herself the hurt.

He went in and automatically she poured his drink. She had on a scarlet and orange skirt which swayed and flared as she walked. It was seductive. Now that he had made up his mind to leave her he felt a strange, urgent longing to make love to her again. He turned towards the window and looked out at the noisy street, sipping his drink. Her flat was on the first floor, level with the thickly flowering horse chestnuts which lined the street, and he could almost touch the blossoms through the open window.

'I've something to tell you, Derek; I hope you're going to be pleased.' Her voice was hesitant, almost lost beneath the roar of the bus which accelerated into the stream of traffic outside.

'What is it, Tina?' He turned and smiled to make it easier for her to tell him.

She hesitated for a brief moment, and then, 'I'm going to have your baby.'

The smile stuck on his face for a moment, wooden. Then slowly it faded as he felt the draught cold from the window behind him. Christ Almighty! How could he have been so stupid? But surely, surely, she had been on the pill? Taking a deep breath to steady himself he smiled again; he must reassure her.

'Are you absolutely sure?'

'Well, I'm nearly sure. I haven't had a test or anything, but . . .'

'Then you must. Once we know we'll be able to decide what to do.'

He was wondering how much it would cost; and then of course he would want to send her away for a really good holiday. But she was still talking, rushing on, not listening to him, her eyes panicking suddenly . . . divorce . . . marry her . . . keep the baby . . . divorce . . . divorce Janet

'*No!*' His voice came out much louder than he had intended. Oh Christ, why had he let it go on so long? Why had she not understood? Why had he ever mentioned children to her at all? He cursed himself silently as he turned back to the window, to give himself some time, not able to look at her frantic face. No. No. There was no way he was going to allow her to blackmail him like that, to force his hand, to betray Janet any more. He set his teeth grimly. He was fond of the girl; he even loved her still, in a way, but Janet had to come first.

Later she ran from the room crying, defiantly shouting that she wanted to keep the baby with or without him and she had slammed her bedroom door in his face. He reached for a cigarette, shaken, expecting to hear her sobs from behind the door. But the bedroom was silent. After a few moments he stubbed out the cigarette. Automatically he glanced at his watch. It was time to go back to the office.

Should he say anything before he went? Better not. In a day or so he would ring her; he would see she lacked for nothing whatever she decided but he would never see the baby. Whatever happened he would never do that to Janet.

With a shrug he gave a final glance round the room and slowly he walked out, carefully closing the front door behind him.

THE WIFE

Rows with Derek at breakfast always left me quivering with resentment and hurt. By and large they followed the same pattern each time, as though they had been scripted for us by a hack writer, and later I would try and shrug them off, pouring myself another coffee, my hand shaking a little. Glancing at my watch I could time him exactly. Two minutes to the door to collect his briefcase and coat, three minutes out to the garage. Another three to start the car and crunch slowly backwards up the drive – then silence.

I nearly always had twenty minutes or so to spare from that

moment before I left to catch the commuter train to my office. I could not bear the traffic and the crawl for hours through the suburbs as Derek could, I am too impatient, so I would never accept a lift with him.

This time the quarrel had ended on a conciliatory note. He had apologised, trying humorously to rationalise. 'I must be seeking the immortality of sons or something,' he had laughed as he refolded the paper to fit into his briefcase. I groped in my bag for my cigarettes, frowning. That throw-away comment had reached me where so many other arguments had failed. He was after all so much older than I and it meant so much to him, having children. But then, I reminded myself crossly, I had never had any desire for a family, and had made that clear before we married. He taunted me with the description 'high-powered business woman' and I knew from him it was no compliment, but that is what I was, and I revelled in it.

'Morning Mrs H.' Maggie's cheerful voice echoed through the hatch from the kitchen. I stood up slowly and taking my cup and my cigarette went thoughtfully out to her.

'It's cold this morning! You wrap up warm, dear, and watch out for the ice on the way to the station!' My cleaning lady was a cheerful, plump, motherly woman. I watched her take off her coat and hang it behind the door and suddenly I wanted to confide in her, ask her opinion. I took a sip from the cup. It would be foolish of course and all round the village in no time. 'Have some coffee, Maggie. It's still hot.'

'Thanks, dear. You know, I will this morning. It'll warm me nicely.'

'Maggie.' I was strangely embarrassed, not knowing how to put it. For so long I had been used to people – friends, above all relatives – saying, 'And when are you going to start a family?' to which I replied indignantly that it was none of their business. But we had been married, what, eight years now, and the questions had for the most part stopped. Except from Derek.

'Maggie, do *you* think I'm wrong not to want children?'

She gaped at me for a moment. Then she grinned comfortably. 'Well, each to his own way, that's what I say. We can't all want babies I suppose; and it would be wrong for you to have one after all this time if you didn't want it – not that you wouldn't love one if it came. I was only saying to my Harry last week, what this house needs is some little ones. Mr H, he'd be a lovely father.' She was pouring herself some coffee and she crossed to refill my cup at the same time. 'You enjoy your job too much though, don't you, dear?'

She began to stack the breakfast things. 'You'll miss your train if you don't hurry.'

'I suppose I could have a baby and go on working. People do. They get nannies or au pairs or something.'

She beamed going to the sink with the loaded tray. 'I'd give you all the help I could too. Love kiddies, I do.'

I set down the cup and reached for my coat. 'Don't say anything to anyone about this Maggie, will you? I am still thinking about it.' I pulled a wry face as I buttoned my coat and she smiled confidentially.

'Mum's the word, Mrs H. Now you run for your train, or you'll miss it. And mind the ice!'

It was a busy day and went reasonably well. At six I closed my desk diary and put it away with a sigh. Then I stood up and stretched. Outside, the evening was black, but the towering office blocks were bright with thousands of lights. London throbbed at this time of day and I loved it. I grabbed my handbag and made my way out to the Ladies to patch up my make-up. It was one of the days Derek was going to be late home; he was under a lot of pressure at the office and two or three nights a week he had been out till after midnight. In a way it was a relief. It meant I had no need to switch from thoughts of international currency exchange to worries about whether Maggie had done all the shopping and remembered to turn on the oven. I could go on being myself for the evening and not pretend to be more domesticated than I was.

The evening was mine. I slung my bag over my shoulder and ran down the steps to the entrance hall. Digby, the commissionaire, dapper as always, wished me a knowing goodnight as he opened the door and I was outside. I took a deep breath of the cold damp air. It has a strange quality all of its own, London air. Not sharp like country air; not sweet like that of the hills. It has a bitter, sour smell that combines traffic fumes and hurrying people and wet scummy pavements and the excitement of the lights, the noise and the constant vibrant hurry. I adore it.

I thought of Derek stuck in that smoky boardroom in the City and I suddenly felt very benevolent towards him, poor darling. He always worked so hard.

Then I thought again of my plan. It was late-night shopping and I had decided to do a little research into my own psyche! The thought had come to me gradually as the day had progressed and I had faced it with equilibrium. It was, after all, the sensible way to analyse my own state of mind.

I pushed with the crowds into the store and allowed myself to be steered at random between counters stacked high and unattractively with Sale goods. Once or twice I stopped and allowed myself to be tempted but I was restless. I was suddenly eager to get on with what I had come for. I made my way to the escalators and let them carry me up out of the crowds. One, two, three, four floors. Why so high? It was much quieter up there. The crowds were thin. I stepped off the moving concourse and stood and looked around. Before me stretched lines of cots and prams, elegant, glittering and empty. I swallowed. I hadn't expected it to be quite so soulless. Slowly I began to walk.

For ten minutes I wandered around that department, out of the prams towards the soft toys, the tiny clothes, the powder and the rattles. There were no real babies there. I suppose it was too late for them to be out. I glanced at my watch. It was after seven. Once more round the display of baby buggies, each with a fluffy teddy bear as occupant, and I made thoughtfully for the *Down* sign.

I could feel myself frowning as I descended slowly into the crowds again. The visit had not been in any way decisive. I had not been repelled by what I saw and I must confess that I had been scared that I might be, but I hadn't been won over, either. I thought about all the babies I knew. The trouble was that I didn't actually *know* any. I always inspected from a safe distance, usually a little distastefully, shrinking from the sour milky smell so many of them seemed to have.

'For Christ's sake, Janet,' Derek had said in one of our earlier rows, when he still had the energy to go into the practicality of things. 'You needn't even look after it if you don't want to. Just give birth, that's all I ask. We'll get someone from the village to come in. I can afford it. Damn it, *you* can afford it, if you insist on going on working.'

'If you want to know, the idea of being pregnant repels me,' I had retorted, to hurt him. '*You* don't have to go around looking like the back of a bus, suffering from varicose veins and God knows what else for three-quarters of a bloody year!'

Poor Derek. It was to his credit that he had stuck so gently but so firmly to his guns for so long. Not that I had seen it like that. I had been on the point of leaving him over it, and yet. . .

The problem was a straight choice. I loved my husband and my home. Even more I loved my job and my independence. I loathed the idea of having to go to anyone and ask them for money and if I gave up work I would in a sense be giving up my right to be an individual – even if it was only for a few months or so.

That was the way I saw it.

I put my key in the lock and pushed open the front door.

The house was warm and welcoming. Nothing had changed of course. It was still home. With a grateful sigh I kicked off my boots and wandered into the living room to turn on the lamp. In the winter Maggie lights the fire before she leaves in the afternoon and she had done it today, not realising I would be late home. It had died to embers. I threw on a couple of logs and poured myself a drink.

In theory three months off work should be no problem. But there was always Ronnie Maxton. Ronnie, who had come in as my assistant, waiting, watching, full of drive and an ambition which I had straightaway pinpointed as ruthless. I am good at my job, but when it comes to it, if I took maternity leave Ronnie would still be there ready with his own schemes.

I lit a cigarette and began to pace up and down the hearth-rug. Would there be a place for me when I went back? The logs were blazing up now, on their bed of ash, shooting sparks up the chimney, scenting the room with the lovely fragrance of burning apple. I threw the half-smoked cigarette into the red heart of the fire.

I had a long leisurely bath and wandered into the bedroom. The rain had stopped earlier and when I drew back the curtains and glanced out I could see the black sky was pierced with a myriad shimmering stars and the garden was glittering with frost. I hoped the roads would not be too icy for Derek when he drove back from his meeting.

I kept my contraceptive pills in the bathroom cabinet. Last thing each night I would take one meticulously before I cleaned my teeth. Tonight I took them out and looked at them, turning the unopened new pink-and-white packet in my hand. It was the right moment, as far as I understood it, to stop – If I was going to stop. I took a deep breath.

I didn't have the courage to throw them away. I took the packet into the bedroom and tucked it into the back of the top drawer of my dressing table. It didn't seem somehow quite so irrevocable an act as putting them in the waste bin.

I was asleep when Derek came home at last. I woke when

he tiptoed into the bedroom and then out into the bathroom again and I lay there thinking sleepily, listening to the bath water flowing, watching the wisps of steam curling across the landing in the hall light and disappearing into the dark. Then at last I could lie still no longer. I got up and pulled on my dressing gown.

He looked so tired. I stood and watched him as he cleaned his teeth. Then he stood, stooping forward over the basin, gazing for a long time at his reflection. He looked haggard and my heart went out to him.

'You're working too hard, Derek,' I whispered, hardly realising that I was speaking out loud. 'Poor darling. I wish you would take a few days off and let up for a bit. Shall I get you a hot drink?'

He was still looking in the mirror. As if half asleep he raised his arm and rubbed the steamy reflection with the sleeve of his bathrobe. Our eyes met for a second in the glass. He turned.

'Janet.' He looked so anguished that for a moment I was afraid.

'What is it?'

'Do you have to go away this weekend?'

I jumped. This weekend. The two-day conference I had been looking forward to so much. It had slipped my mind altogether. For a moment I was tempted to let Ronnie go and keep the weekend free for Derek, but I knew that just this once more I had to be there.

'You know I must.'

His shoulders slumped a little and suddenly I desperately wanted to tell him what I had done; about the pills in the dressing-table drawer, but I knew I must keep it a secret. Supposing he had been right when once, not so long ago, he had said I would soon be too old to conceive. Suppose I had been too long on the pill? Supposing tomorrow I panicked and changed my mind?

He sat down suddenly on the edge of the bath looking pitifully defeated and I went to take him in my arms. I could at least promise him that I would allow no more weekends to come between us. Slowly his arms came up and round me, and at his touch I felt relaxed and happy – more so than I had felt for years.

We both began to be happy again after that. Derek seemed a different person and it was weeks and then months since we had had a row. He stopped coming home late, as well. I suppose the urgent order had been finished at last; and now that I no longer, guiltily, saw criticism and sarcasm in his every word we talked happily without the hurtful, loaded comments.

I was content – most of the time. Sometimes I would panic though, as I had known I would. I would sit in my office clutching the edge of my desk, feeling the sweat breaking through the careful make-up on my forehead, unable to bear the thought of giving it all up. Those days I would bring work home, clutching my briefcase like a talisman. Then after a few days the curse would come and I would relax again, perhaps even a little disappointed, knowing that it hadn't happened this time.

Slowly winter passed. I watched the birth of spring, a time I had always loved, with the swelling buds in the garden and the slow emergence of the bulbs and then the glory of the daffodils and narcissi in the orchard. It was a glorious season.

When at last it happened there was no panic and no doubt. I found that I knew quite calmly that this time it was for real. I waited for two months, hugging my secret, then I went to see Dr Forbes.

It was a sunny spring day, glorious with streaming clouds, the milky horse chestnut blossom outside the surgery shower-ing a confetti of white petals on to the pavement as I walked home up the lane. It was hard not to tell Maggie, though I think with her unerring woman's instinct she guessed the second I had said I was taking a few days off work.

'It's a celebration, is it?' she enquired when I began to

prepare the supper that afternoon; all Derek's favourite things.

I nodded, trying to hide my excitement and she didn't ask any more.

He came home early, but the moment he entered the front door I realised that something was very wrong. He had the grey hunted look of the winter again and he went straight to the drinks tray and poured himself a large Scotch before he said hello.

Only then did he smile, acknowledging with a brief widening of the eyes that he liked my new dress.

'What is it, Derek?' I kept my voice carefully neutral as I poured myself a drink.

'Oh sorry, I should have got you one. It's nothing, Janet. A lousy day at the office, that's all.'

I didn't press him. He poured himself another drink and walked over to the fire, kicking the logs, so that the sparks shot up. It was still cold in the evenings and I had lit the fire to make the room more attractive, knowing how much he liked it.

He picked up the poker, the hand holding the glass resting on the mantelpiece and began to draw patterns in the dead white ash round the edge of the fire and I sat down pretending not to watch him, trying to ignore the selfish little lump of disappointment which had firmly lodged in my throat. I had for so many months been consciously and unconsciously preparing for this moment that I had forgotten that Derek knew nothing about it; had had nothing particular to look forward to this evening. It was obvious that he was in no mood for a celebration.

He did his best to hide his mood and his obvious worry. I wanted him to tell me what was wrong, so perhaps I could help him, but I knew better than to ask. I had kept my secret so long I could keep it another day or two.

We ate the celebration meal in a silence broken only by

the quiet record which I put on in an attempt to dispel the tension in the room. He did not seem to notice the choice of his favourite food, or the wine, which he drank fast and desperately. I had no inkling of what was really wrong. Until the next morning.

The post was early. He brought it as usual to the breakfast table, two for me, two for himself. I saw him turn one of the envelopes over and over, puzzled, as though not recognising the hand. I kept my eyes on my plate. He had slept badly, tossing and turning and getting up at least twice in the night and I had hoped that the coming of the morning might persuade him to confide in me. But no.

He picked up his knife and slid it into the envelope. He pulled out a sheet of pale blue paper and read it slowly. I sipped my coffee.

He put the letter back into the envelope without comment and tucked it into the newspaper beside his plate. Then he drank his own coffee and rose, glancing at his watch as usual. 'I must go Janet. Usual time tonight, darling.' He smiled, a strained, absent smile and picked up the newspaper to put it in his briefcase.

The letter fell out of it to the floor unnoticed and I said nothing. Had I, even then, instinctively guessed what was in it?

My Darling Derek, it said in a loopy, so very feminine hand. *I am so sorry that I misunderstood what you wanted. I truly thought it would make you happy. Please forgive me. We have had such a lovely two years together –* Two years! *– and I love you so much. I could not bear it to end like this. I want very badly to keep the baby, but I promise I will make no claim on you now or in the future. Just love us a little, and keep in touch. You will have my love always, Tina.*

I put the letter carefully back into the envelope and only then did I notice that it said *Private* on the top left-hand corner.

It was my own ignorance which hurt most. The fact that I had trusted and believed and been proved naïve. I poured myself another cup of coffee, my hand shaking so much I slopped it on the table cloth. Then as I sipped it I felt a sudden constriction in my stomach. I set down the cup with a crash. I was shivering suddenly and there was no doubt at all, I was going to be sick. And I was already late for my train.

The Inheritance

LOOKING DOWN at her empty cup Jacqueline fixed her attention with determination on the muddy dregs in the bottom; she had made up her mind it would not be right to show any emotion at all when her turn came. Out of the corner of her eye she saw her mother's hand beginning to shake as she opened the letter and the sight unnerved her. The solicitor's letter held no surprises for Mrs Percival of course; she knew exactly what she had inherited. Her hand was probably shaking because the letter had reminded her of her own mother's death and Jacqueline could tell from the strained expression and the two white dimples beneath her cheekbones that her mother was determined not to cry.

'This letter concerns you three.' She looked up at her children and sniffed. Then she smiled wanly. 'I hope you'll be pleased. Great-Grandma has left you all something. Debbie, you and Greg, you each get five thousand pounds.' She glanced at each of the twins in turn. 'That's a lot of money,' she added unnecessarily. 'And you must be careful what you do with it.'

Debbie and Greg stared at her open-mouthed, then Greg let out a whoop of delight. 'I can get that new racing bike at last.' He launched himself from behind his plate of scrambled eggs and planted a kiss on his mother's head. Debbie seemed to have been struck dumb. She sat there with a glazed look on her face and then slowly began to crumble a piece of toast between her fingers onto the table cloth.

Once again Jacqueline began to gaze earnestly into the depths of her coffee cup. She swallowed. She was by a long way the eldest, and had been the acknowledged favourite.

She closed her eyes and breathed deeply as her mother chose that moment to set the letter down amongst the plates and empty cups and sticky knives and blow her nose. Then she glanced up. It came almost as an afterthought. 'Granny has left you her clock, Jackie, of course.'

Jacqueline waited expectantly.

Her father at last emerged from behind the paper. He refolded it noisily and glanced down at his watch. 'Come on, twins; I'll drop you off at school if you're quick. Jackie, you're going to be late for work again.' He stood up, obviously unmoved by the news; perhaps he hadn't heard it at all; dropped an absent-minded kiss on his wife's hair and strode from the room, followed by his two younger children, who were trying with scant success to keep the triumph out of their faces.

Jacqueline sat where she was, her eyes fixed on the letter. Her mother hadn't picked it up again. Her mother was standing up. She had begun to stack the plates.

'Come on, Jackie; get a move on. You heard your father.' She was bustling; efficient; trying to make up for the blown nose.

'Is that all?' Jacqueline's voice came out at last, strangled.

'Is what all, dear? Come on, come on.' Mrs Percival had swept the letter away and thrown it on the dresser.

'The clock. Don't *I* get any money?' She knew it was a dreadful thing to say. Swallowing guiltily she stood up.

As expected her mother turned on her. 'All? All! That clock was your great-grandmother's most treasured possession! She adored that clock!' She burst suddenly into a storm of noisy tears.

'I know.' Jacqueline was anguished. 'I'm sorry; I don't mean to be ungrateful; it's just that I hoped – well, I hoped for some money like the twins. Then I could pay for the modelling course and give up that job with Mr Grenside . . .' Her voice tailed away as she saw her mother's lips tighten into their accustomed thin line.

Mrs Percival groped for her handkerchief once more. 'Oh Jackie, can't you get that ridiculous idea out of your head. Your father and I must have told you a hundred times. You've got a good job with Grenside. It's solid and respectable and it's well-paid. Modelling is so insecure. It's not the glamorous life you think, really it isn't. I wish you wouldn't keep mentioning it.'

Jacqueline knew better than to argue. She turned and disconsolately began to shrug herself into her coat. It wasn't as if she had expected any money in the will at all; none of them had. But in the glorious few minutes between hearing of the twins' bequest and her own she had known real, ecstatic hope. For a moment she toyed with the idea of trying to borrow the money from the twins, then she shrugged it aside. There wouldn't be a chance.

When the clock was at last delivered Jacqueline retired with the brown paper parcel to the privacy of her bedroom and sat down with it on the bed. She remembered the clock clearly. It had always sat in its battered leather case on the chest of drawers in her great-grandmother's bedroom, surrounded by sewing boxes and bags of old stockings and patent medicine bottles. The white face, startlingly clear and precise in the surround of scratched red morocco through which it peered, had seemed to her to be insufferably pompous. 'That's my most treasured possession.' Great-Granny's voice echoed back to her as she began to fumble with the string. 'That clock is a little beauty. It belonged to my grandfather you know, and one day it will belong to you Jacqueline, as you're the eldest.'

Jacqueline patiently coaxed the string from the parcel into a neat coil and dropped it on her bedside table. Of course, ever since she could remember Granny had been saying that. Most of the family things would go to Mum and then probably to Greg, just because he was the boy, but the clock would come to her.

She removed the paper and threw it on the floor and there was the clock, its face as prim as ever, peering from the case. For once it was wrong. Its hands had stopped together at midday – or was it midnight? Gazing at it Jacqueline wondered suddenly if it had stopped the moment Great-Granny died, never-to-go-again.

'It keeps perfect time, that clock. Perfect time.' Her great-grandmother's voice sounded in her ears.

Taped inside the case was an envelope. Inside was a key.

So all it needed was winding.

She smiled at the clock and then child-like, stuck her tongue out at it. 'Supposing I never wind you up again. You wouldn't be so smug then.'

She put it on her own chest of drawers and instantly was reminded of the rather sour old-people smell of her great-grandmother's bedroom. Her own began to take on a different look. All it needed was the thick stockings and the bottles of linctus. Shuddering she picked it up. Immediately the room became itself again.

Eventually she wedged it into a gap between some books on one of her shelves. It held them upright nicely.

She never gave it another thought until she knocked her alarm clock off the bedside table. She shook it hopefully and was rewarded with an ominous rattle; no tick. She dropped it off at the jeweller on her way to work and that evening pulled Great-Granny's clock from its position between Dylan Thomas and Jilly Cooper. She blew off the dust. It wouldn't have an alarm of course, but with a noisy twin on either side of her she didn't really need one.

She pulled the envelope off and took out the key. Surprisingly it was exquisitely chased gilt. Tiny and delicate.

Gingerly she undid the leather case. Inside, the clock nestled down into a velvet lining, its gilt handle folded neatly down on a glass top. Gripping it, she lifted the clock out of its case and sat it on her bedside table beside her lamp.

She looked at it for a long time.

The gilt winked and glittered in the lamplight, untarnished and perfect. All round the sides and corners the clock was decorated with a tiny glittering inlay of coloured enamels, and around the face was a ring of minute diamonds. It was exquisite. Inside, through the glass panels at the top and round the sides, she could see the intricate details of the movement which gleamed like gold. Liberated from its case at long last the white ivory of the face no longer looked prim. It was beautiful.

With a shaking hand Jacqueline fitted the key into one of the two holes at the back and began to wind. The tick was surprisingly loud for such a small clock. She put the key into the other hole, expecting it to move the hands, and the clock chimed; a delicate silvery chime followed by twelve mellow velvet notes.

The clock was alive and she was enchanted.

She kept glancing at it as she changed from her office skirt into her jeans. Then she knelt down beside it and rested her finger lightly on the glass top. It vibrated with energy.

It was a long while before she called the rest of the family.

'In all the years I remember that clock I've never seen it without its case,' her mother exclaimed. 'No wonder your great-grandmother made such a fuss about it.'

'It's lovely, Jackie, you lucky thing.' For the first time Greg seemed to have a moment's regret about his share in the bequest, over which he had not stopped crowing unkindly.

'Are those real diamonds?' Debbie had fallen to her knees before it to get a better view as it stood on the low table. 'Oh Jackie, it's lovely. Why on earth have you left it so long to take it out of its case?'

'That clock must be worth a fortune, Jackie,' her father commented, frowning. 'I suppose we ought to see about getting it insured. Unless you want to sell it, of course?' He glanced at her and winked. 'I reckon that would pay a good bit towards that course you were hankering after.' He grinned.

'Roger!' Mrs Percival turned on him. 'How could you suggest such a thing. Sell grandmother's clock! Of course she wouldn't. I've never heard such nonsense. She must keep it forever.' She sat down heavily on the bed and groped for her handkerchief. 'It's the most beautiful thing I've ever seen.' She sniffed. 'And to think that none of us realised . . .'

The modelling course. Jacqueline looked at the clock and then at her father.

'How can we find out what it's worth?' Her heart was beating with excitement.

'I can take it up to town with me on Wednesday. I should think I could find someone to give me a rough idea.' He leaned forward and picked it up. 'Pretty thing. But better sold, I'd say, if it's worth anything.'

It was worth a great deal. The jeweller to whom he showed it respectfully mentioned Sotheby's or Christie's and padded the clock with several layers of corrugated cardboard before allowing Mr Percival to carry it home. Once there, through tact or natural caution, he said nothing to his wife, waiting for his daughter to come in.

Jacqueline went straight to her room, flinging the curtains shut and turning on the light and gas fire before beginning to unbutton her dress. She was in her dressing gown when her father knocked on the door.

'It's more money than one could ever hope to be handed, Jackie,' he said quietly, after he had told her. They sat side by side on the bed, gazing at the clock, as with a small important series of clicks and whirrs it prepared to strike the hour.

'It's the most beautiful and valuable thing I've ever owned.'

301

Wistfully Jackie pulled her dressing gown closer round her.

'It would buy you that course, Jackie, and leave you a nest egg to put in the bank.' Mr Percival put his arm round her. 'I know how much you've wanted to have a go at modelling, love. I think you deserve the chance. You've got a lovely figure and face. You've got what it takes, I'm sure of it.' He smiled at her fondly.

'Mummy doesn't think so; she's always been dead against it.' She frowned.

'Your mother's a sensible woman. She knows how much hard slog and possible heartache is involved.' He got up and, with his back to the fire, he stood looking down at her. 'She's wanted to save you from disappointment, Jackie, and I agree, up to a point. But,' he sighed. 'There's another way of looking at it. After all, faint heart never won fair lady, and all that.'

Jackie smiled at him fondly. 'You think I should have a go?'

'I think you'll wonder for the rest of your life if you could have been a cover girl if you don't. Better know, one way or the other.'

Jacqueline stared at the clock. There was a strange lump in her throat. 'The awful thing is,' she said suddenly, 'I can't bear the idea of selling it.'

'No. It's a beautiful thing, certainly.'

'I collected my alarm clock today.' She dived into her bag and brought out a box. She stood the clock up beside her bed. 'It works now; it's accurate. It only cost a couple of pounds to mend. It has an alarm. It's really much more useful in every way . . .'

Mr Percival smiled. 'But it doesn't have a pretty chime and glitter with diamonds, eh?'

'Oh Daddy, I don't know what to do. If I sell the clock I'll have the money, yes. But supposing I am a lousy model? It would be such a waste. I could never buy another clock like that.'

Mr Percival rubbed his chin thoughtfully.

'As I see it there's no easy way to decide, love. I know what I'd do. I'd sell. I know what your mother would do. She'd keep it for sentimental reasons. And she'd keep it even if she were half starving.' He shook his head slowly. 'But there's no real hurry, is there? If I were you I'd think about it for a while.'

Jacqueline sat on the bed gazing at the clock for a long time after he had gone downstairs.

For half an hour she thought, listening as twice the clock chimed the quarters; then slowly she reached under her pillow for the magazine. It was folded back as always at the modelling school's advertisement. *For further particulars, write to. . .*

There was no harm in writing. After all, it didn't commit her to anything, did it? Carefully she filled in her name and address. Then, hungry, she turned out the light and went downstairs.

Dance Little Lady

THE YACHT was in the bay again, anchored off the point, as I had hoped she might be. For a moment I forgot the need to hurry as I stood at the tall bay window of my bedroom and stared at it, hugging my dressing gown around me. The breeze off the sea touched my skin and I shivered. I was thinking about the evening to come.

'Only a few people this weekend, darling,' Sylvia had said anxiously as she met me off the train. 'It won't be too tiring.'

It is strange how solicitous some people are when they know you are recovering from a broken love affair; as if you had been ill. Except that I was the one who had broken it off, because for me it had never really existed. I was grateful, though, for her gentleness. I liked the woman my father lived with, even though I hated my father. It was because of her I still came home. Her, and the money my father paid for my London flat.

I turned reluctantly from the window. My hopes of a quiet weekend, swimming and sailing on my own while I thought things out, were gone. Instead the weekend had to be endured. But somehow the presence of the yacht, out there on the water, comforted me. I had seen her there several times that summer, always with the same man on board. I had surreptitiously studied him through binoculars. He was tall, fair and tanned. The opposite of Ben.

Dear Ben. I was still fond of him in spite of all the things he had called me. Perhaps he was right; perhaps I was immature and frigid; perhaps I did live in a dream world – my fantasy about the skipper of that white yacht rather proved that – but was it so very terrible to reject the cynicism and world weariness that people like Ben, and my father, wore round them like a cloak? I was sure the man out on that yacht was different; an independent spirit.

My father's guests were assembled in the drawing room when I went down. The only car I had recognised when Sylvia brought me home had been my brother David's Alfa and I saw him now with two other men by the open French windows. Sylvia was by the sideboard; with her was David's wife, Betinne. My heart sank. I loathed my sister-in-law.

She looked me up and down as I accepted a glass of champagne from Sylvia. 'I hear Ben ditched you, Anna,' she said. 'I can't say I'm surprised.' She sipped her own drink. 'Don must be relieved though, if it means you can dance attendance on his guests.' She managed to make her words sound suggestive.

I saw Sylvia frown, but I didn't want her to defend me. I hastily turned to look round the room. 'Where is Father? I haven't seen him yet.'

'Don is next door. With Parker Forbes,' Sylvia said quietly.

'*The* Parker Forbes,' Betinne emphasised. She was still watching me with a rather strange look in her eye.

Parker Forbes; the multi-millionaire; owner of half the West End of London. My father had been trying to pin him down to a deal for ages and his name had been the most frequent topic of conversation at weekends for months.

Sylvia was eyeing me anxiously. 'I think you'll like him, Anna. He's very attractive. And he likes music.'

Suddenly I understood. The urgent invitation home; the sudden concern over my welfare; the interest in my break-up with Ben. And I had thought Sylvia was on my side!

Once before my father had done this; he had invited a

colleague home and then proceeded to throw me at him for the entire weekend. I had been younger then, and more naïve. The man had taken pity on me; laughed at my gaucheness, and signed anyway. But I had a feeling Parker Forbes was different. His reputation had percolated through even to my particular corner of the College of Music.

I turned away without a word, conscious of their eyes following me as, sickened, I crossed the room towards David. I should have walked away then, but I knew my brother would cushion my shyness as he always did and sure enough he reached out and pulled me close for a hug. 'Anna, how's the college? I don't see enough of you these days,' and he introduced me to his two companions.

David was the only person in that house who knew me as I really was; who knew me in London, in my own world, away from father's wealth and the shallow pleasure-seeking life he led. In London I had my own career with music. Ben had almost bridged those two worlds but something had gone wrong. I eyed the two men standing with us. They were typical of father's colleagues; wealthy, brash, hard-drinking, laughing a little too much – and I sighed. The whole weekend to be got through.

I did not meet the other guests until dinner. Melanie Whittacker, the wife of one of David's companions, was a strangely mousey woman; quiet, cowed I suspected by her boorish husband. I was immediately sorry for her. With her were two other women: Naomi who I gathered was a model and Jane Peters. The final two guests were Robin Hamilton, the journalist – and Parker Forbes.

Robin sat opposite me. He was a tall, attractive man, tanned, fit, charming – the kind of man who makes every woman instantly aware of him, and knows it. Betinne was hanging on his every word as he regaled her and Melanie Whittacker with a stream of scandalous gossip, but I got the feeling that he did not reciprocate her enthusiasm. Once, looking up, he caught my eye over the glow of the candles and I was almost sure he winked. I felt a quick thrill of pleasure and was instantly furious with myself.

I had no chance to think about it, though, as my attention was once more drawn back to my father and Parker Forbes.

'You must get Anna to take you out onto the terrace later, Parker,' my father was saying for the second time. 'Let her show you our Sussex moon . . .'

I couldn't believe that he could be so blatant! I glanced desperately round for David, but he was talking at the other end of the table. There was nothing I could do except smile and nod and pretend that I agreed.

And I was still pretending half an hour later when Parker edged me towards the French windows and we stepped out with our coffee cups in our hands, into the velvet night. It was heavenly to get away from the hot cigar smoke and fumes of the wine. The sea air was balmy, softened with honeysuckle and the sweetness of new-mown hay.

He wasted no time. 'I had no idea that Don had such a beautiful home,' he murmured. We had paused at the edge of the terrace looking down across the lawn towards the sea which I could hear sighing gently against the rocks. 'And such charming ladies too. How long has he known Sylvia?'

'A couple of years,' I replied. Sylvia was the latest, and by far the nicest, of the succession of girlfriends my father had lived with since my mother had left him ten years before. Ma now lived with a horse breeder in Argentina. I never blamed her for going. My father had always been a ruthless, selfish bastard. I only wished I had had the strength of character and the courage to turn my back on him as well.

Parker and I began to walk again, slowly this time, towards the summer house which Sylvia had had perched on the top of the low cliff. I could feel the dew beginning to soak through my thin sandals and dragging at the hem of my skirt. Somewhere near a gull called in the night.

'Do you like her?' he asked curiously. He still hadn't looked at me.

'Very much,' I answered.

'I imagine she takes a lot of work off your hands. Don told me you used to act as his hostess.'

I laughed uneasily. 'I was never very good at it I'm afraid.'

'I can't believe that.' His voice was caressing. 'In fact, had I know what a welcome his house would have for me I would have been doing business with Don months ago.'

He turned to look at me, a long appraising glance which swept slowly up and down me leaving me feeling naked and self-conscious, then he took the cup out of my hand and put it down on the step of the summer house with his own. He was much taller than I, and powerfully built, and as his hands came down on my shoulders pulling me towards him I felt a surge of real fear.

'Mind if I join you?' As the cool, deep voice from the darkness interrupted us Parker released me abruptly and turned, his face set and angry. The journalist Robin Hamilton strolled towards us, the glowing butt of a cigar in his hand. He stopped, and stood looking at the view about three feet from me. 'You must not catch cold, Anna,' he said quietly. 'That dress is soaking, dragging in the dew.'

'You're right.' I could have kissed him from sheer relief. 'Excuse me, Parker, but I think I will go in.'

I didn't wait to see Parker's face. I flew towards the lights of the house.

My father cornered me ten minutes later. His handsome face was harsh.

'Anna? I thought you were looking after Parker?'

I liked the looking after bit! 'I was. I came in.' I faced him. 'I'm not going to let him make passes at me, Don, just to make him more amenable to your schemes. The man is detestable!'

My father's face darkened visibly. 'And you don't like it? What the hell are you, Anna, a twelve-year-old virgin? For God's sake grow up. Do you realise what Parker's signature on that agreement means to me?' We were standing in the

308

corner of the dining room where I had been finding myself some more coffee and we were alone, but with a glance over his shoulder towards the open door into the hall, he dropped his voice to an ugly whisper.

'You be nice to Parker, Anna. You hear me? Everyone in this house pulls their weight and if they don't they're out, understand?' He stared at me for a full twenty seconds then he swung on his heel and left me alone in the room.

Mechanically I finished filling my cup and carried it over to the window seat. But the drink stayed untouched as I gazed at the coloured reflections in the glass.

The sound of the door closing behind me made me turn. It was Betinne. 'I saw Don leave you,' she said softly. 'He looked livid. What did he say?'

'Is that your business?' I snapped.

Her face was flushed and had a predatory excitement about it. 'It is if it involves Parker.' She stepped nearer. 'He wants to sleep with you doesn't he? He couldn't keep his eyes off you at dinner. I was watching. Doesn't Don like the idea?'

'You know very well what Don wants,' I retorted.

Betinne came and stood very close to me. 'And little miss pure pants doesn't like the idea?' she breathed scornfully.

'Would you?' I blazed at her and then suddenly I saw. The wide grey eyes, the large deep pupils gazing at me, the naked hunger in them. 'You would, wouldn't you?' I answered my own question quietly. 'You would sleep with him.'

'Sleep with him,' she echoed sarcastically. 'Of course I'd sleep with him; I'd do anything he wanted. Have you any idea how much money that man has? How much power?'

We stared at each other for a moment. I felt sick.

'Poor David,' I said at last.

'Leave David out of this!' she hissed viciously.

'Well you obviously have,' I retorted. 'Look Betinne. If you want Parker Forbes then you have him. Don will no doubt be delighted as long as some woman in this family nets him. But count me out. Please!'

I pushed past her, my cheeks flaming with heat, and let myself into the hall just as Robin Hamilton came back from the garden. I saw him look at me swiftly then glance over my shoulder into the dining room. Then he grinned. 'Hi. I hope you didn't mind me interrupting you out there.'

'You saved my life,' I said with rather more vehemence than I meant. 'That is –'

'I understand,' he said, laughing quietly. 'You needn't explain.' He hesitated. 'Your sister-in-law looked pretty heated in there.'

'She was.' I had no intention of telling Robin Hamilton, or anyone else for that matter, what I had quarrelled with Betinne about, but his presence soothed me as we went into the drawing room where the Whittackers were seated with my father and David. The four of them were laughing. My father looked up and I saw his glance harden as it swept over us. Then he stared out towards the terrace. Following his look I saw Sylvia out there with Parker. As I watched Betinne joined them.

The next day dawned hot and beautiful. After breakfast most of the house party collected towels and broad-brimmed hats and beach bags and headed for the rustic flight of steps which led down the cliff to our private beach. To my intense irritation Parker sat down beside me. He grinned.

'Pity we were interrupted last night, Anna. I was going to suggest a midnight bathe perhaps; an assignation under the stars? I tried your door later. Why do you lock it?' He was speaking in a low confidential voice but I could see Robin watching me, a quizzical expression on his face.

'Because I need my beauty sleep,' I managed to retort with a smile. I could feel my skin crawling as he leaned towards me and put his hand on my ankle, stroking it gently. His palm was damp.

I moved away a little and it was then that my father's shadow fell across us. 'I hope my daughter is entertaining you, Parker,' he said softly. 'We aim to keep our guests happy, don't we Anna?'

I looked up and at that moment I felt real loathing for my father but I was still so conditioned by my upbringing, by what we are taught are good manners, that I merely smiled stiffly. 'Of course,' I said. I wriggled out of Parker's reach and jumped to my feet. 'We aim to please always, don't we Don?' I ran towards the water. 'Come on Parker. Let's swim!'

The water was ice cold. Parker did not move. It was Robin who followed me, pacing me easily as I made for the raft which was anchored about fifty yards off the beach. He grabbed it as I pulled myself up onto it, and looked up at me.

'He can't get you here, eh?' He shook the water out of his eyes, laughing. We both glanced towards the beach where Betinne, oiled and sleek, had taken my place on the rug beside Parker.

'My father –' I stopped abruptly, biting off the words. I had been about to confide in him; about to tell him what my father was doing, but something stopped me. Robin was a journalist after all. And who could resist the kind of headline my story could generate?

Robin grinned. 'Stand up for yourself, kiddo,' he said quietly. 'You're a free agent, remember?'

He gave me a long searching look, then he dived and was swimming back towards the beach. Robin Hamilton, I thought, knows exactly what is going on. And I had a feeling he was on my side. I watched him reach the shore and wade out of the water to grab a towel. He was extremely handsome as well as being nice and I found myself wishing suddenly that he was the one my father wanted me to seduce! The thought made me smile to myself. If Ben knew what had crossed my mind he would not have believed it. Physically Ben and I had not been a success; perhaps that was because any man to whom my father introduced me was suspect.

Beyond Robin, I saw Betinne roll over onto her stomach

and reach behind her to unhook her bikini top, cushioning her heavy breasts in the sand. It would only be a matter of minutes before Parker would be asked to oil her back. I almost envied her her casual sensuality. But Ben was right after all. I did not seem to know how to let myself go. Or was it that I had not yet met the right man? Almost unconsciously I found my eyes searching once more for Robin, then with a sigh I shifted round so that I could lie and watch the sea. The yacht was still there, her dinghy lying astern. I could see two brightly coloured towels fluttering from the rigging. If I was really a free agent, I thought ruefully, I would have been out there in my own little sailing dinghy thumbing a lift out of Don's world forever. But I didn't have the courage, then.

The heat was building. We ate a cold luncheon in the shade of the cedars on the lawn and then the guests drifted off towards their rooms for a siesta. I followed suit.

My bedroom was shaded by the soft pink curtains and I slipped out of my sundress to lie naked on the cool sheets thankful to be out of that blazing sun. Two seconds later I got up. I had forgotten to lock the door. I ran across the carpet and reached to turn the key, but it had gone. Puzzled I searched for it on the carpet, thinking it had fallen out, then I opened the door and groped for it on the outside. It wasn't there either.

As I stood there, not wanting to believe the suspicion which had flashed through my mind, I heard another door open in the corridor.

I grabbed my bathrobe off the chair and was knotting it around me as my door began to move.

Parker was wearing a navy and maroon striped silk dressing gown and a great deal of cologne, and, I was fairly sure, not much else. He came in and closed the door behind him, then triumphantly he felt in his pocket and produced the key. Locking the door he turned to me and grinned.

'Don said he hoped we'd get to know each other better

this afternoon,' he said softly. 'What do you say we give it a try?'

There was no fear or revulsion in me this time. As he walked towards me and put his hands on my shoulders as he had done before I felt nothing but white hot anger. His strength was enormous as he pushed me back against the wall but he wasn't expecting me to give more than a token resistance. As his mouth closed over mine I brought my knee up into his groin with all the force I could muster, my fingers clawing for his eyes. Then I dived for the door, fumbling desperately with the key.

Behind me he was doubled up, groaning. He made no attempt to follow me as I fled down the hall, but instinctively I made for the attics where I used to hide as a child, knowing that no one would find me in that network of old interconnecting lofts.

I stayed there a long time. It was hot under the roof and smelled of wood and dust and it was completely safe, but I knew I would have to come down eventually, if only to catch the last train back to London. There was no way I was going to spend another night in my father's house. Ever!

It was only the sound of the gong in the distance which made me realise how late it really was. Cautiously I went down at last. The house was deathly quiet; when I peered into my room it was deserted and the key was still in the door. Thankfully I went in and locked it, then I had a slower and lay down on my bed, trying to think.

It was Sylvia who came. 'Anna?' She knocked gently. 'Anna? Are you there?'

I got up and let her in. 'I'm not coming down,' I said defiantly. 'I have a terrible headache.'

I could see her eyes on me and there was real concern in her face. I wondered if Parker had said anything. On the whole I suspected not. It would not do his image much good if it became known that one of his victims had fought back. And won.

'Anna dear.' She sat down on the bed. 'I'm sorry. I know what you must be thinking; your father is a little insensitive at times.' She was looking lovely in a silvery evening dress which showed her tan. 'Please come down.'

'I really do have a headache,' I said. 'The weather is so thundery. I'll be all right in the morning.' I refused to meet her eye.

She sighed and stood up. 'I'll ask them to bring something up for you, shall I?'

When she had gone I relocked the door and went to stand by the window. There was no breath of air and, I realised suddenly, it was true: my head was splitting but I was still determined to go. I would drive myself to the station in my old Mini. I left it at the house during the week as it seemed pointless to keep it in London, but it would then get me to the train. And it would give me time to lie down for an hour, to let my head clear.

I was about to go back to bed when there was a furious knocking. It was my father. 'Anna, open this door at once!'

I obeyed him, waiting defiantly as he strode into the room. 'What the hell have you done?' he shouted. 'Parker is threatening to leave the house!'

'I warned you, Don.' For the first time in my life I wasn't afraid of him. I saw him for what he was, a ranting, bullying, weak man, terrified of failure. 'If Parker wanted your deal nothing would stop him signing,' I said, and I realised it was true. 'If he's looking for an excuse to back out it is because he has no faith in you, not because I refused to sleep with him.'

My father's face was puce.

'If you are determined that one of your family should prostitute herself for you then ask Betinne. She's more than willing,' I went on. 'I'm going back to London tonight.'

My father controlled himself with an effort. 'You are not. You are going to apologise to Parker. I don't know what happened between you but my God Anna you are going to apologise.'

His gaze swept across my dressing table where my handbag stood open. He dived for it, rifling through the contents. 'You needn't think you're going to creep out of this house. You're staying here until I tell you to go.'

Speechless, I watched him stride from the room and slam the door behind him. For one incredulous moment I thought he was going to lock me in, but I heard his steps move off down the hall. I ran to my bag and stared into it. He had taken my money, my return ticket and my car keys.

I sat down on the bed. My legs were shaking, and I was more angry, I think, than I have ever been in my life. I was more or less a prisoner.

I suppose I slept at last from sheer exhaustion, but when I next opened my eyes my headache had gone and the room was growing dark, and I could hear the sound of voices and laughter outside my window. I got up and went to look out. The dinner guests were all out on the terrace below me with their drinks. I counted them slowly. No one was missing; Betinne was talking to Parker in the corner by the wisteria. I saw the gleam of gold around her throat as she laughed up at him. Nearby I could see my father. He was watching them intently.

The yacht lay quite still on a sea which looked like oiled silk. The dinghy was gone. He must have come ashore, probably to the pub on the quay in the village a mile down the coast. I could see the reflection of the boat wavering gently below her. Beyond her, the arms of the bay had become indistinct in the darkening haze. Great black clouds were building in the distance and I heard a faint rumble of thunder as I turned from the window. I had awakened knowing exactly what I meant to do.

I slipped some jeans and a T-shirt on and pulled on some rope-soled espadrilles, then I let myself out into the empty corridor. If my father thought to keep me in his house till Parker came for me that night he was mistaken. I had other ideas. The kitchens were deserted; the staff had tidied up and retired as usual as soon as they had finished clearing away dinner so I was able to let myself out into the yard unnoticed. My old bicycle was still there – the tyres didn't even need pumping.

It took me ten minutes to reach the quay. I leaned the bike against the wall and peered down into the water. It was moving gently in a subdued swell as in the distance I heard another faint rumble of thunder.

I walked down to the end of the jetty where several small dinghies were tied, and carefully lowering myself into one of them, undid the painter and felt for the oars. I was awkward with them at first, out of practice and, I must confess, a little panicky when I saw the door of the pub open and the light flood out over the water as three figures walked down to the edge of the quay. I was expecting to hear angry shouts at any moment, but none came. I settled down to a steady pull, glancing over my shoulder to make sure I was heading in the right direction as I felt the drag of the tide. I think I was a little mad, that night; I would never dare to do such a thing again. But at that moment I felt no fear, only excitement and a sense of incredible freedom. The fear only came when it was too late to do anything about it.

My hands were blistered before I was half-way there, but I gritted my teeth against the pain and went on. I think if I had stopped for a rest my nerve would have failed, but always out of the corner of my eye I could see the blaze of lights on the cliff which was my father's home. The sight of it spurred me on.

There was a ladder over the side. I grabbed it, shaking with exhaustion, and pulled myself up onto the deck. Behind me, the dinghy tossed like a cork without my weight to steady it, bumped its way down the white side of the yacht, and then disappeared into the darkness. I watched it go with an almost detached relief. Now I could not go back if I wanted to; I was marooned.

I turned and made my way down into the cockpit. The main hatch had been left half open and I peered down into the darkened cabin, cursing myself for not thinking of bringing a torch. I knew he had light – I had seen it flooding from the portholes in the dark, but I didn't want to draw attention to myself too soon. I stepped down into the companionway and held my breath, listening, wondering for the first time what I would do if he had left someone on board, but the boat was silent. Uncannily silent save for the occasional gurgle and slap of water down her sides and once more an ominous growl of thunder in the west.

I reached out, feeling my way forward, and my hand found a rack just inside the hatchway; amongst the charts was a large rubber-cased torch. I switched it on and the beam of light flooded the cabin.

She was a beautiful yacht, fitted out to sleep five, with two main cabins, a shower cubicle, a galley and a forward sail locker which was large enough for the fifth bunk. The whole boat was immaculately tidy, everything stowed neatly into place, a chart already fixed to the chart table. Above me a halyard had begun to tap against the mast and I felt the floor beneath me move a little as a wave slide beneath the hull. The wind was rising.

I went out into the cockpit and, switching off the torch, looked around. The sky was black now – black with cloud that blotted out the moon and stars, leaving only the riding light at the masthead showing as the boat began to turn and tug at her anchor. I strained my eyes in the direction of the shore and then I saw it – the outline of his dinghy already half-way out towards the boat, the white dip of the oars showing against the black water.

My heart gave a sudden little kick of fright and I turned to go back into the cabin. My nerve had failed at last and I found myself desperately looking round for somewhere to hide. It wasn't a logical decision; the sensible thing would have been to show myself at once, and if he was angry ask him to put me ashore, but I was no longer thinking logically. The anger which had sent me flying from Don's house, the thundery air pressing down on the boat, my aching head and bleeding hands and the image of Parker, his aroused body naked beneath his dressing gown as he pushed me against the wall, all combined to reduce me to a frightened animal and like a frightened animal I looked for a dark corner to hide in. The quarter berth was the obvious place – the berth opposite the chart table which was half settee but which slotted down under the cockpit, so the sleeper could insert his legs to obtain a full-length bed. I wriggled down into that space now, relieved to find it quite roomy, and pulled the two berth cushions behind me, blocking me from sight. Unless he actually moved those cushions I could not be seen. It was an uncomfortable position. I could not sit up nor stretch out, I had to lie curled up in the darkness, listening to the beating of my heart above the slap of the water on the other side of the thin planking by my ear.

There was a slight lurch as the dinghy came alongside and I heard the thud of rubber soles almost immediately above my head. Minutes later the cabin was flooded with light; the cushions were not after all big enough to block me in entirely and I shrank back, praying he would not notice that they had been moved.

'Check everything's stowed and put out those lights as soon as you can. I want to save the battery.' His voice was so close I thought for a moment he must know I was there and be talking to me. I held my breath. He spoke with a distinct public school accent, but the voice was already moving as his footsteps ran over the deck. Someone else was in the cabin near me. I bit my lip, not daring to move, wondering who was with him. I had never seen anyone on the yacht besides him.

A female voice, husky, attractive and American, called out, 'Pete? Surely we can wait till morning. That guy in the pub said there was a gale warning, and I sure as hell don't like the sound of that thunder.'

The footsteps approached once more. 'Not afraid are you, Sam?' His tone, from the cockpit now, was mocking. 'I thought you told me you were prepared to risk everything to get your hands on that much dope. You shouldn't have got involved if you couldn't take the pace. The pick-up is arranged. And I'm going to make it. If you want out, you can swim for it.' His tone made the hairs stand up on the back of my neck.

The girl swore softly. 'Okay, okay. I guess you know what you're doing.'

Minutes later the lights went out and I heard the hatchway close. I was trapped and very afraid. Independent spirit this man might be; there was no doubt he was also potentially very dangerous and I cursed myself miserably. But there was no way of escape.

My hiding place was growing uncomfortably hot; I eased my position slightly and moved one of the cushions to give me some air; then I heard the roar and clap of loosened canvas overhead as the main sail was hauled up. Minutes later the thundering stopped as the sails filled, the yacht listed sideways and from my point of view downwards, and we were obviously on course out of the bay. She hit a heavy swell as soon as we were clear of the headland and the noise of the sea became deafening. In despair I cradled my head as best I could in the crook of my elbow and closed my eyes, trying hard to concentrate on anything other than what was happening to me. A long time later I heard the hatchway being slid back and the lights came on in the cabin. Above my head I could hear the drumming of rain on the decks.

'Coffee or soup?' I heard the woman's voice call. I did not catch the response, only the roar of the wind and waves, and suddenly very loud above them the crash of thunder.

The boat seemed to be slamming hard into wind and I could see the woman now as she made her way up the cabin towards the galley, clinging on to every handhold she could find. She was wearing dripping yellow oilskins, but her head was bare – her hair was long and blonde. She slid back the galley door and wedged herself in the corner whilst she fumbled with matches and locked a kettle into place on the gimballed cooker. The roar and smell of the bottled gas flame and the lights in the cabin were strangely comforting against that terrible background noise of the elements. I studied her face from my hiding place, trying to pluck up the courage to come out and throw myself on her mercy. She looked as though she was in her mid-twenties, although her face was strained and drawn and there were dark circles beneath her eyes. She did not look particularly sympathetic. On the whole I was not hopeful.

She stayed with the kettle until it boiled, then she made two mugs of coffee.

'Pete?' she yelled. 'Come and have it down here!'

There was no response. With a sigh she drank one of the mags, pulled up the hood of her oilskin and came back towards the hatchway. 'Come on Pete, I'll take a turn while you have a break,' she called, and she vanished out of my line of vision.

I held my breath as another figure appeared. He too was dressed in dripping oilskins, but he peeled his off, leaving them lying on the cabin floor. Dressed in a sweater and jeans he was, as I had seen through my binoculars, tall, rugged, fairly good-looking with, I now saw, sun-bleached hair and piercing blue eyes; his face like hers was hard and he had a deep frown on his brow. He pulled his way up to the galley just as the woman had done and collected his mug, then to my terror he came back and sat on the quarter berth only about eighteen inches from my head. He only had to glance my way – I froze, holding my breath as he sipped from the mug and then leaned forward gazing intently at something ahead of him. The chart table of course.

He worked for some time, making careful measurements and calculations, then at last he threw down his pencil, and leaned back. With a grunt of surprise he felt around behind him for the cushions which should have been there, then he turned and looked straight at me.

For a moment I don't think he believed what he saw; then I saw his face darken with anger.

'Who in the name of God's own Hell are you?' he whispered. He didn't give me a chance to extricate myself from my hiding place with any dignity. He lunged forward and grabbed my arm, pulling me headlong onto the floor of the cabin where I lay for a moment at his feet, too winded and too stiff to move.

'Well? I asked you a question!' he yelled at me again.

'I'm sorry,' I heard myself stammer. 'I'm so sorry. I did it for a joke.'

'A joke!' His voice rose in anger.

Shaking with fear and embarrassment I tried to pull myself up but the narrow space and the motion of the boat made it almost impossible, and I found myself kneeling at his feet clutching at the chart table to steady myself.

'I really am sorry,' I said again, trying to control my voice as I heard it waver like a child's. 'I thought I would stow away for fun; you have so often anchored off the beach near our house. I didn't mean any harm.' There was a brilliant flash of lightning from outside, filling the cabin, dimming the light for a moment, then a clap of thunder immediately overhead. I felt myself flinch but he did not move. There was no softening in his face, no sign of humour.

Behind him the hatch slid back and the girl's head appeared, dripping with rain. 'Did you say something, Pete? Christ this storm is bad! I wish you'd come up –' she broke off in astonishment as she suddenly noticed me.

'It seems we have a stowaway,' he said.

She went on staring for a moment, then she pushed the hatch right back and climbed in, to sit dripping on the companionway steps.

Pete too had not taken his eyes off me, but he swore at her sharply. 'You're supposed to be on watch, Sam,' he said.

'There's nothing on the radar,' she retorted. 'Nobody is such a bloody fool as to be out on a night like this; we're out of the shipping lanes and there's no point in having self-steering gear if you don't use it. Who is she?'

He raised an eyebrow. 'Who indeed.'

I swallowed, trying to regain a little of my composure, but it was difficult kneeling there between them on the hard lurching floor. 'My name is Anna Marshall,' I began. And I went on to try and explain.

They both listened frostily as I explained how I had taken the dinghy and hidden while they were in the pub. When I had finished there was a moment's silence broken only by another roar of thunder from above.

'What are you going to do with her?' Sam asked at last. She said it quietly but her tone sent a shiver up my spine.

Pete was watching me closely. 'I'm sure you are intelligent enough to realise, Miss Marshall,' he said, 'why stowaways are not welcomed on this boat.'

I had heard enough to know that. My eyes were fixed on his face, but I shrugged. Then I glanced at Sam, and I saw something – excitement – flickering behind her eyes. 'She's scared Pete. Scared as shit!'

'So she should be, we don't take passengers.' He moved forward slightly onto the edge of the bunk and I felt myself shrink back in terror, but he was craning to look out of the half open hatchway. Abruptly he reached down for the oilskins. 'The wind's veered. I'll have to go up. Watch her, Sam.'

He stepped over me and vanished up the companionway, pulling the hatch closed after him.

The girl was watching me half fascinated, half, I was sure, afraid herself, now that Pete had gone. I took my chance and pulled myself up onto the bunk where he had been sitting. I felt less at a disadvantage off my knees. I gave a feeble smile. 'You couldn't spare some of that coffee you were making, could you?'

She stared at me a moment longer and I thought she was

going to refuse but she stood up and groped her way to the galley. A second later she was back with a mugful. She handed it to me without speaking and I drank it gratefully. It was only just warm and very bitter but it comforted me a little.

'Thanks,' I said.

She was still watching me in silence when Pete reappeared some minutes later.

Sam turned to him. 'You can't throw her overboard, Pete. That would be murder.'

'And aren't you prepared to murder, sweetheart, for a million pounds?' he asked her sarcastically.

I saw her lips tighten till the flesh round her mouth drained of colour but she shook her head. 'Not murder, Pete.'

He looked at me for a moment – he had not taken off his waterproofs this time – then he stooped and caught my elbow, pulling me to my feet. I cried out with fear, but instead of dragging me up on deck he pushed me in front of him towards the bows of the boat. 'You'll have to forgive us if we deprive ourselves of your company Miss Marshall,' he said with meticulous politeness. 'Until I decide what to do with you. It's a wild night as you cannot have failed to notice and I need Sam to help me sail this tub.'

He pushed me into the forward sail locker and pulled the door shut behind me, leaving me alone in the dark. I had already seen there was a padlock on the outside of the door; I did not need to hear the click to know he had locked me in.

The spare berth was furnished with a plastic-covered foam mattress; apart from the neatly stacked sailbags which more than half filled the small space, it was empty. There were no portholes.

I sat down hugging my arms around me to try and keep warm as the tears began to slip down my cheeks.

Later I wrapped myself in one of the sails; the cold crackly Terylene was little comfort but it was better than nothing and I must have dozed a little for I awoke to find the motion had lessened. I could hear feet above my head. I peered up half expecting the forehatch to open but it didn't. Instead I heard a deafening roar as the anchor chain began to run.

We had been rocking gently for some time when the sound of an outboard engine came to my ears. It drew close, hovered for a while then drew away again. Then at last the lock rattled and the door was pulled open. The light which streamed in was blinding after the darkness.

'Good morning Miss Marshall. I trust you slept well.' Pete reached in and took my arm.

This time we were going on deck. He propelled me up the companionway into the cockpit and, dazed, I glanced round. Sam was standing at the wheel. The oilskins were gone; she was dressed in shorts and a striped T-shirt, her blonde hair blowing in the sun. She grinned at me.

'I hope you can swim,' she said.

I tried to struggle but his arms were round me, lifting me over the rail, and there was nothing I could do to save myself. No time to think. I heard myself scream and then the icy water closed over my head.

I fought it madly, choking desperately until at last in a haze of bubbles I rose back into the air and only then did I realise that I was less than a hundred yards from the shore. As I began to swim I glanced over my shoulder at the yacht. Her sails set, she was already drawing away on a starboard tack. Only Sam turned to see if I had surfaced. The yacht, I noticed suddenly, had no name.

I lay on the beach until my clothes dried on me and I stopped shaking, then half faint with exhaustion and hunger I made my way up over the sand towards the dunes. My head throbbed but I was so grateful to be back on land and in one piece I could ignore it. I slipped and staggered as I walked but there at last was a road and in the distance I thought I could see a house.

I was still staring at the road sign incredulously when a lorry drew up beside me with a squeal and hiss of brakes. The driver leaned down from his cab and grinned. '*Salut!*' he said.

I stared at him. The first thing that came into my head was a sob of disbelief. 'This isn't France!' I said.

I saw the easy smile vanish off his face. He looked at me hard for a moment, taking in my crumpled, salt-stained clothes and tangled hair, then the huge panting engine was silenced and he opened his door, jumping down beside me. He was a tall man, in his forties, broadly built, with brawny arms and his face as he looked down into mine was gentle and concerned. 'You are English, yes? What do you mean this is not *La France*?' His accent was heavy.

I shook my head trying to blink back my tears; he would never believe me. No one would ever believe me.

But he did. Two minutes' gentle probing revealed to him that I had no money, no papers and had not eaten for nearly twenty-four hours. The last news seemed to cheer him slightly. It was something he could put right.

That French *routier* restored my faith in men. The vast lorry stowed safely off the road, he escorted me into a small restaurant in the next village and proceeded to order what seemed to me to be a feast.

'There. Better. Yes?' He said at last. We had not spoken while the soup was on the table. It was scalding, full of onions and cheese and quite beautiful.

'Much better.' I managed a quite presentable smile. I had borrowed his comb and washed the salt off my face. 'I don't know what I should have done if you hadn't arrived.'

He leaned forward and put his brawny arms on the table, pushing the plates aside. 'Now, when we are finished you will telephone home, yes?' He poured me some more of the *ordinaire* wine.

'But I was running away from home,' I protested. 'If I ring – '

He interrupted with a very Gallic shrug. '*Bien sûr*. But to run away without money; without passport; that was not well planned, eh?'

The *patron* took away our soup plates and replaced them with succulent helpings of fish dressed in a rich sauce.

I sighed. 'You are right. I will have to ring my father,' I said. It seemed a terrible thing, after my terrifying bid for freedom, to have to admit defeat.

'This father he is a tyrant, yes?' Jean-Pierre was watching me. I could see a flicker of amusement in his eyes. 'This I do not understand. I thought English girls were, how you say, liberate.'

'Liberated.' I smiled back. 'They are, most of them.'

'*Bon*. Then perhaps you can phone someone else. Your boyfriend?' He tore a piece of bread from the baguette which lay between us on the red and white chequered cloth and began to chew it thoughtfully.

Boyfriend. Ben? What would Ben say if I rang him and told him that I was marooned in France without money or passport, wining and dining with a lorry driver after being thrown overboard by drug smugglers? The only thing missing was the shark-infested sea!

I saw him grin. 'You have thought of something funny yes? That is good. You are not unhappy any more. Things are never so bad as they would seem, yes?'

'Yes,' I agreed. Suddenly I knew what I was going to do. 'I have thought of someone,' I said.

We had a *café filtré*, then at last we commandeered the *patron*'s telephone and made the call. I don't know who answered but when Jean-Pierre went back to our table he had summoned Robin Hamilton to the phone.

'Robin? It's Anna. Listen I'm in France.'

'I thought you were in bed with a headache!' I could hear the amusement in his voice over the phone. 'Did you do a bunk?'

'Sort of. I'll explain later. Robin, can you come and get me? Can you bring my passport and some money?'

'Where will I find them?'

'You mean you will?' I was incredulous for a moment.

'The party is appalling without you and I can be on the next hovercraft. Where do I find your things?' His voice was matter of fact as though he was asked things like this every day. Perhaps journalists are. Behind it I could hear the sound of music and laughter.

When I rejoined Jean-Pierre he had ordered another carafe of wine. '*Tout va bien?*' he asked.

I nodded. 'I told him where I'd be, just as you said. Are you sure you don't mind . . .' I was embarrassed suddenly. This complete stranger had become a friend in the space of less than two hours; a real friend. His lorry was empty and he was on his way home for twenty-four hours' rest before taking a load back to Paris, and he assured me he could think of no more delightful way of passing some of the time than with me!

We met Robin at seven that evening. He had taken the ferry to Boulogne and hired a car there. In the back was one of my own suitcases. He had gone to my room, rifled my drawers and cupboards and made his own selection of clothes. I saw Jean-Pierre eyeing him with obvious approval and I was pleased. I didn't think I was going to regret throwing myself on Robin's mercy. Nevertheless I was sad when Jean-Pierre had to go. One day, we promised, we would visit him, but before then I had a way of life to change.

When he had gone Robin produced my passport from his pocket and handed it to me. 'There you are,' he said. 'But you also need money. It was conspicuous by its absence in your handbag.'

He was looking at me closely. 'Do I get an explanation?'

I nodded. 'I rather think you do. Also, probably, a good story. I owe you a lot for coming like this.'

He grinned. 'You do indeed.' He opened the door of the red Renault for me. 'But first of all, I think, a change of clothes and dinner. I've checked us into a hotel.'

It was a double room.

'One of the things I owe you?' I asked, looking round. Strangely I did not feel angry.

He swung my case onto the bed and went to push back the shutters. Outside the street was noisy with traffic; two men were having an argument immediately beneath the wrought iron balcony; the air was full of the sound of their shouting and the smell of French cooking.

He turned and leaned with his shoulder against the wall, looking at me. 'Not unless you want,' he said. 'I could just about restrain myself to a chaste neighbourliness, provided I get my explanation; I am not quite such a lecher as Parker. Do I gather you told him where to go? The atmosphere at your idyllic home has not been all sweetness and light since you left.'

'Did Don lose his contract?' I had taken my silk négligé from the case.

Robin shrugged. 'Still not signed as far as *I* know. He'll get it though. Parker doesn't do business entirely with his balls. He'll make Don sweat but if he got as far as going down to Sussex, he'll sign.'

To my surprise I found I didn't really care. The house; Don; they were already in the past, as were, I suspected, my flat, my allowance and my car! I had a leisurely bath and then we went out to dinner.

By half-way through I was beginning to realise that I liked Robin Hamilton very much. He was unlike any other man I had known; relaxed, humorous, totally unconventional and, for the first time I found, as his fingers closed over mine on the table, a man whose touch did not leave me rigid with dislike. On the contrary I felt an unmistakable tingle of excitement.

There was a lot to talk about that evening and some of it involved the police. Robin was not prepared to ignore the method of my arrival in France. He took it very seriously indeed.

And he used the story. It made the headlines in most of the papers in England, but as far as I know they never caught Pete and Sam.

The other story, the one about a businessman who tried to sell his daughter for a contract, Robin kept to himself.

In our bedroom that first night together, as I waited for him to come upstairs from phoning his paper and Don, to tell him where I was, I went once more to the window and looked out. The sound of an accordion floated up from the café across the street and I could hear laughter and the sound of singing. I thought for one short moment about Ben. It was without regret.

When Robin returned at last he came over to the window and put his arms around me. 'I told Don, among other things,' he said softly, 'that you and I were driving on down to the Riviera for a few days.'

I turned to look up at him. His face was only inches from mine. 'I should like that,' I said.

He smiled. 'No strings attached. We'll see how it goes, shall we?'

I remembered Ben and all the strings that had surrounded that relationship and laughed. 'No strings,' I agreed, and I was surprised to realise that I really meant it. I was content to see what time, and the freedom to be myself at last, would bring.

'I told Don that his little Anna has grown up,' Robin added. 'She makes her own decisions from now on.'

'She does indeed,' I whispered. 'And one of my first is about you.'

While I was waiting for him to come upstairs from his phone calls I had changed into my négligé, and now, loosening the belt I let the pale blue silk slide gently from my shoulders to the floor. Robin had not packed any night-dresses, so of course I wasn't wearing one.

Rosemary and Thyme

THE SOUND OF THE FLUTE had taken her completely by surprise. It was as pure in its way as the sound of the robin's song which was cascading with icy beauty across the garden. This was not a small child painfully practising before school, this was adult music, expert, complex. Elizabethan. Shivering, as she listened, Lesley glanced down with distaste at her mud-caked gardening gloves. They were cold, clinging to her fingers, no longer comforting against the earth. Peeling them off she stooped and picked up her thermos. A secret indulgence this: steaming bitter coffee, redolent of past breakfasts, but here in the cleansing air of dawn safely apart from memories. Sipping, she could feel the darkness of her mood lifting and dispersing with the music.

Beyond the herb beds and the low box hedges she could see the sea. The sun, hard silver behind bars of dawn cloud, threw no heat yet across the glitter of the water. Behind her, in contrast, the churchyard wall was smothered in warm blossom. Espaliered pears clung unpruned the whole length of the soft old red brick and as she turned to watch a wren darted in and out of the white flowers.

From the yew tree behind the wall the robin was pouring out its heart to the dawn, the sweetness of the song a sharp counterpoint to the sudden harsh ringing cry of a gull over-head until, as though indignant at being outclassed by the music of the flute, it stopped singing and with a flirt of its tail vanished.

Unable to contain her curiosity, Lesley put down her mug and tiptoed across the beds, brushing aside the delicate fronds of rosemary with their veil of blue flowers. At the wall she reached up and cautiously she peered over. She could see nothing. The shadows in the depths of the churchyard were thick and dark. Suddenly the music stopped.

'Oh no!'

She had spoken involuntarily and half embarrassed she waited, expecting some response from the musician.

None came.

The silence unnerved her slightly. She had expected a voice, or a face amongst the holly branches, or even the sound of retreating footsteps. Uncomfortable with the intensity of the quiet she raised herself on her toes and peered further over the wall.

'Hello?' she called.

At the sound of her voice a blackbird hurtled out of the hollies near her, shrieking in alarm. Otherwise there was no sound.

Turning, she followed the wall to where an old wooden gate led from the garden into the churchyard itself. She pushed at it. It was swollen and stiff to open but with a protesting creak it allowed her to pass. Beyond the wall, where a few moments before she had stood and listened to the music, the sun was gaining strength. A small streak of gold touched the clouds.

The gravel path was thickly overgrown, but still it crunched beneath her feet as she moved cautiously forward. The church was locked. The old ivy-covered graves slept in silence.

The music when it came again was quieter, sadder. She listened, turning slowly round, trying to work out where it was coming from.

Beyond the church the path wound between the graves

331

towards the lych gate and the lane which led up from the village.

Slowly she walked on, following the music towards the avenue of majestic yews and a tangled thicket of old rose bushes. Leaving the path she walked on feeling the dew soaking, ice cold, over the top of her boots from the long, uncut grass.

The young man was standing looking down at a newly dug grave. Tall and slim he appeared to be dressed entirely in black. In his hand she could see the long outline of the instrument he had been playing. She stopped. He had his back to her, he hadn't seen her yet; she could still turn back. She hesitated, unwilling to leave, but not wanting to intrude on his obvious grief.

Seconds ticked by. Beside her the robin, reassured by her stillness, hopped out of the ivy which clung around the stone coping of a vault and came to rest only two feet from her. It bowed and half spread its wings and danced across the arm of a cross near by. Distracted, she watched it for a few seconds. When she glanced back at the young man, he had gone.

She shrugged. He must have looked round and caught sight of her. Slowly she made her way back towards the gate, conscious of the newly rising sun throwing warmth through the still-bare branches of the trees. She could understand grief too raw, too new to be shared, but at the same time she was overwhelmed with regret for the beauty and emotion of the music which had gone with him.

She did it automatically, as she would have done for a friend, conscious that she had scared the mourner away, putting together in recompense the nosegay of rosemary with its intense blue flowers, the gaudy bells of lungwort, cowslips and sweet violets, then retracing her steps, she followed the path towards the grave, her own offering to whoever lay beneath that soft black earth, a bright, fragrant bouquet in her hand.

The robin led the way, bobbing ahead with flirtatious friendliness, its beady eyes fixed on her face.

The church door was open. Someone must have been there to unlock it while she was preparing the flowers. Unable suddenly to face the thought of meeting anyone, of speaking, embarrassed by the presumptuousness of her little posy for the unknown grave, she tiptoed on the grass, following the path between the yew trees past the vault to the tangled rose bushes. Now the light was stronger, the shadows gone, she could see how old they were – great thick woody stems, most of them dead, or only sustained by suckers, threaded with thistle and goose grass, entwined with ivy. Beyond them there was an old grave, surrounded by railings, the stone moss-covered, cracked and crumbling. She glanced round, lost. Surely it was here she had been standing when she saw the young man. Feeling foolish suddenly she cast around, searching for the mound of newly turned dark earth.

'Can I help you? Are you looking for someone?'

She spun round with an involuntary cry of surprise at the diffident voice behind her. A man, painter's overalls over his thick green sweater, stood there on the path. He was about her own age she guessed, and about her height, but stocky, his thick curly hair awry, his face lit by a friendly smile. 'Sorry. I startled you.' His voice was low and musical.

'I didn't hear you coming.' Her uneasiness had been caused not so much by his sudden appearance as by the seeming disappearance of the grave. It had thrown her out of kilter. She had lost her bearings totally.

'I'm painting over some damp patches in the church.' He shrugged. 'Any job, you know, when one is temporarily unwaged.' His humorous scowl at the euphemism made her smile. 'You must be Mrs Davis?' His head to one side, he surveyed her with open curiosity. 'I saw you coming through the gate from Stables Cottage. You are very much a mystery lady. Everyone in the village is falling over themselves with curiosity about you.'

'Are they?' She stared at him, half her mind still on the grave behind her, half shocked by this revelation. It was threatening. Intrusive.

He read her mind with ease. 'I'm sorry. It's none of my business either. I'll leave you to it. Unless,' he hesitated, his eyes going to the flowers in her hand. 'Did you want help finding a grave? Whose is it?'

'I don't know.' She felt foolish as she had known she would. 'I was here earlier. I saw someone –'

It seemed easier suddenly to start from the beginning, and strangely, now that she had started talking she wanted to go on, wanted to end the self-imposed loneliness of the past weeks. She told him about the garden, the cold dawn, the hot coffee, the music drifting across the churchyard wall.

When she had finished he was looking puzzled. 'I don't quite understand. I'm not a great authority on local funerals, but I don't think there's been a burial here for months. So many people go to the crematorium these days. There are certainly no new graves.'

'Perhaps the grave was months old then.' She gave a wry smile. 'I'm not an expert on them either. Would they still look new?'

He grinned. 'All I know about graves is to be found in *Hamlet*, I'm afraid. "Water is a sore decayer of your whoreson dead body," and all that. The latest village graves are on the far side of the church, near the path. They certainly wouldn't be down here. These are all ages old.' He gestured towards the dead roses. 'I'll show you if you like –'

'No!'

He frowned, surprised at her vehemence.

'It was here. Near the yews; the roses. It was here.' She pointed to the railings.

> '*Mary Elizabeth Weaver.*
> *Born 3rd May 1672. Died 5th August 1696*'

he read, squinting at the inscription almost worn away and covered in lichen, and he shook his head. There was a long pause. 'I don't know of anyone in the village who plays the flute or the recorder. Not properly. Not if you don't count the school kids.' It was said absently as though he were mentally scanning a list of names. 'You are sure it wasn't a tape?'

'I saw him. He had the flute in his hand.'

'A visitor then. Come to see the grave of an ancestor?'

'It was a new grave.' She put her hand to her face wearily and he could see the earth encrusted round her nails. The sight made him feel strangely protective. She was very beautiful this stranger who had bought the cottage so close to the centre of the village but who remained so determinedly an enigma. Beautiful and sad.

The sadness vanished suddenly as she turned to him and her face lit with a smile. 'I must have been imagining it. Dreaming.' Crouching down she put her hand through the railings and laid the posy on the grave. 'There. She can have them with my love.' She stood up again and turned to him. 'Are you very busy? If the damp patches can wait come and have a cup of coffee. Then you can tell the villagers that you've met me and earn lots of Brownie points!'

He laughed. She had read his mind, but only to a certain extent. He would not tell them anything. He sensed a secret here to be guarded and cherished.

'I'd like some coffee. Thanks.'

Her cottage was comfortably furnished, the kitchen separated from the living room by only a few oak studs. Sitting down at the round pine table he was able to stare appreciatively around her whole domain, then watch as she put the kettle onto the stove. There were so many questions he wanted to ask but he knew he would ask none of them. He would wait for her to volunteer.

She took two heavy earthenware mugs down from the dresser and went to the fridge for a jug of milk. 'You are my first visitor from the village and I don't even know your name.' She had her back to him as she fished in a biscuit tin and brought out some flapjacks which she arranged on a plate.

'Philip. Phil.'

'And does Phil have a second name?'

He grinned. Enigma for enigma. 'He does.'

'But I'm not to know it?'

'My turn for a question perhaps?' He helped himself to a biscuit as she pushed the plate towards him.

'Fair enough.' She sat down too as they waited for the kettle to boil. 'Fire away. Just one.'

'Do you live here alone?'

She nodded. The barrier was closing around her again. The friendliness, the banter, they were good, but why had he homed in on the one thing she could not discuss? Because it was the most important thing in her life, of course. The gap at her side. The empty place in her bed. The missing laughter even in this house that had never known him, that she had thought would comfort her after the aching emptiness in the home they had shared.

Phil was watching her closely and she had a feeling he could read every thought passing through her mind. He turned to look out of the window. 'You're working on the old herb garden. I used to visit it when I was a boy. I loved the smells. It seemed so strange that you could stand in such a warm, safe, fragrant place and yet look out to the sea and watch the cold squalls of rain racing across the waves in the distance.' He paused. She didn't say anything so he went on. 'My parents lived on the other side of the church, in the old rectory. When my father died my mother bought a cottage up the other end of the village so when I was made redundant in the City I came back here for a bit to help her sort things out.'

'And you live alone with your mother?' Standing up she began to make the coffee.

He smiled and nodded. 'Three years of marriage and a fairly good-tempered divorce under my belt. Once bitten twice shy.'

There was silence. This was the moment to tell him. My

husband died. That was all she had to say. No need to talk about the hospice and the long weeks as she sat and watched the man who was her whole existence slip slowly beyond reach. Just the bare facts.

Outside the window the robin perched on the budding wisteria and burst into song. Phil smiled. 'He's followed us from the churchyard. Nosy fellow. Look at those bright eyes.' The moment had gone.

She nodded. 'I'll find him some crumbs.'

Pushing wide the casement she held her breath suddenly. 'Phil, listen!'

The beautiful haunting melody from the churchyard was drifting across the garden. In silence they listened for several minutes, then, his finger to his lips, Phil stood up and silently he opened the door. They crept down the path towards the gate and round the church, following the direction of the sound.

The young man was standing where she had seen him before, near the grave of Mary Elizabeth Weaver. But now the railings were missing, the headstone gone. The earth was newly turned. On it lay Lesley's posy of spring herbs. As the young man played they waited motionless, seeing the tall slim body, dressed all in black, sway gently in rhythm to the music, absorbed as they were by the beauty of the sound.

Lesley realised suddenly that she was clutching Phil's hand. They were both holding their breath. Behind them the robin bounced cheerfully into the hollies and, puffing up its scarlet breast feathers, it began to sing.

The young man lowered his instrument at last. He stood for a moment, looking down at the grave then he half glanced back over his shoulder as though he too could hear the cheerful song of the bird. For half a second more the vision remained, then a squirrel ran along the path in front of them and they realised he had gone.

Lesley slowly released her companion's hand. She took a deep breath. 'Tell me you saw him too.'

'I saw him too.'

She stared at him, her eyes wide, her face suddenly pale. 'He was a ghost.'

He nodded. 'I think he must have been.'

'But not frightening.'

'No. Just sad.' He smiled.

'That beautiful music!' She was strangely breathless. 'Trapped in time. Still existing.'

'We're privileged.' He looked at her. 'I hope it's comforting. To know people can come back. Can still love each other beyond whatever boundary it is we cross when we die.'

So he had guessed. Perhaps the villagers with their gossip and their grapevine already knew. She nodded. 'It is.' For a few seconds she thought about it, reassured as he had meant her to be, but then she frowned. 'But where is *she*? Where is Mary Elizabeth? Why haven't they met out there beyond the boundary?' She began slowly to walk forward towards the grave. Standing staring down through the railings she focused on the bunch of herbs. 'But perhaps he did find her.' She was talking to herself now. 'The music. The shadow of the man. They are just echoes. Images in the mirror. That's all.' She turned to face him and the sadness in her eyes had gone. 'We were idiots. We should have tried to tape the music. If there's a next time shall we have a go?'

He liked the 'we'. He could feel comfortable with that. And he could live with the shadows. 'What was your husband's name?' It was the right time to ask. He made no attempt to step closer to her.

'Jeff.'

He could see it was an effort even to say it.

He nodded. 'Lesley, I must get on with my painting. Would you come out to supper one evening? Perhaps go to a concert?' He gave wry grin. 'We both like music. It's a start.'

He could see her considering. She was staring at the robin, perched now on the railings round the grave. Suddenly she smiled. 'You're right,' she said slowly. 'It's a start.'

Flowers for the Teacher

I SHUT THE FRONT DOOR thankfully behind me and stood
for a moment leaning against it, gazing round the cool living
room of my tiny cottage. Almost at once I began to feel calm,
it was so peaceful in there.

It had been the most terrible week since I had taken over
as the teacher at the village school at Sherbridge. There had
been times when I had thought I would never survive until
Friday at all. And it was all due to one new boy who had
arrived at half term.

His name was Paul Danefield and he was eight. He was a
small sturdy child with freckles and his sole aim as far as I
could see was to reduce the school to chaos and me to tears.
He had very nearly succeeded in both.

With a sigh I dropped my books on a chair and went to
plug in the kettle. I was worn out. Kicking off my shoes I
ran my fingers through my hair and gazed out of the kitchen
window at the lavender and sweet marigolds in the bed outside. Then someone knocked on the front door. I was
tempted not to answer, but as I had soon discovered when
I moved to Sherbridge, the teacher was considered public
property rather as the district nurse was. If I was in I was
available. And they would all know by now that I was in.

I opened the door to a tall young man in a smart grey suit.
Puzzled, I tried to think who he was. I knew most of the

villagers by now, and certainly all the parents, but I could not remember having seen him before.

'Miss Stanley?' His voice was low and even. 'I wonder if I might have a word with you. My name is James Danefield. It is about my son, Paul.'

My heart sank, but I smiled and beckoned him in, wishing I had thought to put my shoes on again before I opened the door. I felt ridiculously defenceless in bare feet.

'I expect you can guess why I'm here.' His grey eyes surveyed me rather grimly and I saw them taking in my dishevelled hair and my toes at a glance. He rather obviously disapproved of what he saw.

'I assume you want to discuss Paul's work,' I said rather weakly. I was about to add, 'And his rude uncouth behaviour,' but I bit back the words, not wanting to antagonise the man.

The kettle lid was beginning to jump up and down next door so I offered him a cup of tea. He accepted, rather curtly, I thought, and waited, his lips pursed, as I went through into the kitchen.

As I made the tea I found a comb in the drawer and my sandals under a chair so I was feeling slightly less untidy when I carried the tray into the living room.

'We haven't met before, Miss Stanley.' Mr Danefield refused to sit down and stood watching me pour out, his back to the fireplace. 'As you know it was my sister you saw at the time Paul joined your school. He has no mother.' He hesitated a moment as though wondering whether to tell me what had happened to her. Then obviously thinking better of it, he went on, 'And I have been away in London for the last few weeks.'

He took the cup I offered him and stirred it absently. 'Miss Stanley, I am extremely concerned about the way you have been treating my son.'

'I beg your pardon?' I looked at him blankly.

'He is a sensitive and unhappy child,' he went on as though I hadn't spoken, 'and he is still upset at having lost his mother.

I am most perturbed to find that you have been picking on him, making an example of him before the whole school and even using corporal punishment.'

'I've what?' My tea slopped into the saucer as I dropped my cup onto it. I was furious. 'Is that what he's told you? Well, I've news for you, Mr Danefield. Your son seems to me to be anything but sensitive. He has been going out of his way to wreck the school and everything I'm trying to do. He's unpleasant, rude, disobedient and spiteful. Ever since he came there's been nothing but trouble. And I have never, ever, used corporal punishment on him or any of the children!'

I was shaking with anger. I had managed to keep my temper all week in spite of Paul's single-minded attempts to make me lose it, but this was the last straw.

Mr Danefield put his cup down rather deliberately, his tea untouched. He looked at me for a long moment without speaking, his handsome face quite without expression, then he said, 'I am sorry, Miss Stanley, but this is obviously a matter for the school authorities.' Without another word he walked out and closed my front door behind him.

I stood gazing after him in disbelief for a moment and then I threw myself full length on the sofa and burst into tears.

How could I have been so stupid as to say all those things to him? Where was all my training, my tact, all that I had learned in psychology lectures, even my own natural politeness? How could I be such a fool? I loved this job and I loved Sherbridge and now I should probably be dismissed because I had lost my temper after the most awful week since I had finished my training; the sort of week every teacher dreads and prays will never happen. What I should have done was discuss things rationally with the child's father. Perhaps Paul *was* sensitive; perhaps his behaviour *was* solely due to his unhappiness. Why hadn't his aunt explained to me about his mother? I racked my brains trying to remember what she had said, but I am sure she had only told me that both his parents were away.

Worn out by tears and exhaustion I fell asleep eventually on the sofa and it was almost dark when I awoke at last and looked around me. The tea on the tray beside me was stone cold and a milky film had formed on the liquid in the cups. I shuddered at the sight, and picking up the tray went slowly into the kitchen. Through the open window came the smell of night-scented stock and the sound of the flitting bats as they squeaked in the dusk.

Instead of being the relaxed, happy weekend I had hoped for the next two days were a torment for me. I saw James Dane-field in the village on Saturday afternoon, but either he didn't see me, or he pretended he didn't. He was dressed more casually this time, in a roll-neck sweater, and as he was chat-ting to Mrs Crowell outside the baker's I saw, with an unexpected little pang of misery, that he had a very attractive smile. But it was not directed at me.

Paul came to school as usual on Monday and I thought he seemed a little subdued. Certainly he was far better behaved and I had no need of my careful resolution to treat him with kid gloves.

Tuesday was the same and it really seemed as though the class was settling down again. But I couldn't relax. Every day now I was expecting a letter or a visit from the school authorities, for I had every reason to think that that cool grim-faced man meant every word he said about informing them. And who would take my word against his?

Then on the Thursday something very strange happened. Paul was very late. I had begun to think that he would not be coming when I saw him slinking into the back of the class. As he offered no apology or explanation I decided to ignore him until break and then ask him what had happened, but to my astonishment, as soon as the others had been dismissed I saw him making his way of his own accord towards my desk. His face was tear-stained and he was holding something behind his back.

'Good morning, Paul,' I said quietly. To my surprise I felt my heart going out to the child. He looked so crestfallen and unhappy.

'Please miss,' his voice was almost a whisper. 'I brought you these.' From behind his back he produced a bunch of wilted flowers. 'I'm sorry I've been naughty, miss.' So saying he turned and fled.

I was so touched and astonished I just sat there for a while, looking down at the bedraggled posy, gently separating out the bruised stems of pansies, primulas and buttercups from a few straggling pieces of grass. The little boy must have been clutching them tightly all morning. Eventually I fetched a jam jar for them from the cupboard and putting them carefully in water I set it on the front of my desk.

I noticed Paul's face light up a little at the sight when he returned to the classroom, but for the rest of the day he sat in silence and at the end of school he shot off on his own before any of the other children had left their desks.

I was still debating what had happened after I had had my supper that evening. I was sitting by the open window reading in the last of the daylight when there was a knock at the door.

It was James Danefield again. But this time he was wearing an open-necked shirt, and he carried a large bunch of red roses.

'Miss Stanley. I am sorry to call so late. I wonder if I could have a word with you?' I saw his eyes drop immediately to my feet which were yet again bare. 'I . . .' he hesitated. 'I want to apologise.' His face reddened slightly and I saw what a tremendous effort it was for him to say it.

Standing in front of the fireplace as he had before, still holding the roses, he smiled at me for the first time.

'I had a word with Mrs Greville who lives next door to me. Her son shares a desk with Paul, I believe. She seemed to agree with your view of Paul. So I tackled the wretched child about it and he admitted having lied to me, and having been badly behaved and rude to you. I hope you will forgive us both for our ill manners.'

He looked amazingly like Paul as he pushed the roses at me, half smiling, half embarrassed. I almost expected him to turn and run away as his son had done, but he didn't. He sat down on the sofa.

'I owe you an explanation,' he said, pulling a wry face. 'My wife and I have been separated for some time, and our divorce came through six months ago. She remarried recently and Paul feels it very badly. She doesn't really want anything to do with him, you see, although he does visit her once a fortnight.' He paused, as though looking for words. 'I think Paul was misbehaving because he wanted to attract your attention. He was seeking affection, although he was going the wrong way about getting it.' He glanced up at me under his long eyelashes. 'Besides telling me that you beat him . . .'

'I never did,' I interrupted indignantly.

'I realise that now. But besides that, you know, he told me you had hair the colour of polished conkers and that you were very beautiful. Quite discerning for a child of eight, I should say.' He grinned and I felt myself blushing scarlet.

'But of course,' he went on, 'he also said that "Miss" had this terrible temper, which goes with hair the colour of conkers.'

'And I obligingly proved it for him last time you came over.' I was contrite. 'It's I who should apologise, Mr Danefield. I should never have said those things to you, even if they were true. Poor little Paul. I should have realised there was something wrong.'

'Please, call me James.' He stood up and held out his hands to me. 'Will you have dinner with me on Saturday? We'll forget all our mutual apologies and start again from the beginning, and we can work out a plan for what to do with my errant son.' He smiled down at me and I could feel myself melting in the warmth of his charm.

Of course I should have said no. I should have insisted on a strictly parent-teacher relationship and politely sent him on his way. But I found myself smiling back at him. 'I'd love to,' I replied. 'Thank you for asking me.'

'Fine. I'm glad.' He beamed at me. 'But there is just one thing.' He hesitated and I saw a mischievous look come into his eyes. 'The restaurant where I plan to take you has some really rather nasty gravel in the front. It might be advisable, possibly, to wear some sort of shoes . . .'

He was already making for the front door, but the cushion I threw caught him on the shoulder. Laughing, he picked it up and tossed it back. Then he was gone.

I gathered up his beautiful roses and almost danced into the kitchen to find a vase for them. Perhaps my job at Sherbridge was not doomed to a premature end after all. And perhaps . . . But I was not going to build any dreams just yet. I would just wait and see what happened.

A Family Affair

PART ONE

THANKFULLY I CLOSED THE DOOR on the dusty New York street and ran up the steps to my cousin's apartment.

'Minna?' I called as I let myself in. 'Would you believe, Martin has let me come home early!'

I worked for Martin George, the world famous ecologist and TV personality, and I adored the job, but the hours were long and erratic: my work had to be my whole life, except for Chris of course. Chris and I were close, but not lovers. Maybe that would come later, but for the moment he was that rarest of animals, a male friend. And for once I could call him and tell him I could make it, shower and actually have time to relax for five minutes before he could get from his advertising offices on Madison Avenue to the brownstone where I was temporarily sharing my cousin's apartment.

'Minna, are you home?' Puzzled by the silence I checked my watch. My cousin's job was as regular as mine was variable and she should have been back an hour before.

Then I heard a sob.

I ran into the living room and found her, with her head in her arms, on the couch. She was crying.

'Uncle Julian phoned from England,' she sobbed.

'Pa?' I stared at her, feeling cold fingers run down my spine. 'What's happened?'

346

'It's Grandfather. He's dead!'

Stunned I sat down beside her, unable to say a word, and silently we held hands. Grandfather had meant so much to me. With my mother dead, and my father virtually an invalid from a bad heart, Grandfather had brought me up, his home at Kingley Manor my home, his world my world. Only in the last few years as I had grown up and he had become frail had he allowed Pa and me to move out of the manor house into one of the old farmhouses on the estate.

When I had recovered enough I rang my father back. 'He died in his sleep, Kate,' he assured me. 'It's the way he would have wanted to go. And he didn't want you to fly back for the funeral. "Tell the kids to hold a wake with the air fare money when I go," you know yourself that is what he said.'

Strange that home-loving Grandfather's three grand-children should all be living in the States when he died. I, because I followed Martin and my job around the world, Minna because she had never lived in England – her mother had married an American, and she was as American as the Empire State Building, and Richard. Our cousin Richard Bradshaw, the only son of Grandfather's only son, an enigma, and if the gossip columnists were to be believed, a jet-setting millionaire, lived somewhere near Boston. Neither Minna nor I had ever met him, and neither of us thought of contacting him now. If he had wanted to keep in touch with his family, no doubt he would have done so, but like his father, who having met and married the Boston-born heiress to the Bay View millions had cut off all contact with Kingley, Richard had never as far as I knew made any attempt to see Grand-father, or visit the family home.

So the shock was doubly great when the will came through. Pa had phoned us again as soon as he knew what it said. 'Minna has been left Gatehouse Farm and the home Pad-docks, and some money,' he shouted down the phone. Father always shouts on telephones. 'And you, sweetheart, get our beloved Kingley Farm and also the whole of Kingley Woods and the Marshes – and some money too.' He chuckled.

'And the main estate?' I asked. 'The manor house?'

There was a short silence. 'Richard gets all of that,' he said bleakly. 'Richard gets everything else!'

'It's so unfair!' Minna stamped her foot when I told her. 'What the hell has he done to deserve it! He never even visited grandfather! And he's as rich as Croesus already!'

Privately I agreed with her, but I was so overjoyed with my own bequest, our home and the woods and marshes I had adored since I was a child, that I didn't think too much about the main estate. Neither Minna nor I were business-minded, nor were we farmers, and I had always secretly thought the manor house too big and spooky ever to be really a home. If Richard were a businessman, he could run the estate and welcome.

Chris, when I mentioned my cousin to him, to my surprise knew all about him, and he whistled.

'He owns half of Boston, for Chrissake,' he said, when I told him over a hamburger lunch about the Bradshaw inherit-ance. 'Hey, Katie honey, you'll soon be out of my class!' We laughed together as we walked hand in hand down the street, and suddenly I began to feel better about grandfather's death. He would not have wanted me to grieve.

'So, you're a rich girl now,' Martin said jovially when I told him my news. 'You won't want to work for me any more!' He looked at me, his ruddy face twisted with mock sadness, his gold-rimmed spectacles twinkling, and I laughed.

'Of course I will, you know that. And I'm not rich. The money wasn't all that much, but I haven't told you the best bit.' I could hardly contain my excitement. 'I now own King-ley Marshes!'

He stared at me. 'Do you now,' was all he said. It was enough. In the world of conservation that name was famous – the last resort of several endangered species of flowers and butterflies. 'We'll do a TV special on it,' Martin said, and I was overjoyed.

Two days later Martin and I had to fly to Palm Beach and between spells in the conference centre and the sweltering TV studios I managed to find time to go shopping in anticipation of my money coming through, to buy what Martin laughingly called 'rich-lady' beach clothes, and to lie on the sand collecting what I hoped was a fairly respectable tan. By the time we were back in New York my hair had bleached out to honey highlights and I was quite proud of the way I looked. But my happiness was short-lived.

Minna had disappeared.

Frantically I called everyone I could think of, appalled at the smelling mouldy food I had found in the kitchen, and the unmade bed in her room, which was so unlike her, but no one knew where she was. She had not checked in at work for over a week. In the end, after tearfully consulting Martin and Chris I called the police department.

They were not interested. So many people disappear in New York, what was one more to them? They confirmed that her body had not been identified in any morgue, nor was she in any hospital as far as they knew, and presumably they slotted her name into a computer and forgot about her, leaving me shivering at all the unimaginable horrors which might have happened to her as I prowled the apartment and waited.

I had to wait two days before the phone rang.

'Hi! Is this Katherine Parrish?' a deep, unfamiliar voice drawled.

Listlessly I said that it was.

'My name is Dave Conway. I'm PA to your cousin Richard. Listen, Kate. Can you get up here to Salem? Minna is here, it's kind of a family reunion, and Richard would so like to meet you . . .'

I had already stopped listening. Minna was safe! And the enigmatic Richard Bradshaw had at last come out of hiding.

Martin agreed to give me a few days off – we had long ago

decided that he owed me months and months of overtime if
truth were known – and Dave Conway arranged to pick me
up by car. 'I'm in New York on business, and I have to make
one short call on my way back, but I'd sure like to have your
company,' he said. I needed no persuading.

Deliriously happy now, I whirled round the apartment,
cleaning it like a new pin – I hadn't had the heart before –
and then I set to, organising myself. I spent some more of that
not-yet-arrived money on some new clothes and fashionable
shoes, I had my hair done, and I was ready.

Dave was due to pick me up at Martin's downtown office
and exactly on time a beige Cadillac slid to a halt outside the
building.

Dave was tall, very thin, with grey hazel eyes, and utterly
charming. I felt relaxed with him at once. He admired
our chaotic office, shook hands with Martin, who responded
with his usual warmth, and at last he bent to pick up my
two new bags. I was following him out of the door when
one of the telephones rang, and automatically I reached
for it.

'Kate? Thank God I caught you!' It was Minna. Her voice
sounded strangled and hysterical.

'Minna? What is it? Where are you?' Astonished I stared
down at the receiver in my hand, then I put it back to my
ear.

'Kate! For God's sake don't go. You mustn't –' There was
a gasp and the line went dead.

I replaced the receiver and stared up at Dave. 'That was
Minna,' I said. I had gone cold all over.

He was watching my face closely and I had the sudden
feeling that he knew exactly what Minna had been trying to
tell me.

'Poor Minna,' he said, shaking his head. 'I'm afraid she has
not been well. How did she sound?'

I saw Martin's worried frown in the distance, but my eyes
were taken up with analysing Dave's expression. 'She sounded

hysterical,' I said cautiously. Minna was one of the calmest people I knew.

Dave nodded. 'She has had some kind of a virus up at Bay View. She is on the mend though, you've no need to worry.' I wanted to believe him, but a strange foreboding was tugging somewhere at the back of my mind. It did not last however as Dave gave an apologetic grin. 'She was so sure she was infectious, poor thing, that is why we didn't call you up before, but the doc says she's not. I guess it'll do her more good than anything else to see you.' He stooped once again to pick up my bags.

I had no reason not to believe him. Reassured, I said good-bye to Martin and followed Dave down to the car.

As it slid silently and effortlessly through the heavy New York traffic and out onto the freeway I sat back in my seat and prepared to enjoy the journey. Dave was a good companion, handsome, amusing, strangely gentle in some ways for a high-powered businessman, and prepared to talk about his employer.

'He never saw his family in England,' I explained. 'I expect Minna told you. So he is a great mystery to us all. What's he like?'

He pondered a minute, swinging the car out to over-take a huge truck. 'He's quiet; strong; clever; a bit of a loner.'

'He's not married?' I asked innocently. I knew that much. Every gossip column invariably described him as 'eligible bachelor millionaire Richard Bradshaw' but I wanted Dave to confirm it.

'Nope; he's not married. And not likely to.' For a moment his good-natured grin vanished. Then it was back. 'He lives mainly at Bay View, but he has houses in France and Long Beach too.' He guided the car expertly round a long bend. 'You'll love Bay View. It's an old colonial place; our English guests always feel at home there.' He gave a throaty chuckle. I was liking Dave more and more. He made me feel relaxed and happy and I forgot my nervousness about meeting my millionaire cousin at last.

We stopped for lunch at Hertford, then Dave had a short meeting at one of the office blocks in the city centre. Afterwards we drove on through the hot afternoon towards Boston.

Bay View was every bit as breathtaking as Dave had promised. Entirely surrounded by a high wall, on the edge of the ocean, the estate was invisible from the road. We slowed before the enormous iron gates and miraculously they swung open before us, closing as soon as we were through. We drove up the long tree-lined drive and there was the house.

It was a large, square, white-painted building with three storeys topped by an elegant balustrade. Innumerable windows flanked by immaculately painted shutters, porticoes and pillars marked it out as a beautiful piece of early nineteenth century architecture. The velvet lawns, glorious grounds and clustered stables and outbuildings showed it was the home of a very rich man.

We swept up to the front door and drew to a halt. As Dave helped me out of the car the door was opened by the most beautiful woman I had ever seen. She was tall and painfully thin, with high, angled cheekbones and enormous dark eyes. She stared down at me from the top step. 'So, the country cousin is here,' she said softly.

I was stunned by the hostility which oozed from her as we stared at each other and I could sense that I was going scarlet, feeling already gauche in the pale linen dress of which I had been so proud.

'Let me introduce Jacqueline Overton,' Dave said quietly at my elbow.

Taking a deep breath I held out my hand as I mounted the steps. The woman's clasp was ice cold. 'I am Richard's fiancée,' she said.

I felt my mouth drop open. His fiancée? Why had Dave made no mention of a fiancée; surely he had said that Richard was unlikely to marry? I turned to him reproachfully but already he had moved to the back of the car to fetch my cases and I found myself entering the huge cool hall, carpeted with scattered Persian rugs. Jacqueline went without pause towards the sweeping staircase and mesmerised, I followed her.

'Richard is not back from Boston yet,' she said over her shoulder as she went up ahead of us. She had a way of talking in short, clipped sentences which required no reply. I was aware suddenly that Dave was no longer anywhere in sight.

I cleared my throat tentatively. 'How is Minna?' I enquired. 'I had half expected her to be on the doorstep waiting for me.'

Jacqueline stopped so suddenly that I almost bumped into her. 'Minna?' she said.

I was two steps below her on the stairs, and she looked down at me with withering scorn.

'She is here, isn't she?' I said. I could hear the uncertainty in my own voice.

'No,' she said. 'She's not here,' and she resumed her way upstairs.

I followed her, almost running. 'But she phoned me! David said –'

'What did Dave say?' She turned on me again. 'Minna Munro is no longer here. Richard didn't need her any more.' I thought she was going to say something else, but after a second she merely turned and continued up the stairs, leaving me to follow her, all my doubts and suspicions flooding back. If Minna wasn't there, where was she, and why had she tried so desperately to phone me?

Jacqueline stopped outside a door in the long, deeply carpeted corridor. 'Ring if you need anything,' she said haughtily. 'The housekeeper will help you,' and so saying she turned away, sweeping out of sight along the passage.

I opened the door and went in. The room was flooded with sunlight and I stared round, my delight for a moment obliterating my fears, quite dazzled by the white carpet and drapes and the lovely soft velvet of the chairs. A huge bowl of damask roses stood on the dressing table, filling the room with their heady scent.

Beyond the bedroom was a bathroom. Both bathroom and bedroom were equipped with enamelled bell-pulls. I hesitated, then defiantly pulled one.

Almost at once the door opened and a figure appeared, a tall dark-haired woman in her fifties, dressed in impeccable black. Her austere features did not betray the glimmer of a smile as she looked me up and down. I had the feeling she was judging me and was uncomfortably uncertain about the decision she had reached.

'Good afternoon Miss Parrish,' she said, in a strong Bostonian accent. 'I am Edith Marlesford, Mr Bradshaw's housekeeper. I trust you have everything you need?'

She sounded as if she were challenging me to find fault with something if I dare, and my question about Minna froze on my lips. I found myself giving her a tentative smile. 'The room is lovely, thank you. I was wondering if someone could bring up my cases.'

She bowed slightly. 'They are on their way.'

'When will my cousin return from Boston?' I asked.

'About eight, I believe,' she said. 'Dinner is at nine. There is one other guest here at present. Mr Calder, from England like yourself.' She paused, then almost unwillingly she went on, 'Perhaps you would like some refreshment brought up to your room now? Some iced tea?' It was obviously a great concession and gratefully I nodded assent.

An hour later, showered, changed and refreshed I leaned on the low window sill looking out into the deserted gardens, wondering what I was expected to do until Richard returned. I was not inclined to seek out the beautiful Jacqueline.

There was a phone beside the bed and on impulse I dialled Chris in New York. I had to talk to someone.

'How is it?' he asked. 'What's the tycoon like?'

I laughed nervously. 'He's not here yet, but his house is

fantastic.' It was reassuring to hear Chris's voice. I had begun to feel very lonely.

'Chris,' I went on. 'Minna isn't here.'

I could almost hear him shrug. 'She's probably had enough of the high life and come home. I shouldn't worry; I can't help thinking you'd have a lot more fun without her, Kate.' I might have known he would not take my worries seriously.

We talked for a few minutes more, then, my courage bolstered, I set off to explore the house. Slipping down the staircase I peered into first one cool high-ceilinged room, then another. All were spacious, all impeccably furnished with English antiques, and all deserted. Eventually I found some doors which led onto the lawns and I slipped outside with relief. I was tempted to take off my shoes and run barefoot on the velvet grass but somehow I resisted. I was still too awed by my surroundings.

I had been wondering where Dave Conway had got to all this time, and then in the distance I thought I caught sight of him, sitting on the edge of a stone fountain. I ran towards him with relief.

'Dave, thank goodness, I thought you'd abandoned me!'

The figure turned slightly and I recognised in embarrassment that it wasn't Dave at all, but a tall broad-shouldered dark-haired man with brilliant blue eyes; he was the most attractive man I had ever seen. He rose courteously and held out his hand. 'Katherine Parrish, I presume,' he said in an impeccable English accent. 'I'm sorry to disappoint you. Were you feeling very abandoned?' There was a hint of a smile in his eyes.

Flustered, I gave a little laugh. This was obviously the other guest, Mr Calder, and now I was close I saw no resemblance to Dave. Where Dave was charming and quiet with relaxed understated good looks, this man exuded a kind of vibrant magnetism which was almost palpable.

'Lost is a better word perhaps,' I said, confiding in him in spite of my shyness. 'I wasn't sure what I was expected to do until my cousin returns. I could find no one in the house.'

He nodded. 'How very remiss of everyone. I must apologise. Dave has his own quarters at the back. I expect he is there, and Jacqueline is probably resting.' He tightened his lips slightly and I received a strong impression that he did not like Jacqueline. 'So,' he went on with a smile, 'allow me to show you round the gardens. It will help to fill in the time before dinner.'

He slipped the note book he had been writing in into his hip pocket and gestured towards the vista of lakes and flower beds which led down towards the sunset.

I walked beside him, conscious every second of how attractive the man was as I wondered how he fitted into the household. He obviously knew who I was but had made no attempt to introduce himself. 'You must be Mr Calder?' I asked tentatively at last.

'Must I?' He turned his blue eyes on me and grinned. 'If you say so.'

That smile was irresistible. I found my own unease evaporating. 'Are you a colleague of my cousin's?' I asked as I followed him over the grass.

'Something like that,' he said unhelpfully.

'Have you known him long?' I persisted. My curiosity about Richard was at fever pitch now that I was actually in his house.

'All my life, I suppose.' He led me around the corner of a huge hedge and we stopped, looking down the broad grass terraces to a view of the distant sea.

'What is he like?' I asked.

He seemed to consider for a moment, his thumbs hitched into his belt. 'Hard,' he said. 'In fact, he's really rather a swine. You mustn't trust him.'

I swallowed. I had not expected such an outspoken assessment of our host, and it threw me; I was not sure how to take it.

'But you like him,' I stammered at last.

He considered for a moment. 'No,' he said. 'Sometimes I don't like him at all.'

I stared at him in complete silence. He was gazing into the distance, and for a second I received a sharp impression that he no longer knew I was there. I felt my skin suddenly grow cold as if a shadow had swept across the bright garden.

'There you are!' A woman's voice interrupted us and I swung round to see a tall red-haired figure appearing from the shelter of the hedge. She was dressed in a low-cut, green evening gown which revealed every detail of her fantastic figure. She eyed me with open antagonism.

'Is this the other cousin?' she asked, slipping her arm possessively through my companion's. Until that moment, I realised suddenly, he had not bothered to turn to face her.

'This is Katherine Parrish,' he agreed, his voice hard now. He swung round to me. 'Katherine, let me introduce Sara Dashwood.'

I held out my hand uncertainly. 'Please, call me Kate,' I said.

The woman ignored my gesture. 'Hi Kate,' she said dismissively, and one of her hands crept up to the front of his shirt and as I watched, fascinated, it slipped inside, caressing his chest possessively. 'What about coming in for a drink?' she whispered huskily. She could not have made it more clear that I was in the way.

I could feel my cheeks growing scarlet but Mr Calder gripped her wrist firmly and pushed her away. 'Good idea,' he said calmly. 'Katherine, you must forgive Sara. Her manners are not all they might be.' I caught my breath at his acid tone and was in time to see the vindictive look she flashed me, but he went on coolly. 'You don't mind if I call you Katherine, I hope. It suits you so much better than Kate.' His glance was warm and appraising, and I began to feel better but a moment later he had crushed me by his next remark. 'May I suggest that you should go and change now, Katherine. Dinner is in half an hour,' he consulted the wafer-thin gold watch on his wrist, 'and we like to keep it formal here.'

I fled.

Luckily I had brought a long dress with me and trembling with humiliation and rage I slipped into it, conscious that next to Sara and Jacqueline I would indeed look like some hick country cousin. I swept my long hair into what I hoped was a more sophisticated style and clipped my antique pearl studs into my ears. I was studying myself in the mirror when there was a knock at the door.

It was the housekeeper once more and I saw her eyeing me critically as she stood in the doorway. It was impossible to judge what she thought. Her face was as demonstrative as marble.

'If you are ready, Mr Richard would like to speak to you before dinner,' she said. So, he had returned at last.

I followed her down, my heart hammering with fear. I was no longer looking forward to our meeting.

The huge dim study was illuminated by a single alabaster table lamp which threw a pool of warm light on the leather-topped desk by the window. Two men were seated in the room and as I appeared they both rose to their feet.

To my relief my companion from the garden was there, dressed in a dinner jacket. With him was a much older man. I looked round, puzzled. I had imagined Richard to be in his thirties – certainly no more.

'Katherine, there you are. Allow me to present John Calder, my English lawyer,' my Mr Calder said. I had not missed the quick look of admiration which he flashed in my direction as he took in my dress and hair.

I stared at him. 'I . . . I don't understand. Mr Calder? But then who are you?' Then overcome with embarrassment I understood suddenly. 'You mean you are Richard? But why didn't you say?' I felt anger sweep over me as I saw the amusement in his eyes.

Impassively John Calder, the real John Calder, produced

a glass and put it into my hand. 'A drink, Miss Parrish,' he murmured. I took it, but my gaze had not left my cousin's face. 'I thought you were an American born and bred,' I went on. 'You don't sound American!'

'Indeed?' He replied at last, and his tone was suddenly icy. 'I can't think why I should.'

Once more he consulted his watch. 'Please, sit down Katherine. There is some business I wish to discuss with you before we dine.' He snapped his fingers. 'The papers, John.'

Obediently the other man reached for a leather document wallet as I seated myself in a chair near the desk and arranged my skirts around me as calmly as I could. The hands I clasped around my glass were trembling slightly as I surveyed my cousin's face in the lamplight. He was still the most handsome man I had ever seen, but the humour in his eyes had vanished. His face was hard and unemotional as he took the sheaf of papers from his colleague and came round the desk to sit on the edge of it, facing me.

'I have here deeds making over to me your share of the inheritance at Kingley,' he said. 'I have arranged that you have life tenancy of the farmhouse where your father lives at present – I am not interested in the building – but I want immediate possession of the land so that the woods can be cleared and the marshland drained. I am prepared to give you the current market value for the acreage in cash. You may of course have an independent valuation if you wish.'

I stared at him, unable to speak for a moment in my surprise. Then I felt the first white hot anger clamp down on my heart. His eyes had lost their charm; they were as hard as steel. Rising to my feet I put down my glass, shaking my head. 'I am sorry Richard. I am not selling.'

He did not seem surprised. 'I have paid Minna five hundred thousand pounds for her share,' he said softly.

I gasped. 'She agreed to sell?'

'She agreed.' He picked up his own glass and drained it.

I thought of Minna's phone call, her sobbing voice, her strangled warning and I felt suddenly very sick. 'Where is Minna?' I asked sharply. 'I want to see her. What have you done to her?'

'Done?' He raised an eyebrow coldly. 'I have done nothing other than make a rich woman of her. As to where she is, I assume she has gone back to New York.'

They were both looking at me and I could see nothing but menace in their faces. A picture of the lovely marshes at home, the sun reflecting on the golden reeded water flashed before my eyes and I shuddered violently. 'No,' I repeated again, looking wildly round. 'No, I will not sell.'

A gong sounded somewhere in the depths of the house. It seemed to dispel the sinister atmosphere which was building round us. Almost magically Richard's face cleared and he was once more all charm. 'Dinner,' he said quietly. 'You may of course have as much time as you need to consider your decision, but I should like your signature before you return to New York. Let us leave business now. My chef would be very upset to think that we even contemplated such a thing when one of his meals was in the offing. Allow me to show you the way . . .' His hand on my bare shoulder was warm and firm, his touch electric as he ushered me towards the door.

The others were already gathered in the dining room. To my relief Dave was there, handsome in a blue tuxedo, between Sara, her flaming hair glowing in the candlelight, and Jacqueline, thin and exquisite in silver lace.

We took our places and I found myself staring around the table, my hands still shaking, as the two uniformed maids served the soup course. What kind of man was my cousin? Handsome, charming, undeniably attractive to women as I myself had found, but it was he who had said he was hard and unlikeable, even to himself. I glanced from Sara, whose eyes were fixed possessively on him, to Jacqueline, who was toying listlessly with her food and I frowned. A fiancée and a mistress, if I read the signs aright, under the same roof, and at the same table. Was it possible?

I turned to Dave in some relief as he began to ask me about my job and somehow I managed to get through the meal, conscious the whole time of the silence of the other two women and my cousin as I chatted lightly with Dave and Calder, describing my work and the life I led with Martin. It was a very uncomfortable hour. Afterwards, coffee was served outside by the swimming pool and I found myself seated beside Richard. He was watching me carefully. 'You really care about your work?' he said.

I nodded. 'You must see why I cannot sell that land. It is a wildlife sanctuary of enormous importance,' I said earnestly.

He beckoned a servant over and asked for a cigar. I watched him flick his gold Dunhill into life. 'Unfortunate, but it can't be helped,' he said thoughtfully after a moment. 'Draining the marshes doubles the efficiency of the main estate.' He blew a column of fragrant smoke into the night sky.

'I'll never sell,' I said quietly.

I saw his eyes gleam. 'You will,' he said. 'I'm prepared to pay you half a million sterling for it. That is way over the market price for that acreage of uneconomic land.'

I stared at him, but he wasn't looking at me. I followed his gaze and saw that Sara was standing at the edge of the swimming pool, a brandy balloon in her hand, talking to Dave. Even in the twilight of the pool lights she looked voluptuous.

Abruptly I hauled myself to my feet from the low chair, overcome with a stifling sense of claustrophobia. I looked down at Richard, conscious that behind us everyone had turned to watch me. 'I told you, I am not going to part with that land,' I said softly. 'Grandfather intended me to have it; he knew what it meant to me, and I am going to hang on to it. Now, if you don't mind I should like to leave. Perhaps someone could drive me to the airport?'

Richard had not moved from his chair. He crossed his

ankles lazily, seemingly engrossed in the glowing point of his cigar. 'Tomorrow,' he said.

'I should like to go tonight,' I insisted, my voice rising slightly.

'You can't, Katherine, I'm sorry. The gates are locked on a time switch at dusk.' He smiled up at me, all charm once more. I licked my lips nervously trying to keep calm. 'But surely you can override it?'

'I can. But I don't choose to. Not tonight.' He stretched out comfortably and tapped a gobbet of glowing ash onto the paving stones. 'You must restrain your urge to leave until morning,' he said. 'If you are consumed with restlessness, why don't you have a swim?' He indicated the warm aquamarine water at our feet, and once again I saw the amusement in his eyes.

I was trapped. Trapped in an awful silken web of luxury.

Trying to hide my agitation I went over to the serving table and helped myself to more coffee, conscious that he was watching me, a slight smile on his lips. Then angrily I turned away and walked to the edge of the pool, whilst behind me Sara had slipped into my vacated chair at his side. I heard her soft laugh as she leaned towards him.

I made my way over to Dave and we wandered out of earshot on the far side of the pool.

'You've got to get me out of here,' I whispered urgently. 'Please, help me.'

He looked at me. 'I'm sorry, Kate, I can't do that.'

My heart sank, but I was determined not to show it. 'You said Minna was here, ill,' I whispered accusingly, 'but she's not, and now I find myself being kept here against my will! What the hell is going on?'

He had turned away to stare back across the pool, to where Richard and Sara were talking, their heads almost touching as they leaned towards one another in the low chairs. Calder and Jacqueline were strolling about on the terrace engaged in deep conversation, no longer interested in me.

'I understand Minna decided she was well enough to return home,' Dave replied guardedly.

'Now that Richard has got his way?'

My voice had risen slightly and I saw him frown. 'I don't know what you are suggesting, Kate – '

'Oh yes you do,' I interrupted. 'I am suggesting that she was kept here a prisoner until she signed over her farm. How he forced her I don't know, but she rang me to warn me and I took no notice, fool that I am.' I paused bitterly. 'And now I am a prisoner here in my turn!'

He looked at me in astonishment. 'A prisoner? Oh Kate, come on. You're imagining things.'

'Am I?' I caught at his arm. 'Then why aren't you prepared to help me leave?'

He sighed. 'Of course you can leave, Kate. In the morning. I'll drive you to the airport myself if it will make you feel happier, and you can take the first plane back home then. I promise.'

And with that I had to be content.

As soon as I decently could I excused myself and made my way to my bedroom, conscious of several pairs of eyes following me as I left the terrace and disappeared into the house. For a moment I wondered if anyone would follow me, but I was alone as I made my way through the darkened rooms to the stairs. Only then did I allow myself to run. I fled towards my room, finding to my relief that there was a key in the lock, and turning it, I slipped it under my pillow.

I kept telling myself that my suspicions were unfounded; that I was becoming paranoid if I thought Richard intended to find some way of forcing me to sign his wretched piece of paper, but I could not rid myself of my strange terror. Some instinct told me that I was in danger and nothing I could do would dispel it.

I had been in bed for less than twenty minutes trying to make myself relax between the cool peach-coloured silk sheets when I heard a knock at the door. I sat up, my heart thumping with terror, and clutched the sheet tightly to my throat. 'Who is it?' I whispered.

There was no answer, but as I watched, horrified, I saw the handle turn and heard a key in the lock on the outside. Whoever was there had a duplicate of my own and was using it to enter the room.

The door opened slowly and I saw the tall figure of the housekeeper silhouetted in the doorway.

'I'm sorry to disturb you,' she said, 'but Miss Sara would like to see you before you go to sleep.'

To my relief she had not made a move to enter the room.

'As you see I am already in bed,' I said, defiantly trying to keep my voice steady. 'Perhaps you would tell her I'll see her in the morning.'

'She would like to see you now,' the woman repeated mechanically, and there was something in her tone which defied argument. With a sigh I reached for my robe and pulled it on. I could not think what Sara Dashwood could possibly have to say to me.

I followed Edith Marlesford down several passages until we reached a door. She knocked on it once, then left me.

There was a murmur from behind the door and I pushed it open and went in.

Sara, dressed in a short nightdress which left nothing to the imagination, was lounging on a huge double bed, a glass in her hand which she waved at me languidly as she saw me.

'Come in and close the door,' she said.

I did so, staring round me in astonishment, half expecting to see Richard there, but she was alone. The walls of her room were hung with deep red silk and the bed itself repeated the colour in a darker shade. The only relief came from the windows which were wide open onto the garden so the moonlight flooded into the room.

She sat up and put down the glass. 'You'll have to sign, you know,' she said.

I was staring at her in horrified fascination. The long

elegant arms and legs curled languidly on the soft covers and her flaming hair hung provocatively over the low neckline of her nightdress.

'May I ask why it should interest you what I do?' I said, pulling myself together with an effort. I felt as little as a rabbit must feel confronted by a snake.

'Everything that interests Richard interests me,' she said softly. She smiled. 'If he wants your land, he'll get it one way or the other, believe me.'

I felt a return of my earlier fear, but I was determined not to show it. Tearing my eyes away from hers I walked across to the window and stared out.

'He's going to be unlucky this time,' I said firmly. 'That land means too much to me to sell it, and you can tell him as much.'

'Then you're a fool!' The scorn in her voice was like a whiplash. 'You're no match for him!'

Was it jealousy, I wondered, which made her so hostile? Well, however possessive she was, she had no need to fear me; there was no way I ever wanted to see my cousin Richard again.

I opened my mouth to say so, but she had risen from the bed in one sinuous movement and came to stand beside me. 'Do as he asks, Kate Parrish,' she hissed, her green eyes glinting in the moonlight. 'Otherwise something unpleasant could happen. You might have an accident and be found floating face down in the pool, or you might find yourself cornered in some lonely New York street and beaten up! It's happened before, you know.'

I gasped. 'You're not serious,' I said weakly. 'You're just trying to frighten me. He would never do such a thing!'

She gave me a withering look and then she smiled, a long beautiful smile which left me chilled to the marrow. 'Richard does anything he likes,' she said huskily. 'Do you want to know how you'd look when he'd finished with you?' Before I could speak she reached down and with one quick movement she had pulled her flimsy nightdress up and over her head. She flung it on the floor and stood before me naked, the moonlight shining coldly on her ivory skin. Her body was disfigured with bruises.

For one whole minute I could not drag my eyes away from the marks on her flesh, then I was running for the door. Appalled and terrified I was afraid I was going to be sick as I heard her laughter echoing up the passage behind me. I fled back to my room, slammed the door and locked it with shaking hands. Then, taking no chances, I wedged the back of a chair beneath the handle before I staggered trembling to the telephone.

I misdialled twice before I reached Chris.

'Kate? Do you know what time it is, for Chrissake?' he said as I sobbed his name into the receiver.

'Chris! Chris, you must come and fetch me, please,' I begged.

'Honey, it's three in the goddam morning!' he repeated patiently. 'Look, I couldn't even get to you for three or four hours. You've had a nightmare, Katie. Come on now, calm down!' He was beginning to sound irritated. 'If you hate it there so much leave, okay? Take the first shuttle out of Boston in the morning and I'll meet you at the airport. No sweat. Now go back to bed, Kate!'

There was no point in arguing. I knew he did not believe me. Trembling I climbed back into bed and pulled the bed-clothes tightly round me. But I could not sleep a wink. Every time I closed my eyes, all I could see were those livid bruises on Sara's pale skin.

The first tentative rays of light were beginning to steal across the carpet when someone tried my door-handle once more. Somehow I stopped myself from screaming out loud as I crawled, aching, from the bed.

'Who is it?' I stammered.

There was a faint knock. Then I heard a whisper. 'Let me in, quickly. It is Jacqueline.'

366

'What do you want?' I answered suspiciously. I edged towards the door, my bare feet silent on the thick white carpet.

'I want to help you. I can get you away.'

Her voice, from the keyhole, sounded distant and very tired.

Cautiously I pulled away the chair and put the key in the lock. Jacqueline was dressed in jeans and a thick roll-neck sweater, her dark hair pulled back severely from her face. Her skin was paper white and her eyes had a drawn, haunted look which was inexpressibly painful to see. She slipped into my room and pushed the door silently shut behind her.

'Get dressed as quickly as you can,' she ordered quietly. 'My car is round the back.'

I did not bother to argue. I wanted more than anything on earth to be out of that house. Grabbing my clothes I ran to the bathroom and dressed, then flinging my things into the cases I put on my thin coat and I was ready. She had been watching me silently and now, with her finger to her lips, she tiptoed towards the door.

The corridor was deserted, and holding my breath I followed her through the sleeping house to the polished gleaming kitchens where the back door stood wide open. Outside stood a sleek red two-seater Mercedes. We climbed in without a word, pulling the doors closed silently, then she started the engine. I was sure the throaty roar would bring heads to every window in the house, but there was no sign of life as she swung away, the gravel spurting beneath the wheels, and headed up the drive, the headlights cutting swathes of brightness through the fresh silent dawn.

The gates opened at the touch of a button on her dashboard and then we were outside Bay View at last.

Only then did I feel I could breathe. I leaned back on the pale leather upholstery with a sigh.

'Why are you helping me?' I asked at last.

She did not take her eyes off the road, but I saw her

knuckles whiten on the wheel. 'Richard has ruined enough lives,' she said briefly.

'Won't he be angry with you?' I asked.

She gave a harsh humourless laugh. 'It doesn't matter if he is. There is nothing more he can do to me,' she said.

Already the car was slowing down and she drew into the side. I saw we were on a lonely road which overlooked a sea that was grey and endlessly empty. She opened the door and got out.

Then she bent and looked in at the window. 'Take the car, Katherine,' she said. 'I shall walk back along the beach.' She smiled for the first time. 'Don't let him catch up with you. He always ends up getting his way and it's time someone stood up to him. Good luck.'

Already she was threading her way down through the steeply growing undergrowth towards the shore. She did not look back, and I did not wait to watch her go. I had to put as many miles between myself and Richard Bradshaw as I could before he found out that I had gone.

PART TWO

Slipping across into the driver's seat I started the engine and gingerly began to ease off the handbrake. The Merc was the fastest car I had ever driven and for a moment I was tempted to take it all the way to New York, but the traffic was becoming heavier, and my nervousness was increasing as I craned in the mirror, wondering if I had been missed. I headed straight for Boston in the end and the airport, where I abandoned the Mercedes and caught the first available flight to New York after phoning Chris to come and meet me. He was there too; dear, dependable solid Chris, ready by now to listen to my story but still not prepared to believe more than half of it.

'Kate honey, Richard Bradshaw is as sound a businessman

as I ever heard of,' he said as he drove me into the city. 'There is no way he'd resort to the sort of things you are describing.' He laid a huge comforting hand on my knee. 'Come on. You need a good night's sleep, that's all. You'll see it differently when you've had a do'nut and some coffee.' Chris's universal panacea!

He dropped me off at the apartment, then he swung away from the kerb, already late for a business appointment, leaving me to let myself in. Pushing open the door I stared round cautiously. There were flowers in the room; things had been moved.

'Minna?' I called. 'Minna, are you there?'

She was lying face down on her bed, her hair tumbled over her shoulders, and for one awful moment I thought she was dead. Then I saw her drag herself almost unwillingly to wakefulness.

'Kate?' she murmured blearily. 'Are you all right?'

We hugged each other in silence for a long time. Then, over black coffee, she told me her story.

She too had been driven up to Bay View by Dave Conway in the beige Cadillac. She too had been ordered to sign over her inheritance. But she, eventually, had given in.

'Richard's a fiend, Kate,' she said weakly. 'He was so charming, so nice at first, then he changed completely. He became hard and cruel, and yet he was offering so much money.' She looked at me earnestly. 'More money than it was worth, Kate. And it's not as if Kingley means as much to me as it does to you.'

'I understand, Minna,' I said. She looked so miserable and guilty. 'I only wish we had never met him. Either of us!'

She nodded mournfully. 'If you really don't want to sell you'll have to get right away!'

I stared at her. 'I have got away,' I said warily. 'You don't think he'll try again?'

But of course I knew in my heart he would. Our fight was only just beginning.

She stood up pushing her hair off her face. 'Kate, I think he'll keep at you till he gets what he wants. He's that kind of man. And he knows where you live so you're not safe here any more.' I could hear the hysteria in her voice. It was very near the surface.

'What shall I do then?' I asked, feeling her panic beginning to creep through me. She was right of course. I was no safer in this apartment than I had been in my locked bedroom at his house.

It was my boss who solved the problem. Martin listened attentively to my story then he scratched his head.

'It seems to me, Kate, that it is time you took a vacation,' he said thoughtfully. 'Put yourself right out of his reach for a while. I can spare you a little now the series has finished. Why not take a month; that'll give him a chance to simmer down. And while you're there,' he grinned knowingly, 'you can do some preliminary research on our documentary.'

I stared. 'You mean I should go home? To Kingley?'

'Where else?' he said.

Chris agreed with him, though I could see he still thought I was over-reacting, and so without giving myself time to think I went to Pan Am and booked my flight to England. Only when the huge jet was safely in the air would I be safe again.

I settled back into my seat in relief the next day, looking out of the window at the beautiful misty morning and resolved, as the plane soared up over Long Island, that at last I could relax.

It was as the stewardess was serving coffee that I happened to turn to look back down the aisle and my heart stopped beating. On the opposite side, two rows back, sat David Conway.

He smiled at me apologetically. 'Hi,' he said. 'Richard's orders. He didn't want you getting lost or anything. Not before you've signed the documents, anyway . . .'

Far below, the mist and cloud had vanished and I could see the sparkling blue miles of the Atlantic Ocean. Why had

I ever thought Kingley would be safe? It was so obvious that I would go there and so obvious that he would follow.

Dave kept close to me through customs and out into the huge concourse at Arrivals and there for a moment I thought I had lost him; but I wasn't quick enough. As I scanned the ranks for an empty cab I felt a hand on my arm.

'If you're going to Kingley you might as well let me drive you,' he said. 'I've a hire car waiting for me, and it'll be much easier.'

Easier for whom, I wondered, but in the end I gave in. There was no point in pretending I wasn't going home, and I had no real fear of Dave. It was my cousin Richard I was afraid of.

With a sigh, I settled back on the smart leather upholstery and let him drive; he seemed to know his way round London and out into the dark countryside. Once I even felt myself doze off, worn out by the long journey, and was jerked into wakefulness only when we stopped at a service station for coffee. There, facing each other across a checked tablecloth, we talked about my cousin.

'Is he really so hard?' I asked, stirring my cup obsessively as I watched his face.

He scratched his ear. 'He's a very clever businessman,' he said.

'And he's ruthless?' I prompted.

He looked very serious. 'Yes,' he said slowly. 'He's probably the most ruthless man I've ever met. It doesn't do to cross him. Many a tough opponent has discovered that.'

Tougher than me, he was implying.

'You make him sound a very unpleasant person,' I said frankly. I could feel the almost familiar creep of fear playing over my skin once more, as it seemed to at every mention of Richard Bradshaw's name.

Dave shook his head. 'No. You've met him and you know better than that,' he replied. 'He's charming; he's a good friend. The best. But he makes a bad enemy and,' he looked up and held my gaze for a long moment, 'Kate, in case you should get any ideas about it, he dislikes women.'

I felt myself colour. I had found him attractive, I had to admit it. I swallowed nervously. 'What about Jacqueline and Sara? For a man who hates women he has more than average under his own roof!'

He gave a slow smile. 'Perhaps women like him,' he said cryptically.

A sudden suspicion crossed my mind. 'Are you telling me he's gay?' I asked.

He gave a harsh laugh. 'Oh no, Kate,' he said. 'He's not that.'

It was late when we reached Kingley and he dropped me off at the farm before driving on up to the old half-timbered manor house which now belonged to my cousin. One look at my father told me that I should never be able to confide my worries to him; he had grown so frail since I had seen him, his white hair a silver cloud around his head, his face paper white and thin as he greeted me. He drew me into the kitchen and made me a mug of hot milk and gradually the old house began to envelope me once more in its usual warm peace, so that for the remainder of that night I slept soundly for the first time since I had come across Richard Bradshaw.

Next day I went up to the manor, approaching it with some trepidation, afraid that seeing it with Grandfather gone would be more than I could bear, but it was just the same, a huge rambling Elizabethan building, the small leaded windows letting in little light, and it was still pervaded with the faint scent of burning apple boughs and, perhaps, a little of my grandfather's pipe.

I was greeted with open arms by Hill, the butler, and Mrs Dawson, Grandfather's cook-housekeeper, and was left in no doubt at once that they had no reservations about Grandfather's will. 'Of course we are all looking forward to meeting Mr Richard,' Hill said slowly. 'I hope that perhaps he will one day make his home here, but meanwhile he has appointed a first-class manager to take care of the estate.' Mrs Dawson nodded agreement. 'And that nice Mr Conway,' she said beaming. 'So American, Miss Kate, and so charming!'

I smiled to myself. They were right about Dave and what was the point of worrying them with my doubts about Richard?

I enjoyed the next few days enormously. The weather was heavenly and I took a horse each day from the Kingley stables and rode out across the land: my land, where the marshes stretched out towards the sea, ringed by woods hundreds of years old where the sunlight dappled through the young leaves onto carpets of bluebells. The air smelled of sweetness and salt and the warmth of the soft sunlight, and I blessed Minna for suggesting I came.

My happiness was reinforced by the visit I had made to the family lawyer.

Old Mr Kenton had stared at me in amazement when I had told him a carefully edited version of my story. 'Well, of course I knew your cousin Minna had made her share of the inheritance over to Mr Bradshaw,' he said. 'Frankly, it did not surprise me. I understand she has always lived in the States and she can have no emotional ties to the land, but there is no way the will can be broken, Katherine, other than by agreement. The bequest was quite unconditional.'

'So Richard cannot force me to part with Kingley Farm?'

He stared at me, his faded eyes concerned. 'There is no question of it. Kingley Farm and Marshes are yours and yours alone. That is definite.'

And without my consent Richard could not ever lay his hands on them.

Richard himself arrived at the Manor two weeks later. I had heard nothing of his arrival and was quite unprepared when the ringing of the phone brought me in from the garden where I had been weeding the rose beds whilst Father was resting.

'Oh Miss Kate!' It was Mrs Dawson on the line, and I

could hear she had been crying. 'Mr Richard is here and he has sacked us all!'

For a moment I could not believe my ears, then I knew what I had to do.

'I'm coming straight over,' I said.

It was beginning.

It was less than a mile up to the manor house and it looked the same as usual as I drove up, the mellow timbers and pink-washed walls dozing in the sunlight. Only the sapphire-blue Rolls Royce outside was different and I knew that already I had become a stranger there.

I went in without knocking, instinctively making for my grandfather's study.

Only when I was several feet into the room, propelled by my anger, did I see who the sole occupant of the study was. Sara Dashwood was poring over some papers on the desk. Her eyes widened as she recognised me and a slow smile spread across her features.

'Kate!' she said, her low voice purring. 'Welcome!'

I could feel my muscles tensing with dislike, but somehow I managed to smile. 'Is Dave Conway here?' I asked as pleasantly as I could. I was wondering if Jacqueline too had come to England, and if Richard had ever found out about her part in my escape.

She shook her head. 'Sorry Katie. Dave drove to London to collect some papers. He won't be back until tomorrow. Richard is here though. But I expect you know that. *Richard!*' She raised her voice only slightly to call him and I realised that the door into the library was open.

Seconds later Richard appeared. He was more handsome than ever, dressed in an open-necked blue shirt and slacks, his face deeply tanned, and I felt my heart give an illogical little jump at the sight of him.

'So, Katherine. How kind of you to call,' he said quietly. I had forgotten what a pleasant voice he had, but something in its tone frightened me.

I was not going to give my fear its head, however. This was, or had been, my territory, and I had a mission.

'I should like to speak to you alone, Richard,' I said looking pointedly at Sara. She had moved behind me to the door and as I watched she reached for the key and turned it. She smiled at me sweetly. 'Just in case you feel like leaving suddenly again,' she said. She tossed the key onto the desk and walked into the library.

I bit back my anger at her childishness. 'I came to speak to you about the staff,' I said stiffly, turning back to Richard.

He sat down on the edge of the desk watching me attentively, but as he said nothing, I went on: 'They have been with my grandfather for years. Kingley is their home. You cannot sack them.'

He raised an eyebrow. 'Grandfather is dead, Katherine. His ancient retainers are no use to me. But I assure you I am not as hard as you think. I am not completely insensitive. They are all being given pensions.'

'Money isn't everything!' I retorted hotly, wishing he wasn't so damned attractive. 'They are broken-hearted. They were looking forward to working for you.'

He gave a faint smile. 'Then I'm sorry to disappoint them, but I'm not a charitable institution.'

'Then you should be,' I said. 'It is part of the duty of a landowner to care for the people on his land.'

'I'll tell you what,' he said helpfully. 'Supposing I make cottages available for them on the estate and increase their pensions, would that appease you?'

I looked up suspiciously and met his glance. 'Is there a catch?' I asked.

He laughed softly. 'Of course,' he said. 'Your signature in exchange for their peace of mind.'

Somehow I controlled my anger. 'Just why do you want that land so badly?' I asked. 'It's right on the edge of the estate, and its clearance doesn't affect the efficiency of the rest of the place at all.' I held his gaze as calmly as

I could and was incensed to see the humour in his eyes.

'Maybe it does, maybe it doesn't,' he said. 'My reasons are not relevant.'

'They are to me,' I retorted. 'You can't ride roughshod over people like this!' I had begun to pace up and down the carpet. 'There is more to life than money! There is such a thing as beauty and kindness and loyalty and – love!' To my shame I could feel tears of anger pricking my eyelids.

He hadn't moved from the desk but I could see his eyes following me. He was grinning. 'You know, I can't help admiring you,' he said. 'You've got a lot more spirit than a great many of my business opponents. I like that in a woman.'

'That's not what I've heard!' I said sharply.

His eyes narrowed. 'Have you also heard that I am never defeated in a business battle?' he murmured. 'I think I shall enjoy defeating you, Katherine. It is a pity that Grandfather's old servants must suffer for your intransigence.'

'They won't suffer!' I had already thought what I was going to do. 'They can come to Kingley Farm.'

He laughed out loud. 'And how will you pay them?'

'From my inheritance. Grandfather left me some money too, you know.'

'I know exactly how much money Grandfather left you,' he said. 'If you spend it on a pack of idle servants you will be left penniless.' He stood up and walked over to the open window. The scent of the grass and fresh earth drifted in across the sill and I could see him breathing it in. Then he turned back to me.

'You really care about them, don't you,' he said.

'They are family to me,' I replied. 'I've known most of them since I was a baby.'

He was looking at me rather quizzically. 'Sentiment is not something I admire,' he went on. 'It leaves people vulnerable. But you have courage and as you said, loyalty, which I do admire. It makes you a worthy opponent. I suggest we take our battle of words further. But not here. Over dinner at the White Hart which I hear is not a bad hostelry.'

I was speechless for a moment at his change of tactics, but not so Sara, who had obviously been listening from the library the whole time. She erupted through the door, her green eyes blazing. 'You promised you would take me there tonight!' she accused.

Richard gave her a look of pure contempt. 'Another time,' he snapped. 'This is business.'

I should have turned him down there and then, but something made me agree to go out with him. Partly I think it was to get back at Sara, whom I had begun to dislike excessively, partly because now that my anger rather than my fear was uppermost, I had almost begun to enjoy sparring with him. But most of all, if I admitted the truth to myself, because I was finding him more and more attractive.

He drove me home first and waited in the Rolls whilst I changed. I did not ask him in to meet my father, who was in the event still asleep anyway, so I left him a note, then having donned a cream linen dress and my pearl earrings, I made my way out to the car once more.

Richard had obviously made up his mind not to mention our quarrel at all, nor did he mention Jacqueline. Not once did he antagonise me as we sat opposite each other in the candlelight and, baffled by his change of tactics, I found myself relaxing under his charm, almost enjoying myself as I sipped the wine.

In one corner of my mind I kept reminding myself that this man was dangerous and I must not trust him, but slowly my caution, and my antagonism, were slipping away. Without my noticing he ordered a second bottle of the Chateau Lafitte and, with my cheeks burning from the candles and the warmth of the room, I drank far more than I was used to. At last I saw the flames begin to blur and waver before my eyes and I caught myself nodding dangerously close to them. Finally Richard reached across the table and touched my hand and I jerked myself upright as if he had stung me.

'I'm sorry,' I said.

'You're tired.' He looked concerned. 'Perhaps it would be better if I took you home?'

I must have dozed again on the drive back for when I awoke we were drawing up outside the Manor.

'I thought you were taking me home!' I said, looking round in alarm.

'A coffee first, I think,' he replied firmly, and I had no alternative but to allow him to help me out of the car.

He was still holding my arm as we walked slowly up the moss-covered steps when the oak front door swung open and Sara stood there framed in the light of the hall.

I would have stopped, but Richard did not hesitate, urging me on until we passed through the wisteria-covered porch. Only then did I see the expression on Sara's face.

She was laughing. 'So, you got her drunk,' she said gleefully. 'How very clever. I might have known it wasn't the pleasure of her company you wanted!'

I drew back but Richard's arm was round me, propelling me forward into the study, and as I watched Sara slammed the door behind me. This time, when she had locked it, she dropped the key triumphantly into her cleavage.

Richard pushed me into one of the chairs then he turned to her. 'Go and make some coffee,' he said curtly, and I was aware that he had her by the elbow and was hustling her towards the door to the library beyond which lay the kitchens. Closing it behind her he strode back to me.

My head had begun to ache unbearably. 'You got me drunk deliberately,' I managed to say. 'I had begun to trust you.'

He laughed softly. 'That was a bad mistake, Katherine,' he said. 'No one should ever trust me. But I assure you, I did not get you drunk deliberately. I had imagined you would have a harder head than this. Why should I want to, anyway?' He sat down on the arm of my chair very close to me. 'Did you think I wanted to seduce you?' He was still laughing as his head dropped close to mine. 'I assure you, if I want a woman, I'll take her. I don't need to get her drunk!'

His lips were firm and warm, and I did not resist as his hands moved gently over my shoulders to slip inside my dress, caressing my breasts. All I knew was that I wanted him more than I had ever wanted any man in my life before.

'What the hell is going on?' Sara's sudden hiss of fury pierced my dazed thoughts and I shrank away from him, but he merely straightened up slowly and turned to her, mildly annoyed.

'I suggest you learn to knock on doors,' he said with awful quietness.

'And I suggest you stick to getting her signature!' she almost spat at him.

Shock cleared my head a little and I staggered to my feet, ducking under his arm. He did not appear to notice. They were regarding each other with too much anger and I was beginning to wonder if she would physically attack him when the silence between them was broken by the doorbell.

'See who that is!' he ordered abruptly.

She glared at him, then began to fumble in her blouse for the key. When she finally found it and opened the door I shot out of the room after her.

'Are you leaving so soon?' Richard had followed me into the hall, but he made no effort to restrain me.

'I am indeed,' I said as Sara pulled open the door and I saw the way of escape appear across the moonlit gravel before me. On the doorstep stood Dave Conway.

'I thought I'd come back tonight after all,' he said.

'Good.' Suavely Richard blocked his way. 'You are just in time to drive Katherine home.'

I saw the surprise on Dave's face, but already I was past him. 'There's no need,' I called over my shoulder. 'I'll drive myself.'

'You're had too much to drink,' Richard shouted sharply. 'Let Dave take you.'

I swung to face him. 'These are private roads. I'll be a

danger to no one but myself, and I seem to have sobered up astonishingly,' I replied.

He was still standing in the hall and the light showed he was smiling. 'You have indeed,' he said. 'Very well. We'll continue our little talk another time. And conclude our business transactions then as well.'

I held his gaze for a moment across that narrow stretch of gravel and I did not like what I saw there at all. All his charm had vanished. He was once more my antagonist and a dangerous man.

I accomplished the drive home without mishap and found my father waiting up for me.

'Katie! I was worried. Did Richard not drive you back?'

I shook my head. 'I had my car at the Manor so he dropped me there.' I didn't want him to see my face, but it was too late.

'Katie? Is something wrong? Have you and Richard quarrelled?'

There was no use denying it. I was too agitated. 'I suppose we have,' I admitted. 'Nothing serious, but I do think I should go away for a few days. Just to calm down a little.' I forced myself to laugh, as I knelt beside his chair. 'Will you promise me something so I can go? Will you have Mrs Dawson and Hill to work for you here?'

He smiled sadly. 'So it is true that Richard has sacked everyone up at the Manor?'

I nodded.

'Is that why you quarrelled?'

I nodded again and he reached for my hand. 'It's his decision to make Katie, but I should like people to help here. We'll afford it somehow.'

I only managed four hours' sleep. By eight next morning my case was in the car and I was driving through waist-high mist towards the main road, an enormous sense of relief bolstering me. Without my signature my woods were safe and as long as I was out of reach, Richard could not win.

* * *

I had not told my father where I was going. Sally and Duncan Graham were my best friends and the only people in England I could think of to whom I could tell my story. It was a good two-hour drive to their house and I found myself glancing constantly in the driving mirror for the sign that I was being followed, but as far as I could see there was no one behind me and with every mile I felt happier and more relaxed.

Coffee with a slug of Scotch was their first remedy. Then they listened intently to my story.

'My God, Kate! The man sounds a fiend,' Sally said with feeling. 'Yet if I read you right,' she looked at me sideways, 'you fancy him, don't you?'

I could feel my cheeks growing hot. 'Is it so obvious?' I said. She laughed. 'Only to an expert like me.'

Duncan was frowning, however. 'I think you could be in real danger Kate,' he said. 'Not of your life or anything like that, but I suspect a man like that knows how to put the pressure on. He sounds most unsavoury to me.' Something Minna had echoed every time I had phoned her.

The Grahams' solution was immediate. They were leaving for a holiday at their Scottish cottage, and I should go with them. Duncan seemed to think that once I had dropped completely out of Richard's sight, I would be safe. 'He'll get tired of the new estate and get involved in some new deal, then you can slip home,' he said with a grin.

Twenty-four hours later I was ensconced with them in a stone-built cottage on the west coast of Scotland, a lifetime away from Kingley and Richard Bradshaw.

But my relief was all too short-lived. After dinner that first evening as we sat with our coffee around the crackling driftwood fire I asked Duncan if I could ring my father. I let the dialling tone purr in my ear for a long time before I admitted no one was going to answer and hung up.

'Surely he could have gone out?' Sally said, shrewdly watching my face.

I shook my head slowly. 'He practically never does. And even if he had, someone should be there.'

I tried again an hour later and finally, just before we went to bed. Then I rang the Manor. An American voice answered.

'Who is that?' I asked cautiously. The receiver felt clammy in my hands.

'David Conway. May I help you?'

'Dave? Listen, do you know where my father is?'

'Kate? Where are you?'

'Never mind where I am. Where is my father?'

There was a short silence, then I heard him say cautiously, 'Kate, I think you had better come home.'

I felt panic beginning to mount in my throat, and I knew my face had gone white. Sally had risen to her feet and came to stand beside me, her hand on my arm. Somehow I managed to repeat my question.

'He's in Switzerland, Kate.'

'*Switzerland?*'

Duncan had stood up and came to stand beside Sally. They both had their eyes fixed on my face.

'He had a bad turn, Kate. Nothing too serious. Richard heard about it and naturally he wanted to help. He had a specialist come in and they arranged for Mr Parrish to be taken to a clinic in Switzerland.'

'Where is it? Give me the address.' My voice was shaking.

'I can't do that Kate,' he said softly. 'Richard has all the details. He's in New York just now, but he'll be back on Friday. You'll have to speak to him. In person, Kate.'

'You can't go!' Sally said later. 'It's a trap, you must see that.'

I knew she was right. And I also knew that I had no choice. Richard had found my weak point. Miserably I repacked my case and asked Duncan to drive me to catch the first train from Oban next morning.

Dave was waiting for me at King's Cross with the Rolls. 'I don't usually get involved in Richard's personal affairs, Kate,' he said as we threaded our way through the traffic. 'But in business I know him. He is completely ruthless honey, and without sentiment. He doesn't understand or care what you feel about that land. To him it's acreage on a piece of paper; more for his empire. You are a challenge and so, true to form, he's found your Achilles heel and gone straight for it.' He glanced across at me, his hazel eyes worried. 'Don't fight him, Kate. For God's sake. Do I have to spell out what I'm trying to say?'

'He'd actually hurt my father?' My fingers had twisted my skirt into a fan of tiny pleats.

For a moment he didn't answer. Then he nodded slowly. 'He stops at nothing to get what he wants honey, believe me.'

I believed him. I sat in a coma for the rest of that drive and, persuading Dave to drop me off at the farmhouse alone, I walked up the drive feeling as though the weight of the world were on my shoulders.

Mrs Dawson was in the kitchen and the place was full of sunlight and flowers with the kettle singing on the hob. But the house was empty without my father and I knew I was beaten.

Late that afternoon I went for a walk over my land and realised that I was saying goodbye. The bluebells still scented the shade of the oak woods and the marshland smelled of salt and sweet grasses and I stood for a long time watching the redshanks running about on the mud, their slender feet making light tracks which stayed a minute then vanished as if they had never been. 'Forgive me,' I whispered into the wind. 'Forgive me, for what I'm going to do.'

I walked back slowly, the setting sun in my face, and made my way back home exhausted and defeated. Mrs Dawson was waiting for me by the gate, her kind face wrinkled with worry. 'Miss Kate, you've been so long.'

'I'm sorry. I had to think by myself for a bit,' I said. Then I added hopefully, 'Has there been any word from my father?'

Any word which would bring reprieve.

She shook her head. 'Only Mr Richard phoned.' The tone of her voice told me what she thought of him. 'He said he was expecting you to dinner at the Manor.'

I dressed carefully in a long dress of palest eau de nil and piled my hair into a chignon. My car was still at Sally and Duncan's house, but Richard had said he would send the Rolls and I found myself smiling faintly at the chauffeur as I stepped in, feeling like Marie Antoinette as she mounted the tumbril for her last ride through Paris.

Richard seemed to be alone in the study – as far as I could see the only room in the house which he used – and I glanced round, expecting to see Sara somewhere in the background as usual, but no; there was no one else there. I was not sure whether or not I should be relieved.

I looked him straight in the eye as he rose to greet me. 'So, you've won. I suppose you think you're very clever.' I did not try to keep the bitterness out of my voice.

I was astonished at the way my heart had started to jerk uncomfortably somewhere under my breastbone at the sight of him. He was casually dressed in a cord jacket with a cravat at the open neck of his silk shirt and looked unbearably handsome. But I was determined not to be won over. 'It must be marvellous to be so rich you can ride roughshod over everyone and everything,' I went on relentlessly, 'manipulating lives, as if they were pawns on a chessboard.'

He had begun to smile slightly and I could feel my eyes blazing with anger.

'You are not a good loser I see, Katherine,' he said softly. 'Perhaps a drink would help a little?'

It was champagne.

I threw my purse down on a chair and took the tall tulip glass from him with as steady a hand as I could manage.

'I may not be a good loser, Richard,' I breathed, 'but I'm not a stupid one. I have to have proof my father is all right before I sign anything at all.'

He was watching me closely and now he sat down on the

corner of his desk. Putting his own glass down on the blotter, he folded his arms. 'And you also want to see the colour of my money, of course.'

'Of course.' It hadn't even crossed my mind, but I wasn't going to let him guess that. My eyes were fixed on the spray of tiny bubbles rising from his glass, too small to stain the royal blue blotting paper beneath them as they landed.

He laughed quietly. 'You know, Katherine, I'm almost disappointed in you. I had thought you would hold out to the death.'

I looked at him at that. 'My own perhaps,' I whispered. 'But not my father's.'

He picked up his glass. 'Then let us drink to his recovery,' he said smoothly. 'What proof do you want that he is safe and well? Will your own eyes convince you?'

I nodded.

Without a word he swivelled to pick up the phone on the desk. After a few murmured orders he turned back to me. 'We have time to eat a quick dinner, then the car will call at your place so that you can collect your passport,' he said, and he picked up his glass.

If only it could have been under different circumstances I would have enjoyed that flight in the executive jet across France. The sky was clear and starlit and the ground far beneath us bathed in silver moonlight as we cruised towards Switzerland and my father. It was too late to visit him when we arrived and a car whisked us into the centre of Geneva where hotel rooms were awaiting us, and I was shown with meticulous politeness to a private suite.

Exhausted, I fell asleep almost instantly and was only awakened by the chambermaid bringing a breakfast of coffee, croissants and black cherry jam.

Richard was waiting for me in the foyer. He greeted me with a brotherly kiss on the cheek. 'It's an hour's drive,' he said cheerfully. 'I've rung the clinic and your father is expecting us.'

I had never been to Switzerland before, and the beauty of
those circling mountains took my breath away. In spite of
my determination not to unbend towards Richard in any way,
I could not prevent myself exclaiming in delight as the hired
BMW drove us ever higher. The clinic was huge, white
painted and obviously excessively expensive, and my father,
greeting us in the muted, flower-filled reception room, looked
better than I had seen him look for years.

'Richard, my boy,' he said after he had hugged us both. 'I
don't know how to thank you. I've been given a new lease
of life!' He turned to me and pulled my hair playfully. 'I had
got the impression from you Katie, that this chap was some
kind of Machiavellian monster. What were you thinking of
you naughty child?'

'I can't imagine,' I said dryly.

We spent a couple of hours with father, wandering slowly
in the gardens, and then we went back inside. As Richard
said goodbye and went out to the car I lingered behind for
a moment.

'You really are happy to be here, Pa? They are looking after
you?' I asked.

He kissed me on the forehead. 'Reichman is the best there
is in his field, Kate. I couldn't be in better hands. I don't
know how I can ever thank Richard. This place costs a fortune
you know.'

I smiled. 'He's glad to do it, Pa.'

'And you're in love with him, Kate, aren't you?' He was
looking down into my face, his eyes reflecting all the pride
and joy he had always shown me. I opened my mouth to
deny it, but I knew suddenly that it would spoil everything
for him if I did. Instead, I managed to smile. 'Perhaps a little,'
I said. 'It's early days yet.'

'He's a good man, Katie, you could do no better,' he said
hopefully. 'And he adores you, you know, I can see it in his
eyes.'

*　　*　　*

386

By tea time we were once more circling the airport back home. The Rolls was waiting outside the terminal. At the wheel was Sara, her hair glowing above a black shirt and tight white jeans. She was laughing as she saw us emerge from the building. 'What, no cuckoo clocks and duty free brandy?' she said as she gunned the car viciously into life. 'I am surprised, Kate. And was the beloved parent alive and well?'

'That is enough Sara!' Richard's voice cut like a whiplash across her sarcasm and she fell silent, but my eyes met hers for an instant in the driving mirror and I saw the flash of triumph in them with a sinking heart.

I asked to be dropped off at the farm, but Richard refused. 'You have a small duty to perform before you go home, Katherine. A signature, remember?'

How could I forget?

At the Manor I headed for the study automatically, but Sara barred my way.

'There's a room for you upstairs,' she said. She eyed my suit as if it were something the cat had dragged in. 'I'm sure you would like to freshen up and change before dinner.'

I took a shower and slipped on the shantung dress which I had in my overnight bag. I brushed my hair down on my shoulders and carefully applied some make-up, then taking a deep breath I made my way back downstairs.

Richard was alone in the study. There was no sign of Sara, nor, I noted, Jacqueline. He too had changed and was now formally dressed in a dinner jacket. A new bottle of Krug stood already opened on the desk and when I appeared he poured out a second glass.

'To our business deal,' he said.

The windows were opened onto the twilit garden and I could hear a blackbird singing in the distance. The sound was somehow heart-breaking in its beauty.

'Well,' I said sharply, wishing I were not so conscious of how handsome he was looking. 'Let me sign and get it over.'

He glanced at his watch. 'Calder should be here soon. He's

on his way down from London. He has the papers with him.'

I put down my glass untouched. 'You should be feeling very pleased with yourself,' I said sadly. 'The fact that you are going to destroy so much that is beautiful and irreplaceable means nothing to you?'

'Should it?' He strode over to the window and glanced out.

'Haven't you enough money?'

Turning he looked at me. 'Does anyone ever have enough?'

I closed my eyes, hoping I wasn't going to cry. I had no arguments left.

John Calder arrived, dapper and cool in spite of his long drive, and produced a sheaf of legal documents from his brief-case. One by one they were put before me and one by one I signed, hardly seeing what I was doing through a haze of tears. Then all the papers were locked away in the safe behind Grandfather's portrait on the wall.

Richard pushed a scrap of paper towards me as I turned away. 'Don't forget your cheque, Katherine. Better put it somewhere safe.'

I picked it up without looking at it and slipped it into my pocket.

Calder and Richard drank more champagne, and then the former took his leave, shaking hands with us both in turn. 'I am so glad this has ended happily,' he said as he made his farewells and he slipped unobtrusively from the room. Outside the blackbird was still singing.

Richard was watching me closely. 'You look a little pale,' he said. 'Dinner won't be long.'

I shook my head. 'I don't want any dinner. I'm going home.'

He was at the door before me, his hands on my shoulders. 'I insist. You can't disappoint the chef. Then you can go home.'

I was too tired and too miserable to argue.

Only when we were seated once more in the huge, gloomy

dining room, lit by candles in the two silver candelabra, did I notice that Sara was still missing.

'Isn't your lady friend joining us?' I asked wanly as Richard poured white wine into two crystal glasses.

'She is not.' His voice was suddenly uncompromisingly hard.

'I can't believe she approves of you dining with me alone,' I said.

'She has no say in the matter,' he replied sitting down and picking up his napkin. 'She's locked in her room.'

I stared at him, shocked out of my apathy. 'You're joking!'

'Am I?' He met my gaze steadily for a moment. 'I wonder.'

The door opened and a maid appeared with the hors d'oeuvres. Only when she had gone did I look at Richard again. His eyes were gleaming maliciously in the candlelight. 'I hope you are going to eat this time. You've been picking at your food ever since I met you, and you are already too thin for my liking,' he said.

'Indeed,' I retorted. 'Well, if Sara is the shape you like, you can keep her. I'll never have a figure like that!'

He looked thoughtful. 'She is beautiful, that's true, but stupid. Very stupid.' He grinned. 'And a real bitch.'

'You haven't really locked her in?' I persisted uneasily in spite of myself. I wasn't at all sure that he was joking.

One of Grandfather's crested silver forks gleamed in his hand as he toyed with a minute curl of smoked salmon. He looked at me for a long moment, then he raised his glass. His face was alive with amusement.

'I did. She has a vicious temper. I gather she told you I beat her,' he went on conversationally.

I felt myself grow cold. 'Do you?' I asked.

He laughed and the sound made my skin crawl. 'I always beat my women,' he said softly.

There was a long silence in the room as, seemingly unconcerned, he continued eating.

'I don't believe a word you say!' I said at last.

He looked up. 'Don't you? You should see your face!'

Despite my feelings, I smiled. 'All I can say is thank God I am not one of your women, so I need never find out the truth.'

'Ah, but you are,' he said.

'I beg your pardon?' I stared at him.

'You are one of my women, Katherine,' he repeated softly.

'How do you make that out?'

'I've bought you, sweetheart. Body and soul.' He laughed again and I felt the hairs rise on the back of my neck.

'That cheque in your pocket,' he went on. 'Only half that money was for the land; the price I originally offered you. What do you think the rest is for?'

I stared at him for one full minute, then I reached into my pocket and unfolded the cheque, holding it to the candlelight so that I could read it.

It was made out for one million pounds sterling.

'Don't tear it up my dear, will you.' His voice came from miles away beyond the glow of the candlelight. 'You've signed now, and I shall not write you another one for less!'

For a moment I remained where I was, paralysed, then I pushed my chair back and stood up. 'You're crazy!' I cried. 'Quite, quite crazy!'

Again that low, pleasant laugh. 'Quite, quite possibly,' he echoed, 'but not too crazy to be able to collect what is mine.'

And with that he rose and began to walk towards me round the long table. . .

PART THREE

I found I could not move. Paralysed, I watched as Richard approached me round that long Georgian dining table, his face illumined by the flickering candles. My brain had ceased to function – then he touched me. His hands rested lightly on my elbows, and he drew me to him without a word. Obediently I lifted my lips to his and felt his kiss burning against my mouth. Slowly his arms slipped around me, holding me against him so tightly I could barely breathe, and I closed my eyes, feeling my whole body come unwillingly alive at his touch, powerless to resist him.

But somewhere, somehow, my mind was fighting back. This man was my enemy; however masterly a lover he was, however much I wanted him, nothing could change that. He was in search of conquest and only when I was completely his would his craving for power over me be satisfied. It was not me, Kate Parrish, whom he wanted. I had been a rival and I had to be completely defeated.

Besides, he was engaged. The thought broke the spell and at last I regained the power of movement. I began to struggle, pushing him away.

'How could you!' I managed to say. 'Doesn't it make you feel just the smallest bit guilty, making love to every woman who crosses your path, when you have a beautiful fiancée waiting for you in the States?'

He stiffened imperceptibly, then he let me go. 'I no longer have a fiancée,' he said, his voice cold. He walked across to the window and leaned out, his elbows on the sill.

'You mean you broke it off?' I asked incredulously.

There was a long silence. 'You could say that she broke it off,' he replied after a moment.

'All right then, what about Sara?' I flung at him. 'Your mistress is upstairs in this very house!'

He turned and gazed at me. Then he began to shake his head in mock despair.

'Mistress is such a quaint term; but are you going to make me get rid of all my women, Katherine?'

This time I could have moved, but I didn't try. I wanted him to kiss me again.

As his arms closed round me I heard the telephone ring in the distance. For a moment I thought he would ignore it, but reluctantly he pushed me away. 'I'll be back,' he whispered, touching the tip of my nose with his finger, and he was gone.

Seconds later he reappeared. He looked mildly amused rather than annoyed. 'It's for you,' he said.

The phone was in the study and, still dazed, I followed him and picked up the receiver.

'Kate? It's Chris. Can you get over here right away?'

'Chris?' For a moment I was non-plussed. Chris. My dependable, nice American Chris, ringing me at Kingley Manor? 'Where are you?' I stammered.

'I'm over at your place. Mrs Dawson here told me where you were. Look, Kate, you've got to get back here quickly.'

'Is something wrong? Is it Father?'

'I'll tell you when you get here.'

'Chris? Chris, *wait* . . .' I shouted, but he had hung up.

Richard was watching my face. 'What's wrong?'

Shaking my head, I was still staring at the phone. 'I don't know. I must go back . . .'

I expected him to argue, but to my surprise he offered to drive me home straightaway. Like me he obviously thought it must have something to do with my father.

At the farm he helped me out of the car. 'Do you want me to come in?' he said, his voice unexpectedly gentle.

I shook my head, and without a word he climbed back into the Rolls. 'You know where I am if you need me,' he said. 'Remember the plane is there if you want to go to him,' and he was gone.

I stood for a moment, watching the tail lights disappearing up the long tree-lined road back to the Manor, then I went into the farmhouse. Chris was sitting in the cosy living room, drinking coffee. There was no sign of Mrs Dawson. He rose as I went in, and I was enveloped in a huge bear hug. 'Kate honey, have I missed you!'

'Chris, what is it? Is it Pa?' Unable to think of anything else I stood, my hands clutching Chris's shirt-front, trying to read his face.

'Hey, relax honey. Why should it be to do with your Pa?' He guided me to the sofa and pulled me down beside him. 'I was sorry to hear from Minna that he'd been ill, but I understood from your nice Mrs Dawson that he was at some swanky clinic in Switzerland.'

'He is.' I was beginning to breathe evenly again. 'But what did you want to tell me so urgently then?'

'I'll tell you.' He reached for his coffee. 'Do you want some of this stuff? Okay, now, listen. Just before I was due to come over here, I had dinner with your boss, and he told me he'd been doing some research into your precious Kingley Woods.'

I felt my heart sink. What would Martin think of me when he heard I'd sold out?

'He's discovered the reason your millionaire cousin is so all-fired eager to get his paws on that land.'

'Don't tell me, Chris. It's too late,' I said desperately.

He stared at me. 'Too late?'

I nodded. 'I sold.'

For a moment I thought he was going to have a fit. His face went puce, then white. 'Why, for Chrissake?' he managed to say at last.

I got to my feet and feeling in my pocket I found the cheque and threw it down on the coffee table in front of him. 'There's the reason,' I said bitterly.

He reached for the piece of paper and opened it, and his mouth dropped open. 'One million. One lousy million! Kate, Martin has discovered that several years ago test borings were done on that land. There is oil under there.'

I gasped. 'And Richard knew that?'

'Sure he knew.'

For a moment I was too stunned to speak, then suddenly I began to laugh. Chris stared at me as if I had gone off my head as, too weak to explain, I threw myself back on the sofa, the cheque in my hand, and waved it at him.

'Only half this was for the land,' I spluttered hysterically. 'Half a million for the land. The other half was for me!'

It took him a minute to follow what I was saying, but eventually he understood. I have never seen Chris angry before, but this time I thought he'd hit the ceiling.

'The bastard!' he yelled, beside himself. 'The lousy, no-account bastard! Who the hell does he think he is anyway? My God! When I think . . .' He was beyond speech for a moment. Then he went on. 'When was this, anyway?'

'Just now,' I said with a harsh little laugh. 'You called up just as he was about to haul me off to bed.' I didn't add that, seduced by wine and candles and kisses, I would probably have gone without too much of a struggle. His next words however left me completely cold with horror, every ounce of bitter laughter drained from my body.

'I knew he was a shit,' he said slowly. 'But this takes some beating. Did he tell you his fiancée killed herself a couple of days back?'

Outside an owl had started hooting in the old walnut tree on the side lawn. It was the only sound in that room for a long time.

'Jacqueline?' I whispered at last.

'Jacqui Overton. That's right.'

'How?' Stiffly my lips framed the question.

He hesitated for a moment. 'She shot herself. Hey, Katie, I'm sorry honey. You look shattered. I didn't realise you knew her.'

I shook my head. 'I only met her once, but . . .' My eyes had filled with tears. 'She was kind to me, in her own way.'

Her last words to me had come flooding back. 'There is nothing more Richard can do to me,' she had said and I remembered suddenly the despair I had seen in her eyes.

I looked at Chris bleakly. 'You know, I would like that coffee after all,' I said huskily.

I did not sleep that night. I had shown Chris to the spare room and with one look at my face he had kissed me good-night and meekly closed the door behind him. I went to my own bed alone. My head was whirling with images: Jacqui, her face white, her eyes great aching pools of misery; Richard, his handsome profile stone-carved against the candlelit velvet curtains; my father, his eyes bright and happy above lips which still showed that tell-tale tinge of blue; and Sara, her mouth scarlet, laughing at me, laughing as she was dragged away by some of Richard's minions; and above all I kept seeing my woods and marshes, bright and sun-filled no longer, disfigured by a choking blanket of oil.

When I awoke it was raining. I lay for a long time listening to the regular splatter on the window then I dragged myself, my head splitting, out of bed.

Chris was sitting at the kitchen table demolishing a plate of bacon and eggs. I slid into the chair opposite him and tried to smile. 'How long can you stay?' I asked.

Mrs Dawson put a cup of coffee before me. 'Do you want bacon, Miss Kate?' she asked. I could see her eyeing my face doubtfully.

I shook my head. 'Just coffee thanks.' My hand was shaking as I picked up the cup.

'I'll stay as long as you like,' Chris said gently. 'And the first thing I'm doing is driving you to the bank to pay this in.' He reached into his pocket and produced the cheque. He laughed quietly. 'You know I found it on the floor this morning! You must get it cleared before our friend changes his mind and cancels it.'

I grimaced and reached for the wooden sugar bowl. 'I'm going to return it to him.'

'No, you're not.'

'Chris! I told you what the money was for!'

'Okay, so you pay the cheque in and write him another for half the sum.'

I had never thought of that.

My triumph was short-lived. Two days later I received my cheque to Richard through the post. It had been neatly torn in half and in spite of myself I was once more a millionairess and in his debt.

I told Chris, tears of frustration in my eyes, and he gave a dry laugh. 'Don't worry, honey,' he said. 'We'll win.'

Leaving Chris sitting in the garden I walked over to the stables and borrowed a horse, determined to gallop the misery out of my system, feeling the wind and rain and sun in my hair and on my face, but I was to wish bitterly that I hadn't. Automatically I took the bridle path which led round the acres Minna had sold to Richard, already shimmering green beneath their crop of winter wheat, and headed towards my woods. One more ride, surely, could do no harm, and Richard wasn't there to see me; I had heard that he had gone back to Boston.

But at the edge of Kingley Wood I had to pull the horse to a rearing halt. Instead of the broad soft leafy path I was used to I was confronted by a solid wire fence which led off in both directions as far as I could see into the distance. I stared at it. He must have had men working to fence off the wood at dawn the day after I had signed it over.

I walked the horse home, no longer interested in where I went. All I wanted was to go away and never see Kingley again.

Chris provided a temporary solution. 'We'll go and see your father,' he said. 'Spend a week or two in Switzerland. It's best like that, Katie, surely?'

Mutely I nodded. I had already heard the distant whine of a chainsaw echoing across the fields and I knew I could not hang around to watch those great oaks fall.

The flight to Switzerland was very different this time. I could not bring myself to touch the money in the bank, so we went economy, a pedal plane, as Chris laughingly called it, full of tourists and children and harassed stewardesses, and then hired a Hertz car to take us out to the clinic.

My father had a small private room on the second floor, a bright room full of flowers, and he seemed astonishingly well. At his recommendation Chris and I found ourselves rooms at the inn in the local village which we could use as a base for exploring the countryside.

'It looks to me as if you need this air as much as I do, Katie,' Pa said gently as I sat beside him on the window seat in his room. The doctor to whom I had spoken on our arrival had said he was so much better he would be able to go home within a few weeks. 'But I'm disappointed not to see Richard.' He looked at me searchingly. Chris had gone off to collect some newspapers.

I tried to keep my face impassive. 'He had to go to Boston on business,' I said, as calmly as I could.

'I see.' He was still watching me. 'I like Chris, of course, but I had hoped, Katie, that you and Richard –' he stopped as I jumped to my feet.

'No, I'm sorry, but there can never be anything between Richard and me!' As I said it I realised that I would have given my right arm to have been able to please him. But I never wanted to see Richard again.

Luckily Chris appeared at that moment, a pile of newspapers under his arm. 'Hi,' he said. 'I took the chance to ask them to bring up some coffee and pastries. I hope that's all right?' He looked from one to the other of us, obviously puzzled by our silence. 'Would you like me to go away again?' he asked humbly.

I grabbed his arm. 'Of course not. I was just telling Pa that Richard had gone to Boston.'

'Such a pleasant young man,' my father muttered defiantly.

Unfortunately Chris heard him. 'You're kidding,' he said. 'After the stunt he pulled over those woods!'

I aimed a kick at his ankle, but it was too late. My father rounded on him sharply.

'What are you talking about?'

Chris ignored my frenzied signals. 'He forced Kate to sell him her inheritance, that's all,' he said. 'The man is an unprincipled bastard.'

My father had gone white. 'You've sold the marsh, Katie?

It's not true? I can't believe it. Your grandfather wanted you to have it forever.'

'Pa,' I took his hands in mine. 'Don't be upset.'

'Upset!' He rounded on me. 'What made you do it? What in the world made you do it?'

I could not reply, but Chris stepped in. 'Why do you think Richard had you brought here?' he said quietly. 'The man has proved himself an unscrupulous blackmailer!'

For a moment there was complete silence in the room, then my father clutched at his chest. Through a haze of horror I saw his face go white and then blue as he began to stagger towards the bed, gasping for breath.

'*Chris!*' I screamed.

He had the presence of mind to press the bell and within seconds the room was full of doctors and nurses and Chris and I were hustled away.

'Oh Kate, I'm sorry.' Chris was holding his head. 'I never thought! I never realised . . .'

'It doesn't matter,' I heard myself say tonelessly. 'You weren't to know.'

Later the doctor came and spoke to us. He was very reassuring. 'He'll be fine after a good rest,' he said kindly. 'Come and see him tomorrow, for five minutes only.'

We walked slowly towards the inn with heavy hearts. I had not realised just how precarious my father's health was, but I could not be angry with Chris. He was on my side, after all.

We walked into the bar at the inn and ordered ourselves a drink. There seemed nothing else to do.

Seated in silence at the table for a while we watched the coming and going of the other guests, then Chris idly pulled one of the American newspapers out of the bag he was carrying, and opened it.

I heard his gasp and looked up. 'What is it?'

'Kate, you're not going to believe it!' he said, his voice

shaking. He folded the paper and pushed it towards me, his finger pointing at a double column article at the bottom of the page. The light was dim, but I could just make it out. The headline read: *Boston Murder Enquiry*. Below it there was an account of Jacqui's death and the police decision that it had not been suicide after all, but murder. There was a photo of Jacqui and another of Richard. I reread the last paragraph: *Police said last night that they were anxious to interview the deceased's fiancé, millionaire businessman Richard Bradshaw, at present believed to be visiting his family estates in England. They admitted that he could not be ruled out as a suspect...*

The room had started to spin and I closed my eyes, not realising that Chris had left the table until he returned with a brandy and pressed the glass into my hand.

'Drink it,' he ordered softly. Then he took the paper back and scrutinised it again, shaking his head.

I went to my room shortly afterwards, and spent the next hour sitting in a daze on the bed, staring at the wall. It was not possible. I did not believe it. Whatever I thought of Richard, whatever I had said, I did not, could not, believe he was capable of murder. Whatever Sara and David had said, and Jacqui herself, the man I knew, the man who had held me in his arms, could not be a killer.

I was only brought back to myself by a knock at the door. It was Chris.

'Kate, there's a David Conway in the bar asking for you. He went up to the clinic and they told him we were here.'

I heard myself gasp.

'If you don't want to see him, I'll tell him to get lost.' Chris was bristling with suspicion at once. But I shook my head. 'I'll come,' I said. 'Give me one minute and I'll come down.'

I washed my face and ran a comb through my hair. Then I went to join them.

Dave was looking tired, but reasonably cheerful, I thought. 'Seen the papers?' he said.

I nodded, sliding in close to Chris on the bench.

'Mrs Dawson said you'd flown out to see your father,' he went on. 'I thought I'd better come right out and reassure you. Needless to say Richard had nothing to do with this dreadful business. You do believe that, don't you?' He glanced first at me, then at Chris, his hazel eyes warm and sincere.

Obviously we both looked doubtful so he went on. 'You didn't know about Jacqui, Kate. There's no reason why you should as Richard protected her the whole time, even keeping up the pretence that they were engaged. She had a big drug problem, and she had tried to kill herself a couple of times before.'

I stared at him. 'But the paper said –'

'The papers say Richard is suspected of murdering her,' David said softly, 'because the police received information – anonymously of course – that he did.' He paused, his eyes steadily on mine. 'Hell has no fury, someone once said, and the woman Richard scorned was Sara Dashwood!'

'*She* told them he was a murderer?' I repeated, scandalised.

'She did. He had given her her marching orders, stupid bitch, and she got her own back very neatly.'

'Then he can prove he's innocent, surely?' I asked in a whisper.

He gave me a reassuring smile. 'He'll manage somehow.'

My head was reeling with the implications of what he had said.

'What made him decide to get rid of Sara at last?' I asked after a moment.

He looked at me, his head a little to one side.

'Can't you guess?'

Something in his expression made me blush. 'For Jacqui?' I murmured.

'No, for you.' For a moment we sat in silence looking at

each other. Then abruptly he stood up. 'Let me get us all another drink,' he said.

'What was that last bit about?' Chris said as Dave headed for the bar.

'You know as well as I do,' I said sharply. 'But I never thought he'd actually go as far as telling her to go!'

'You asked him to?' He raised an eyebrow.

'I asked him what the hell he meant by trying to seduce me with a fiancée –' I stopped abruptly, then I went on, 'and at the same time another woman upstairs in the same house.'

'I see.' He didn't sound convinced.

David returned with three drinks. 'I've got to get going,' he said. 'I'm booked on a flight from Geneva this afternoon.'

'It was good of you to come here.' I could feel the strain showing on my face as I forced myself to smile.

He grinned. 'I just wanted to put your mind at rest. And the two most important things I haven't even mentioned yet. First, whatever happens Richard wants you to know that your father's bills at the clinic will be met. And second, the Kingley Wood trust is all but set up.'

'The Kingley Wood trust?' I echoed blankly.

He nodded. 'The land he bought from you.' He stopped and stared at me, his puzzlement showing clearly for a moment. 'He's put it in trust in perpetuity as a conservation area!'

I felt my mouth drop open. 'Are you *sure*?'

'I'm sure.'

'You mean he didn't know about the oil?'

'He knew.' He laughed at the look on my face. 'I don't know what you've done to him, Kate Parrish, but it's the first unbusinesslike move I have ever known him make! He could have made millions from that deal.'

I thought about that statement a great deal that night as I lay alone in bed, staring out of the open window at the moonlight reflecting on the soaring mountain peaks outside my window.

* * *

The next morning Richard's face was on all the front pages. *Millionaire Sought for Murder of Fiancée*, screamed the head-lines. Chris looked at me across the breakfast table. 'You believe Conway? That he's innocent?'

I nodded. 'He's ruthless, Chris. But not a murderer!'

Chris looked sceptical. 'I'm sorry, Kate, but I'm not con-vinced. I'm just glad you're right out of it here. You may have lost your land, but at least *your* life is safe!'

'Chris. We've been unfair to him.' I could feel myself grow-ing hot with indignation. 'He's saving the land. He's not going to let it go for oil.'

'So Conway says.' Chris raised an eyebrow. 'Sweet, inno-cent Kate. I don't know what the rules in Britain are, but sure as hell, if your government wants that oil, they'll get it, no matter what kind of rare bird has built its nest on top of it. They'll shift that bird's ass so fast – and who'll get the money, while he's bitterly regretting the betrayal of his attempt at conservation? Mr Richard Bradshaw!' He did not lighten the remark with a smile. Pushing his chair back he stalked out of the dining room, and left me with my thoughts.

I was completely torn. My head kept telling me that Chris was right. Richard was hard, ruthless, unsentimental at his own admission, and capable of violence. Hadn't I seen Sara's bruises with my own eyes? But my heart kept telling me that inside he was not like that at all, that perhaps he had become a little fond of me and that whatever or whoever he was, I had to admit at last that I had fallen in love with him.

And Chris knew it.

Two days later, after a spate of reporting in the press and on the TV news which I had watched at the inn, trying to hide the shaking of my hands as I saw the handsome face of my cousin on the screen, Chris insisted that we go for a walk.

'I'm going back home to New York, Kate,' he said.

'But Chris –' I stared at him.

'No, Kate.' He took my hands in his and held my gaze steadily. 'Honey. You've got your father here, and no doubt

Conway will keep you in the picture about Bradshaw. I'm not going to stay and watch you destroying yourself over a man like that. If you need me, call me, but as long as you're in love with him, don't bother.'

Had I been as obvious as that? Overcome with remorse I threw my arms around his neck. 'Oh Chris,' I cried. 'I didn't mean to hurt you. But you and I –' I hesitated. 'It was never –'

'I know, Katie.' Gently he disengaged himself. 'And I hope it all works out the way you want.'

Two hours later I watched him climb into the local taxi and disappear out of sight.

I was very sad when I made my way up to the clinic that afternoon. Chris had been my prop and reassurance. I knew in my heart that I hadn't been fair to him, but already I missed him desperately.

In the corridor near my father's room I was waylaid by a doctor. 'Only ten minutes today, Miss Parrish,' he said. 'Your father is not feeling very strong.' He frowned. 'I gather he has learned more news which appears to have upset him considerably. I don't know if you can reassure him at all?' I had of course told him how much Chris regretted his indiscretion and about the Trust. It had cheered him and seemed to be helping him on the road to recovery. I had not mentioned a word about the murder.

Of course he had been bound to find out. In a way I was surprised he had not heard already.

Sure enough, as soon as I went in he groped under his pillow for a newspaper and showed it to me. 'You knew, Kate?'

I nodded. 'He's innocent of course. And he has a cast iron alibi. It will all be sorted out soon, you'll see.'

He seemed reassured, but I could see he was still unhappy. 'I don't understand it all, Kate. He seemed such a pleasant man and I had such hopes . . .' he went on after a moment.

He surveyed my face wistfully and I felt myself blush scarlet.

'It'll all work out in the end, Pa,' was all I could say and I patted his hand.

I didn't stay long, but as I left he brought me up in my tracks. 'Kate, I want you to go back to Kingley till this is all over,' he said.

I stared at him. 'But I want to be with you!'

He smiled rather wanly. 'I'm in good hands here; I couldn't be better off. But there is no one to take care of things at home. I'm sure Richard has an efficient manager but it's not the same as one of the family being there.'

In the end I had to agree with him. 'Okay. I'll fly straight home.' I kissed him fondly. 'If you promise to get completely well soon.'

'I promise,' he said.

The estate looked quite fabulous beneath the June sun. I stood and looked about me as I climbed out of the car, sniffing the sweetness of the honeysuckle and pinks and the soft air, so different from the biting purity of the mountains.

My father's worries, at first sight anyway, seemed groundless. The estate was working like clockwork under the direction of Richard's astute manager and the houses were being efficiently run. In fact Mrs Dawson had lavished so much love on Kingley Farm I wondered if she would polish away some of the furniture altogether. The woods and marshes had been completely fenced and as far as I could tell, allowed to go their own way, although the solicitor told me no further progress could be made on forming the trust without Richard's signature. Of Richard there was no word. He had vanished into thin air.

I had begun to relax, lying on a deckchair beneath the apple trees in the soft sunshine, feeling the warmth soaking into my skin, when Mrs Dawson brought me the news. Her normally gentle eyes were hard and excited.

'They've got him!' she announced. 'It was on the eleven o'clock news. He's been arrested in New York and taken to Boston where he's being charged.'

I looked up at her, thankful for my dark glasses which must have hidden some of my expression, conscious of the terrible despair welling up in me.

'You sound glad, Mrs Dawson.'

She nodded grimly. 'He's been nothing but trouble, that man. I'm glad he's going to get his come-uppance,' she said.

I had forgotten that he had sacked her from the manor.

I was glad that it was her evening off. The gleam in her eyes for the rest of that day had been more than I could bear as she stomped around with her dusters almost singing her triumph. My own heart was heavy. Several times I thought of picking up the phone and calling David at Bay View, but each time I stopped myself. If there were news, he would tell me soon enough, and anyway what was Richard Bradshaw to me?

I stayed out in the garden long after Mrs Dawson had gone, wandering around the lawns in the dusk. Then at last I went in. The house seemed very empty without her or my father there and restlessly I paced from room to room, touching the old oak furniture, running my finger lightly across the back of the books, blowing the powdering of pollen which had fallen from the bowl of flowers onto a polished table.

Slowly it began to grow dark. I turned on the small table light and tried to read, but my mind wasn't on my book.

When I heard the knock at the door I glanced at my watch. It was after eleven. I padded out to the hall and listened. There was no sound from outside, then the knocking came again, loud and insistent.

'Who is it?' I asked.

There was no reply. For a moment I didn't know what to do, but the wild hope had shot through me that it might be Richard; that the news had been wrong and that he had managed to reach home – and me.

With shaking hands I pulled back the bolt and eased the door open. For a moment I could see no one in the darkness, then a figure lurched out of the shadows. It was a woman.

With an exclamation of surprise I stepped back and tried to

push the door shut in her face, but she was too quick for me.

'I want to talk to you, honey,' Sara said thickly.

'I can't think why.' I looked at her in distaste. She was wearing a low-cut, tight-fitting green dress and she reeked of alcohol as she threw out her arm to steady herself against the wall.

'I thought you'd like to hear the news,' she said. 'Get me a drink.' She pushed past me into the living room and stood staring round. 'So this is where the little country cousin lives. I might have known it would be all chintz and schmaltz.' The look she threw round the quiet, much-loved room filled me with wild anger, but I managed to restrain myself.

'We don't all have the same tastes,' I said quietly.

'Except in men, it seems!' she flashed back at me. Her red hair was dishevelled and her skin had a damp white pallor which was most unattractive.

I took a step back. 'I'm not sure I know what you mean,' I said cautiously.

She laughed. 'Oh come, you're not as stupid as that. You were determined to get your hooks into Richard the moment you set eyes on him. Well, I've come to tell you, you're not going to get him.'

She threw herself down on the sofa, exposing a great deal of white thigh, and dropped her little clutch bag on the cushion beside her. 'Have you got any bourbon?'

I shook my head, feeling myself stiffly awkward in my dislike and disapproval. 'I can't see why you've come, and I think you should leave now,' I said. I moved hopefully towards the door, but she didn't attempt to rise. She eyed me insolently from beneath her eyelashes and smiled.

'You know who told them that Richard killed Jacqui?'

'I know,' I said quietly. 'And I also know it's a lie.'

'How can you be so sure?' Her eyes were gleaming in the lamplight. 'Richard is a schizo.'

'He's not a murderer,' I said as witheringly as I could. 'And you know it.'

'You know where Richard is?' she asked.

'I heard he's been arrested.'

She stretched her arms out along the back of the sofa and I heard the rasp of her nails in the heavy material.

'He was, but they released him on bail.' She narrowed her eyes. 'He's not supposed to leave town, but he's jumped it already.'

Again that chilling laugh.

'How do you know?' I was watching her in fascination, knowing that she was enjoying every moment of my discomfort but unable to stop myself asking.

'Because I called him up.' She moved her head to one side. 'He didn't want to speak to me, but I made him listen.'

There was something incredibly sinister about her, sitting there on the sofa, exuding malice, and I could feel the goose flesh creeping across my skin as I watched her.

'I suppose you're going to tell me what you said?' I went on unwillingly.

She was still enjoying herself. 'I sure am.' Stretching out her elegant legs she crossed them. 'Haven't you got anything at all to drink?' she repeated, and I suddenly realised that her hands were trembling.

'There's some Scotch in the sideboard,' I said guardedly.

'It'll do.'

I poured her some, and as an afterthought poured myself a small one as well. I thought I needed it.

She drank hers at one gulp and let the empty glass fall negligently onto the cushions. 'Richard is a fool,' she said, almost affectionately. 'A goddam, bastard fool.'

Her eyes were closing.

'Why don't you go home, Sara?' I said softly at last. I didn't want her falling asleep on my sofa.

'Home,' she said. 'Home? Do you know where home is? Richard thinks it's California.' She gave a strange, bitter giggle. 'But it isn't. It's Brooklyn.'

'What did you tell him on the phone, Sara?' I asked patiently, bringing her back to the subject.

She seemed to drag her eyes open with an effort. 'I told him I was going to kill you.'

For a moment I was speechless, conscious only of those brilliant, lazy green eyes watching me. 'It was a test,' she went on, enunciating each word carefully. 'To see if he loved you. If he dropped everything to come to you, I'd know.'

'And did he?' I whispered.

She smiled. 'When I rang that old fool Marlesford, he'd left for the airport.' She groped for the glass and lurching to her feet, moved towards the bottle. 'Bad luck for you,' she murmured, raising her glass in a toast.

'I'd have thought it was good,' I said with a spark of defiance. 'If it means he loves me.'

'What it means, honey, is that I really am going to have to kill you!' She said it so softly I hardly heard the words. 'And the beauty of it is,' she went on, filling her glass with elaborate care, 'that he will arrive here just in time to collect the rap.'

'You're mad,' I stammered, panic beginning to run up and down my spine.

'Very probably,' she said sweetly. She drained the glass and set it down on the table, staggering very slightly as she walked over to the sofa. Then she picked up her purse.

'Poor little Katherine,' she went on, half scornfully. 'His two million bucks didn't get Richard very far did it? Did he get any change out of it at all I wonder?' The laugh she gave was unmistakably crude.

I was eyeing the phone, wondering desperately if I could get to it; she was too drunk to reach me, I was sure of it, and if she did I could fight her off, but I had not anticipated the horror of the next two minutes.

Casually she pulled open the flap of her purse and reached inside.

Seconds later I was staring, mesmerised with terror, at the

barrel of a small revolver, and I heard the slight click as she eased off the safety catch.

PART FOUR

The gun was weaving in the air and Sara, with a laugh, brought up her other hand to steady it. My mouth was dry; I could not believe that this was happening to me.

I knew I had to talk, to distract her somehow, but terror had clamped down on my vocal cords and I could not utter a word. The smell of Scotch was overpowering in the room.

'If Richard comes, he won't come alone, you know,' I managed to gasp at last. 'And if you hurt me, he'll know it was you.'

'I intend him to know it was me,' she said with emphasis. 'If it weren't for the cops, I'd sign my name on your corpse.' Suddenly her eyes filled with tears. 'You lousy little bitch,' she shrieked. 'If you hadn't come along he would still have loved me!'

She was beyond reason. Taking two steps forward, clutching the gun in front of her she knocked against the table and let out a string of curses. Then she fired. Again and again she squeezed the trigger and, my ears ringing with shots, I waited to die. Only when four or five useless clicks showed that the gun was empty did I realise that she had missed me completely. Perhaps she had not really tried to hit me; a lifetime later we found five bullets embedded in various parts of that room.

Once the gun was empty she hurled it towards the chimney, where it knocked a pretty Staffordshire figurine off the mantelpiece and fell amid a shower of porcelain into the empty hearth. Then she threw herself face down on the sofa and began to cry.

I stared at her, too shaken for a moment to move. Then, dazed, I made my way towards the phone.

I called the Manor. It was by far the closest and the estate manager had seemed a solid, dependable man. All I wanted was someone to come. Anyone. Quickly.

A familiar voice answered the phone however and I felt a quick surge of relief.

'Dave? Is that really you?'

'Sure.' He sounded sleepy. 'Who's that?'

'It's Kate. Dave, can you come over to the farm? Sara's here. She tried to kill me!' And suddenly I started to cry.

'Where is she now?' He was fully awake at once, his voice clipped and urgent.

'Here. In the living room. She's drunk.'

I heard a low mutter at the other end of the line.

'Kate? Open the front door for me, then get the hell out of there. I'm on my way!' A second later I was listening to an empty line.

I met Dave at the gate. He drew up in one of the estate Range Rovers and leaped out. 'Are you okay?'

I nodded. 'Just a bit shaky. She missed me.'

'*Missed you?*' He stared. 'Are you telling me that she had a gun?'

'A revolver. In her purse.' I gave an unsteady laugh. 'I don't think she knew what she was doing.'

'Like hell she did. You wait out here.'

He strode past me and disappeared into the house. Moments later he was back. 'Okay. Come on. She's passed out for the moment.' His face was grim as he led me in and shut the front door. He took me into the kitchen. 'Now, tell me what happened exactly.'

Briefly I explained, and he gave a silent whistle. 'Of course we knew she had told the cops Richard killed Jacqui, but this is unbelievable! You say Richard has jumped bail?'

'So she said.'

'Christ!' He was gnawing the joint of his thumb. Then he reached for the wall phone.

He dialled Bay View and then Boston airport. At the latter they confirmed Richard's jet had filed a flight plan for London and taken off two hours before.

Dave put his head in his hands. 'What a mess,' he said. He looked up and gave a wan grin. 'Come on, Kate. Black coffee, then I'll take the lady home.'

'What'll you do?' Automatically I took down the jug and reached into the fridge for the coffee beans.

He shrugged. 'We'll keep her up at the Manor till Richard comes and then let him decide. I'm sure he's plenty of ideas about what to do with our Sara.'

I did not like the look of the grim expression which had clamped down on his features at all. 'Aren't you going to call the police?'

He shook his head. 'And have them waiting when Richard lands? No way, honey. This is a private matter.'

'You think *she* killed Jacqui, don't you?' I said after a moment. The idea had been hovering at the back of my mind since the first moment I had seen her gun.

Dave was plugging in the grinder for me and I couldn't see his face. 'It had occurred to me,' he said guardedly. 'She was over there when it happened.'

Almost unwillingly I found myself glancing over my shoulder towards the door as the roar of the grinder echoed through the house, terrified she would awake. But seconds later when Dave switched it off, I once more heard the rhythmical snores coming from the living room where Sara lay sprawled on the floor.

'She won't wake, Kate,' he said, catching my glance with a sympathetic grin. 'It'll take her hours to sleep off that lot. I've known lushes like her before. You've nothing more to fear, I promise.'

I turned back to him. 'It's almost as if she hates him now,' I said softly. 'Did he really beat her, Dave?'

He gave a harsh laugh. 'If he did, which I doubt, it's because she likes it. Oh come on, Kate! What kind of man do you think he is?' He reached out and put his hand under my chin. 'Richard's okay, honey. Business, he's ruthless in, even dangerous; but he's no Bluebeard.'

I wanted so much to believe him.

He carried Sara, who was still asleep, out to the Range Rover and put her in the back, then he turned to me.

'Get some sleep if you can, and I'll call you in the morning, okay?'

I lay a long time, tossing restlessly, listening to the ticking of my little clock in the dark, watching the sky slowly grow light behind the curtains. Then at last I must have fallen asleep for the room was brilliant with sunshine when I was awoken by the shrilling of the phone.

'Kate?' It was Dave. 'Richard has sent his plane for you. It arrived in the night and it's all right; he didn't come himself. I told his boys there is no panic and you're okay but they're anxious to get back. How soon can you be ready?'

I blinked up at the ceiling. 'You mean he wants me to fly back to the States?'

'Looks like it. I think you should go, Kate.' There was something in his voice which did not brook argument. And suddenly I didn't want to argue. I had been thinking about Richard almost without ceasing for weeks now, and all I wanted was to see him again, to find out if my love for him was real; if the love he felt for me existed at all.

Richard's plane was waiting at the local airport and it seemed hardly any time before I was ensconced alone in state in the cabin, being served breakfast and fragrant coffee as we winged our way out across the Atlantic. I was completely relaxed. The quiet tough men who had driven me to the airport looked competent to deal with any eventuality and I could understand Richard being content to send them to save me from Sara.

From Boston, after a minimum of formalities they drove me straight out to Bay View. I had hoped that Richard would be at the airport, but there was no sign of him, and by now the silence of my escorts was beginning to worry me. I had had time to think on the long flight; time to have second thoughts.

Why in heaven's name had I agreed to come? I had not been in danger any longer from Sara at home, but now, what was I heading for? My obscure longing to see a man who, even though he protested his innocence, had been charged with murder, had brought me, in the company of strangers, back to the States. And suddenly I was afraid again.

But it was too late to turn back; my escort would see to that.

Edith Marlesford greeted me at the door of the mansion and showed me to the room I had had before with the same gloomy silence, which she broke only when I asked her if Richard was in the house. Shaking her head she said reluctantly, 'I don't know where he is at present.' That was all, and turning she left me to myself.

I looked round the room with a shiver, remembering my last brief visit; that one night which I had spent sleepless with terror under Richard's roof. And I thought about Jacqui. I was in a bedroom only two doors away from the room in which she had died. I didn't want to stay. Miserable and afraid, I did not even unpack my case; I dragged a comb through my hair and sat on the bed thinking, then I reached for the phone and dialled Minna's number in New York. There was no reply, so I tried Chris's. It rang and rang in the silence, and then I heard a click. 'Chris Hannaway is out just now,' came the voice, mechanical and without animation. 'At the tone will you leave your name . . .' I hung up without a word, conscious suddenly that I was crying.

I would have sat there all day had not Mrs Marlesford knocked, and after a moment entered the room again. She looked to be in an even blacker humour than before.

'The police are here,' she said grimly. 'They want to speak to you.'

'To me?' I felt my stomach turn over apprehensively. 'Why?'

She shrugged austerely. 'They're downstairs.'

Literally shaking, I followed her.

Two men were standing in the dining room, gazing out of the windows across the garden towards the ice-blue pool. They turned as I came in. 'Miss Parrish?' one of them asked. I nodded. He had a note book in his hand and consulting it he went on, 'You are Richard Bradshaw's cousin from England, I understand? May I ask when and where you last saw him.'

I stumbled through his questions, doing my best to answer, not understanding where they were leading. The men were bland, seemingly only half interested. Then suddenly came one sneaky as a knife: 'I gather someone tried to kill you too, Miss Parrish?' The hard brown eyes were no longer evasive. They bored into my skull.

'How do you know that?' I said, shaken.

'We get to hear about most things, in the end,' he said laconically. 'Now, you recently sold some land in England to your cousin. Is that right?'

I nodded.

'As did a third cousin, Miss Minna Monro?' He was looking at his note book.

I nodded again.

'And neither of you wanted to part with your property?'

'Well, no, but –'

'Pressure was brought to bear on you, and in the end you agreed, Miss Parrish, isn't that right?' There was a moment's silence. He put his note book away and looked me straight in the eye. 'Did Bradshaw try to kill you?'

'No! No, you've got it all wrong!' Desperately I tried to explain. I told them about Sara and the gun, floundering as they asked question after question. How many shots had been fired? What time was it? Why hadn't I called the British police? Why had Sara hated me enough to want to kill me? And again, when had I last seen Richard?

At long last they went. I was left with two pieces of information, both of which frightened me. One, that by admitting my attraction to Richard, I had somehow perhaps implicated myself, and two, that Richard had not been seen since he was released on bail. He had completely disappeared.

As the front door closed on the two police officers I stood uncertainly in the hall and wondered what to do. The house seemed deserted. Then I heard a distant sound from somewhere at the back. Hesitantly I made my way towards it and found myself in the huge gleaming kitchens. Edith Marlesford was making coffee, her back to the door, and I stood for a moment watching her in her absorption with her task. Eventually I cleared my throat. 'I . . . I'm sorry.' I found I was stammering. 'I . . . I could smell the coffee . . .'

She turned quickly, a jug of cream in her hand. 'Did they give you a rough time?'

Collapsing into a chair at the kitchen table I nodded wordlessly. She eyed me, then she brought the percolator to the table and produced two shallow French coffee bowls. 'What did they say?' she asked sharply.

I was too tired and too upset to be on my guard. Sipping the coffee gratefully I poured out the whole story yet again, conscious that her black eyes never left my face. When I reached the bit about Sara I saw the malicious gleam increase.

'And you told them all that?' she asked.

'I had to.'

She laughed out loud. 'They'll call the English police and that will fix that lady for good. Save Mr Richard the trouble of doing it himself, and good riddance to her!'

Something in the way she said those words made me stare at her.

'You do know where he is?'

She looked away. 'I might. I might not.'

Cupping my hands round my bowl and sipping the coffee gratefully I watched as she stirred her own. She drank it black, without sugar or cream, and yet she stirred it endlessly, gazing down into the black eye of the whirlpool she was making with her spoon.

'Will you tell me something?' I asked after a long silence. She put her head slightly on one side. 'What?'

'Did Jacqui kill herself or was she murdered?' I held my breath as I waited for her reply, knowing instinctively that she would have the answer.

There was a further long pause. Then: 'Richard wanted her dead, honey.'

I felt myself growing cold. 'You mean he did kill her; it wasn't Sara at all?' I breathed.

She laughed out loud. 'Oh it wasn't Sara!'

'Then it was Richard?' I persisted. I was sick with horror.

Shaking her head she smiled down at her coffee. 'Not with his own hands. Richard gives orders and they are obeyed.'

Somehow I stood up. 'What's the difference?' I cried in despair. 'He's the killer! Even if he got someone else to do it. He killed her!'

Blindly I turned for the door and ran out into the hot sunlight. I had to get away. I had to leave that evil, frightening house.

But I had forgotten the security which surrounded the estate. Pounding across the yard I dodged through the stables and ran as fast as I could across the grass towards the distant gates, only to find them locked fast. Sobbing, I beat feebly on the heavy painted iron with my fists, but I knew it was no good. I was trapped.

Edith Marlesford found me there and I felt her arm slip stiffly around my shoulders. 'Come back to the house, honey,' she said calmly.

Too exhausted to argue, I went with her, allowing her to lead me back to my chair at the kitchen table. I sat there, still crying silently as she busied herself once more with a new brew of coffee.

'I know it's a shock, honey.' She was talking softly, almost to herself. 'You're an English lady, not used to our way of doing things. Not like that trash, Sara. She was good for nothing, that one, and Jacqueline. Useless. Not the right ones for Mr Richard at all, either of them.' She put the freshly filled coffee bowl down before me. 'There, drink that.' Sitting down opposite me, she put her hand over mine. It was ice cold. 'You've nothing to fear, Katherine,' she said again. 'Nothing at all. He likes you.'

I drank the coffee slowly, half listening to her almost hypnotic voice droning on, reassuring, soothing, wondering sleepily why the events of the last two days and the long flight had left me more exhausted than I had thought possible. I no longer felt I could cope with what was happening to me as a warm drowsiness began to creep through my veins.

With an effort I pulled myself together and forced myself to listen to what she was saying, propping my head on my elbow as I tried to focus on her face.

'I've always taken care of Richard, since his momee died,' she was explaining. 'I've known what's best for him since he was five years old. Hundreds of women have chased him; but none of them were good enough. I've gotten rid of them all. Then Jacqueline came along. She was too dependent, too weak. She wouldn't let him go so easily, so I had to make her.'

I stared at her, trying to keep my eyes open with an effort, my brain struggling as I tried to understand. 'What are you saying?' I murmured.

She laughed, almost gaily. 'Don't you know?' she asked.

'You killed her?' I whispered. '*You* killed Jacqueline?'

'It was what he wanted,' she replied complacently. 'I've always been the instrument of his wishes. That's what I'm here for.'

Her face was swimming before me, in a haze, as I tried to stand, and I realised suddenly that I couldn't.

'What have you done to me?' I heard myself crying. 'You've poisoned me. In the coffee!' My mind had gone numb; I wasn't even afraid as, smiling, she rose slowly to her feet.

'No, no,' she said reassuringly. 'Not poison. I'm not going to hurt you, Katherine. You are the right one for him. I knew it the first time I saw you. You are what he needs; the others were wrong, but not you.' She was coming round the table towards me and I could do nothing but watch. I felt her arm go round my shoulders. 'Come, I'll help you to bed. This will help you sleep, honey, that's all. You're overwrought by everything that's happened.'

I seemed unable to argue. Her grip was surprisingly strong and I could feel her almost carrying me along the hall and up the stairs towards my bedroom. There she helped me to the bed and I fell on it heavily, my eyes closing. I heard the rattle of the curtains as she shut out the sunlight, then she came back to the bedside and I felt her removing my shoes. 'There, Katherine Parrish,' she said from a long way away. 'Relax and you'll soon be comfy.'

Dimly I realised that she was pulling off my dress, then the rest of my clothes, and I felt the satin sheets cold against my burning body. Her hand brushed my breast for a moment, caressing my skin, then gently she pulled the cover over me and tucked me in. I was unable to struggle, unable to move as I fought in vain against the terrible sleepiness which was overwhelming me.

'This'll keep you safe and quiet, honey,' she murmured, bending over me and touching my hair. 'Ready for him when he comes home . . .'

Through eyelids heavy as lead I saw her tiptoe across the shadowy carpet, remove the key from the lock and, taking it with her, slip out of the room. Seconds later I slid into unconsciousness.

When I awoke the room was almost dark. I lay there for a while conscious only of the painful throbbing behind my eyelids, feeling the numbness slowly ebbing from my limbs as gradually I remembered where I was.

'So, she's waking up.'

Only when I heard the voice did I realise at last that some-one was sitting on the bed beside me and, as my eyes grew used to the gloom, I recognised Richard. His weight on the sheet was pinioning me to the bed, but I was suddenly painfully conscious that beneath the smooth satin I was naked.

He laughed softly and I felt the whisper of fear begin to play once more about me. This man was a murderer.

'I'm glad you decided to pay off your debt after all,' he said, still smiling as he reached out and touched my cheek with the back of his hand. 'You are beautiful, Katherine. I can see why Mrs M is so taken by you.'

I shrank away from his touch, but the sheet held me fast and I found I could not move as he leaned forward over me and began gently to kiss my lips.

So I did not resist or turn my head away. Perhaps I was still drugged; perhaps I had realised even then that I could not fight him, but slowly I felt a quick tingle of desire mingling with my fear. Even as I realised it Richard released me and straightened up with a grin. 'There is no time for this now,' he said standing up. 'Do you feel strong enough to get dressed? We must hurry.'

Hurry, before the police could find him. I stared at him, trying to see a murderer in the face of the man I had imagined myself in love with; a man who was prepared to let others kill for him; a man with the blood of a beautiful, helpless woman on his hands.

'The police know I'm here,' I stammered at last – the first words I had spoken to him since a lifetime ago he had driven me back to the farm with his cheque for a million pounds in my pocket.

'Ah yes. The police.' He picked up my clothes and tossed them to me.

'They are probably watching the house,' I stammered, sit-ting up, the sheet pulled up to my chin. 'They'll catch you, you know. You mustn't stay . . .' I realised for the first time that behind the curtains the sky was dark. I must have been asleep for hours.

He was watching me closely, his expression inscrutable, but for a moment I thought I saw a smile hovering behind his eyes. 'I don't intend to stay. And they're not going to bother me where I'm going.' He paused, then he corrected himself slowly. 'Where *we* are going, Katherine.' Gently but firmly he unfolded my fingers from my sheet and pulled it back. Then he smiled and reached to touch a strand of my hair which lay curling across my bare shoulder. 'Hurry up, my love. Put on that dress and come down. My car is at the door.'

I watched as he left the room, a tall, slim figure in immaculately cut jeans, and I shivered suddenly as I remembered the burning touch of his hands on my skin and realised that I did still love him. But how could I love a murderer? How could I have borne such a touch?

My fingers trembling, I reached for my clothes and began to put them on. I pushed my feet into my sandals and stood shakily up, grabbing my bag, then I ran for the stairs. The front door stood wide and outside, drawn up before the steps, I recognised the red Mercedes, the same car Jacqueline had driven when she rescued me before from Bay View. There was no sign of Richard.

I looked round cautiously, and then tiptoed out onto the steps. In the light from the porch I could see the keys in the ignition. Without another thought I ran down, pulled open the door and threw myself in. The car started at the first turn of the key. I slammed down the accelerator and hurtled down the drive as if all the hounds of hell were after me.

The tall iron-bound gates were still closed, but I remembered the button on the dashboard in time. At a touch the heavy green wings began to swing slowly open and I could see the black ribbon of the road stretching away into the darkness beyond.

I turned the car southbound with a squeal of tyres and drove with my foot flat on the boards. After the first hour I stopped glancing in the mirror to see if I was being followed; after two I dared to pull in for gasoline and picked up a sandwich and a paper cup of coffee to help keep me awake. It was the early hours when I reached New York and only as the traffic thickened and swirled around me, sucking me with it closer and closer to the heart of the city, did I feel safe at last.

Even so, I did not dare to go to Minna. It was the first place Richard would look. Instead I swung the car through the streets, threading my way towards Chris's apartment. It was three in the morning when I rang his bell.

For one awful moment I thought he wasn't there, then at last I saw a light come on in the hall and he swung the door open.

'Hi Chris,' I said.

'Kate!' He did not seem pleased to see me. 'What the hell are you doing here?'

'Oh Chris I'm sorry. You've got to help me!' I slipped past him. 'It's Richard!'

I heard a murmured curse behind me, but he closed the door to my relief and I watched as he put on the chain. 'What about Richard?' he said wearily. 'I thought it was all sorted out.'

'Sorted out?' I swung round on him. 'Chris! It's a mess!'

'It's that all right. I saw the old witch on the TV news last night.'

I was stunned for a moment. Then I heard myself repeat: 'On the news?'

'Sure. Edith Marlesford.' He must have noticed my blank face. 'Don't you know? She gave herself up to the cops last night. Confessed everything. Richard is in the clear.'

I sat down abruptly on the chest by the door. 'Richard is not under suspicion any more? Not even for wanting Jacqui dead, for incitement or whatever it's called?' I was dizzy with relief.

'Not for anything. Hell Kate, I thought you were the one who believed in him!'

Yes, I had believed in him. Hadn't I?

'Oh God!' I said. I grabbed the phone and with shaking hands I punched out the number to Bay View while Chris stared at me in astonishment.

A man's voice answered; not Richard.

'Who is that?' it asked suspiciously.

'It's Kate Parrish. I must speak to Richard.'

There was an infinitesimal pause. Then the voice asked: 'Where are you calling from, Miss Parrish?'

'Never mind where,' I said. 'Can I speak to him?'

'I must know where you are Miss Parrish,' the voice went on relentless.

'No chance. Look, just tell him I'm sorry. But if he'd explained what had happened perhaps it would have been better!' I said, my hurt and anger slowly building as I realised that he had deliberately let me go on thinking the worst. 'Tell him I'll mail the car keys!' I hung up.

My hands were still shaking as I pushed away the phone. Why had he not told me? Why had he let me go on thinking the police were after him?

Miserably I preceded Chris into the living room, then I stopped dead, jolted from my thoughts. A woman's clothes were scattered over the carpet.

'Oh hell, Chris! You've got someone here.'

'Top marks!' He reached into the pocket of his robe and brought out a pack of cigarettes.

Strangely I found I didn't mind. I smiled at him apologetically. 'Chris, I don't want to cause any hassle. I just had to have somewhere to go tonight, somewhere he couldn't find me. Tomorrow I'm flying back home.'

Behind me I heard the door open. A tall blonde girl appeared, swathed in a bed sheet. She gazed at me in silence.

I sighed. 'Sorry to intrude,' I saw awkwardly. 'Look, can I just fix myself some coffee, then I'll go.'

'Hell, no. You can stay,' Chris said at last. 'If you don't mind the couch.'

Maggie turned out to be very nice. She made me coffee and then made up a bed on the couch. I fell into it without bothering to undress and was asleep in seconds.

I slept, too, most of the way back to London and was still too desperately tired when I reached home to do any thinking.

My faith in Richard had not been strong enough. I had not believed in him at the end and he had seen the terror in my eyes. I did not even know if he had loved me, but if he did, it was my own fault that I had lost him. My own fault that I would never see him again without both of us realising that for a few short hours I had believed him a murderer. And this was something I could not bear to face, and something I could forget only in the oblivion of sleep.

When at last I let myself in at Kingley Farm I looked round in disbelief. Was it really only the day before yesterday I had scribbled that quick note to Mrs Dawson, packed my bag and left? I tried to count up the hours on my fingers and gave up.

'Is that you Miss Kate?' Mrs Dawson called from the kitchen, just like any other day when I came in from a ride or from the garden. 'I've just put the kettle on for tea, my dear.'

I went into the warm, sunny room and stared round. It was full of flowers and the smell of baking, and after the nightmare I had lived through in the last day or so the sheer relief of being home made me want to cry.

There was something I had to do, though, before I could rest. I waited until Mrs Dawson had gone outside to hang some sheets in the sun, then I grabbed the phone.

A secretary answered. Yes, she said. Mr Conway was still at the Manor.

'Kate?' He came on the line slightly breathless. 'Thank goodness. Are you home?'

'Never mind where I am,' I said, automatically cautious, though it could not matter any more now. 'What has happened to Sara?'

'She's in hospital. A complete nervous breakdown. Your police came and interviewed her, but they say it's up to you whether you want to press charges.'

'Oh no,' I said hastily. I hesitated. 'Dave? Have you heard from Richard?'

He laughed. 'I have indeed. I gather you kidnapped his Merc!'

I wondered what else Richard had told him.

'Kate,' he went on. 'Do tell me where you are. I want to see you.'

'You and who else,' I retorted. 'I'm in Scotland, Dave, so tell Richard to forget it for now, okay?'

Of course he would find out where I was within seconds if he wanted to, but I wanted a breather; the chance to compose myself, and put my thoughts in order.

Richard's face was still haunting me as I walked up to the marshes, climbing through the double threads of barbed wire which surrounded them and wandering in the gold and peace of the English summer, but I thought perhaps I was winning. I would be able to put the memory of what might have been behind me.

I was still thinking about him so much that when the phone rang that evening for a moment I was convinced it would be him. I almost did not answer it at all, then at last I picked it up and waited cautiously for someone to speak.

'Kate? Kate, are you there? Hello?' A familiar voice crackled over the wire and I found I was breathing again.

'Pa! Are you all right?' I had phoned him that morning as I phoned him every morning.

'I'm just fine, Katie. The doctors are very pleased with me.'

His voice sounded strong and confident. 'But I'd be better if you came over here again for a few days!'

It seemed a wonderful idea. Joyfully I put down the phone. I had lost Chris; I had no hope of Richard, but at least I still had my father.

He was propped up in bed when I reached the clinic at last, his colour better than I could remember seeing it for years, his eyes sparkling with pleasure.

I kissed his forehead. 'You look very pleased with yourself,' I said, laying the huge bunch of freesias which I had brought him on the bed cover. 'I expected to find you looking pale and interesting and you sit here looking as if you could beat me in straight sets at tennis!'

He laughed. 'I feel as if I could,' he said softly. 'I have a surprise for you, Katie, my love,' he went on.

'Oh?' I looked at him suspiciously, but he merely went on grinning at me. 'No,' he said, maddeningly. 'Not yet. Tonight.'

And with that I had to be content for the time being. I returned to the clinic at seven, having been lucky enough to secure a room at the inn after a cancellation, and went straight up to my father. He was sitting in a chair beside his bed, dressed in a new silk dressing gown and on his knee was a box wrapped in gold paper and tied with scarlet ribbon. I eyed it. 'No one told me it was Christmas,' I said with a smile.

He beamed at me. 'Well, it is,' he replied. He held out the box to me. 'Open it and see.'

I took it and shook it gently. It felt as if it were empty. With a suspicious look at my father I began to untie the ribbon and peeled off the paper. Beneath it was a plain white box which, when I took off the lid, was empty save for an envelope. Behind me the door opened and I heard someone enter, but my attention was on the envelope on my knee and I did not look up. As I tore it open I glanced up only once and caught sight of my father's face. He looked radiantly happy.

I could not make head or tail of the closely typed pages which I drew from the envelope. 'What is it?' I asked bewildered.

The voice which answered was not my father's.

'It is a deed making you co-trustee of the Kingley Marshes Sanctuary,' Richard said softly from the window seat behind me.

For a moment I did not move, then, slowly, I turned and look at him. 'How did you know I was here?' I asked when at last I had found my voice.

He smiled enigmatically. 'Shall we say I guessed,' he said.

My father chuckled. 'Rubbish. He came and told me to call you.'

'And you did?' I swung back to my father.

'Of course.' Pa was looking very pleased with himself.

'I told him the whole story Kate,' Richard said, standing up. 'Even the sorry tale of how I bullied and frightened you. I've apologised to him and now I want to do the same to you. I should have realised you would be terrified. It was unforgivable of me.'

I could feel my cheeks beginning to burn. 'I was not terrified!' I denied hotly.

Smiling unrepentantly he bowed slightly. 'You were apprehensive, should I say. But I still want to apologise.'

'So I should hope,' I said, beginning to recover from my shock. 'You are the most overbearing, tyrannical, unscrupulous man I have ever met.'

He laughed. 'To all that I plead guilty,' he said. 'And I promise, I will try to reform.'

'And you must let the man take you out to dinner, Kate,' came my father's voice from his corner. 'Alas, I cannot join you as yet, but I dare say you will find enough to talk about without me there!'

He was right of course. But there were still several things

that bothered me enough to make me pause, once we were outside on the beautifully raked gravel on the forecourt of the clinic.

'I know what you are going to ask, Kate,' Richard said, facing me and taking my hands. 'I never even hinted to Edith that she do that terrible thing. You must believe that. Jacqui had everything to live for at the end. She had agreed to go away for a cure, and she had met someone I believe she could have loved. I had nothing to gain by wanting the poor girl dead.'

I did believe him. But there was something else.

'And Sara,' I said softly. 'I saw her bruises.'

The sadness on his face vanished and I saw a malicious twinkle appear in his eyes. 'Still afraid I might beat you?' He tucked my hand comfortably beneath his arm and began to walk towards the car. 'Well, I must confess that, much though she deserved it, I didn't lay a finger on her. Those bruises, Kate, came from a fall she had when she was drunk.'

I should have guessed.

'Any other problems, ma'am?' He was opening the car door for me and helping me in. 'Because if there are I would rather sort them out now. This meal is going to be one which is not interrupted by telephone calls, or quarrels, or trans-Atlantic flights or you falling asleep and setting fire to yourself in the candles.' He leaned down to tuck my skirt out of reach of the door and I felt his lips brush my hair.

I pretended to think. 'Actually, there is one other thing that's been worrying me,' I murmured demurely, hoping he could not see how fast my heart was beating at his touch. 'I don't like the colour of your Rolls Royce.' I looked up at him, my eyes wide. 'I really don't.'

Taking several paces back he looked at me hard, then he shrugged. 'I can see you're going to be a tough lady to please,' he said cheerfully. 'Okay, we'll get a new one on our wedding day, and you can choose the colour. How does that appeal?' So saying, he climbed into the driving seat of the hired car and we set off down the road towards the mountains.

Networking

'THAT'S IT. That is absolutely it!' Denzil Johnson threw the front door of his flat shut behind him, sent his briefcase skidding up the polished pine floorboards and headed for the bottle of Scotch. He poured himself a hefty dose.

'Meg! Meg? I'm home.'

His wife put a cautious head round the door. She smiled nervously. 'I know, darling. I heard your key in the lock. Bad day?' Her face registered careful sympathy.

'Bad! Bad? It was bloody terrible!' He flung himself into a chair, swallowing the Scotch down with ostensible effort as if he disliked the taste.

Meg emerged further, ready to retreat if necessary. Her husband's adrenaline count had to be treated with caution these days. One approached him rather as one might the dial on a jammed steam engine.

'Was it Carter again, Den? The man's a swine. A perfect swine.' Coming from her, the epithet sounded genteelly judicious in the extreme.

Denzil was still fuming. 'Him and just about everyone else in that firm. They're unethical, Meg. They're immoral. If they don't want me on their staff why don't they say so? Why don't they transfer me, or make me redundant and pay me the whack they damn well owe me instead of this endless war of nerves. More Scotch.' He held out his glass.

Meg unscrewed the bottle slowly. 'Shall I put some water in this time, darling?' she asked hopefully.

He shook his head violently. 'No way. Milk and water – that's been my trouble all along and that's enough. Never again. I'm going to fight them. From tomorrow I'm going to fight. They can't do this to me Meg. Either they employ me or they transfer me to Bristol or they make me redundant. They are not going to chase me out. It's happening all the time, now, you know: putting pressure on people to make them resign. It's appalling! I'm going to fight, and fight all the way.'

His wife walked over to the window and drew the curtains against the glare of the recently lit street lamps outside. The table was already laid for supper but she ignored it with a sigh.

'TV darling, or are you going jogging this evening?' she asked in a conciliatory tone.

The tone did not this time have the desired effect.

'Neither. Hell, neither! I mean it this time, Meg. I'm going to fight. And before anything else I'm going to put the fear of God into those guys at work. What I need is a good QC.'

'Oh no, Denzil.' She was alarmed suddenly. 'We can't afford to take anyone to court, you know we can't.' She picked up the Scotch again. It was for herself this time.

He laughed wryly. 'Oh no, not to take them to court. Or a tribunal. I just want someone to talk to them. Someone who will shake them into taking me seriously. The very words "Queen's Counsel" will terrify them. *Terrify them*.' He repeated the words, almost lasciviously.

Meg took a sip of neat Scotch. He didn't usually go this far. His fury was usually dissipated after a drink and a day-dream, while she steamed the potatoes, about the lovely garden they could have if Carter would only recommend him for a transfer to the Bristol branch.

She swallowed. 'You'd have to pay him, darling.'

'So, I'll pay him if I must. But surely we *know* one, don't we? Doesn't your mother know a QC? She knows just about every bloody person in London!'

He put down his glass and set about loosening his tie, slipping it noose-like upwards over his head and leaning back at last in his chair, his eyes closed. A muscle twitched spasmodically in his cheek.

Meg looked at it, worried, unsure as to whether or not to take him seriously this time. She decided he probably did mean it, for he had thrown her a challenge and she knew it. And family solidarity demanded that her mother know a QC.

She glanced at the phone. No, she wouldn't do it now. Perhaps later, when he was in the bath. She didn't want him to overhear the conversation, larding it with provocative comments from the wings, antagonising her mother before she had consulted the inimitable address book which lodged somewhere in the deeply recessed memory banks of her brain.

He had opened his eyes and was watching her. For the first time he had noticed her wan, tense expression and he frowned as he leaned forward.

'Meggie, I'm sorry. I'm a boar. Go on, tell me. I'm so obsessed with the office I can't think about anything else. How was the dentist?'

She smiled radiantly. 'The dentist was last week, Den.'

For a moment his face fell. Then he laughed. 'Forgive me?'

'Of course I forgive you. Shall I go and put the food in the oven now darling?' She dropped a paper-light kiss onto the top of his head. In spite of everything, she noticed, his hair was as thick and boyishly ruffled as the day she had first met him.

It wasn't until he was safely in the bath that she rang her mother.

'Mummy? It's Meg. Do you happen to know any QCs?' She frowned as her straightforward query was greeted with an outburst of near hysteria.

430

'No dear, no one has murdered anyone. Yet. I just wanted to know. For Denzil.'

She turned, the receiver still pressed to her ear, and parting the curtains she gazed down at the dark street below. It had begun to rain.

'No Mummy. Uncle James was a solicitor. It's different. And anyway he's dead.'

Her mother was obviously scraping the bottom of the barrel. She decided to cut short the flow of reminiscence which had been let loose the other end of the line before it reached her mother's last parking fine outside Harrods – a case which had in any case been undefended, and undefensible.

'Look Mummy, I must ring off. There's someone at the door –' time-worn, time-honoured excuse, ' – if you think of anyone let me know, there's a dear.'

She hung up and took a deep breath. It wasn't often her mother was stumped for someone who knew someone. . .

If only there was some other way she could help Denzil in his war with Carter. Moral support from behind the lines did not seem to be of much use at the moment.

She had a sudden brainwave and dialled before she could change her mind.

'Mary? It's Meg. Yes, I know, hasn't it been ages? You must come and have dinner with us soon.' She blanched visibly. 'All right, next week. Yes, that would be nice. Look Mary, didn't you go out with a barrister before you married David? Do you still know him by any chance?'

Her lips twitched imperceptibly at Mary's indignation.

'No, of course not. No, well, we wanted a QC and I remembered . . . what? Oh no, I don't think Denzil wants to use his solicitor. It's not that kind of *legal* thing. We want a QC who's a *friend*.'

She hung up wearily and reached for her diary, cursing her own weakness. She had let them in for a boring dinner party and achieved nothing into the bargain.

She jumped as the sitting room door opened. Denzil

appeared, wrapped in a bathrobe, glowing gently from the bath.

'Meg. I've had an idea. There's a chap I was at school with. I'm pretty sure he was a QC last time I heard. I think I'll give him a buzz.'

Meg lowered her eyes and shut her diary. 'That's a good idea, darling.' She hesitated. 'Den, why a QC? What's wrong with asking our own solicitor?'

He was rifling through the phone book. 'Doesn't pack enough wallop,' he commented absent-mindedly. 'Need the real thing for those bastards at the office.'

'But I gather you're only supposed to get an introduction through a solicitor, darling.' She did not dare tell him yet about the dinner party.

'Rubbish. Straight to the top, that's my motto.' He ran his finger down a page, squinting.

'Ellis. Let's see. Here we are. This must be him. I'll try.'

He punched out the number slowly and deliberately as he always did, with the action of a seasoned executive.

'Hello, is Fred Ellis there? What? Mr Justice Ellis? Oh no. I'm sorry, must be the wrong man.' He hung up swiftly and glanced at his wife rather sheepishly. 'Too much wallop,' he commented dryly.

It was as they were at last climbing into bed that the phone rang. Meg glanced at her watch. It was nearly midnight.

'You go.' Denzil pulled the sheet up to his chin. 'If it's for me I'm out.'

She gave him a withering look and padded barefoot into the sitting room, groping for the switch of the table lamp as she picked up the phone.

'Yes, who is it?' She tried to sound as though she'd just been woken up – an instinctive ploy to make the caller feel guilty. It didn't work. It was her sister. 'Jill! do you know what time it is? Yes I know I called Mummy. No, Denzil isn't in trouble. He just needs a . . . what?'

She gripped the receiver more tightly. 'You know one? Who?'

She listened intently as Jill explained a tenuous but definitely real line of contact and reached excitedly for her diary.

'But are you sure he knows he owes Don a favour?' she asked slowly as she wrote. Don was her brother-in-law.

She was reassured and a few minutes later was hurrying back to the bedroom.

She eyed her husband's recumbent and snoring form. 'Jill and Don have asked us to go for drinks on Thursday,' she announced triumphantly. 'They've got a QC lined up for you.'

She was answered by a snort.

At nine the next morning her mother was on the phone again. This time she was excited. She had obviously spent the night in deep communion with her address book.

'I've just remembered, darling,' she announced before Meg could draw breath. 'Your brother's godmother's husband was a QC. I think he's retired, but that won't matter will it? It's just as good, I'm sure. I've asked them over for tomorrow. Make sure you come early then Denzil will have plenty of time to talk to him . . .'

Mary called back at ten forty-five. 'Meg. You know, I thought about what you said yesterday and it did seem a super excuse to call Roland. He remembered me, and he sounds fabulous – a very *rich* sort of voice, I thought –' there was a short pause on the line while she licked her lips. 'And guess what? He's just been made a QC. So everything's perfect. He's agreed to come to have drinks with us Friday at six. All right? Of course I didn't tell him about Denzil wanting to speak to him, I mean how could I? I'm sure it's unethical or something, but you'll have to work that out . . .'

Meg put down the phone and stared at her diary. No one could say she hadn't tried. Three QCs, three days running!

She gave a little secret smile and picking up the phone

dialled Denzil's work number. It was a while before he came on the line, but when he did he sounded breathless.

'Meg? The most fantastic news!'

She stiffened suspiciously. 'Den, you haven't found a QC have you?'

'QC? What are you talking about? Good Lord, no, forget all that. Darling, I decided to take the bull by the horns and I went and saw the MD himself this morning and asked for a transfer. And guess what. He's agreed. No questions, no arguments. He said because of my seniority I can have the next posting there and one is coming up in about three months' time. It was as simple as that.'

As simple as that? She glanced down at her diary.

> Wednesday: Mummy's QC – 7.30
>
> Thursday: Jill's QC – 8.30
>
> Friday: Mary's QC – 6.00

She closed her eyes and taking a deep breath began to count slowly to ten.

When the phone rang again a little while later she automatically reached for her diary. There was only Saturday left. This week.

'Meg dear? It's Aunt Hattie. Your mother tells me you're anxious to find the name of a Queen's Counsel. Well, I happen to know one. He's a most delicious young man . . .'

I wonder how many QCs there are, Meg thought to herself idly as she listened, and reaching for her pen she began to doodle round the tiny picture of the moon which appeared on the page heralding the start of the following month.

Catherine's Cat

THEY WERE THERE AGAIN. The eyes. High up on top of the old-fashioned wardrobe in the corner of her room. Gleaming in the dark. Golden. Elliptical.

Of course, she knew they were really the locks on the suitcase, catching the reflection from the street lamp outside her window, but sometimes in the long sleepless nights as her aching lids refused to stay shut she would half focus on them and know that up there there lurked a big hungry cat.

With a shiver she pulled the duvet up over her mouth and nose leaving only her eyes exposed, eyes which refused to close. Soon she would hear her mother and father coming up to bed; the footsteps on the stairs, the quiet talking, sometimes laughter – always discreet, always thoughtful, not wanting to wake her up. It was reassuring, hearing them there, sensing them close, just across the landing. She didn't like it when she was upstairs by herself. It was frightening; lonely.

She heard their bedroom door close. In a few minutes it would open again and one of them would go into the bathroom. Sometimes they would run the bath before they shut the door, going backwards and forwards between the two rooms and sometimes, very faintly, she could smell the sweet lavender of her mother's bath oil. It comforted her to think that they were there so close. Within call if something awful should really happen. Her eyes went quickly from the thin bright line down the side of her bedroom door to the top of the wardrobe again.

It was still there, the sleepy cat; watching. Tonight it seemed more alert than usual; the eyes bigger. She glanced hastily out of the window, hardly daring to move her head lest she draw attention to herself, and saw the light outside in the street. It too seemed brighter. It was blue instead of a softer yellow. Perhaps they had changed the bulb. She looked back at the cat and heard a soft unmistakable growl.

Her heart thudding with fear she shrank back into the bed, trying to slip out of sight, trying to shrink herself to nothing. She didn't dare hide completely though. If she stopped watching it might move – leap down from its high perch and attack.

It had never done it yet but there was always a first time for everything – her father had told her that.

She could hear its tail swishing now – a rhythmic brushing against the wood of the wardrobe door and then in the silence she heard the slight rasping as it flexed its claws.

'Mummy –' Her call was so quiet it was no more than a whisper. She was too afraid it would hear her. 'Mummy, can you come here.'

If she called as her mother came out of the bathroom she might hear; might come straightaway, but then supposing the cat leapt and landed on her mother?

She ducked even further out of sight, not daring to call out again, her eyes red with staring.

'Frances? Come on. What are you doing in there? Did you fall asleep in the bath?' Her father's sudden call was shockingly loud. She tensed, waiting for the animal to jump, but it didn't move.

Couldn't move, she reminded herself sternly. It was after all a suitcase. Just a suitcase.

'Frances?' His voice was sharper, somehow more anxious. 'Are you all right?'

She held her breath.

Her father's footsteps padded across the landing and she heard the bathroom door open. 'Frances!' His call was peremptory and a little afraid. 'Frances!' It was louder again. He had come back out onto the landing. It sounded as if he were just outside her door. 'Frances!' The word was quieter yet louder as though he were speaking with his lips to her keyhole, yet not wanting to awaken her. Her eyes went up automatically to the cat. It watched sleepily, not moving.

'Frances!' It was a whisper this time but her door was opening – the crack of light widening cautiously as it pushed with a slight shushing sound across the pile of the carpet. The cat's eyes disappeared.

'Frances, are you in there?'

'Daddy?' Catherine sat up. 'Daddy, what's wrong?'

For a moment he hesitated then he groped for the light switch by the door. In the sudden brightness Catherine screwed up her eyes, blinking.

'I thought Mummy was in here,' he said slowly. 'I'm sorry, pudding. I didn't mean to wake you.'

'I wasn't asleep.' Catherine clutched her duvet more tightly.

'No.' He sounded suddenly bleak.

She stared at him. He was wrapped in his dark-blue dressing gown and his legs and feet were bare. She glanced at his legs and then averted her eyes. They were very white with black hairs growing on them. 'Where's Mummy gone?' she asked.

He gave a small tight smile, his hand going back to the light switch.

'Downstairs. I expect she's gone to make us some cocoa. Back to sleep now, pudding. God bless. I'll see you in the morning.'

The light clicked off and the door closed. The room was suddenly in total darkness. She froze, not daring to move.

The cat opened its eyes.

'Frances? Where are you, darling?' She heard her father's voice as he ran downstairs; the soft thump of his bare feet on each step. '*Frances*!' The anxiety was real now, sharp, although fainter. 'Oh God, please Frances, no. I can't live without you.'

Catherine's fists were knotted into the fabric of the duvet cover. She pressed her face into it, where it draped across her knees, to stop the scalding tears before they ran down her cheeks.

The house was silent. In the bed she began slowly to rock backwards and forwards in her misery, her loneliness and terror like an ice wall around her.

On the wardrobe the cat moved slightly. A paw flexed on the fretted wooden gallery above the doors and a deep groove appeared in the richness of the wood.

'Frances! Frances, my darling, I love you! Don't you see. I love you!'

Catherine stiffened. The voice was very loud once more, clear in the stillness of the night. It came not from the house but from outside her window. For a moment she couldn't move, then she pushed back the duvet and slid out of bed, running to stare out, shocked and terrified to see her father, still in his dressing gown and bare feet, standing in the middle of the road. Behind him the garden gate swung open, the path clear in the light of the street lamp. The road in both directions was completely empty. His hair was tousled and his face, clearly visible in the blue cold light, contorted with pain.

Her fingers clutched at the window sill so tightly her hands were white and bloodless; her attention was focused so hard on her father she did not hear the thud as the cat leapt down and stood for a moment on the carpet near her bed. It regarded the child's thin shoulders with an air of detached, almost academic interest and then it leapt onto the bed. Turning round once it settled down, the long tail brushing the floor on one side, a huge velvet paw casually draped over the other. It watched her sleepily, its eyes slowly closing, its nose resting comfortably on the soft black fur of a forepaw.

Catherine swallowed hard, trying not to cry, empathising with her father's pain and not able to articulate her own.

'Mummy?' The whisper was strangled.

After several minutes he turned and walked back towards the house. She could see his bare feet on the gritty tarmac of the road in the lamp light and she stared fascinated by this terrible abnormality in a life which had seemed so sane and ordered for every day of her existence.

He came through the gate and left it open as he walked slowly back towards the house. As he reached the front door, so like the others in the suburban avenue with its blue and green stained-glass flowers let into the panel above the letter box, he passed out of her sight.

Catherine didn't move. She heard him close the front door and knew with some part of herself that he was leaning against it, defeated, and sobbing silently.

She didn't dare move. Her world had crumbled. The love and security with which she had been surrounded all her life had gone. Reality was the loneliness of the darkened bedroom, the hungry angry cat lying on the wardrobe waiting to pounce.

She stared down the road with eyes blinded by tears. It was still empty.

'Daddy?' Her lips framed the word but she knew he couldn't come. She was no longer the centre of his world; she was no longer the centre of any world. He had forgotten her.

When she at last turned from the window, cold and stiff, trembling in every limb, she did not even look at the wardrobe; nor did she notice the shadow-like black shape taking up so much room on the end of her bed. Crawling under the pillows she burrowed out of sight and began to sob again. It was only as she was falling asleep that, stretching out a little, she felt the solid weight on the duvet near her feet and, taking comfort from the warmth, without further conscious thought, snuggled down against it.

She did not know how long she had been asleep when she was awakened by the sound of a door banging. She tensed, her eyes, swollen by crying, still tightly shut.

'Frances?' Her father's voice in the distance was croaky with exhaustion.

Catherine crept out of bed and went to the door. Pulling it open she peered out. The lights upstairs were all on. From where she stood she could see the top of the stairs and the banister around the head of the stairwell close to the bath-room door. In the bathroom the water for her mother's bath had long ago gone cold. Only a slow monotonous drip from one of the taps broke the silence.

'Frances? You came back?'

Behind her only a large oval indentation and a few black hairs on Catherine's bed cover showed where the cat had lain.

'I couldn't do it, Freddie.' Her mother's voice was barely audible.

Catherine crept across the landing and crouched down, peering through the banister rails. Her mother was standing just inside the front door, her hair wet with rain. When had it started raining? She was dressed in her old jeans with a heavy blue sweater and her red woollen jacket that Catherine liked to dress up in sometimes because on her it came down to the ground. Her mother's face was white and strained – it was to Catherine's shocked eyes no longer the face of the beautiful young princess-like figure who had figured in so many of the child's fantasy games, but that of an old ugly woman.

'I'm sorry for all the things I said.' Frances hadn't moved any further into the hall. Her hands were pushed down into the pockets of the jacket and her shoulders were hunched defensively. 'It was hateful of me.'

'They were true.' Freddie was sitting on the stairs with his back to Catherine and he had not stood up. He looked defeated. They were both, Catherine realised suddenly, frightened. She bit her lip. Her world had started to spin again; parents are never afraid.

'I am boring. I am stuck in a rut. You could have done much better than me. Everyone always thought that.'

'No!' Frances was shaking her head. 'No, Freddie –'

'Yes!' He buried his face in his hands. 'And I am too old for you. I always knew it. But I loved – love – you so much.' He looked up.

Catherine chewed her lip. She pressed her face closer to the bars. She could feel her father's pain; his absolute despair. Her eyes narrowed as her gaze went to her mother. For the first time in her life she was seeing her as a separate thing – a frightening, unpredictable stranger. She studied her mother's face with hostile intensity, noting the pale, unmade-up skin, the huge shadowed eyes with mud-coloured circles under the lower lids, the thin almost paper-coloured lips, usually so joyously scarlet and full, and she registered an infinitesimal shiver of dislike. Frances's hair was hanging round her shoulders in rats' tails, dripping down her neck and she pushed it away with cold near-lifeless fingers. 'I think I'll go upstairs and have a bath.' Her voice was lacklustre and defeated.

'Why did you come back?' Freddie was still sitting on the stairs. To go up to the bathroom she would have to climb over him.

She stood still, her hands spread in a gesture of helplessness.

'Wouldn't he have you?' Freddie's voice was suddenly harsh.

Her eyes went to his and Catherine noted dispassionately that they were now brimming with tears. 'I never reached his house.'

There was a long silence. Freddie didn't seem to know what to say. His shoulders had slumped as he sat there below her and Catherine saw the sharp angles of his bones beneath the blue towelling of his robe. Above the collar his neck rose, thin and defenceless, and above that his tousled hair. As if he could feel his daughter's gaze he ran distracted fingers through it and then sank his head once more into his hands. 'You could still go.'

She drew in her breath sharply. 'Do you want me to?'

'No.' He raised his head wearily. 'No of course I don't want you to, but I don't want you to stay if you're unhappy and it's all over between us.'

'It's not all over, Freddie. It was never there.' She turned back towards the front door and put her hand on the latch. For a moment it stayed there, then it slid away. Frances leaned forward, her forehead resting against the leaded panes of coloured glass, her hands hanging limply at her sides. 'I don't know what to do.' It was a child-like call for help.

'Stay. Please stay. Think of Catherine.'

Catherine's grip tightened on the banister rails until her hands hurt.

Frances turned wearily. 'Catherine wouldn't even miss me. She's always loved you best.'

Freddie didn't say anything for a moment, then he shrugged. 'That's silly. She loves both of us.'

'No.' Frances shook her head violently. 'No. She's never loved me. She's a cold uncaring child. I sometimes can't believe I even gave birth to her. She'd be much happier if I weren't here. Then she could have you all to herself.'

'Frances!' His voice was stronger suddenly. 'You don't know what you're saying.'

'No?' There was a strange half-sneer on Frances's lips. 'Do you want me to ask her?'

Catherine shrank back out of sight. She was very cold. Climbing unsteadily to her feet she crept back along the landing towards her bedroom door, her skin like ice beneath her thin cotton pyjamas.

The room was very dark; she was half-way across the carpet before she remembered the cat. She glanced up at the wardrobe. The animal had gone. She could see the wall clearly. No suitcase. She frowned, distracted. Had her father moved it? Then she heard the growl.

She found she couldn't breathe any more. Turning slowly back towards her bed she saw the huge black shape sitting there, saw the golden almond-shaped eyes with dark diamond slits, and heard the knife-like claws unsheathed, massaging the soft pink candy stripes of the duvet. She could smell the feral warmth of its fur.

Slowly it stood up. Arching its back with casual luxuriousness it jumped off the bed. Only a few feet from her now, it stood with its shoulder level with hers, its head raised almost at a height with her own.

She moistened her lips nervously with her tongue, her eyes on the cat's, and it echoed the movement revealing for a moment two hooked, white canine fangs.

Then it moved.

Anaesthetised by her fear Catherine stayed where she was. Only her eyes followed the cat as it padded once round the room before coming to a stop beside her and pressed its huge head against her, nuzzling her shoulder. Her small hand went cautiously to the ruff of stiff fur behind its ears and as she began to scratch it she was rewarded with a barely audible, deep vibrating purr.

'Catherine! Wake up. You'll be late for school.'

Her mother's voice cut through her dream like a serrated knife. For a moment Catherine lay quite still, then cautiously she opened her eyes.

Cold sunshine flooded into the bedroom; on the top of the wardrobe the old suitcase was stacked as usual beside her grown-up brother's empty rucksack and a broken kite.

She turned to look at her mother. Frances's face was pale beneath her make-up and she looked tired, but otherwise she was much as usual, bustling over to the stripped pine chest of drawers and pulling the top drawers open for clean blouse and knickers and socks. She tossed them onto the bed. 'Five minutes. Breakfast is almost ready,' she said and turning she went out of the room.

Catherine sat up in bed, hugging her knees, her eyes on the suitcase. It was a dream. It had to have been a dream. All of it.

She sat down in front of her bowl of cornflakes without enthusiasm, her eyes going to her father's place.

'Where's Daddy?'

'He caught the early train.' Her mother retrieved two pieces of toast from the toaster and juggled them into the rack. 'I'm driving you to school this morning.' She was the same as usual, apart from the funny blurred look on her face – efficient, slightly impatient, impersonal, trying to read the headlines of the paper as she drank her instant coffee and poured Catherine's hot milk from the saucepan.

'Mummy, can we have a kitten?' Catherine unscrewed the honey jar and stuck her knife into the grainy waxy sweetness, knowing it would call forth a cry of anger from her mother who had carefully put a long-handled spoon beside the jar.

'What, darling?' Seemingly engrossed in the paper Frances had not noticed the honey.

'A kitten. I would so love to have a kitten.'

'Mm.' The noise was too non-committal to be a yes; it was a reflex action, no more, and meant her mother hadn't heard.

'Daddy says I can.' That was chancing her arm and she knew it.

'What?' Frances looked up and threw the paper on the table. 'Come on. You're going to be late. Go and brush your teeth. Quickly.' She hadn't heard a word about the kitten. Not a word. 'Have you got your satchel? Don't forget your history book. It's in the dining room still, and your ballet things are in the airing cupboard.'

They were the things she always said. Normal, naggy, caring things. The kind of things mothers always said.

Catherine slid from her chair, still chewing on her toast. 'So, can I have a kitten?'

Her mother heard. She frowned. 'No, of course you can't have a kitten! What a ridiculous idea.'

'Daddy said –'

'I don't care what Daddy said. I say no. Now go and clean your teeth.'

Catherine walked sedately out of the room and up the stairs. Going into the bathroom she reached for her pink toothbrush and then the tube of paste. Carefully she cleaned her teeth and rinsed out her mouth, then she walked back across the landing and into her bedroom. She took her blazer out of the wardrobe and then she looked up.

'Mummy doesn't like kittens,' she said softly but clearly. 'I don't think Mummy likes cats either.'

The animal was lying, head on paws, surveying her through sleepy eyes. Its tail, hanging down the side of the cupboard, twitched slightly, softly stroking the polished walnut.

She could feel it now, the soft ruff of fur, the warmth, the coils of steel-strong muscle, relaxed and pliant beneath her fingers, the heavy head beside hers on the tear-hot pillow as she cried herself to sleep and she stared up at it unafraid. It was the first time she had seen it in daylight. It was huge; big enough to eat someone.

She smiled as she buttoned her blazer. 'Mummy doesn't like me either,' she said, her tone conversational. 'That's because Daddy likes me best.'

The cat blinked with lazy interest.

'Catherine!' Her mother's shout on the landing made her jump. 'For goodness' sake, hurry!'

'If you're hungry, you could probably eat her, you know.' She said it quickly under her breath, half afraid, half defiant, a last-minute instruction as she turned towards the door. Opening it she glanced back. In a patch of early morning sunlight the suitcase on the wardrobe had changed from shadowy black to the rich chestnut of old leather.

Sitting in her classroom Catherine glanced across her neighbour towards the window. The sun was shining brightly now and the heat was striking through the glass. The roar of traffic in the busy road outside was muted into a muffled continuous sound which with the heat of the sun falling across her desk made her feel very sleepy. It was Monday, the day her mother hung out the washing on the line in the narrow back garden, the day she would go into Catherine's room and change the bed linen so that tonight, Catherine's favourite night, the sheets and pillows would smell of flowers and grass and fresh country things.

Her mother would be going into the bedroom, alone, unsuspecting, her arms full of clean pillowcases and clothes and with her back to the wardrobe she would set them all down as she always did, on the small frilled stool which stood in front of Catherine's dressing table. She might glance up into the little mirror and catch a glance of the black face with the golden almond-shaped eyes as it sprang, she might not. She might never know what had attacked her at all.

'Catherine?'

All they would find would be a pile of clean laundry and perhaps her mother's silver bangles, lying on the carpet near the bed.

'Catherine, what is it? Are you ill?' Miss Pitman had heard the child's strangled gasp and seen her eyes fill with tears. She put her arm round Catherine's shoulders and squatted down beside her chair. 'What is it, sweetheart? What's wrong?'

Catherine's face was white and she was shaking. The other children in the class looked at her with interest. 'She's going to be sick,' a small voice announced from the end of the row with the certainty of long experience and with some satisfaction.

'No she's not, Edward.' Miss Pitman put her other hand gently over Catherine's. 'What's wrong, Cathie? Aren't you feeling well?'

Catherine shook her head. She was trembling too much to speak.

There was a procedure in place for occasions such as these

and it was set in motion without delay. While Catherine was led to the sick room the class was put on its honour to do some copying in silence and as on all occasions before she and Miss Pitman had reached the corner of the passage the noise behind them was crescendoing out of control; but for once Miss Pitman did not storm back to fling open the door and shout, without having to even look who it was, at young Edward and his two best cronies. The child beside her was worrying her too much.

She sat her on the bed and put a professionally cool hand on Catherine's forehead to feel skin burning like fire. 'What is it, Catherine? Where are you hurting?'

Catherine shook her head, incapable of speech. Before her eyes she could see clearly her mother's dismembered body, an arm lying near the dressing table, a foot on the bed where the cat had taken it to eat, holding it meticulously between two soft velvet paws, as it licked delicately at the toes, its eyes half shut in concentration.

Mrs Harriman, the principal, summoned from her mathematics class, frowned thoughtfully. 'Has something happened at home to upset you, Catherine?' She bent down a little in front of Catherine putting a hand on each shoulder, peering through circular spectacle lenses which enlarged her eyes into startling blue-irised globes.

Catherine nodded between hiccuping sobs.

'You must calm down and tell me so I can help. What's happened? What has upset you so much?'

'I've done something,' Catherine's words were all but inaudible, 'terrible.'

'You've done something terrible?'

She nodded miserably, hiccuping in earnest now, her eyes swollen and red.

'What have you done, Catherine?'

The quiet authority in the headmistress's voice was beginning to calm her. Catherine took a deep shuddering breath. Her hot hands kneaded the front of her pleated school skirt into a damp crushed rag. 'Mummy's dead.' The words were so quiet, so indistinct, at first, that neither woman thought she had heard aright.

Mrs Harriman collected herself visibly. 'Did you say there was something wrong with your Mummy, Catherine? But I saw her this morning when she brought you to school. She looked fine.'

'I've killed her.' The words were clearer this time, almost defiant. 'I killed her,' she repeated. 'Because she doesn't love me.'

Miss Pitman turned away from Catherine to the table near the window. Picking up a box of tissues, she pulled out a wad and put it into Catherine's hand. 'Blow your nose, sweetheart, and stop crying,' she said in her most bracing voice. 'Of course your mother loves you. How silly.' She raised an eyebrow in the direction of her superior. 'Do you think we'd better ring home?'

Mrs Harriman nodded. 'Give her a drink. I'll be back in a minute.'

It was a long minute. A mug of cocoa and two digestive biscuits later, with reinforcements sent to quell the two teacherless classrooms, Miss Pitman and Catherine were sitting side by side on the sick room bed and slowly the story was emerging.

Miss Pitman hid a smile. 'So, you told this panther or whatever it is, which lives on the wardrobe, that it could eat your mother, because your mother doesn't love you any more?'

Catherine nodded.

'And because you didn't love your mother any more either?'

Catherine nodded again.

'And you wanted to punish her?'

The nod was so small it was hardly visible.

'And now you're sorry you told the cat it could hurt her because you really love her very much.'

The nod this time, eyes huge, fixed desperately hopeful on Miss Pitman's face, was unmistakable.

Miss Pitman smiled. 'Catherine, the cat won't have attacked your mother! I'm sure you'll find she's safe and sound. It knows you really love her, just as it knows she really loves you. You know,' she stopped, wondering how far she dared go in reassuring the child on the subject of parental rows, 'grown ups do sometimes say things they don't mean at all when they are cross and it sounds to me as if your mummy and daddy were a bit cross with each other, doesn't it. I don't think they meant you to hear their quarrel. I think your mummy would be very upset indeed if she knew you heard her say something she didn't mean about you.'

'Does the cat know?'

Miss Pitman smiled again. 'Oh yes, the cat knows. The cat knows everything, because I think some of the time that silly old cat is just a story inside your head.'

Catherine surveyed her solemnly. Surely something inside her head could not scratch the wardrobe with its sharp claws; tear at her duvet cover the way it had.

'Anyway –' Miss Pitman reached once more for the biscuit packet and passed it to her. 'You'll soon see your mummy is all right.'

She glanced up as the door opened. Sarah Harriman's face was white as she beckoned Miss Pitman out of the room. In the hall she pulled Miss Pitman away from the door and began to talk in an urgent whisper. 'There was no reply from the house so I rang the father at his office. They told me there he had been called to the hospital. His wife has had an accident.' She glanced over her colleague's shoulder towards the closed door of the sick room and lowered her voice even further. 'They think she was attacked by some kind of animal.'

The women stared at each other for a moment in silence as her words sank in and the shock registered on Miss Pitman's face. The word which she finally chose to relieve her feelings was not one usually heard even in the playground.

'Quite.' Sarah endorsed it without the flicker of an eyelash. 'So, what do we do?'

'Is she badly hurt, do they know?'

'All they know is that Freddie Carter dropped everything and raced off to be at her bedside.'

'You'd better ring the hospital.' Miss Pitman bit her lip. 'I'll go back to Catherine.' She hesitated. 'She says it was a cat; a cat to which she made the suggestion that it eat her mother.' There was another short pause. 'I suppose it could be a real cat – some moggy she's enticed into her bedroom?'

Her headmistress narrowed her eyes. 'What do you mean it *could* be a real cat? What else could it be?' They held each other's gaze for a moment and both looked away simultaneously. 'Look, go back to the child. Stuff her with biscuits. Take her back into class if she's calmed down enough. Tell her her mummy is out shopping and can't come and get her for a while – anything. Anything. I'll see what I can find out.'

Freddie came to collect his small daughter two hours later. Before he was allowed to see her, Sarah Harriman showed him into her study.

'How is your wife?' She studied his face, noting that though he was tired and obviously under some strain he was equally obviously not prostrate with grief. Inwardly she sighed with relief even before he spoke.

'She's okay. They're keeping her in over night. She's got one or two deep scratches but most are superficial. She's very shocked, though.'

'What was it, do you know?'

Sitting behind her desk, she was playing nervously with her pen.

'The police think a stray cat must have got into the house but there was no sign of it when we went back to look.'

'A stray cat.' Sarah nodded slowly.

She looked down at her blotter. 'I see.' She glanced up again and took a deep breath. 'I think it's possible Catherine may have enticed it in. She has been telling us a little about it this morning, but she's obviously been very upset.'

In the car going home Freddie glanced at his daughter's face. It was still a little puffy from her earlier storm of crying when he had told her what had happened to her mother, and he noticed not for the first time how heartbreakingly like Frances she was.

'We'll go home and have tea, then later we'll go to the hospital to see Mummy, okay?' He smiled at her, changing down as they reached the corner of their road, wondering yet again just how such a little girl was going to live with the trauma of her guilt and her pain, if as Mrs Harriman seemed to think, Catherine knew about the cat.

Catherine nodded. She had grown more and more quiet as they approached the house.

'What is it, sweetheart? There's nothing to be afraid of.' Drawing up outside he reached for her hands. 'The police have searched every corner of the house and the animal has gone.' So had the blood. He had cleaned it up himself before setting out to fetch Catherine. He looked at her hard for a minute and then he turned away to gaze out of the windscreen. He hadn't reached for the door-handle. 'It must have sneaked in when Mummy was hanging out the washing, or,' he hesitated, 'did you let it in, Cathie? Had you been giving it some milk or something?' The police had found the black hairs on his daughter's duvet and noted the deep jumping scratches on the top of the wardrobe from which the creature had leapt onto Frances's back. The lacerations across her shoulders had been ferociously deep.

The puzzle had been where the cat had gone. Frances had not seen it at all. Flinging the clinging creature from her back with a scream she had run from the room, half fallen down the stairs and locked herself, shaking and hysterical, in the kitchen. From there she had phoned a neighbour before she collapsed, and the neighbour taking one look at her unconscious friend and her blood-soaked sweater had called an ambulance and then the police. No door had been forced, no window was open more than a crack, yet the cat was undoubtedly gone.

'No one is cross, sweetheart. You couldn't have known it had a vicious streak. I'm just relieved it didn't hurt you as well.' He put his arm round her and she snuggled against him, comforted. 'That was it, wasn't it? You let it in.'

Catherine shook her head.

'You didn't?' He looked down at her with a frown.

She shook her head again. 'It's always lived here. In my room.' She waited for her father to say something and when he didn't she took a deep breath and she began to speak.

At the end of her story he was sitting staring sightlessly out of the windscreen. For a long time he said nothing and at last, timidly, she touched his hand.

'Daddy?' She was very afraid.

He turned to her and the sorrow on his face was so great she had to look away. 'I'm sorry,' she whispered. 'I'm sorry.'

'Darling, it's me who should be sorry. Mummy and me. We had no idea you were there listening. No idea at all.' He bit his lip, still making no move to get out of the car. It was as if he were afraid to go into the house.

He sighed. 'Listen. You have to believe me. You have to. Mummy loves you as much as I do and that is so much it would drown mountains.' He managed a smile. 'She only said she didn't love you so much and you didn't love her because she knew how cross it would make me! Grown ups do that every now and then, you know. Just to wind each other up. It's a sort of game they play. Then they make up and everything is all right. They know none of the things they said meant anything.' If only it were true. Please God, let it be true.

His hand on hers was ice cold and shaking slightly. She reversed the grip, taking his in her own two hot little palms and trying to give him comfort.

'I didn't mean her to get hurt. Truly.'

'I know you didn't. Cathie, it's not your fault. The cat didn't listen to what you were saying. It couldn't have!'

But even as he said the words he wondered.

Inside at last he gave her hot cheese on toast on her knee in front of the television, not arguing when she refused to go to her room, until she had been home for an hour and he couldn't stand it any longer. He reached down for her hand. 'Come on. We're going to check it out upstairs.'

She shook her head.

'Yes. We need to look at your room, find you a night light so you're never scared in the dark again, and look at this silly old suitcase.'

It was where it always was, on top of the cupboard. For a long time they both stared at it, then Freddie collected her dressing table stool and put it in front of the wardrobe. 'Hold it for me so I don't fall off.'

'Careful.' Her mouth was dry with terror.

'I will be.' He grinned at her.

Standing on tiptoe he reached for the worn leather handle and gave it a tug. It didn't move. He tugged again, realising he was going to have to lift it over the small ornate parapet which ran around the top of the wardrobe. For a moment it resisted then at last he dragged it free and swung it down, surprised at its weight. 'This old case belonged to my father,' he said to her as he laid it down on the floor and knelt before the huge brass locks. 'It went all over the world with him. Look at the labels.' He glanced up at her. 'There's nothing to be afraid of, Cathie. The case is empty.'

She had backed away, her hands tightly clasped together behind her back, her face like chalk.

He was struggling with the locks now, fighting them back, sure it wasn't locked, until at last one clicked back and then the other.

He stared down. The child's fear was infectious. Suddenly he didn't want to open it.

He had an irrational feeling that the cat was inside; but how could it be?

'When we've put this away up in the attic where it belongs, we'll go and see Mummy shall we?' He smiled up at her.

She nodded wearily.

'I don't think we'll tell her about all this, do you, Pudding?' he went on carefully. 'I think it's a special secret thing between you and me. Poor Mummy thinks it was just a silly old wild cat from the garden. I think it's better that way, don't you?' She also thought the cat was some kind of punishment for what she had done. His hand was on the lid of the case and Catherine was watching it, mesmerised.

'See this lovely old leather? That's why the case is so heavy; almost too heavy to lift even though it's empty. We should be glad modern suitcases are so light. In the old days they were all like this unless they were made of cardboard.' His fingers stroked the surface and rested one by one on the torn stickers. 'Look. India. Burma. China. What memories the case must have.' He bit his lip. All places where big cats roamed free.

Taking a deep breath he began to ease back the lid. Slowly it rose, revealing nothing but a rubbed faded lining and a few nondescript bits of rubbish. Tickets, a hairpin, an old envelope. The smell inside the suitcase was of old leather, dust and musty long-forgotten cologne.

For a long time Catherine and her father stared down into the case, then he let the lid fall shut. Neither of them had noticed the clump of black hairs caught in the inner buckled straps.

Pulling down the attic steps Freddie humped the case up out of sight and came back down again shutting the trap door behind him.

'Right?' He dusted his hands together. 'Now, we'll go and see Mummy. And I think you'll find she's got an idea for you.' He smiled. She had been devastated in the hospital about her harshness to Catherine that morning, remembering only her small daughter's crestfallen face and her tears, so resolutely held back as she walked into school. She would do everything in her power to make it up to the child, as she would to him. 'I think, as Mummy is a bit off cats at the moment, that it might involve a puppy.'

Catherine gave a gasp of delight but half-way down the stairs she stopped and glanced back. Obviously her father hadn't heard the click of claws on top of the trap door or the small querulous growl, but then perhaps she hadn't either.

Stranger's Choice

THE SUN WAS SLANTING through the feathery branches of the larch tree. Fiona stood for a while in the dappled shade, looking down at the broad sweep of the river at her feet. It was a still, gentle evening. Behind her she could see the stones of the old kirk nestling up in the wooded slopes of the hill.

Her heart beat fast and she checked her wristwatch. Half past, the minister had said. She clutched her music case a little more tightly and sat down on the river bank to wait, trying hard to think of anything but the coming test and the tunes she had so carefully practised.

Setting the case down on the grass as gently as she would had it contained some of the eggs from her mother's hens, she picked up a sprig of larch cones. Nervously she twisted them between her fingers, picking off the tiny scales. Then a bird caught her eye as it swept low over the water, just skimming the surface with its beak before it angled sharply up into the wood and disappeared. Fiona shivered. That was how she wanted to play the organ. The low easy skimming, the swift, controlled flights of ecstasy, the breathless, dizzy grace. She looked down at her hands. They were sturdy and red from the gardening, not the kind of hands to produce ethereal music.

From across the trees came the echoing single note of the clock striking the half hour. Fiona scrambled to her feet in horror. Her watch must have stopped. She began to run up through the dim woods, fighting her way between the closely planted firs, her sandals sinking into the soft carpet made by their needles.

The hillside was very steep, and when at last she arrived at the little grey-built kirk she was breathless and dishevelled. There was no sign of Mr Seton, the minister. Her heart sank. She knew he was a busy man. It had only been with reluctance that he had agreed to come and hear her play this evening at all. Indeed he had not even seemed to want to admit that the position of organist would be free when Sandy Gregor moved away. She knew he thought her too young for the post. To him, as to everyone else she was still Mrs Macrae's 'wee Fiona'.

Ducking into the low porch she listened for a moment to the noisily squabbling birds in the roof beams. They had an untidy nest up there, she saw, with two gaping beaks protruding from it. The sight made her smile as, cautiously, she pushed at the heavy door. To her surprise it was unlocked.

The kirk was very still. She thought for a moment it was empty, then she noticed a figure sitting on one of the benches to the side, near the organ. She approached on tiptoe and nervously cleared her throat.

He did not appear to hear her. He was dressed in his customary black suit, his head resting on his hand, his shoulders hunched. For a moment she stood beside him in awed silence, not knowing what to do. Then she spoke softly.

Slowly the man raised his head, and he gave her a grave smile. It was not Mr Seton.

'Oh, I'm sorry.' Fiona backed away in alarm, seeing the grey, tired face and red-rimmed eyes. 'I shouldn't have disturbed you. I thought you were the minister.'

Again the same smile. 'Think nothing of it, lassie. It was time I was leaving anyway.' He looked around the empty building, his eyes dwelling momentarily on the bowl of daffodils and narcissi before the lectern. The sun slanting through the tiny panes of glass in the west window was casting chequered patterns across the floor, lighting the blooms in a glorious radiance.

The man smiled. 'This is a beautiful place, young lady,' he said, his voice sad. Rising to his feet, he began to make his way towards the door. Then he paused and looked back.

Already Fiona, preoccupied with her own worries, had made her way to the organ and was running her fingers soundlessly over the keys. Her stomach was tied in a nervous knot, and she wondered suddenly if she would be able to remember a single note if Mr Seton came.

'Do you know how to play it?'

She jumped as the stranger's words carried back to her beneath the echoing roof vault.

'A little.' She smiled nervously. 'I've come to play for the minister, to see if I'm good enough for the services.'

'Indeed.' The man slowly retraced his steps. He stood behind her for a moment. 'Play something for me now.'

'Oh I couldn't.' Fiona was embarrassed. 'Besides, I must wait for Mr Seton.'

'He won't mind. Come on. I want to hear some music.'

Fiona slipped uncomfortably into the seat, then she let out a stifled cry.

'My music! Oh, I've left my music down by the river.' She looked round, anguished. 'Oh what am I to do?' The easy tears were already brimming in her eyes.

'Hush, hush.' The man put a gentle hand on her shoulder. 'Look there's plenty of music there, on the shelf.'

'But it's not mine,' wailed Fiona. 'I had it especially prepared. I had practised special things.' A tear fell on the keyboard and she hastily dabbed at it with her handkerchief.

The man chuckled. 'I'm thinking that these are the tunes you'll be asked to play: hymns and carols, not organ sonatas and party pieces.' He reached down a pile of tattered folios and began slowly to leaf through them.

Fiona watched him miserably. It had all gone wrong. She knew now that she would fail the test. She would never be able to play; her hands were shaking too much. Once again she was Mrs Macrae's wee Fiona and she wanted to run back to her mother's house.

The man looked over several pieces and then she saw him pause at one. He frowned and then gave a little laugh. Placing it before her, he smoothed back the page. 'Play me that,' he commanded.

Sniffing, she tentatively ran her fingers over the stops, and then slowly, softly, picked out the tune, touching in an occasional chord to give the music depth. It was something she had never heard before – sad, haunting and very beautiful.

Gradually she became absorbed in the music. She forgot herself and her mother, and the reason she was in the kirk. She did not even notice as the strange man, after listening for a few moments, his eyes distant with memory, slowly made his way back to the door and let himself out into the still evening.

Neither did she notice when a while later Mr Seton slipped into the kirk, still panting from his climb through the wood.

Not until the notes of the final chord had died away did she become conscious once more of her surroundings. Mr Seton rose from the seat he had taken at the back of the kirk and walked slowly up the aisle. 'That was very beautiful, Fiona,' he said. He reached over her shoulder and took the music. 'A strange choice though, I think, for the kirk. A lovely song, but more suited for a lover's wooing than one of my services.'

Fiona blushed. 'I'm sorry, Mr Seton. That gentleman chose it for me. And he took it from the music here by the organ, so I thought it was all right.'

'Indeed.' Mr Seton's eyebrows shot up, but he seemed amused. 'In that case I must have a wee word with Sandy Gregor before he leaves. I think it's time he had a sort through the music.' The minister himself picked up the pile of scores, and after a moment handed her another. 'What gentleman was that, Fiona?'

'He was in the kirk when I arrived. I disturbed him, thinking it was you, but he wasn't from these parts at all. I told him I'd left my music down by the river and he chose that song for me to play for him.'

'Indeed.' The minister smiled once more. 'I'm sorry I didn't see him. It seems he has a sense of humour, your strange friend. Enough. Play me the *Crimond* there, and we'll see how that sounds.'

Fiona sighed with relief. This was something she did know. She wished Mr Seton wouldn't stand quite so close behind her, checking every note she played, but on the whole she thought she got through it well enough. Her nervousness had not returned. He seemed pleased. She played two more hymns for him and that was all he wanted.

She sat quietly on the narrow seat, her sandals tucked well up on the crossbar, waiting for him to speak after she finished the last piece. He had retired during the last couple of verses to the end of the nave where he stood, his hands behind his back, seemingly lost in thought.

Then at last he spoke. 'Well, Fiona. I think you've got yourself a job, my dear, if you'd like it.' He smiled. 'I had no idea you had such a talent. My congratulations.'

Blushing, Fiona wriggled from her place and almost skipped down between the rows of empty seats to where he stood. Solemnly he shook hands with her.

She followed him out of the kirk, paused while he locked the door and went with him across the mown grass of the graveyard in the gradually dimming light.

'Will you go back by the river, Fiona, to collect your music?' The minister grinned at her mischievously. 'I know you won't make a habit of leaving it there before service.'

'Oh I won't,' Fiona agreed with him fervently. 'Indeed I won't.'

She stood and watched as he made his way out of the gate into the lane, then slowly she turned once more into the fragrant larches. Below her the evening sun, reflected in the river, turned the waters to a broad sweep of red gold.

Her music case was where she had left it on the river bank, the leather damp with dew. Clutching it to her she stood for a moment gazing out across the water.

She could hear someone singing. The voice, distant and melodious, seemed to be coming from further down the river. She strained her ears to make out the tune above the sound of the water: gradually she began to distinguish the notes. He was singing the love song she had played in the kirk.

She strained her eyes in the gloaming to see him. Was that a figure standing further down river near the rocks? She wasn't sure. Already the sound of the music was fading.

Raising her hand she waved in its direction, although she knew he couldn't see her.

'I'll never know who he was,' she reflected with a strange certainty, 'but maybe I'll play that tune for him again one day.' Whoever he was, his quiet smile and gentle choice of music had won her back her confidence and given her the job of her dreams.

She turned away from the water slowly and once more clutching her music case to her heart she began to make her way home in the dusk.

Aboard the Moonbeam

I STRETCHED LUXURIOUSLY and lay looking up at the dappled white reflection playing over the ceiling. It puzzled me for a moment. Then I remembered. I had arrived late the night before at the old house on the edge of Chichester Harbour. Outside my bedroom window stretched a vast expanse of ice-rimmed water.

Pulling my dressing gown around me with a shiver, half of excitement, half of cold as my feet met the floorboards beneath my bed, I got up and went over to the window to look out. It was early morning still and the harbour was deserted. Over towards the east the water was tinged with red from the morning sun. On either side cats' paws flecked the water into slate and silver shadow.

A solitary boat, large and black, was moored across the channel. I gazed at it fascinated for a while, lost in a dream, and then forgot it as I heard a call from downstairs.

My cousin, Jim, was in the kitchen.

'Granny stays in bed till lunch,' he explained, 'and I'm driving into town, so there's nothing for you to do but relax, and get well.' He smiled.

I was not really ill but long months of glandular fever had left me exhausted and depressed. My great aunt, Andrea, who had already offered Jim a home, now said she would be glad to have me for a few months as well. I think she guessed how lonely and unsettled I was and she knew how much I had loved my childhood holidays in her house.

After Jim had gone, I settled back to enjoy a second cup of coffee in the peaceful dining room, and inevitably my thoughts went back to Graham.

I looked ruefully at the engagement ring on my finger. It was a little loose still. We had never got round to having it altered to fit me properly. Dear Graham. He had said nothing; neither had I, but I had a feeling that when next we met it would be for me to return that ring. He had been too eager to go back to New Zealand without me, had too easily accepted my reason for postponing the wedding. Indeed he seemed almost relieved when I said I would not follow him until later.

This time I had not cried when we parted. There was a tight restriction in my throat, but also, unaccountably, a sense of sudden freedom.

I was so immersed in my thoughts that it was a moment before I realised that someone was knocking on the side door. A young man stood outside, a muffler pulled well up to his chin. I supposed him to be one of the local fishermen.

'Morning.' He stared at me, obviously wondering who I was. 'I just thought I'd let you know. *Moonbeam*'s signalling.'

'*Moonbeam*?' I stared at him, bewildered.

He nodded. 'Is Jim here? 'E always goes over.'

'He's gone up to town.' That at least I could answer.

The man scratched his head. He looked worried. 'Might be urgent. 'E don't often signal.' He saw that I still didn't understand. 'Chap lives over there on the *Moonbeam*.' He indicated the black hulk I had noticed earlier. 'Your Jim rows over most days and takes him food and papers and that. Edward Avon, that's 'is name, has an emergency signal if 'e needs help.'

'Why can't he come here?' I was indignant. It seemed a strange, one-sided arrangement to me.

'Broke 'is leg. Mrs Andrea, she offered to have 'im to stay, of course, with 'er heart of gold, but he wouldn't 'ear of it; didn't want to put 'er out, so 'e said. Never mind. I'll see if anyone from the village can go over.'

'I know how to row.' I don't know what made me say it. Perhaps I was curious. Perhaps it was the light way this young man assumed that I would be of no use. 'If you show me where the boat is I'll go over and see.'

'You sure you can manage?' He looked at me hard from piercing blue eyes.

I grinned. 'Give me one moment to fetch my jacket.'

I followed him out into the exhilarating autumn sunshine, down to the edge of the quay, and climbed into the rowing boat which was tethered there. He pushed me off and I managed quite well on the whole, as I pulled at the oars with unaccustomed muscles, a fixed grin on my face as he stood to watch me go. To my relief he only stayed a minute, I suppose to make sure this town woman really could row, and then he turned and hurried away towards the village.

It was much further than I thought across the harbour. I rowed slowly, losing my breath in the brisk salty wind, cursing the fact that I hadn't remembered to bring any gloves. My fingers turned red, blue and white in turns, and soon I felt my strokes beginning to fail. I had forgotten my own stupid weakness, and the fact that this harbour, unlike the lake at home where I had learned to row, had a tide.

As I felt myself weaken I kept glancing over my shoulder towards the singularly misnamed *Moonbeam*, where she lay black and forbidding against a bank of reeds. Uncomfortable waves of panic began to crawl up and down my spine as I wondered whether I could get there at all, and what would happen to me if I didn't. The tide had such effortless hidden strength as it swept up the broad channel, bringing with it great lumps of green spinach-like seaweed.

Eventually I did get there, even though for a while I had the strength only to hang gasping onto one of the heavy mooring ropes, slimy with weed. Then at last I began to swing my little dinghy round towards the ladder which hung over the side. I was beginning to call Edward Avon all kinds of rude names under my breath. Didn't the silly man have a mobile phone, or a radio or something sensible like that? Why didn't he appear and at least help me up his beastly ladder? I wasn't sure I had enough energy left to climb it on my own.

I squinted up at the flag hanging from the stumpy mast above me. On it there was a pretty yellow boat, and it was flying upside down. That was the signal, I supposed, as I scrabbled my way feebly around the side of the boat with frozen hands.

At last I reached the ladder and managed to pull myself up precariously onto the slippery deck. I looked around. The boat seemed deserted. Making my way to the cabin door, I tapped on it, shaking with cold. There was no reply so I pushed it open and peered in.

The cabin was neat and warm, an oil light burning above the table. In the corner I could see a bunk and on it the huddled form of a man, the plaster cast encasing his ankle dragging at an awkward angle on the floorboards beside the berth.

'Hello, can I come in?' I was surprised by the tremor in my voice. My teeth were chattering.

He did not stir. I supposed he was asleep and timidly stepped down into the cabin.

His pillow was soaked in blood.

For a moment I had to fight off a wave of terrified faintness and nausea and then miraculously I was clear-headed again. Very gently I touched his head, easing back the fair hair, which was matted black with blood. He groaned as I touched him, but he didn't open his eyes.

I sat down at the little table for a moment, trying to decide what to do. I hadn't enough strength to row back for help. Of that I was sure. Somehow I had to attract the attention of someone in the village.

He let out another groan and I pulled myself to my feet to go to his side. Somehow I had to help him myself. Eventually, very gently I managed to sponge away most of the blood. He seemed to have a deep cut on his temple and a massive, spreading bruise across his forehead. Cautiously I lifted his heavy cast up onto the bed and straightened his legs, throwing a rug over them. At least he looked more comfortable.

It was as I tried easing the blood-soaked pillow away and replacing it with a cushion that he suddenly opened his eyes. They were clear slits of silver in his weather-beaten face. He looked at me blankly for a moment and then he smiled.

'I'm sure you can't be an angel,' he said clearly. Then he mumbled something I couldn't make out and closed his eyes.

I looked down at him, amused. 'I'm afraid I'm not,' I was about to reply, but I could see he had slipped away into unconsciousness again.

He was, I guessed, about thirty, perhaps a little more, and his face had a pleasant, thoughtful expression as though he were puzzling out some strange but not too unpleasant problem. There were little laughter lines at the corners of his eyes.

I was worried. Obviously he needed a doctor, and obviously I shouldn't really have touched him at all. Supposing he had a fractured skull? I quickly tried to put the idea out of my head as I searched fruitlessly for the radio or phone which I had already guessed he didn't possess and then went back out onto the freezing deck and looked around for the way to make another signal. Aunt Andrea's house seemed so far away now, across the still water, and the village, the other side of the point, turned nothing but stone walls to the cold harbour view. I could see no signs of life.

Perhaps I should after all row back for help. I went to the ladder and peered down uncertainly.

The rowing boat had gone.

There were tears in my eyes as I made my way back into the cabin. How could I have been so foolish; so stupid? I wondered if I had even tried to tie it up. I suspect I had been so relieved to get to the ladder I had stepped out of the little boat and forgotten it.

'There she is again.' The voice was slightly muffled but more coherent this time. 'I dreamed I saw a lady, and she tried to walk away with my foot.'

I laughed. 'Well, I picked it up onto your bed. I'm sorry. I hope I didn't hurt it.'

'Bunk.' He smiled disarmingly.

'I beg your pardon?' I was indignant. Was he being deliberately rude?

'You don't have beds on boats, you have bunks.' He held out his hand. 'Come nearer, young lady; you have your back to the light and I can't see you. You're not the district nurse I suppose?'

I wasn't sure if he was being facetious. 'I am not. I am staying with Aunt Andrea and when we saw your signal I came to see what was wrong. Jim, who is my cousin, had already left for town.'

He looked a little puzzled.

'Signal? Andrea?' He put his hand to his head, and winced suddenly. 'I remember now. I tripped on deck with my stupid foot, and hit my face. There was blood everywhere. My foot hurt like hell, and I was scared. I put the signal up hoping to catch Jim before he left. Then I remember coming back down and the pain, and then . . .' he shook his head. 'I suppose I blacked out for a bit.'

Gingerly I reached out and touched his forehead. 'The bleeding has stopped. Have you a first aid box anywhere? I think I ought to put something on it until the doctor comes.'

I bit my lip suddenly as I remembered the dinghy, and my inability to call the doctor now.

'What's wrong?' His eyes were acute now that he was completely conscious.

'You'll think I'm such a fool. I've lost my boat. I didn't tie it up properly when I got here.'

To my surprise he let out a shout of laughter. 'Thank God!

467

You're not as efficient as you look. Don't worry, your boat will go for help without you. The tide will take it straight back to Andrea's. Then they will come and fetch you. I did that myself once just after I came here.'

'Haven't *you* got a dinghy? Then I could go back in that,' I said a little stiffly. 'Or a phone?' I didn't much like being laughed at. 'Or do you always rely on other people?'

'Now, now.' He tapped my hand reprovingly. 'I do have a dinghy, as it happens, but it is on deck, and I doubt if you could lower it on your own into the water, however strong and capable you are. Modern technology I eschew. It has its uses, I admit. But I did not envisage having any need of it.'

I withdrew my hand, where his own had casually come to rest, and backed away from his bunk.

'In that case shall I put on the kettle? I suppose you have one of them? Where did you say the first aid box is?'

His eyes twinkled. 'If you're thinking of making tea, I'd rather have medicinal brandy. And I prescribe it for you, too . . .' he paused, his head on one side. 'Does my angel of mercy have a name?'

'Christine,' I mumbled. 'Christine Harper.'

'Well, excellent Christine Harper; if you proceed through there,' he pointed vaguely to a door, 'to what would in your landlubber language be called the front end of the boat, you will find in a locker, or cupboard, which probably has the door open, a selection of bottles. Scrabble about a bit and see what you can find. And Christine –' he called after me as I made my way to the door, 'there's a box of plasters on the sink.'

Gingerly I let myself into the next cabin and gasped. It was flooded with light. Nearly half the roof had been replaced by an enormous skylight. There was an easel, a table, and everywhere paints, canvasses and jam jars of brushes and pencils and palette knives.

Shutting the door behind me I went over to the easel and examined the picture on it. It showed a flock of geese paddling about on the saltings. Eagerly I turned other paintings towards me. Most of them were of birds, although some showed boats and harbour scenes. It was the most fascinating room, and immediately explained a great deal about Edward's solitude. I found a small unopened bottle of brandy in the cupboard as he had predicted, behind a few empty beer cans and several bottles of turps and linseed oil. Collecting the elastoplast I returned to the main cabin.

'You're a painter!' I remarked rather foolishly, holding out the bottle to him. He was sitting up now, his head in his hands.

'Full marks for observation.' He grimaced slightly as he reached for the brandy. 'I'm more of an illustrator actually. The glasses are in the locker over there.'

I found them, and seeing how his hands were shaking, took the bottle back and poured out two small measures myself. Sitting down next to him I handed him a glass.

'I hope Aunt Andrea won't be terribly worried when the rowing boat drifts back without me. I didn't tell her I was coming here. She was still in bed when I left.'

'Your Aunt Andrea is not a worrier,' he smiled. 'At least not until you've spent the night here with me, then she might.' He chuckled.

I glanced at him sideways. 'Do I gather you have a reputation then?'

'I do.' He sounded quite pleased about it. 'The villagers think I live a life of utter debauchery over here, partly because people always think that about painters; partly because they saw my sister here in her bikini last summer. But, alas, I live like a hermit. Or did until now.' He looked at me speculatively. But I could see the twinkle was still there.

'I see I shall have to watch out.' I was beginning to enjoy his teasing manner. 'I can always swim for the shore if you get too persistent.'

We both looked down at his cast, and laughed.

'You'll outrun me for a while yet, Christine, so don't risk

hypothermia on my account. When are you getting married?'

I was astonished. His sharp eyes had missed nothing. Ruefully I twisted the ring on my finger. 'I don't think I am. My fiancé has gone back to New Zealand and I have a feeling I shan't be following him.'

'I'm sorry.' His voice was suddenly gentle. 'What went wrong?'

I shrugged. 'What does go wrong? We'd been apart for several months and when he came back we just didn't seem to be so right any more. We couldn't discuss things as we used to. The spark had gone, somehow.'

'And you came down here to make up your mind?'

I nodded. 'And to convalesce. I've been ill.'

'What a pair we are.' His voice was suddenly bright once more. 'More brandy?' He held out his glass.

We were on our third 'dose' and I was beginning to feel extremely light-headed when there was a loud knocking on the side of the boat. A moment later we heard heavy footsteps on deck.

'Anyone in?' a hearty voice called out. I looked at my companion wide-eyed.

'Come on down, Mac. It's Dr Macintosh,' he laughed at me, and then turning to the doorway, 'Are you psychic, or did you see me fall through your telescope?'

A large, jovial-faced man stepped cautiously down into the cabin. 'Neither. I gather you need me young man, but if you had any memory at all you would have remembered that I was coming over to see you this morning anyway.' He turned to me with a smile and stuck out a huge hand. 'Christine Harper, I presume. Your aunt asked me to look in this morning to give you a quick check-up, but you had gone out. I might have known Edward here would have enticed you over.'

I was indignant. 'Why did she want you to see me? She never mentioned it.'

'Oh just to catch up on your list of ailments.' He laughed

reassuringly. 'I gather you've been poorly for some time. But if you've the strength to row across here and indulge in a drunken orgy with this reprobate . . .' He grinned, leaving his sentence unfinished.

'Have one, doctor, while there's still some left.' Edward held out the battle.

The doctor poured himself a tiny measure, but his attention was already on Edward's head. He set down the glass untouched and made his patient lie down, thoroughly examining him as I watched. 'Did the lady hit you over the head?' he enquired thoughtfully as his fingers gently touched the wound.

'She did, doctor.' Edward's voice was mournful.

I could see the two of them were good friends, and very much on the same wavelength. And I was beginning to feel outnumbered.

'Does this convince you you're not fit to stay here alone?' the doctor said as he sat back at last, after putting on a dressing. He picked up his glass.

Edward shook his head. 'I'm unrepentant. Did you come to take off my cast?'

The doctor laughed. 'You've a while yet I'm afraid, before you can start thinking of that.'

When he stood up to go, I was making ready to follow when Edward took my hand.

'You will come again, Christine, please? I get so few visitors.'

'That's because you threaten to throw them off your boat,' Dr Macintosh commented over his shoulder as he climbed out of the door.

'Shut up, Mac.' Edward's voice was quite threatening. 'Please, Christine?'

'I'll think about it,' I said with a grin. I was beginning to like this Edward Avon – and his doctor – very much. 'But perhaps I'll get Jim to row me over next time. It might be wiser.' I ducked out under the low door before he had a chance to argue, and gingerly followed the doctor down the ladder into his motor launch.

Two days later I went into Chichester and posted my engagement ring to New Zealand. I was not going to follow it.

I visited the *Moonbeam* two or three times in the safely recovered dinghy, with Jim at the oars, and then as I regained my strength and nerve for rowing I began to do the trip on my own. The first time I did this Edward was awaiting me on deck, balancing with a walking stick near the rail. As I climbed the ladder he presented me with a little book on knots.

'Now,' he commented, 'you're not coming in until you've learned to tie a bowline and having done so have looped it over the appropriate bollard – or knob to you.' He grinned.

'And knobs to you too,' I retorted. But I obediently sat down in the freezing wind and twisted the dinghy's long painter into the correct knot.

Two weeks later when I arrived, still slightly breathless from the rowing, he greeted me on deck, jubilant. His cast had been removed.

'Now there's no escape,' he gloated with a grin. 'Even if I still have to hop I can go faster than you.'

But we both knew by now that he would not have to run. My initial attraction had swiftly developed into something much deeper, and although neither of us ever mentioned it I sensed that he felt the same way.

Autumn turned to winter and at last Christmas Eve arrived. I rowed over to the *Moonbeam* in the morning, a small Christmas tree propped up in the bow of the dinghy. He was coming to spend Christmas Day with us at Andrea's house, but I wanted the celebration to start early, with just us two there.

Carefully tying the dinghy to the ladder I climbed it and hauled the tree up after me.

'So now she wants a garden on board too!' He was looking

at me through the open cabin door, his eyes laughing as he watched my exertions.

'More like a forest,' I retorted. 'You might come and help.'

I had a box full of decorations and together we set up the tree in the main cabin. It took up an awful lot of space but it did look beautiful.

'Now,' he commanded. 'Make the coffee. I'm busy.' He retreated into his studio and closed the door.

'Make it yourself,' I answered back happily. There was something else in the dinghy which I wanted to fetch. His present.

The door reopened and he appeared, frowning. 'Did I hear you disobeying orders?'

'You sure did.' I stuck my tongue out at him.

'You realise that this is mutiny?' He strode towards me and grabbed my wrist. 'I don't hold with mutiny on my ship. I have ways of dealing with it.'

He had never kissed me before. As his arms went round me and he drew me to him, I felt myself starting to tremble. I did not believe it was possible to be so happy.

He broke away from me abruptly. 'As I was saying, I have ways of dealing with troublemakers.' He fished for a moment in his pocket and then he brought out a slim gold bangle. 'I clap them in irons. It generally keeps them in line.' He clipped it on my wrist, and gave me another quick kiss. '*Now*, will you make the coffee. Please?'

I put on the kettle.

The next morning he rowed across to us dressed, unbelievably, in a smart suit. Just before church he whisked Aunt Andrea away into the dining room. Moments later they reappeared together, smiling.

'This delightfully old-fashioned boy has asked me if he may propose to you, Chris,' said Aunt Andrea, her whole face alight with laughter. 'I said I thought probably that would be all right.' Picking up her prayer book with a little chuckle she went out into the hall, pointedly closing the door behind her.

I looked at Edward. He was grinning. 'As I told you, Christine, I don't hold with mutiny. You do as you're told.' He held out a little box. 'Try it for size, if you please.'

This engagement ring fitted me perfectly.

'Happy Christmas, darling,' he whispered, and he took me into his arms.

Choices

HE WAS TALL for an old man, perhaps over six foot in spite of his stoop, with a large ungainly frame to match his size, his skin dried up, leather-like, desiccated by eighty years of wind and weather and pain. Up and down he plodded, his feet leaving damp circles in the sand, rhythmically sweeping back and forth with the heavy disk on its long handle, slowly, methodically beating the tide back towards the setting sun.

Louise narrowed her eyes. She should have left for home by now. Hers was the last car in the car park on the cliff but still she lingered, watching. There was something so dogged, so determined, in his persistence. She had first seen him earlier in the café at the top of the cliff and had been struck then by his self-contained poise as he sat and drank his cup of tea and slowly reached into his pocket for the coins to pay. The tip he left the waitress was, she noticed, as much again as the price of the drink. He had reached down for the metal detector lying under the table, stooping painfully, and then straightened with a groan.

'Not found your treasure yet, Granddad?' The waitress grinned at him, pocketing her fifty pence.

He smiled. 'Not yet, sweetheart. You'll be the first to know.'

He walked slowly past Louise and out of the café and turned along the path out of sight.

'What's he hoping to find?' Louise had pulled out her

purse and was counting the money for her own bill.

'Gawd knows!' The girl tossed her head. 'Silly old goat.'

Louise frowned. The tone seemed so cruel. The girl was young, her flesh plump and pink and moist. She had her life before her. Surely she could spare a kind word about an old man. What, Louise wondered, would she say about her? A middle-aged woman, still slim, still, she liked to think, attractive, but probably, well, past it! Gathering up her things Louise made her way out and looked after him. Already he had plodded down the wooden steps against the cliff and was walking out across the sand.

She had come out to the beach to think. After all, it was a fair bet at this time of year that it would be empty. All the children were back at school and the guest houses and hotels were emptying fast now that the sun had grown hazy, allowing healing mists to drift up the beach and across the dried gold of the countryside. The shops on the small seafront further along the cliff were one by one being boarded up now, before the autumnal gales hurled the sand across the esplanade and piled rank weed, dredged by the storms from the depths of the sea, onto their doorsteps.

All day she had worried at her problem, tearing it to shreds, tossing the pieces back and forth, hand to hand, like a juggler, watching the alternate possibilities glitter in the sun and spin in and out of reach. Man or career; love or money; adventure or security. Only one. Not both. Not possibly both. If either one had come six months ago without the other there would have been no contest, no problem, but now. . .

The man had come first. Tall, tanned, his hair a short wild tangle of exuberance, his eyes a piercing blue. He was no Lothario. For a long time she had thought he had not even noticed her as he sat at his library desk, surrounded by heavy tomes, scribbling away at his notes. Twice she had found him books from the book stacks in the cellars and carried them to his desk, but the face he turned to hers for a second had been distracted, preoccupied, with – she had glanced at the titles again – the history of South America, the ancient peoples of Peru, the Nasca lines.

When he saw her in the restaurant behind the library however he had come over without hesitation, charming, diffident, apologetic. Magnetic. Within five minutes she was terrifyingly, totally in love.

Love – wild, abandoned, passionate love – always seemed to have bypassed Louise and she had thought she was probably temperamentally unsuited to the state. It was not that men did not find her attractive. They had always pursued her – if sometimes a little more respectfully than she might have wished. Even now she was tiptoeing around the idea of accepting that she was perhaps on the verge of middle age, they still came, still admired, still with the old-fashioned courtesy she seemed to inspire in them, taking her to concerts and theatres and art galleries. They were in fact so respectful that they did not even seem to resent each other. When, as must happen from time to time, one found out about another, there was no bristling of hackles, no flare of testosterone, no drawing of swords. Just a polite, perhaps reproachful, hurt.

Fraser was different. It did not occur to him that to love her would be disrespectful. He did not seem to see her grey hair as a warning or treat her intellect as a barrier or notice her sensible mien. What he had seen was the hidden passion, the longing, the warmth, the desire for romance even she had not known were there.

Galleries and museums, yes. Concerts and plays, no. No time. He took her instead to Avebury, to Stonehenge and to the Rollright Stones, to sites of geomantic significance and electro-magnetic force. He lectured her on ley lines and geophysics and geopathic stress and particles and he was completely honest: he had a wife; a wife he still quite liked. They were not divorced, but they no longer lived together. 'She wanted a home, I'm a wanderer.' He shrugged and smiled. 'I tried. I really tried. I'm still fond of her, but she's found herself another chap. He'll give her everything I can't. So I wish her well.' The way he shrugged had alerted her suspicions though. She would not be going into anything blind.

His other, greater love and one he admitted to freely, was for the planet, for Gaia, for his studies.

She was exhilarated, excited, horrified, dumbfounded by this other passion, by his eclectic intellectual curiosity and what she saw as his blinkered dismissal of recognised science. He was brilliant, shocking, everything she had ever wanted in a man – and he was going to South America in October.

He had told her about that too on the first day they had met; it wasn't until almost the last that he asked her to go with him. She was delirious with excitement, but something in her said, Stop. Consider. Two days later she was offered the post of senior archivist at the City Museum.

The sun was dropping towards the horizon fast; the shadow of the old man grew longer, an ectomorph etched in the sand by the last dying rays. Unconsciously she was following his path, her shadow parallel with his, turning when he turned, walking when he walked as she worried at her problem, tearing at it like some tangle of woven thread.

When he headed up towards her, his back to the sea, she did not at first notice. Her eyes were fixed on the scatter of shells lying in the rippled tide wrack. It was several seconds before she noticed that their shadows had merged and now were one. She looked up, startled. The metal detector was switched off now, at rest, hanging from its strap on his shoulder. The old man's eyes were on the heaped crimson clouds far to the west. 'Be dark soon.' His voice was rich and rumbling, projected from his chest. When she didn't respond he went on. 'I saw you up there in the café drinking Trish's best.' He gave a rueful chuckle. 'Little miss! Bad mouth me, did she, when I left?'

Louise smiled. 'Nothing too awful.'

The chuckle turned into a full blown belly laugh. 'Tactful lady, aren't you! Trish and I understand each other. I've got to know her quite well. She makes a wonderful cheese sandwich with home-made pickle.'

'Do you come here every day then?' Of one accord, companionably, they had begun walking again, slowly, heading away from the darkening sea towards the cliff.

He nodded. 'Most.'

'Have you ever found anything exciting?'

He nodded. 'One or two things. Jewellery mostly, that people have lost.'

'Was it worth much?'

He shook his head. 'I take it to the police. Sometimes I don't hear any more. People take it and that's it. No word of thanks. One or two things I was given when no one claimed them. I got a reward once.'

From the sigh in his voice she received the distinct impression that rewards were not the purpose of his search. She glanced at him sideways and found she was reluctant to probe further. A veil of sadness and of prohibition fluttered between them in the dusk.

'Would a sympathetic old ear help at all?' He glanced at her.

It was her turn to give a rueful smile. 'Is it that obvious?'

' 'Fraid so.'

'I have to make a decision.'

'Does it involve a man?'

She nodded.

'Heart versus head?'

She nodded again.

'If you say "no" will you regret it for the rest of your life?'

'Probably.'

'And all your friends are standing back and falling over themselves not to give advice?'

'I haven't discussed it with my friends.' It was true. In fact she had barely seen any of her friends for weeks.

The old man had glanced at her face and she had the feeling he could read her thoughts. 'Because your friends will back up your head and common sense and you, the you who is at the core of your being, want your heart to triumph.'

She laughed. 'I suppose so.'

'Am I allowed to know the choices?'

'The job of my dreams – one that won't come up again – versus –' she hesitated.

'The man of your dreams? There will be other jobs; you are clearly a talented and intelligent woman. Not the same job perhaps, but others. Will there be another . . .' he paused. 'What is his name?'

'Fraser.'

'Fraser, like you, is a unique human being. There will be other human beings; there will never be another Fraser.'

'You think I should go with him.' Her mouth had gone dry and she realised with surprise that it was with fear at the thought of reaching a decision.

They had reached the steps that led up the cliff and they stopped and faced each other. 'I asked a woman to marry me sixty years ago. She said yes, but then, for reasons unlike yours, but as troubling, she changed her mind. In my unhappiness I went abroad. To India.' He paused. 'I had no way of knowing that she would regret changing her mind and spend forty years looking for me.' Abruptly he turned and began climbing the steep stair, pulling himself up on the wooden handrail. She followed him and at the top he turned and swung round. 'It's her ring I'm looking for down there. The ring she gave back to me down on the beach. I was so upset I threw it into the sea. It was too late when I found out. She was dead.'

'I'm so sorry.' Louise put her warm hands over his cold ones. 'I'm so sorry.'

'Don't be. I'm a silly old goat. That's what Trish calls me. Sentimental. I tell her it helps to pass the time.' He was panting from the climb. 'Shall we go and plague Trish? She's usually open for another half-hour or so, till the market packs up. I'll get her to make us a sandwich.'

Louise stood still as he walked away. The letter she had

written to the museum accepting the job was in the pocket of her coat. She touched it with cautious fingers. Louise: the Louise who had run her life since she was a small child, sensibly, calmly, rationally – successfully – would post the letter now, in the box in the wall beside the café. That Louise always won in the end and she had never regretted it. But the other Louise, the passionate, impetuous, excited Louise; the Louise whose heart had finally rebelled; the Louise who longed to walk on desert sand and sail the turbid waters of the Amazon. What of her?

The old man had stopped. He looked back and saw her draw the envelope out of her pocket. Slowly she walked after him towards the café. In front of the red rectangular box in the old flint wall she raised her hand and held the letter for a moment before its gaping mouth.

He held his breath.

Her hand had begun to shake. She stepped back, staring down at the envelope, then abruptly she tore it in two.

Looking up she smiled at the old man and shrugged. 'Come on,' she said, 'let's have that cheese and pickle sandwich.'

Two's Company

MATTHEW GAZED into her eyes, made sapphire in the candle-light, and smiled as he reached for the bottle of wine. The evening had gone well. They had eaten gloriously and drunk elegantly and Petra had confided in him details of family and friends, of hopes and dreams, of fantasies and fears.

The fears intrigued him. There were so many. The huge eyes with their infinite depths of blue set off by the glossy chestnut curls and skin of creamiest porcelain grew larger and more eloquent with every terror she listed. Acrophobia, which meant abnormal fear of heights, she told him with a certain modest pride, spiders and lifts and thunder and wasps, and above all, ghosts.

'Ghosts?' He wondered, not for the first time, if she were winding him up. Increasingly he thought she was. 'To be afraid of ghosts, you have to see them.'

She smiled. 'I do.'

He risked a long, melting gaze into the fathomless blue and decided that, wound up or not, if he were not to risk drowning he must have her, and soon. The glimmer of a plan was emerging. 'Do you like ghost stories?'

She nodded. Her eyes held his. She did not appear to need ever to blink those sweeping lashes.

First a joke story. She was too serious. He needed to see her relax, to see for sure if she had a sense of humour. There could be no long-term relationship without a sense of humour.

'I could tell you the shortest ghost story in the world,' he said. He paused for a reaction – encouragement perhaps, or even a scowl. She continued to gaze, so, a little laboriously, he went on, ' "Do you believe in ghosts?" asks a man of his companion, on a train. "No," says the companion. "Oh, don't you," says the first man. And disappeared.'

He paused expectantly. It was usually good for a groan, at least.

She greeted the story with silence. Her eyes grew, if anything, larger. He suppressed a sigh.

'Do you have a ghost in your flat, then?'

He topped up her glass again, though she hadn't touched it since the waiter had brought their coffee and now the wine was held from spilling by only the meniscus.

When he had first met this girl at the office party he had assumed himself well in when she agreed to dinner. Now he was uneasy. She had talked too much, lightly, filling silences, but telling nothing. Nothing of her inner soul.

Perhaps she was a ghost herself. Amused at the thought he sat back and surveyed her through half closed eyes. Haloed by candlelight, shimmering in her blue shirt and dark silk jacket, she certainly looked ethereal. He reached out a cautious finger and touched her hand as it lay on the table. It was suspiciously cold and he withdrew with a shiver, almost convinced by his own fantasy.

'I'll introduce you to him, if you like.'

He realised suddenly that she was speaking again in that curiously husky drawl which he had found at first so attractive and now was in danger of finding monotonous.

'To him?' he echoed, puzzled. Some lover? Some husband? Some father then, heaven forbid, who would condemn utterly his politically incorrect motives for taking this beautiful creature to dinner and thence, hopefully, to bed.

'My ghost.' She smiled.

He sighed with relief. 'I'd like that.' He looked sincere. He was sincere. After all, was that not the point of the ploy? His ghost story – his next, real, more frightening and possibly true, ghost story about the fiend that lurked in the attics of the house in which he had been brought up as a child – was supposed to scare her, lead to his putting his arm around her shoulders, apologising for terrifying her, comforting her, reassuring her. Instead she had anticipated his next move for him and was, presumably, not afraid of this her own, private ghost.

'Is he your flatmate?' He asked with a smile. It sounded cool. Not witty perhaps, but at least humorous. And tolerant. No one could accuse him of being – not racist exactly. Corporealist perhaps?

She did not reply for a moment, then he saw the laughter, there at last behind the blue. 'You could say so. There's no one else.'

Now, that was bonus information. A double bonus. An empty flat waiting for them and, at last, signs of a sense of humour. He reached automatically for the bottle to top up her glass again but still she hadn't touched it. He refilled his own instead and glanced round for the waiter. The bill, a taxi back to her place and then with a bit of luck – heaven.

They had to wait for the taxi in the cold, but on the plus side she did not demur when he put his arm around her shoulders to counteract her shivering when at last they settled into its seat.

She lived in Notting Hill. A top-floor flat in a substantial house with pillared porch and white blistered paintwork. There was no lift and he was panting when they reached her door. The landing was dimly lit. He watched her pull her key out of her jacket pocket. 'Why aren't you afraid, living all alone with a ghost?'

He saw her smile, quickly hidden, as she turned to the door and inserted the key. 'We've grown used to each other.'

The flat was in darkness. She groped for a switch and a

shaded lamp came on at the far end of a pale-carpeted corridor.

'Throw your coat here.' She indicated a chair as she led the way into the living room and turned on more lights.

He looked round intrigued. The room was low-ceilinged, cosy, furnished simply with a generous scatter of cushions and throws. He rather liked it. Accepting another glass of wine – so, she did drink the stuff sometimes – and the promise of a coffee when the kettle had boiled, he threw himself down on the sofa and smiled. 'So, where is this flatmate?'

She was choosing a CD from the pile in the corner and he couldn't see her face.

'He'll be along, I expect.'

Soft music filled the room. Nothing he recognised. Strings. A harp. An occasional arpeggio on a pan flute. Taking off her jacket she threw it down and kicked off her shoes. Then she sat down, not next to him, but on a chair several feet away.

And for the first time that evening really looked at him hard.

Embarrassed by the scrutiny he dropped his gaze to the ruby depths in his glass. She smiled. Not bad looking. An eight out of ten, perhaps. Gold credit card – he had used it to pay for dinner, and in his name, not the business's, so money no obvious problem. Good job. He was after all her new boss. Sufficiently unattached or detached to take her out to dinner. His marital status did not bother her; a wife out of sight in the country was a wife out of mind; a ring and a marriage contract were not what she wanted. She wanted intellectual stimulation. Money, excitement, fun, companionship.

And sex of course.

She stretched languidly and saw his eyes flicker away from the wine towards the buttons on her blouse. Performance could only be judged by experience, but he had one or two other little tests to pass before she allowed him to seduce her. She smiled secretly. How strange that it never dawned on men even in this age of equal opportunity that they might be the prey.

'If we're lucky he might not come.' He would of course. He always did.

He looked up, surprised. 'Who?'

'My flatmate.' She did not want him to feel too secure, too comfortable. Not yet.

The trouble was she was fussy about her men. Her real men. She needed to know if he could handle irony. If he had wit and intellect. And courage. So far she was not convinced. His only attempt at a joke had been puerile.

'I'll make the coffee.' She gave him the half-lidded smile which men found enigmatic and headed, not for the kitchen, but towards the bedroom. It was here she kept her books, her flute, her tapes of poetry and drama. And her ghost.

Boris had been there since she had moved in. Companionable, gentle, not frightening at all once she had got used to him. Perhaps a little lonely. He was a friend, a confidant and, when she needed one, a chaperone who could chase away the most persistent of men.

Making sure the door was shut she slipped out of her shirt and trousers, stood for a moment naked in front of her mirror, and then pulled on the green silk wrap which turned her eyes to aquamarine and her hair to living fire.

Then she switched on the tape. Most of it – fifty-five minutes exactly – was silence.

In the shadows Boris watched it all and smiled. He had been lonely before she came, she was right. She had brought interest and sometimes excitement to the stasis of his existence. And she had given her a purpose. She thought she chose the men that stayed, but that was his self-appointed task. A task he performed with care and discrimination.

Matthew ignored the coffee, his eyes fixed, as she had known they would be, on the cleavage artfully revealed by the slippery silk. His physical reaction was, she noticed, a gratifying and unmissable ten out of ten.

He was not sure about the book she had produced though, puzzled by her timing, she thought, rather than appalled by the literary flavour the evening had suddenly acquired. But he acquitted himself well and cheerfully. Almost apologetically he revealed a more than passable knowledge of Chaucer, Jung, Plath and Okri, the cornerstones, in her view, of a broad intellect. Through them she could test briefly and without fuss his knowledge of history, psychology, philosophy, modern literature and politics and mark each out of ten (eight to nine in this case, she reckoned, pleased). That only left the ability to laugh at himself. So many men failed that most crucial test.

She rather hoped he wouldn't.

Intrigued and a little confused by the response his attempt at seduction had evoked, Matthew was nonetheless content. In the restaurant he had marked her down, in his turn, eventually, as scatty and not very bright. A quick lay if he were lucky. No more. Now, given courage by her own environment she had proved herself intelligent, well-read, thoughtful. He liked her for it more and more.

But it was a bit of a turn-off.

Her signals were in conflict: the deep green silk a come-on; the conversation a hold-back. Unmarried and so far uncommitted, he did not yet know that to fall in love with a woman you must first fall in love with her mind. He wanted to take her in his arms, but she was deeply into a new theme now. Universal consciousness.

Perhaps this was where the ghost came in?

Glancing into the shadows thrown by the carefully placed table lamps he smiled, suddenly uneasy.

Recognising the sign she glanced at her watch. It was happening too soon. There were three more minutes of the silent tape to go. There was only one way to fill them.

His lap was very comfortable. His lips tasted pleasantly of wine and coffee. Ten out of ten again, she thought, sleepy now. Slowly, with practised fingers she began to unbutton his shirt. She would be sad if he failed the test. The last three men had failed. But they were wimps and she had let Boris chase them away. Boris's trouble was that he never made a sound. The sound effects she had to provide for him. And they were very subtle. The slightest signs. Footsteps on uncarpeted floors and then in the distance a forlorn, breathy whistle, almost a monotone rather than a tune.

She felt Matthew tense, saw his eyes refocus away from her breast into the corner of the room, felt the gentlest touch of cold cross his skin under her fingers.

'Ignore him,' she whispered. He was there, but Matthew would never see him. She held her breath. The ghostly laugh, especially recorded by her brother with his head in a drainage pipe, had unmanned the others, the wimps. It was coming now.

She had to admit that it made even her blood curdle. For a moment he froze. She felt him grip her arms as though he would throw her across the room, then all at once light dawned. She felt him relax, saw his eyes close as laughter rocked him, felt his kisses on her throat and breasts.

'Thank God, she's got a sense of humour after all,' he thought as he pulled away the last of the clinging silk.

He did not see Boris, a shadow, no more, lurking ever watchful, nodding approval, in the corner of the room.

House of Echoes

Barbara Erskine

The past isn't always dead . . . and buried

When Joss Grant, adopted at birth, inherits Belheddon
Hall – a beautiful old house on the East Anglian coast – it
is like a dream come true. Eager to begin a new life there
with Luke, her husband, and Tom, her small son, she is
also impatient to find out about her newly discovered
family who lived there for generations.

But not long after they move in, Tom wakes screaming at
night. Joss hears echoing voices and senses an invisible
presence, watching her from the shadows. Are they spirits
from the past? Or is she imagining them? As she learns,
with mounting horror, of Belheddon's tragic and dramatic
history, her fear is very real as she realises that both her
family and her own sanity are at the mercy of a violent and
powerful energy which no one, it seems, can control . . .

0 00 647927 8

Midnight is a Lonely Place

Barbara Erskine

'Vivid, romantic and deliciously scary . . . Erskine at
her storytelling best' *Living*

After a broken love affair, Kate Kennedy, a successful
biographer, retires to a remote cottage on the wild Essex
coast to work on her new book. When Alison, her landlord's
daughter, uncovers a Roman site nearby, long-buried
passions are unleashed . . .

In her lonely cottage, Kate is terrorized by mysterious
forces. What do these ghosts want? That the truth about
the violent events of long ago be exposed or remain
concealed? Kate, Alison and her elder brother Greg must
struggle for their lives against earthbound spirits and
ancient curses as hate, jealousy, revenge and passionate
love do battle across the centuries . . .

0 00 647626 0

Lady of Hay

Barbara Erskine

'Barbara Erskine can make us feel the cold, smell the filth, and experience some of the fear of the power of evil men...The author's story telling talent is undeniable'   *The Times*

Jo Clifford, successful journalist, is all set to debunk the idea of past-life regression in her next magazine series. But when she herself submits to a simple hypnotic session, she suddenly finds herself reliving the experiences of Matilda, Lady of Hay, the wife of a baron at the time of King John.

As she learns of Matilda's unhappy marriage, her love for the handsome Richard de Clare and the brutal threats of death at the hands of King John, it becomes clear that Jo's past and present are hopelessly entwined and that, eight hundred years on, a story of secret passion and unspeakable treachery is about to begin again...

'Fascinating, absorbing, original - and hypnotic'
                                                                    She

0 00 649780 2

Child of the Phoenix
Barbara Erskine

The long-awaited new novel by the bestselling author of
Lady of Hay and *Kingdom of Shadows*.

Born in the flames of a burning castle in 1218, Princess
Eleyne is brought up by her fiercely Welsh nurse to support
the Celtic cause against the English aggressor. She is taught
to worship the old gods and to look into the future and
sometimes the past. But her second sight is marred by her
inability to identify time and place in her visions so she is
powerless to avert forthcoming tragedy.

Extraordinary events will follow Eleyne all her days as,
despite passionate resistance, her life is shaped by the
powerful men in her world. Time and again, like the phoenix
that is her symbol, she must rise from the ashes of her past life
to begin anew. But her mystical gifts, her clear intelligence
and unquenchable spirit will involve her in the destinies of
England, Scotland and Wales.

ISBN 0 00 647264 8

Encounters

Barbara Erskine

Longing, revenge, fear, hope and, of course, love - Barbara Erskine's characters experience the full spectrum of emotions in this delightful collection of stories.

Barbara Erskine's acclaimed first volume of short stories brings together over forty tales, all illustrating her extraordinary talent for capturing the spirit of a place and drawing us into the hearts and minds of her characters. Some are humorous, some thrilling, while others are unashamedly sentimental. No one who has enjoyed Barbara Erskine's bestselling novels will be able to resist this captivating collection.

'A marvellous mixture of emotional tales with the emphasis on love'   *Woman's World*

0 00 647068 8